The Greek Ring

A NOVEL OF
ADVENTURE AND ROMANCE

Richard Pim

Grosvenor House
Publishing Limited

The right of Richard Pim to be identified as the author of this
work has been asserted in accordance with Section 78
of the Copyright, Designs and Patents Act 1988

This book is published by
Grosvenor House Publishing Ltd
Link House
140 The Broadway, Tolworth, Surrey, KT6 7HT.
www.grosvenorhousepublishing.co.uk

A CIP record for this book
is available from the British Library

ISBN 978-1-83975-744-0

INTRODUCTION

At a small café somewhere in the whitewashed backstreets of Seville, I sat one early afternoon in September with my black sombrero angled low over the eyes, for the sun's heat is intense at this time of day, and, over a *café con leche*, contemplated my reasons seven years earlier for putting pen to paper.

The Greek Ring was conceived as an illustration of just how powerful and potent the attraction, that can develop between a man and a woman, whatever the difficulties and circumstances of their relationship.

There is another reason for telling this tale, and like the first, it too will remain timeless with age; namely man's eternal responsibility to struggle for a noble cause, despite exhaustion and his basic belief that good must eventually triumph over evil, no matter how desperate the undertaking. We encounter through life individuals whose principles are invariably conducted by the expediency of the moment, and whose loyalty can often be governed by treachery, whatever the disguise. Thus, in the spirit of Don Quixote, I set out to redefine the flame of romance, so that its consuming fire might illuminate a certain truth against the ever-present dark wind of a Machiavellian world.

RICHARD PIM

Seville, September 1994

ABOUT THE AUTHOR

Richard Pim was born in Alberta, Canada. His education included Gordonstoun and Palmer College of Chiropractic, USA. His interests include international travel, particularly in North Africa and the Middle East. Other interests include Egyptology, The Roman Empire, International Politics, Philosophy, and Fencing.

ACKNOWLEDGEMENTS

I would like to express my appreciation to all those individuals who over the years have helped me in one form or another along the path of creating these pages, now collectively entitled *The Greek Ring*. Firstly, I would like to thank those individuals who in the beginning sought to discourage me from embarking on this, at times, difficult and fastidious enterprise. For in the end they only served to sustain my enthusiasm and fortitude to finish the task, no matter how arduous the undertaking.

A special thanks is due to the following individuals who have helped in various capacities over the years: Ann Duvall and Joy Allen, for their typing and patience with interpreting my pencil-written scrawl. Ian Durant, for helpful and constructive criticism. Colin Davies with his detailed medical knowledge as an anaesthetist. Wilfred Hogg, in providing technical information on diamonds and related material. Christian Leigh, for giving me my first fencing lesson and helping to teach me the fundamentals of this ancient sport. Emilia Michaelides-Barr, for offering encouragement and providing balanced opinion over the years. Gary O'Neill, for his faith in my ability to succeed. My brother Jonathan, for giving me my first Thesaurus. India Paton for her technical support including essential computer skills. Lastly, but not least, my parents for their unwavering support, faith, and understanding throughout the long journey towards final completion.

Front and back cover painted by Klara Pim

Love is fiend, a fire, a heaven, a hell

where pleasure, pain, and sad repentance dwell.

RICHARD BARNFIELD (1574-1627)

PROLOGUE

Octavia felt the strength of his arms as Sebastian lifted her slowly to her feet. His muscles bulged with the strain, as she was limp like a puppet whose strings no longer work.

'Octavia…' She was moved by the way he said her name, so deep snd soft. Her near hysteria responded to the calm of his voice. '… You must let your uncertainties go, for faith alone shall ensure your future, you have to believe this'

The Englishman leant forward to kiss her on the mouth, his words echoing through her mind, giving her strength. His kiss was the electricity of life itself. The flame of her soul leapt as if by magic, its fires now burning with defiance against the unknown void that was her only path.

This man's magnetic attraction pulsated through her nervous system and the surge of high voltage was hope regained, once lost forever. Her mind ceased for a moment to build phantoms of fear. Instead, Octavia let his electricity wash through her, bathing her every fibre so that she felt part of him.

This book is dedicated to all those who have
either found the flame of romance, or yet dream
of losing themselves in its consuming fire.

Chapter One

The hands conveyed strength as they worked deep into the girl's shoulder muscles. Slowly, the fingers moved further down, rhythmically kneading her skin towards the soft curves of her hips. The owner of these hands was in no particular hurry to complete his skilled task, now and then pausing to pour more oil over the exposed surface that was the girl's back.

To an observer with a discerning eye for detail, this contented scene illustrated that the Côte d'Azur was not always populated by girls with 'fashionable' figures of the 'half-starved *Vogue* model' variety.

The girl with the blonde hair, who so obviously enjoyed this man's undivided attention, was a living example of an individual who refused to comply with current convention. Without doubt, Rubens would have been glad of her well-endowed shape, for she would inspire as a painter's model.

'Modern Style', dictated by the so-called wisdom of leading fashion houses, has in recent years portrayed a female form to such proportions that *haute couture* is now synonymous with near starvation, perhaps even anorexia. The media has only exacerbated the phenomenon with a relentless campaign that would be incomprehensible to artists from previous centuries, who drew women to a rather more generous scale.

Sebastian North watched the blonde girl until her companion at last exhausted his efforts with massaging and resumed a more relaxed position upon his back. Now it was the girl's turn, she straddled his narrow hips to slowly rub the thick oil into his chest and stomach. Soon the man's eyes were closed against the bright sun; the girl's progress was a little hampered by the man's thick chest hair. However, judging by their contented laughter, the experience must have been one of mutual enjoyment and positive recommendation.

After a long swim, North returned to the beach to find it almost deserted, the blonde girl and her lover nowhere to be seen. He half wondered who she was and where she was from. Perhaps one of the Scandinavian countries or Germany. He was convinced her name would be foreign and exotic sounding.

Sitting on his towel, dripping salt water, North discovered that the sun's heat was a little weaker than before. However, he was still glad of its warmth after the swim. The sun was sinking in the west, its progress slowly turning the horizon red. North recognised another one of those 'picture postcard' sunsets that he had been witness to during his brief stay on the French Riviera. For once, the postcards told the truth. *But for how long?* he thought. It was the end of August, with temperatures in the high nineties still being the norm rather than the exception.

The dark blue sea was smooth and tranquil, only broken by waves of pounding surf and the occasional white foam giving away the position of a hidden reef. Now and again, the shrill cry of seagulls could be heard fighting over some bounty that had been salvaged from tourists. This usually consisted of foul-smelling papers and scraps of half-decayed food.

At last, North stood up, shook his towel free of sand, and started to walk across the beach to his car. The sand was now practically empty, save for a few courting couples, arms entwined. But the blonde girl was not amongst them.

North had travelled from England to the South of France in search of relaxation. The drive had been leisurely, with an ever-increasing sense of liberation as England's oppressive weather gradually relinquished its hold upon the spirit. Through Central France, with the top of his convertible down, the sun seemed to welcome his very presence and be in sympathy with his recent escape. The restaurants and cafés along his route all exhibited a welcoming charm, with excellent food, and of course all the bread was freshly baked and prepared – something beyond the comprehension of so many English palates.

North had been walking for a few moments when something caught his eye, a little way beyond the breakers. It was just a white speck against a dark background. Gradually, it assumed the clear outline of a powerful motorboat. Its direction seemed to be a point on the beach about a quarter of a mile from his present position. North then noticed movement upon the shore. Due to the distance, he could not be sure, but it looked like two figures walking in a hurry towards a point of possible rendezvous with the motorboat.

The motorboat now started to slow down for its final approach through the breakers. The two figures entered the water – one wearing something dark, the other dressed in lighter clothes. They both had to be in a hell of a hurry, as neither socks nor shoes were removed upon entering the water. A man from the motorboat had jumped over the side, his purpose as yet unclear, perhaps to assist with these two new passengers.

North wondered what all the hurry was about, then smiled to himself. The emotions, of course, always tended to run a little higher once one crossed the English Channel.

Suddenly there seemed to be an argument between the two figures. The sleek white motorboat was closing on their position, its passage through the surf now completed. Then, in an instant, after what looked like some kind of struggle that included a lot of arm waving, the lighter figure detached himself and started running straight for North. The distance at which all this activity occurred was such that details were difficult to define, and impossible to make sense of.

The second figure immediately started after the first. Several people had paused from whatever they had been doing to watch the unfolding drama on the beach. It was not unknown for courting couples to chase each other on the sands, but somehow this particular spectacle did not inspire thoughts of flirtatious exuberance. There was an undefined sense of approaching danger that was far more tangible than a passing apprehension.

As the running figure came closer, North noticed that a second person had joined the chase – the man who had previously jumped into the shallow surf from the motorboat. Once close enough, North realised with a shock that the focus of the chase was not a man but a woman. The tall girl had wild, thick black hair and wore only a black and white striped bikini. Her skin was dark, suggesting long exposure to the sun.

North had no time to take in more as she flung herself at him, misjudged the distance, and collapsed at his feet in a heap of panting flesh.

As she fell, she gasped in French, 'Help me, please help me... they will kill me!'

She looked up at him, her dark eyes pleading. North realised the situation must be grim indeed for the girl's face to reflect such terror. Her fear could only be genuine.

North tore his eyes away from her stricken face to her two pursuers, who were rapidly closing the gap in spite of their shoes sinking in soft sand. They both looked very out of place, running along the beach wearing dark suits. The leading man now carried a gun in his right hand, while the man behind him held a knife. Both men were shorter than North's six foot two inches, but this made little difference under the circumstances, as North was armed only with a towel. *It was*, thought North, *not renowned as an effective means of protection against bullets and knives.*

North had to act now if the girl was to have any chance at all. He pulled her up onto her feet, then told her to run towards the silver convertible parked, just visible, four hundred yards away.

He decided that the best means of defence was attack. With the girl on her way towards the car, he sprinted towards the gunman, reasoning that if he could neutralise him first, he might have a chance with the knife man afterwards. Not a brilliant plan, he knew, but it was all he could come up with at that moment.

The gunman slowed his pace, no doubt thinking of how to deal with this unexpected diversion. Then he lifted his gun hand, having obviously reached a conclusion. As he did, North dived to the left, completed a full somersault, then landed on both feet in a crouched position. He heard the crack of the shell's discharge as the bullet passed close to his right ear.

North knew that the next would find its intended target. Upon diving, he had scooped up a handful of fine sand. This he now threw with great force into the gunman's face, rising as he turned from a crouch to his full height. The gun cracked a second time, sending another shell screaming towards North. This time it did find a target – North's left arm; the bullet struck high up, close to the shoulder joint.

North was immediately conscious of discomfort, but no intense, unbearable pain. This, he knew, would arrive soon enough, and be likely to inhibit his left arm with an unpleasant sense of paralysis.

Taking two steps forward, he aimed a sledgehammer of a kick at the still blinded gunman, his foot making contact with the man's solar plexus. The gunman dropped his revolver and his mouth opened like a fish, but no sound came. Instead, he collapsed, writhing in the sand.

Picking up the discarded gun, North turned his attention to the second man, who was now rapidly closing the distance between himself and the still running girl. At a sprint, North started to narrow the gap with the knifeman. He still had no idea what all this was about. His trip to the South of France was intended for relaxation, not this sort of activity, which was starting to pose a great many unanswered questions.

Was shooting someone whom he did not know, and who was now running after a third person whom he also did not know, a real concern of his? Was this something he should be involved in? The man's intentions towards the girl could hardly be termed 'friendly', so on that basis preventing him from reaching her seemed to be the right course of action.

Suddenly the man he was pursuing spun around to confront him. Seeing North's gun, he hesitated, during which time North closed the distance. Then the man lifted his arm with the obvious intention of throwing the knife, holding it by its blade. North sidestepped, then fired twice in rapid succession. The man fell backwards, blood gushing from his face; no doubt the bullet had severed a major blood vessel. It could be safely assumed that his days of chasing girls in bikinis were over for a long time.

North's thoughts were now on the purpose of the two men he had put out of action. *Suppose they were French policemen, trying to carry out their duty? The girl could be some notorious criminal.*

His thoughts were interrupted by the sight of two more men in dark suits, who could only be from the motorboat, running in his direction. They seemed keen on not being left out of the action. There was one more worrisome development: they carried rifles.

As he started after the girl towards the car, the distinctive sound of automatic gunfire was followed by a thud a few yards off to the left. They had found the range with little difficulty. Things were indeed warming up.

Running the last few yards, North tried not to think about his arm, but he felt the warmth of haemorrhaging blood. The girl was leaning against the door, bent over and out of breath. He shouted at her to get in, then as he climbed behind the wheel several more seconds of machine-gun fire sounded. The bullets thudded into the car, and he prayed the fuel tank wasn't hit.

North produced a key from his swimsuit and turned the ignition of the 1956 Bristol 405 Drophead Coupe. The V6 engine rumbled into life, then became deafening as he pushed the rev counter to four-and-a-half thousand, before releasing the clutch. The car shot forward, pushing them both back into their seats, the rear tyres whisking up a storm of loose sand. With his mouth set in a straight line, North concentrated upon the immediate task of putting as much distance as possible between them and their pursuers.

At forty miles per hour, with the RPMs a little over four thousand, North changed into second gear. There was a drop in engine noise, but it did not last, for North's right foot resumed its previous position, pressing the accelerator to the floor. He had not heard any more gunfire but the howl of the engine would have drowned any sound of pursuit. A glance in the rear-view mirror revealed only open road.

The knots in North's stomach eased slightly but his hands, in the position of ten-to-two, gripped the wheel with the same strength as before. At fifty-five miles an hour, he changed into third gear.

The girl made a hissing sound between clenched teeth. *Was this a prelude to conversation?* he wondered. A quick glance showed that her composure was improving. The mirror produced more clear road behind, so North eased up a fraction on the accelerator, then looked again at his new passenger.

The girl's hair was a tangled mass of dark curls that reached well beyond her shoulders. The way she was sitting indicated her height was well above average. In her bikini, she was well-shaped from full breasts to meaningful hips. She possessed very attractive dark, almond-shaped eyes, with well-defined eyebrows. Her mouth was full and sensuous. Her nose was in proportion to the rest of her face, and her chin suggested determination and purpose.

North was aware of growing discomfort in his left arm. The previous dull ache now gave way to burning pain that was going to become increasingly difficult to live with.

'My name is Sebastian North,' he said. 'Now, what the devil was all that about? Who were your friends back there? Not to mention any others left aboard the boat. Friendly bunch of people you hang around with, don't you think?'

'Very funny...' She understood English perfectly, and spoke it with only the faintest trace of an accent. 'My name is Contessa Octavia Delmonte. Those men are members of the Cosa Nostra, sent to kidnap me. You see, I come from a very wealthy Sicilian family, related to the ancient royal line now deposed.'

'Are they likely to try again?'

'I am certain of it,' replied the girl. 'By the way, thank you for your help back there. You certainly made them think twice about continuing their pursuit.' She paused, then said, 'There is possibly another reason for their latest attempt.'

"There have been others?' asked North, surprised.

'Yes, this is the second,' replied the girl. 'My former fiancé, I am sure, has something to do with the incident on the beach.'

'You're going to marry him?'

She did not reply. Her attention caught sight of North's left shoulder, arm, and shirt, covered with blood from the still seeping wound.

'My god, you are hurt badly,' said the girl, shocked at the sight of so much blood. 'We must contact a doctor at once! You can't keep on losing this amount of blood for long!'

North had to admit that his shoulder and arm were now becoming excruciatingly painful, and his driving was positively erratic. He felt the warm trickle of blood running through the fingers of his left hand and down the gear stick. He felt waves of nausea and dizziness so that his eyes started to view the road as if it were deep under water, and very far away. With great effort, he held the road for a moment longer, just long enough to slam the brakes hard. The car responded with a high-pitched squeal from the protesting tyres. The smell of burnt rubber was suddenly everywhere.

The car careered off the road onto grass before coming to an abrupt halt. North felt his eyes close under some invisible weight. His left arm became strangely detached, it belonged to someone else. Then he felt a wonderful sense of relief, pleasant and welcome. He prayed it would last forever.

North was unconscious for only a few moments, certainly not more than two minutes. To him, it seemed an age. He came round because the girl was slapping his face with great ferocity and determination. She was yelling something, but her voice seemed very far away, and he could not make out the words, his thinking still muddled and incoherent.

The girl's intentions became obvious: she wanted him to move to the other seat. With Herculean effort, he responded to the latest assault upon his tortured body by trying to comply with her insistent demands. At last she stopped slapping his face. North took his left leg from the driver's side and pushed it over the gear stick, then the right leg followed.

Now the girl went around to the driver's side to help push him completely onto the passenger side, all the time yelling in what sounded like high-pitched Italian. Somehow, he managed the impossible, and collapsed unconscious into the seat. She leant across and, with a rag from the glove box, mopped his arm and shoulder as best she could. Then, by tying the rag above the wound, she managed to stem the haemorrhaging.

That will have to do, she thought, *until more expert help can be reached*. At first, she found the car hard to drive, a stiff clutch not helping. However, with speed and familiarity, the car seemed to become more responsive to her touch. The girl drove hard and furious, taking unbelievable risks that would make even the insane pause for courage. Her concern now was to find medical attention for this man. From the empty rear-view mirror, she concluded their pursuers had been shaken off, at least for the time being!

He sounded English, but she knew it was sometimes hard to tell; his accent was not strong, so perhaps mid-Atlantic was closer to the truth.

Presently a road sign informed her that Monte Carlo was seventeen kilometres in front of them. She covered the winding road in record time, glancing anxiously as she did at her passenger, whose face had turned a deathly white.

Upon entering Monte Carlo from the Italian side, she chose a side road which took her to the backstreets.

After several more changes of direction and the occasional slowing down for the odd lost or absentminded tourist, she found a particular deserted street lined with expensive villas and stopped the car outside one of the high and imposing gates. Without turning the engine off, she unlocked the gates with a key on a chain around her wrist. She drove the car into the villa's spacious grounds, then ran across a large courtyard that had a bubbling fountain in its centre, surrounded by much green foliage, making it impossible to estimate the building's true size.

Through an archway that revealed a staircase, the girl ran up to a closed door that opened to her touch. She found the telephone she sought, then dialled a local number.

Someone answered. There was much urgency in her voice as she gave several orders in French. Without putting the receiver down, she made a second call. This one was long distance, and she spoke Italian. Running back down the stairs, she retraced her steps to the car and the still unconscious stranger. He was too heavy for her to try and move alone; she would have to wait until help arrived.

On the way back, she had picked up a bottle and filled it with warm water. Then, with cotton wool, she managed to make a reasonable job of cleaning the man's wounds. His blood had at last stopped haemorrhaging, so she slowly removed the pressure bandages with no ill effect.

For the first time, the girl looked at the man who had saved her from danger. He was well over six foot and taken to some exercise, for he looked fit, with well-defined muscles. His hair was cut short and very dark, the face beneath quietly distinguished rather than rugged. She wondered what impression he would leave with his smile and how his laughter would sound.

Ten minutes later, a large Renault passed through the open gates to park behind the convertible and two men stepped out. The driver, balding with grey above the ears, was dressed in a light, well-creased suit. The other man was half the driver's age, dressed in an open-necked, light-coloured shirt and jeans. His hair was curly blond and fell below his ears. He carried a small black bag.

Both men ran towards the left side of the convertible, where the older man conducted a quick examination of his new patient. The only reaction was a muttering to himself and slow shaking of his head.

Octavia gave a brief outline of the events that had resulted in the stranger's condition. The doctor said something to his assistant, and together they carried the limp form of the stranger across the courtyard to a room within the villa.

The doctor gave him an injection, after examining and dressing the wound. His assistant attached an intravenous drip, then Octavia covered the man with a blanket.

'He has lost some blood, but not enough I think to threaten his life. Another half an hour and the story could have been rather different. Your prompt action saved his life, Octavia,' continued the doctor.

'He saved mine, so it was the least I could do.'

'Some blood vessels in the arm were badly damaged, causing the loss of blood. He won't be entering any gymnastic competitions today, but if he rests over the next few weeks, I think he will make a good recovery,' stated the doctor.

The doctor's assistant finished treatment upon the Englishman's shoulder and upper arm with neat bandages, so that the ball and socket joint was fairly well immobilised. Finishing off, the doctor explained that the bullet had passed through the arm close to the shoulder joint itself, without connecting with the bone. Its passage caused enough damage but could have been far worse. The man could have lost the use of his arm.

'It seems you are both lucky to be here.'

Leaving the stranger alone to recover, they made their way once more to the courtyard. Octavia made drinks for the doctor, his assistant, and a strong one for herself. They sat close to the fountain on old wrought-iron chairs.

'Now, what is all this about, Octavia?' asked the doctor.

As she explained the circumstances that related to her encounter with this stranger, both men listened with attention, particularly the doctor who counted Octavia's father among his closest friends.

She left little out, starting with her flight a week previously, from Sicily to Monte Carlo. She'd had to leave her family, whom she claimed were driving her crazy by having her chaperoned everywhere, due to an earlier kidnapping attempt last month in Florence.

Earlier in the afternoon, two men had broken into her hotel room and had waited for her to return. She had been out at the beach all day enjoying the sun, and had done some shopping on the way back. She had struggled, but of course it had been no use. They then drove her to a certain beach. Then, whilst one man stayed in the car, the other walked her across the sand to the breakers and a waiting motorboat. Octavia had decided to struggle in a last bid for freedom, which resulted in the stranger's well-timed intervention. The rest they knew.

Both men – the doctor staring at the ice melting in his drink, his young assistant at Octavia's legs – heard her tale without interruption. When she finished, there was silence, except for the sound of running water from the fountain. Looking up from his glass, Dr. Carlos Lacombe fixed his gaze upon Octavia. She looked more attractive and resplendent than the last time they had met, over three months ago in Nice with her father.

It was then that Baron Delmonte had asked him to help look after his beautiful but disobedient daughter, who did not apparently appreciate the danger she was in. *She certainly*, he thought, *had inherited an independent mind.* However, the doctor sympathised with her position, for it must have been difficult for her living under the constant threat of kidnapping, with her father scrutinising her every move. No wonder she had finally decided to up and go.

The doctor had another drink as he considered the situation. The patient was in no state to be moved, so Francis, his assistant, would stay to keep an eye on the man's progress. Dr. Lacombe could not stay, as there were pressing matters he had to attend to elsewhere.

'Does your father know of recent events?' he asked Octavia.

'I tried phoning him an hour ago, but the line was busy,' she answered. 'Why don't you try, Carlos? You have been close to my father over so many years. It might be better coming from you. He would be less inclined to worry. Our relationship has been terribly strained these last few months.'

Dr. Lacombe agreed to try.

Within five minutes, he was back. 'Your father was not there, but I spoke to your mother. She was very upset at the news and she would like to talk to you.'

Octavia went through French windows to an elegantly furnished room to pick up the telephone receiver. At first, her mother's familiar voice sounded hesitant and faint.

She knew that her mother had not been well, and this added news could only add to her anxiety. Her father, it seemed, was away in Athens on business. Her mother had no idea where he was staying, but said he should arrive back tomorrow. Octavia thought it unlikely her father not to leave at least a phone number.

Her mother was close to tears on the phone as she tried to persuade her daughter to return home, but Octavia was adamant. She would not change her mind in spite of recent events; the thought of returning to her previous claustrophobic environment was too much.

Octavia had not even told her best friend Claudia, who she had met attending the same finishing school in Switzerland. She knew Claudia would have tried to persuade her not to leave her family.

The telephone conversation ended with her mother upset and Octavia determined to carve her own course.

'It's my life and I will do what I want with it.' She put the receiver down, then returned to the courtyard.

Meanwhile, her mother in faraway Sicily contemplated Octavia's last remark. Her daughter had much to experience from life before she could fully understand the meaning of compromise. Octavia's mother knew from her marriage and family that with responsibility comes sacrifice. *Octavia has a lot to become aware of*, she thought.

Carlos was talking to Francis regarding his patient's condition. Seeing Octavia return, he said that he would phone the following day to check on the man's progress.

Due to the urgency of the situation, Octavia had given little consideration to the implications posed by recent events with regard to the authorities.

'Someone has to be notified immediately,' said Carlos.

'The police?' questioned Octavia.

'Well, yes,' replied Carlos, 'but it will be a messy business with this stranger knocking off two members of the Cosa Nostra. And with a Delmonte involved, front page headlines are guaranteed.'

He paused, rubbing his double chin in thought, then his eyes brightened. 'Perhaps there is another way to tidy this whole matter and prevent it from reaching the media.'

Dr. Lacombe had an old friend in the Paris Police Department – something to do with narcotics as far as he could remember, but Inspector Leverett Ladoux never really said what his work involved. Dr Lacombe had not heard from his friend for some years, except for the occasional card at New Year. One notable success attributed to Inspector Ladoux two years ago had been the discovery and breakup of a Marseilles gang who were importing heroin from North Africa for distribution in Western Europe. This particular gang also attained great notoriety for their highly profitable dealings in human cargo, in addition to narcotics. Once discovered, denunciations came from European politicians throughout Western Europe at this appalling traffic in European white women being smuggled to North Africa and The Middle East. 'White Slave Trade Still Exists' ran popular headlines.

A lengthy trial took place that resulted in several senior gang members and scores of others convicted and imprisoned with long sentences. The smuggling ring from Marseilles never really recovered, but two other members caught in Naples escaped and disappeared without trace. The French press went berserk and, with characteristic Gallic language and diplomacy, accused the Italian authorities of total and complete incompetence against organised crime.

The doctor left, telling Octavia that he would see what he could do about the situation with his friend in Paris. She thanked him again for the trouble he had taken with everything.

Upon returning to his villa, Dr. Lacombe telephoned his friend, but there was no answer. When he tried an hour later, Inspector Ladoux answered. It was the same voice he had always known – soft and friendly with an occasional outburst of laughter – but now there was a hint of fatigue.

Inspector Ladoux had just returned from a long day of meetings with the British, German, and Italian Interpol representatives. His comments from the experience were that European unity was some way off from becoming a working reality, assuming that greater integration was indeed possible. He summed up the outcome as far too much inefficient bureaucracy.

The doctor related the evening's events, emphasising his long friendship with Baron Delmonte and his concern for the future safety of Octavia.

Inspector Ladoux thought for a moment, then said he would see what he could do. He had to make some phone calls, but would call back within the hour. His last question was to do with the nationality of the stranger.

'Octavia thinks he is English; she is the only one who heard him speak. His car has English plates and is right-hand drive, so it seems likely. I should have checked his car for any other clues but did not think.'

'Don't worry, Carlos,' said Inspector Ladoux with new confidence, 'it is not too late to achieve a media blackout over this whole unfortunate incident. I also know someone at the British Embassy here in Paris that I think can assist.'

They exchanged a few words of small talk on their respective families before saying goodbye.

* * * * *

North tried to run through what he could only describe as a semi-viscous fluid, which seemed to have an inherent will of its own. Its motives, he concluded, must be hostile. He was trying to escape from something, but his memory remained incapable of supplying a solution, let alone an escape route.

Then he saw the man's face, impassive and without feeling. The eyes, full of hatred, which gave his identity away, for it was the man on the beach from whose hold the girl had escaped.

Someone was holding his arm, apprehending his struggle. Running was becoming increasingly difficult. A gun went off, its report very close and loud. Then a second and third report sounded, thundering so close that deafness seemed a certainty, the shock waves hammering his skull like an echo that refused to die.

After a long time, the nightmare receded, to be replaced by consciousness and burning pain centred around his left shoulder and upper arm. To begin with, opening his eyes let in too much light for the sensitive retina to cope with. His pupils could not respond fast enough in cutting the light exposure.

North heard the door open very quietly. Then he knew someone was quite close, as he could smell perfume – not strong, but definitely there.

'How are you? Is your shoulder painful?' asked Octavia, her voice full of concern.

He remembered the voice, the girl from the beach, but what was her name? Yes, it was unusual, but what was it?

North cautiously opened his eyes, still afraid of the light, only this time the light did not hurt. A single bedside lamp cast the girl in deep shadow. She moved forward, out of the background, so that the lamp now illuminated her face. Her hair was piled high on top of her head to reveal a long slim neck. Her dark eyes were emphasised by mascara, their shape heavily outlined in the Egyptian style, reminding him of Queen Nafertari. Then North remembered her name: Octavia.

'Octavia from the beach, now I remember,' he said.

The girl's face, full of concern, gave way to a smile, directing his attention to the tray she carried. She indicated that he could eat if he wished. Putting the tray down, she rearranged the pillows behind him.

North watched her movements. *A little unsteady*, he thought, *perhaps recent events had taken their toll*. She sat on the end of the bed and watched him eat.

When he had finished, Francis came and examined his patient for any relapse, but found only steady progress. The prognosis was bright, but he had to rest for several days at least. After the assistant left, Octavia cleared away his tray and told North to sleep. This he quickly managed to achieve. The last thing he remembered was the faint fragrance of expensive perfume as she kissed his forehead before leaving.

North woke some twelve hours later. He felt much better for the blissful sleep, which had this time been free from nightmares. Even his shoulder had settled to a dull ache, rather than its previous uncompromising pain.

Francis came and went; once more, his delicate and sensitive fingers changing the dressing with a quiet confidence that inspired faith in his work. He left, suggesting North still retain the present dosage of painkillers.

A little later, North left the bed for the bathroom and a welcome wash. After finishing, he dressed in trousers and a white cotton shirt. The girl must have found them in his car. He felt his chin, which was rough, like sandpaper. Maybe a shave would be in order. He found a razor, brush, and shaving soap, so the next ten minutes were devoted to removing the stubble to smooth skin. He was drying his face when a knock came at the door.

'Come in,' said North, still watching the mirror.

From the reflection, North saw the girl enter the room. She had expected him to be in bed, so she did not see him immediately. He regarded her in profile for just a moment, the large gold earrings contrasting well with her tan. She wore white cotton trousers, very tight, with an indigo blue sleeveless blouse. The silk chiffon was tied in a loose knot at the front, well above the waist, revealing the girl's navel.

North stepped out of the bathroom to face her.

'You should be resting,' she said. 'You are not well enough to be up.' She moved closer to him.

'I feel fine, really, I am much improved.' It was true, he did feel much better, but his shoulder still throbbed with a dull ache.

The girl moved very close, so close that North found himself attracted by her face and momentarily enchanted by her dark almond-shaped eyes. They seemed to melt right through him, as if searching for something. He remained transfixed, not wanting to interrupt the experience.

She suddenly smiled, breaking the spell. 'Thank you for helping me,' she said.

'It was the least I could do in the circumstances...' replied North. 'Anyway, I should be thanking you for looking after my injuries. I very much appreciate all that you have done. If by chance you have any more, how shall I say, difficulties that might require assistance, don't hesitate to contact me!'

The girl laughed at his light-heartedness, then gestured that they should walk out into the courtyard. It was late evening and, typically, the warm Mediterranean air suggested informal conversation and escape from routine. They sat down in wicker chairs near the fountain, its running waters restful and unhurried in their monotonous sound. Octavia poured two glasses of white wine.

'I took the liberty of thinking you might enjoy this wine from Sicily where I come from, though I know much of England drinks gin and tonic.'

'Yes, that's fine,' replied North.

'You are English? Your car has right-hand drive and English plates,' she said, explaining her reasoning.

'Yes, I am English.'

'But your accent...'

'Ah yes, a little more difficult to pinpoint. I have done a certain amount of travelling over the years, and I guess it became lost somewhere between San Francisco and London.

'Have you contacted the police?' he continued. 'The gun shots could not have escaped notice.'

'Yes, I have, but indirectly, through Dr. Carlos Lacombe, who initially attended to your injuries. He phoned a few moments ago to say that he managed to contact an old friend of his in a department of the Paris Police. Apparently, this contact is sufficiently high enough to be able to exert some sort of containing influence over the potential media attention that will inevitably follow.

'He can, I am sure, be trusted to take care of everything, if Dr. Lacombe vouches for him. He will try to keep it out of the papers. There will, of course, be some articles, no doubt – just a mention of "another shooting incident, inspired by continuing gang rivalry". Internal feuding occurs all the time up and down this coast now; it's not like it used to be a few years back.'

After another sip of her wine, Octavia continued.

'Carlos has been my father's doctor for twenty years. He looks after my father, who has a weak heart, whenever he visits the Cote d' Azur and stays at the villa. You can trust him to do what he says he will. I have known Carlos personally since I was a child.'

'What about his assistant?' enquired North, only half convinced.

'I cannot vouch for him, because I had never met him until yesterday, but if Carlos trusts him, he must be okay.'

'Does your father know of recent events?' asked North.

'Not yet, he is away in Athens on business.'

'Don't you have the name of his hotel? Your mother must have a phone number?'

'No, she doesn't. I talked to her earlier.' Octavia became reflective. 'Yes, it is strange that he left without leaving a forwarding address, at least for my mother. He has never done that before and she is quite worried. She was close to tears after I told her what happened on the beach.'

Octavia refilled their glasses. North could see she was troubled.

'I had decided to stay here on the Riviera until you had improved, for this is all my fault, but had no intention of returning to Sicily in the near future. However, I think my duty is now with my mother; she needs me,' she explained. 'Something to do with a Latin temperament mixed with not enough responsibility and too much selflessness. At least, that's what an aunt of mine told me. Maybe she is right.'

North noticed her eyes; the sparkle was gone, to be replaced by anxiety. He stood up and went over to her, picking up her hand, as she had done his earlier. He held it gently.

'I am sure that there is a simple explanation for your father's lack of communication. There is no point worrying unless you have something to worry about,' he said.

The girl looked up at him, her dark eyes suddenly seeming more desperate. Was there a sense of uncertainty, perhaps vulnerability beneath the confident and worldly exterior? Or did North just imagine it? The full impact of the incident on the beach and strain of the last few months perhaps had begun to accumulate.

'You see, Signor North,' she began, 'I was the difficult daughter who, during her growing up, did what she wanted without thinking of her parents. Recently, I realised how I had treated them, but the pressures of being chaperoned proved too much. I now realise how right my father was with his efforts to protect me. After what happened on the beach and my father's strange behaviour, I think something might have happened to him. I must return to Sicily to find out what is going on.'

'Which part of Sicily do you come from?' enquired North.

'Near the town of Cefalù, which is about 60 kilometres east of Palermo. My parents have a 17th century villa overlooking the sea.'

In his imagination, North pictured the villa described, situated upon that rugged north Sicilian coast. It would have extensive gardens. The majestic vistas from its windows must be a constant inspiration for the spirit.

'You have changed your mind? You are returning to your mother?' he enquired.

'Yes, I have been doing some more thinking. I need to reassure her that I am well and to be with her until my father returns. It is my duty. I was being selfish and not thinking of my parents. I will return to Sicily when you are well.'

'I feel much improved and will return to my hotel tonight, so there is no need to delay seeing your mother on my account.'

The girl was distressed. 'You need more time. Carlos said a week at least, maybe two. You have lost a lot of blood. There is no need to rush back. Anyway, I am sure

Carlos's friend in the Paris Police Department will want to contact you, if only to have your account of events.'

'Of course he will.' North told her the name of the hotel, which was not far down the coast. 'He can contact me there. I intend to finish the rest of my holiday for at least another ten days, perhaps more. What happened to my car?'

'I parked it around the back. The keys are in your room.'

"Thank you for all you have done...'

The girl stood up and North observed that she was very tall.

'Why don't you come and visit us in Sicily? My parents would want to thank you for what you have done. In fact, you must come, I insist. There is so much to see and experience on my island, from Norman cathedrals, Greek amphitheatres, to Arab mosques. The fresh food is always a delight to those unfamiliar with its charms, as is the local wine. The endless sunny days, white sandy beaches, turquoise sea, starry nights, and soft cool breezes are all waiting. You would fall in love with my island, Signor Sebastian North, if you gave it a chance.

'Many people think of Mafia when Sicily is mentioned, which is unfair, as there is so much more to my island than the dark hand of organised crime.

'My former fiancé is in Sardinia. We had a big argument and Roberto threatened me, even my family. He said we would never be safe unless I married him.'

'How did he become your fiancé?' intervened North.

'You have to know Sicily to understand that. Sicily used to be run by several influential families that survived the endless tide of fortunes and sometimes near destitution bestowed by history through the centuries. Sicily, in spite of the 20th century, is steeped in tradition that has changed little over the years. As I mentioned, we have been invaded countless times, but have adapted with resilience to whatever the circumstances, in order to survive. We remained constantly suspicious of foreigners and their motives, always on the lookout for the false-hearted and treacherous.

'The arranged marriage for the nobility is still practised with great care, as it had been in previous centuries. My family are no exception to this tradition.'

'So, what happened between you and Roberto?'

Octavia paused, as if searching for the right words to express herself.

'I broke off the engagement to my former fiancé when I threw my ring back at him. He is of noble birth like myself, but his line has degenerated with a strong Mafia involvement that has increased over recent years. I could never be a part of this dark side to Roberto's character. I don't think my parents fully realised how corrupt his family had become. Does that answer your question?'

'Yes. I am sorry for asking. It's none of my business.'

North finished his drink and then said that he must leave for his hotel. He asked Octavia to pass on his profound thanks to Dr. Lacombe and his assistant for all that they had done. He left an envelope with money, in part payment for their attention and dedication.

'Thank you for your most generous invitation to visit Sicily. I would like very much to take you up on it, perhaps sometime in the future.'

North thanked Octavia again for all her help with his shoulder, and they parted in the courtyard with a kiss on both cheeks. She slipped a piece of paper into his hand before he left, saying, 'Perhaps we meet again?'

He had a last impression of the tall Sicilian, with her earrings catching the flickering light from the courtyard lanterns.

He drove the car back to his hotel, situated in a small coastal village not far from the drama of two days before. With relief, he entered his room and was on the bed within seconds. For a while he stared at the ceiling fan, trying to make some sense of recent events, then he drifted off into welcome oblivion.

North woke at 9.30 the next morning. His shoulder felt stiff but there was no pain, and after strong black coffee with fresh croissants served on the patio below, life was definitely looking up. He lingered over his breakfast, enjoying the view and listening to the restless breakers down on the beach.

Back in his room, he found the note that the girl had given him on a scrap of paper. It contained her address. What a strange encounter this was, and how bizarre the circumstances!

Thirty minutes later, North was on a sandy beach with nothing except a towel, sunglasses, suntan oil, bread, cheese, and a bottle of red wine. After a brief dip in the cool water, he dried off and tried to push the last two days out of his mind. He explored the beach for several miles before having lunch from the food he had bought, washed down with the now warm wine. During further exploration, North found several shells of a particularly unusual shape and colour to add to his collection. Then, with the sun casting increasingly long shadows, he returned to his hotel.

North had wished to swim but his bandaged shoulder had prevented all but a dip up to his waist. He had supper very early by French standards, at 6 o'clock at a nearby restaurant. As he ate, North thought for some time about a certain girl from his past. He had nearly married her. He reflected on the good times and possible causes for the eventual and painful break-up. Since then, his business of dealing in antiques on an international scale had flourished. His present holiday was the reward for long hours of dedicated work.

Returning to the hotel, North found a recent copy of *The Times*. There was little of interest: impending strikes at home, and another breakdown of Middle East peace talks. Page four had a long article on the international fight against drug smuggling. Interpol were rumoured to be on the trail of a gang operating in the Eastern Mediterranean, with possible links behind the Iron Curtain, but no arrests yet. North doubted if any major change would result in the slowing of the drugs traffic, even if arrests were achieved. Most would either escape or have charges dropped on a 'technicality'.

The following day, North decided to leave his present hotel and find another further along the coast, for no other reason than a change of surroundings. He would phone through the address of his next hotel in case it was needed for the doctor's friend to contact him with regard to earlier events.

After checking out of the hotel, he was about to drive out of the car park when he found he had forgotten to return his room key. He knew the hotel proprietor from previous visits over several years, and wanted to maintain his good reputation. So, he went back to the reception desk to return his key. He handed it over to

Isabelle, who had only a few moments earlier wished him *bon voyage*.

She produced a slip of paper. 'This message arrived just after you left a few moments ago. It could be important. Someone called Octavia telephoned. Her voice was so low I could hardly make out what she said.'

'So, what did she say?' asked North.

'Come at once, matter of life and death... Octavia...'

'So, what does this mean? You are sure there was nothing more?' he asked.

'Yes. I think she wanted to say something more, but the phone went dead as if she was cut off. She has not tried again.'

From the International Operator, Isabelle established that the call was from abroad, but failed to confirm if Sicily was the country of origin. At North's suggestion, and with further help from the International Operator, the phone number given to him by the Sicilian girl was found to be unobtainable.

The local operator in Palermo suspected another fault on the line. These 'faults' were apparently a regular feature with the Sicilian telephone system. It was also quite impossible to calculate when the 'fault' might be repaired; they were constantly 'over-worked' as it was.

North assumed the girl had flown to Sicily – most likely the previous day – but he had to be sure. With Isabelle's help, he quickly established from the Air France desk in Nice that a Contessa Octavia Delmonte had indeed been booked on a morning flight from Nice to Rome connecting to Palermo.

North again read the message handed to him by Isabelle and thought for a moment or two, before coming to a decision. Then, with Isabelle's by now indispensable help, he enquired as to the first available flight to Palermo. The next one was an Air France to Rome, changing to Alitalia for Palermo, leaving in two hours from Nice. He paid with a credit card, thanked Isabelle for her helpful assistance with a substantial tip, then left the hotel, driving fast for Nice's international airport.

Chapter Two

Alitalia flight 417 approached its final destination with caution, for Punta Raisi Airport has claim to be one of the world's most formidable, in terms of landing a modern jet.

This difficult procedure is not an enviable task amid unpredictable cross winds that blow between sheer-sided rocks and the sea. The wheels touched the runway exactly fifteen minutes later than scheduled. The flight had lasted a little more than an hour from Rome's Leonardo Da Vinci Airport.

North wore a light grey suit, tailored from 100 per cent fine linen of a tropical weight, ideal for hot climates. A white cotton shirt and Royal Air Force tie completed his travelling attire. His luggage consisted of one medium-sized leather suitcase and a flight bag. North did not believe in unnecessary and cumbersome baggage, now such a feature of the modern tourist.

The landing proved pleasantly less of an ordeal than North had been told to expect by the overweight woman next to him. Descending the steps from the plane, he took his first breath of Sicilian air and regarded his fellow passengers with interest. They ranged from short, overweight peasants accompanied by numerous small children, to sophisticated-looking women dressed in the latest fashions from Rome and Milan. Many wore dark glasses against the bright sun, making the men in their Armani suits assume a slightly sinister presence.

There was a certain amount of chaos as everyone waited for their luggage to arrive. There were no Customs, as he had cleared them in Rome earlier. Once his suitcase arrived, North passed through the small arrivals building and once more into bright sunlight.

After locating a taxi in the form of a battered Mercedes, he found the driver half asleep. However, once he saw a potential customer, the man managed to regain full consciousness. North showed the driver the address Octavia had given him, then asked to be taken there.

'*Mi porti a quest indirizzo.*' There followed a brief discussion over the price. North, though unfamiliar with the currency, managed to strike what he considered a reasonable deal – about 50 per cent less than that originally suggested by the driver.

The driver, a greasy specimen with a long droopy moustache and sweat-soaked white T-shirt, started the noisy diesel engine. Leaving Punta Raisi Airport, the Mercedes turned east towards Palermo. The road through Palermo was a nightmare of inadequate signs, numerous road-improvement schemes currently under construction, and every driver's complete disregard for all other cars apart from his own.

Once the outskirts of Palermo faded from view, conditions improved dramatically. The smooth motorway that led to Cefalù provided commanding views of Sicily's rugged northern coast. In the taxi, North reflected on what he knew of Sicily; it was a long time since he had visited its shores.

Sicily – the largest island in the Mediterranean – lies south west of the Italian mainland, separated by the narrow Strait of Messina, about midway between the

Strait of Gibraltar and the Lebanese coast. It can be reached within a day's sail from the North African coast. Because of its strategic location, Sicily has been invaded since earliest times. As a result of these occupying civilisations, Sicily has become rich in history and culture.

The Greeks named Sicily 'Trinacria' or Three Cornered, referring to its three headlands. The present name, Sicily, comes from the Sikeles, who were one of the first people to populate the island. *All these invasions*, thought North, *have contributed in varying degrees to its present make-up, fiery and passionate like the volatile volcanic rock beneath.*

The address had said 'Villa Domitian', with Cefalù below. After passing through this coastal town which exhibited much picturesque beauty and charm, dominated by its magnificent Norman cathedral, they had to be close to the Delmonte Villa.

Instead of returning to the motorway above the town, the car followed a lower and narrower road that hugged the coast. Suddenly, around a corner, they almost passed high wrought-iron gates with hinges set in massive stone pillars. The taxi driver savagely applied his brakes. The car protested with a screeching until it finally came to rest inches from the elegant and decorative structure. A small blue cloud hung momentarily above the road, the smell of burnt rubber strong before the sea breeze finally blew it away.

After paying the driver and watching him disappear in the direction of Palermo, North found that the gates were unlocked. Lifting his suitcase, he set off down the well-kept gravel drive to the Villa Domitian – home of the Delmontes. The long avenue was straight and bordered with cypress and laurel hedges. The Delmontes obviously enjoyed gardening on a grand scale, for intermittently off to either side, smaller avenues ran to citrus orchards and ponds with water lilies, surrounded by large well-kept lawns.

Slowly the villa came into view. Before North could make out its features, he slipped off to the left so that his future progress towards the building would remain hidden by the cypresses. North advanced until he could clearly see the villa's structure; it was a truly magnificent piece of Renaissance architecture. He thought it was a fine example of a structure emphasising well proportioned symmetry and balance.

The facade, when first observed from the avenue, imitated a Roman temple, with its colonnaded portico. It had to be one of the most southerly examples of Andrea Palladio's work. From what North could remember, this renowned architect of the 16th century had designed several famous villas within the region of Vicenza.

On the other side, the villa must have a commanding view of the coast. To confirm this, North carefully made his way through a large patch of dense bamboo foliage that abruptly stopped on a cliff edge. The deep blue of the Mediterranean caught his breath as it sparkled in the late afternoon sunlight. A narrow path zig-zagged down to the water's edge, from which a small jetty ran out for about thirty yards. A powerful-looking motorboat was moored but there was no sign of life.

North turned back towards the villa, his mind preoccupied. Something had happened, but what? Octavia's phone call must have had some relevance to the attempted kidnap in the South of France, of this he was sure. But again, what was the connection? The answer to the puzzle must lie within the villa. At the very least, perhaps a clue or two might be found behind its imposing facades.

Another attempt upon the girl's freedom had taken place on her return to Sicily, he speculated, only this time it had succeeded. Somehow, she had managed to reach a telephone, but once discovered was cut off in mid-sentence. If they, whoever her kidnappers were, had heard her conversation, then it was reasonably safe to assume that he was expected.

North approached the villa with even more caution, using olive trees, a few magnolias, and the thick cypresses as cover. Then he heard a noise but could not be sure what it was. After pausing, everything was still and as it should be. He left his suitcase out of sight under a rose bush. He would not be needing its contents at the moment.

North resumed his approach, but slower than before, his ears straining for a repeat of the earlier sound. Only the seagulls broke the silence with their mournful cries. Then he heard the 'put-put' of a fishing boat far off, its engine noise carried on the offshore breeze.

Then unmistakably, North heard the earlier sound – only this time it was much closer. He stood perfectly still, his ears alert and concentrating, searching for its source. Without doubt, this sound had been man-made.

North had almost given up hope, when a movement caught his eye, and with it was repeated the same sound. It was the tearing of paper that had first alerted him. Moving out from behind a tree was a man eating something. Whatever it was must have been covered in paper so that only tearing its wrapper could reveal its contents.

The man was dressed in dark trousers and a light jacket. His hair was short and dark with a hint of grey, North estimated his age at about forty. There was one other interesting feature: he carried some sort of machine gun, supported by a strap over the left shoulder. The gunman walked, without hurry, towards the villa. North observed his progress until he reached the colonnaded portico, climbed the marble steps, then disappeared inside.

North thought to himself that whoever hired the services of this particular individual was preparing to play for fairly high stakes.

He crept around to the back of the villa, to discover extensive gardens surrounded by a stone wall. Opening a small wrought iron gate to follow a path, he found that these gardens portrayed different themes. One had a pond with a temple watched over by Neptune, carved in white marble. Another had a fountain in the centre of a pool, within the setting of a classical Italian garden. Here, pink hydrangeas contrasted well with masses of white roses.

Once, North almost tripped over a sharp object and discovered a water sprinkler; there were, in fact, dozens carefully concealed. A patio ran nearly the entire length of the north facade. His eyes searched every square inch for movement, his ears strained for sound, but there was no sign of human life.

He waited for five minutes, then another five minutes. It seemed an age, but there is a famous saying that he could not remember exactly, something about 'caution being the better part of valour'.

There was no sign of the man who carried the machine gun, or anyone else. North reached a partially open door situated in the west wing. Once past the threshold, he found himself in a narrow passageway. Before his eyes could become fully accustomed to the inadequate light, the silence was broken.

A woman's voice started shouting obscenities in high-pitched Italian. It came from beyond an archway to his left. North froze, not sure what to make of this interruption. Then he started to move with caution towards the sound. It must be the kitchens, for the unmistakable smell of cooking permeated the air. North's nose identified a typical island pasta dish containing sardines, peppers, olive oil, fennel, and pine nuts, to name but some of the ingredients. Under different circumstances he might have felt hungry. For now, the girl's cries cancelled any appetite he might have had.

Remaining close to the passage wall, North risked a quick look beyond the archway. He saw a young girl in a white apron leaning over a selection of cooking pots and frying pans. *She must be preparing for several people, judging by the quantity of food*, he thought.

So, what had prompted her string of obscenities? North withdrew into shadow, pausing to think, trying to work out his next move. However, he did not have long to wait. During a second observation, the undoubted object of the girl's previous outburst came into view.

A short, stocky man with untidy black hair and a broken nose, which gave his face a hideous and brutal appearance, approached the girl from behind. She must have thought the man might have left her alone, but it looked as if she was going to be mistaken.

Before he could reach her, she heard him, or some sixth sense warned her of his intentions, for she turned around, her face full of panic and terror. The girl tried in vain, with flailing arms, to thwart his attack, but it was hopeless from the beginning. The gorilla, for such was his build, seemed to enjoy the struggle, as an evil grin spread across his overweight face.

The girl screamed as her blouse ripped; at the same time, she moved towards the stove and, with both hands, picked up a frying pan, her intention obvious. North started towards them, deep down knowing that the odds were stacked against him being able to reach the girl in time. But he had to try, no matter what the risk of failure.

The girl managed to lift the hot pan level with her head, but it was an unwieldy object and heavy at this particular angle. Then, with a lightning quick chopping action, the gorilla blocked her arm. The force was so violent that the girl fell, with the pan's lethal contents spilling over her head and chest.

The oil burnt her horribly, the torn apron and blouse offering no protection as it spread relentlessly across her skin. She screamed, putting her hands up to protect her face, but the gesture was too late; irreparable damage had been done. She continued screaming, the echo within the tiled kitchen magnifying the sound to fearful proportions.

North was upon the big man before he was fully aware of his existence, but the gorilla's strength proved too much. With a fist to his right jaw, North fell sprawled across the floor. However, instead of following in his early success, the gorilla turned his attention back to the prostrate girl, her continued screaming having diverted his concentration.

Before North could recover from the hammer blow, the gorilla slit the girl's throat. From the deep wound, a fountain of blood spurted up to arc across the blue and white tiles. The screaming ceased, as if shut off by a switch, to be replaced by an eerie silence.

North knew he had very little time before he would suffer a similar fate. As the gorilla still knelt over the blood-soaked girl, admiring his handiwork, North managed to raise himself up on one elbow. Incredibly, the gorilla still did not leave the girl. With more effort, North managed to reach a countertop with his left hand. He had noticed the carving knife earlier, out of the corner of his eye, and it was on this that he concentrated his attention.

At last, he found its cold steel, but the gorilla must have grown bored with the lifeless girl and now turned his attention towards him. The gorilla was perhaps a little too sure of his position, for he threw himself upon the crouching Englishman, his knife extended forward for the *coup de grâce*. However, this intended blow never realised its target. At the last moment, North rolled over, the knife harmlessly striking the tiles. Then, cat-like, North was upon the big man, plunging the carving knife to its hilt into his back. After briefly coughing up blood with a strange gurgling sound, the gorilla remained completely motionless.

North filled a jug with cold water and, cradling the girl's head, poured some of it over her blistered face and neck in the hope of easing her pain. He did not know if it helped, but he had to do something. A minute later, her breathing ceased. Her throat was a massive gaping wound, blood still seeping from severed vessels. Then even this trickle stopped. Resuscitation was pointless, as the knife wound had been fatal.

North left by the archway through which he had entered the kitchen, into the same corridor, dimly lit from wall-mounted lamps, with just enough light to see its end, marked by a closed door. To one side, leaning against the wall, was a shotgun. North wondered if it had belonged to the gorilla. Opening the breach, he found the chambers contained unfired cartridges.

Slowly, North opened the door, first making sure the safety catch on the gun was off. The gorilla must have some equally unfriendly associates somewhere. After listening for a few seconds, he determined that the room was not full of people – or at least, they were not engaged in noisy conversation. Stepping inside the room, he found its dimensions cavernous, with large windows overlooking the Mediterranean. The view, even in the fading light, was breathtaking with distant lights from boats winking at him as he ventured further into the interior.

Paintings hung on two of the walls; portraits of family ancestors, he guessed. Oriental-looking carpets, many showing leopards in various poses – a symbol of Sicilian aristocracy – covered part of the floor upon which, in a corner, stood a grand piano. Various armchairs and comfortable-looking sofas were arranged at the far end in a way that suggested this was where relaxed after-dinner conversation took place over coffee, and perhaps something stronger. The fourth wall, opposite the tall windows, contained bookcases from floor to ceiling, in which many fine and some undoubtedly old bound volumes could be seen.

Before he could take in any more details, North heard shouting from the direction of the kitchen. He guessed that someone had developed an acute case of incomprehension as to how the gorilla had received a carving knife in the back.

North hid behind the door to await whoever it was, after they had recovered from seeing the kitchen. He did not have long to wait. The partially opened door to the elegant room moved to reveal a slightly-built man with a little grey above each ear. It was the same man that North had seen earlier. At the moment, he could only see his back, thus still possessing the element of surprise.

North decided to challenge the man, who carried a machine gun.

'Don't move!'

The man froze, as if suddenly made from stone. The end of the shotgun's barrel was no more than two feet from the man's spine. North had discovered something that might just prove useful. This particular individual, whoever he was, understood at least some English. North continued his conversation.

'I have a shotgun aimed two feet from your back, so I am sure you appreciate the situation.' North paused a moment to gauge the man's response. He remained motionless as before. 'Drop the gun.'

The machine gun fell to the carpet with a thud, making North feel a little easier. 'Now, lie on the ground, first one knee, then the other.' The man obeyed without hesitation then North kicked the gun well out of possible reach; it was not worth taking any risks.

North came out from behind the door, the shotgun continuously covering the prone man. His head was turned towards North, the eyes watchful like a cornered animal, missing nothing, waiting for an opportunity to escape. *What was he thinking? Would he be willing to talk?*

'Who are you and what are you doing here?' North asked. He somehow had the inherent feeling that he was not going to obtain much information from his questions. And the gunman's initial response confirmed this to be the case.

The unblinking stare of his eyes conveyed a strange, restless unease, and there was a hint of contempt that remained inexplicable. These eyes knew not the meaning of remorse or pity. Then he smiled, as if this would be enough in way of explanation. The gleaming white teeth gave even less away than the previous impassive mask of stone.

North repeated his question, but the answer was the same. North lowered the gun, so that both barrels came into contact with the man's left ear.

'If your attitude remains one of uncooperation, then I will blow your head off. You may recall the gorilla you passed recently in the kitchen. The carving knife sticking out of him did not arrive there by accident. I put it there. I hope you understand.' Without waiting for a reply, North continued, 'Unless I have some answers, I am going to pull the trigger...'

The man's smile vanished as quickly as it had arrived; the cheeks and chin resumed their previous gaunt dimensions. Then the eyes narrowed, calculating North's threat. At last, he reached a decision and his face relaxed to the point of being friendly, with only the eyes remaining impassive.

'I was only carrying out orders... to hold the Baroness and her daughter.'

'Who sent you?' snapped North, full of impatience.

'Major Vasile.'

'And who exactly is Major Vasile?' The name meant nothing to North.

'Major Vasile is a member of the Ceauşescu family. He is related to President Ceauşescu.'

'What interest do the Romanians have here in Sicily?' asked North, more than a little puzzled.

'I don't know everything. All I know is that I was ordered to hold the Baroness and her daughter until Major Vasile returned.'

'Do you have any more friends here, apart from your late comrade in the kitchen?'

'No, just the two of us were sent by Major Vasile.' Somehow, North found it difficult to believe everything he was hearing.

'Where are Countess Octavia and the Baroness?'

'Wine cellar.'

After receiving directions to the wine cellar with the additional help of a little pressure from the gun barrel upon the Romanian's ear, North tied up the gunman with some flex ripped from a standard lamp. Once he had secured and gagged the man, North quickly found the door that led to the cellar. It was locked, but the gunman had supplied the key from his pocket.

Worn stone steps led down to the substantial cellar. An electric light bulb gave an almost adequate amount of light by which to navigate. Still holding the shotgun, North slowly descended, his mind perplexed as to what could possibly be of interest to the Romanian Government here in Sicily.

North tried to recall what he knew of Romania, past and present, which he soon realised was rather little. The present Romanian Government, under the communist dictator Nicolae Ceauşescu and his wife Elena, who many said was the real source of power, was one of the cruellest and most brutal regimes anywhere in the world. The KGB had taught the Romanian secret service not only espionage but the fine arts of torture, which they applied with ruthless efficiency whenever it suited their purposes.

The end of World War II had signalled the birth of Romanian communism and the end of a monarchy which stretched back in history many centuries. The Secret Police enjoyed absolute power over a population whose existence was ever closer to that portrayed in George Orwell's *1984*. The regime knew no morality or ethics, and brought a new meaning to the word 'terror'.

At one time, the population had enjoyed freedom similar to that in the West, but that time was now but a distant memory for a decreasing few. These few remembered being able to pass unhindered beyond Romanian borders, to state what they believed in, to earn money that could purchase commodities in stores that knew no shortages, without endless queues. They had once had pride in their country, but now there was nothing but cynicism and despair. Even the hope of faith and god's divine power was actively discouraged, to be replaced by the new religion of communism.

Russia's satellite states – from the semi-autonomous Finland in the frozen north to Romania and Bulgaria on the Black Sea – created a buffer zone against the West. Moscow always kept its influence over these countries – mostly acquired as a result of World War II – on a short leash. However, in time, one or two, such as Romania under Nicolae Ceauşescu, had tried to pursue a more independent course than that proposed by Moscow. For this 'courageous' action, the West, in their blindness, threw whatever caution they had to the wind in order to embrace this tyrant with open arms.

Subsequently, the CIA learnt much about the true nature of the Romanian Government from an agent who defected from their intelligence service, someone so high up that a contract had been out on him ever since. The information that he brought nearly ten years ago was so valuable that the CIA had kept even his very existence secret until recently.

The 'demonstrated' break from Moscow was staged to gain the confidence of the West and so increase their co-operation in many areas of particular Russian interest. For example, this new relationship resulted in closer industrial ties, which greatly increased opportunities for espionage and subversion.

As North descended further into the cellar, he became aware of a musty smell that seemed to hang in the air. Before he reached the bottom of the staircase, the electric light went out. Did someone turn it off, or was it connected to some kind of timer? North waited, suspended in darkness, but there was no sound. He pulled out his lighter and, with a flick of his thumb, the blackness disappeared.

From the flickering flame, shadows danced across thousands of wine bottles that lined the walls. Two figures, sitting on chairs in the middle of the room, squinted up at North, their features clearly visible from the flame he held before him. Neither could utter a sound due to having the lower portion of their jaws tightly bandaged with tape. Their arms and legs were bound to the chairs with cord.

North immediately recognised the Sicilian girl's dark eyes, her long hair untidy and wild, next to a woman who must be her mother. Within minutes, North had freed them from their bonds.

Octavia had not expected the Englishman to arrive. It was incredible that he had come to her aid a second time! The Baroness, after realising that North was not with the other foreigners who had tied them up, thanked him as only a Mediterranean woman can.

Octavia put her arms around North and squeezed him so tightly that he wondered if she would ever stop. At last, she released him to look up into his smiling face.

'You received my message at the hotel?' she whispered.

'Yes, only a few hours ago. I came straight away.'

She noticed the shotgun.

'Is it yours?'

'Someone upstairs must have dropped it – whoever left it wasn't using it, so I borrowed it. Is your father still abroad?'

Octavia's eyes became large with anxiety at the mention of her father.

'He has been taken to Sardinia. I overheard a conversation in a strange foreign language that I could not place. There were three words I recognised: my father's title 'Baron', 'Sardinia', and *Roxana*, the name of my father's yacht. He must be sailing the *Roxana* bound for Sardinia, which is bizarre, because his last communication to my mother several days ago was something about an unscheduled business trip to Athens!'

'The language you heard was Romanian. It now appears that someone else apart from your former fiancé has a strong interest in the famous Delmonte family. You wouldn't have any idea why?'

'None at all,' replied Octavia truthfully.

'How many of them are there?'

'I am not sure, but I don't think there are more than three. I've seen two, and I heard a third one talking soon after I arrived. I tried phoning you from upstairs but was caught before I could give any details. After that, they put us down here. One of them was a huge fat man with an ugly face; the other was taller and not so heavy.

'Amongst themselves, they used their own language,' she continued. 'I think only the taller man understood Italian. What does all this mean?' cried Octavia.

Her mother sat covering her face with shaking hands, mumbling something that only she knew the meaning of.

'At the moment,' replied North, 'I have no real idea. Maybe the Romanians have started to move into the field of kidnapping as a means of obtaining foreign currency. If this is the case, then it's an interesting venture into "capitalism" from their particular brand of Marxism.'

Somehow, thought North, *there had to be another reason. This explanation did not fit the puzzle.* There would be much easier ways of earning foreign currency, and most of them with considerably less risk of an international outcry than kidnapping members of the Delmonte family.

Octavia, her mother, and North climbed the steps out of the cellar, then made their way to a large formal room that he had not previously seen. After a preliminary search of the remaining rooms, North found no more unwelcome guests, but a car he had noticed earlier was missing. Someone had left within the last few minutes.

Under Octavia's direction, North found a well-equipped drinks cabinet and poured drinks for all of them. When they were settled as comfortably as possible under the circumstances, North continued his line of question.

'Did you learn any other information?' He directed his question at Octavia.

Before she replied, she sipped the strong drink. Normally she never touched spirits, but North had insisted, as she was shaking like a leaf. The whisky did seem to reduce the tension she felt at the bottom of her stomach, and she admitted that she was now slightly more composed than a few moments earlier.

Octavia's mother also drank whisky, the fiery liquid slowly bringing more colour to her previously white cheeks. She was otherwise remarkably relaxed, considering the situation. North noted that the Delmontes certainly seemed to be made from resilient material.

Replying to his question, Octavia said that her mother had sensed for some weeks that something was far from right with her husband. His disposition had been tense and at times unreasonable, which was most uncharacteristic of him. He kept repeating that this was all down to an increase in problems at 'work', but the Baroness said that she did not believe a word of it. She knew her husband far too well. She also knew him well enough not to question him further.

'It could have been those Romanians,' said the Baroness, 'putting some kind of pressure on my husband. Maybe they were involved in the recent kidnapping attempt in the South of France? One of them was always asking as to where my daughter was. They arrived soon after Octavia's phone call from Monte Carlo.'

'Perhaps,' said North, 'they had hoped to persuade Octavia, through you, to return to Sicily after the foiled kidnapping attempt. Maybe the two events are unconnected and Octavia's former fiancé was behind the kidnapping incident, as you suspected previously. Anyway, for the moment this is all rather academic. We need to leave the villa immediately. Whoever left in the Toyota will soon be back. I suspect he will also have some additional friends with which to carry on the struggle. Their attitude, I am sure, will be persistent and far from friendly. Who owns the motorboat moored at the jetty?'

'It's ours,' said the Baroness, her voice steady and even – its tone betraying little of what must be deep anxiety for her husband's safety.

'Right, both of you take a few essentials and meet me here in five minutes,' ordered North.

The women disappeared to their respective apartments to return moments later with a lightweight overnight bag and a small suitcase. Leaving the room, they made their way to the back of the villa, and in silence entered the courtyard. Only the splashing water from the fountain broke the still evening air. They paused for any sign of danger, but the shadows remained unthreatening.

The three figures passed through the archway North had entered earlier, then descended a steep path down the cliff face to the waiting rocks and sea below. The motorboat was moored alongside the jetty by bow and stern ropes. She was fairly large – about seventy feet of wood and epoxy resin construction, North guessed. *Built for speed and little else,* he thought, preferring sailing to speed, but this was obviously not the time to dwell on personal taste.

They had almost reached the motorboat when a rifle shot rang out. The Baroness, who was slightly behind North and Octavia, pitched forward onto the wooden jetty, her small case landing in the water below.

Someone must have a good telescopic sight to pick off a moving target, even if it was an elderly woman carrying a small suitcase, at over eight hundred yards. North grasped Octavia's hand and ran with her the last ten yards to the jetty's edge. Then both jumped onto the afterdeck which was hidden from the villa and cliffs by the wheelhouse.

'Can you start her?' asked North.

'Yes. But—'

'Just do it. I will see to your mother.'

Octavia obediently climbed up into the flying bridge, keeping her head as low as possible.

North undid the long bag he had been holding. It contained the shotgun and a hunting rifle that belonged to Octavia's father. It had been in a gun case in one of the rooms at the villa, and his thinking that it might prove useful now seemed somewhat fortuitous.

Through the scope, North scanned the path they had just left; the first sweep revealed nothing. Upon a second slower search, he spotted a man carrying a gun. The powerful sights clearly picked up his movements even at this distance. However, the boat was a poor gun platform as it swayed from side to side on the gentle swell.

North climbed onto the wooden jetty and, lying down, positioned himself behind a large bollard. The Baroness lay ten yards away, motionless. He feared the worst. Resting the rifle on a wooden box, North soon found the path but no man. A scan of the villa produced the same result. He could not go to the Baroness's aid without eliminating the threat from the gunman.

Then a slight movement caught his eye. Adjusting the focus, North saw a man crouching forward as he ran down the steep gravel path. The light was failing, making it increasingly difficult to follow the man's progress. North focused the crosshairs over the man's chest. He squeezed the trigger slowly, as the slightest tremor at this range would send the bullet wide and into the rocks.

North squeezed the trigger twice, a split second between each bullet. The man dropped from view, which meant he was either dead or had been missed and was thus waiting, out of sight, for another chance to stop the motorboat leaving.

Suddenly the motorboat's powerful engines sprang to life with a deep rumble. Then the fourth shot of the evening shattered the windshield of the flying bridge, sending glass over Octavia who was crouched inside.

Through the scope North hunted for this new source of attack. He estimated it came from in front of the villa. Whoever had left in the Toyota had returned with reinforcements, and sooner than expected. With accurate shooting like this, it was only a matter of time before something vital such as a fuel hose was hit. Immobilising their means of escape was the obvious intention.

North adjusted the range of the scope and patiently traversed the steep path all the way up to the stone balustrade that marked the cliff's edge in front of the villa. Then he saw the second gunman. He was just distinguishable, his head and shoulders silhouetted against the lighter stone of a statue. North remembered that the villa's grounds contained several such examples.

Slowly, hardly daring to breathe, North brought the crosshairs to bear on the man's forehead. He squeezed the trigger, his right shoulder absorbing the recoil. The man's head jerked back in a whiplash action, then disappeared from sight behind the balustrade. There was no other movement. *He must have died instantaneously from the heavy bullet,* thought North.

Taking the risk that the opposition was now neutralised, at least for the moment, North crawled across the wooden jetty to the still motionless shape. Quickly North established that the Baroness's pulse and breathing were non-existent. Where the bullet had struck was unimportant; she was quite dead.

Watched by Octavia, North crawled back to the motorboat, untying the bow rope as he went. Octavia, knowing her mother was dead, felt a tremendous sense of loss come over her. She released the stern rope, then moved the gear lever to reverse.

Suddenly a huge explosion engulfed the jetty, its shock wave blowing out glass and showering the whole area in matchwood. The jetty's once-substantial structure now ceased to exist, its wood scattered far and wide. *How did that happen?* thought North. *Was there a third gunman whose target had been the exposed fuel drums stacked along the jetty's sides?*

North moved towards the girl to take advantage of what inadequate cover was offered by the wheelhouse. With the engines in reverse, he opened the throttles. There was a boiling of foam behind the stern as the twin screws bit. Once clear of the debris, North switched the gear stick to forward. Quickly, the sleek hull was skimming across the water, putting an ever-increasing distance between them and the raging fire that had started. Here and there patches of water burned from where oil or petrol had spread across its surface.

There would be no sign of the Baroness's body after such an explosion and raging fire. A thick black cloud of smoke, fed by the expanding burning slick of hydrocarbons, rose into the still night air. Soon it obscured the jetty's remaining twisted and useless timbers, lying at impossible and crazy angles of defeat.

'I am sorry about your mother,' yelled North above the roar of the diesels. 'It must have been instantaneous; she could not have felt any pain…'

The girl's eyes were wide with fear, and moist from a grief that she could not understand. From her father's strange behaviour to the kidnapping attempts, and now her mother's death; what did it all mean? Where were these events leading? The path of her survival looked increasingly perilous, her destination shrouded with uncertainties.

Once smoke had disappeared behind them, North cut the throttles to 50 per cent of maximum. The powerful engines reduced their distinctive rumble. The racing hull immediately made a more settled approach, its angle now less acute, their white bow wave already becoming less prominent and conspicuous.

North bent over several charts, consulting their information with his navigational instruments and pencil. At last he threw down the pencil to find the girl staring at him, her eyes wide and nervous. Perhaps she was close to hysteria. But somehow, he sensed that she possessed a strange inner resilience that was unusual in one so young.

'I have set a course for southern Sardinia; we won't find many answers to all this by hanging around here. The explosion and the fire will have alerted someone to call the authorities. In any case, the villa will soon be crawling with local police. Thus, Sardinia offers our best chance to discover what the hell is going on, and to find your father. I am so sorry about what happened to your mother.'

Octavia said nothing, her dark eyes still staring at the stranger who had so recently become such an influence in her life. Caution and deliberation would not be accurate descriptions of her natural character. Impulsiveness and spontaneity would be closer to the truth.

Suspicion did not come naturally to Octavia, but through difficult and sometimes bitter experience, life teaches that a girl needs to develop at least a healthy caution towards strange men, particularly if their background and purpose is of an unknown quantity.

Did this stranger represent a lifeline of hope against recent events? Or were there other motives that would account for his actions and ultimately against her interests?

The man smiled, which Octavia found reassuring. She wanted to believe in the sincerity it offered.

'I follow your reasoning,' she replied, 'and agree with your decision in making for Sardinia. The local police here are in the hands of the Cosa Nostra, so I can't see that we can benefit by staying. It is a long time since I visited Sardinia, but I already look forward to seeing its wild and irregular coast once more. Thank you again for your timely help...'

'Don't mention it,' said North, still smiling. 'I was almost thinking that life might be a little predictable and lacked a certain, how shall I say, excitement! However, I think recent events are starting to irretrievably alter my views on life's previous cautious performance, and who knows, perhaps this transformation will turn out to be an interesting diversion.'

Chapter Three

The powerful diesels propelled the boat over the water at slightly less than thirty knots. Her foaming wake creamed out behind her for nearly a quarter of a mile before the dark blue of the Mediterranean resumed its unbroken surface. A green fluorescent glow surrounded the compass, giving a ghost-like appearance to North's features. His eyes were concentrating on the blackness beyond the bow, with regular glances at the compass to confirm their bearing of WNW.

The sea's surface was a millpond of tranquillity. This, combined with a hull built for speed, produced very little vibration, only the wind from the shattered windshield creating some discomfort. However, the night was warm, and North did not find its strength too uncomfortable, as enough glass remained to provide some protection.

Octavia suddenly came up from below deck where she had been trying to sleep, her long thick hair unbrushed, dishevelled, and wild. The wind immediately caught it, exposing her face to reveal bloodshot eyes that had known little rest. The warm wind did, however, manage to dry the tears, but dark rings persisted under her lower lids.

Life has been referred to as a 'testing ground' by philosopher and thinker alike. Some are tested in their youth, some in middle age, and others in their twilight years. Octavia knew that she was encountering great difficulties now, and this was her youth, her beginning. If she had the strength within her to face the future, perhaps with the help of this stranger, she might have a chance of surviving what destiny had in store.

Several hours passed, during which time Octavia managed a few hours sleep. She felt more rested as a consequence, but her anxiety persisted.

The radar screen revealed the position of several ships, but their courses were never close enough to give North cause for concern. It had taken them over twelve hours to cover the near three hundred miles from Cefalù to southern Sardinia.

North did not want to make port in Cagliari itself, as it would almost certainly be watched by Major Vasile's men. So, after consulting the charts, he decided to head for the more desolate piece of coastline at Nora, the site of a Roman settlement on the peninsula. He reasoned that Major Vasile could not possibly watch the entire Sardinian coast all the time for one motorboat. Here, they had a good chance of landing undetected. The map had a symbol donating a historic site. Octavia remembered it was part of the Punic Roman city of Nora, most of which was now under water.

At last they came within sight of the ancient watchtower and the peninsula it had guarded for so many centuries. It was a strange, solid structure, sixty or seventy feet high, made from dark stone.

A few hundred yards from the tower, North saw the remains of a stone pier. Cutting their speed to a crawl, he approached with caution. It was in an advanced stage of disrepair, but there was no other alternative.

Picking a section of the pier that looked reasonably intact, North drew the large boat alongside, their strategically positioned fenders gently touching the rough stone as they slowed to a stop.

Octavia efficiently jumped down with the bow rope and made fast to an iron ring that had not quite rusted through. North, with the engines in neutral, threw the stern rope and she repeated the procedure, this time with another iron ring that had also somehow escaped extensive decay.

'I suggest we go ashore and make some discreet enquiries to see if the *Roxana* has been seen recently. I have heard of her, and a yacht of that size can't slip into a harbour and not be noticed. I am hoping the *Roxana* might lead us to your father. For the moment, I can't think of any other course of action.'

Octavia nodded in agreement. Taking some local currency and his passport, he then hid the guns. North locked the cabin and hatches before leaving. As a last thought, he disconnected the main fuel line to the engine. If anyone wanted to go for a joy ride, it would be a short trip.

North and Octavia quickly found themselves in the middle of what was a reasonable-sized Roman settlement, parts of which were remarkably well preserved. Several areas were cordoned off, with evidence of work in progress. However, for the moment there appeared to be no-one about.

They passed a woman selling postcards and guidebooks, but she did not question them as to their lacking tickets for the ruins. Perhaps it was too early in the day for her to worry about this irregularity. After a few minutes of walking, they found a deserted car park, so they continued their relaxed pace under the morning sun along the road towards Pula.

After ten minutes, a red Fiat drew up, driven by an Australian couple who offered them a lift to Pula. Their blonde hair and suntanned bodies contrasted sharply with the dark and gnarled features of the old woman selling tickets. Their relaxed attitude was a welcome diversion for their new passengers, after their previous days, so full of disturbance and unease.

Pula turned out to be a very small town, with a church and a monument of some sort to the north. After saying goodbye to the cheerful Australians, North decided that breakfast was long overdue, to which Octavia agreed. They found a café that provided tables outside.

They ordered coffee and freshly baked croissants. Octavia did the ordering as her Italian was fluent and would not attract attention. After a few minutes, she struck up a conversation with the waiter – a short man whose waistline strongly suggested a fondness for his food. She managed during the course of their conversation to make some discreet enquiries about the *Roxana*. Apparently, he had not seen or heard of the yacht recently, though he knew it well both by reputation and sight. The *Roxana* was a regular visitor to the shores of Sardinia, particularly the Emerald Coast in the north east.

The waiter left, only to return with the news that a large motorboat belonging to an Italian had been sighted off Cagliari.

So, it would appear, thought North, *that the* Roxana *and Octavia's father have not yet arrived, at least in these waters*. The *Roxana* could have anchored further north, perhaps as far as the Costa Smeralda, still assuming that her destination was Sardinia. *But if so, for what purpose?*

North took another sip of his cappuccino and started to do some calculating. Octavia had overheard the conversation that mentioned the *Roxana* and her father, but she had no idea of a departure time, nor the location of the *Roxana*.

She had arrived at the family villa in the afternoon of September 3rd, and had immediately been held. After finding out who she was, the Romanians had confined her to her room. The following day, she joined her mother in the wine cellar, after being caught using the telephone.

The two men had become very angry with her refusing to tell them who she had been trying to contact. They also questioned her as to the incident on the beach in the South of France, confirming that they had either been involved or somehow knew about it.

It was now the morning of the 5th, and there was no knowing when the *Roxana* had left northern Sicily to estimate its approximate time of arrival in Sardinia – assuming, of course, that this was their plan. Octavia said that the *Roxana* was large and needed a crew to run her. So, if these Romanians were holding her father aboard his own yacht and sailing for Sardinia, then speed and secrecy were not important elements of their plan. If anything, it would appear the opposite, that they were courting attention!

North finished his croissants and cappuccino. Where was Major Vasile? In Bucharest, or perhaps supervising operations from a closer point? Maybe he was on the *Roxana* with the Baron? No doubt he would learn more about this Colonel Vasile and his game in the future.

'Holding the Baron,' reasoned North, 'could be a sort of insurance against us going to the authorities concerning previous events.'

'There is another very good reason,' said Octavia. 'The Cosa Nostra has so infiltrated the police that unless one has connections it is a waste of time going to them. No doubt Major Vasile has his contacts within Police Headquarters at Palermo, which would render any approach to them next to futile. Only a madman would attempt a high-profile kidnapping and what amounted to brazen interference into Cosa Nostra territory, without cooperation from those who wield the real power.'

After settling the bill, North tried for a moment or two longer to solve the puzzle. It just did not make any sense at all to kidnap a well-known and wealthy man upon his own yacht, having tried twice to kidnap his daughter. *They had been successful in holding Octavia and her mother as well, but what is the purpose?* he mused. *Where is the motive? If ransom is the intention, then why hold all key members of the family? Surely it would have been more effective and easier to hold one member of the family, not all three? Maybe having failed twice with Octavia, they decided to see who was in the villa that might prove useful.*

This, of course, did not explain the strange behaviour of her father over the past few weeks, culminating in his recent trip to Athens. *Was Major Vasile's hand at work here, too?*

North thought that their best chance of locating the *Roxana* – and hopefully the Baron – without being discovered was to drive to Cagliari. Major Vasile would have the harbour watched, expecting them to arrive in the motorboat that they had left northern Sicily in the previous evening.

In Major Vasile's place, he would not only have Cagliari harbour watched but any other likely place that they might try to land. Of course, this did rather depend upon the man's available resources. There was another line of thinking: Major Vasile might be ignoring them completely, secure in the knowledge that while he had the Baron aboard his yacht, they would be drawn to him like a magnet, once located.

Octavia wanted to return to the motorboat before proceeding to Cagliari, as she had forgotten her bag of personal effects. North tried to persuade her that it was more important to press on and see if they could discover the whereabouts of the *Roxana*, but the Sicilian girl would not listen.

North soon felt that no matter what argument he posed against returning, she was not going to hear his logic, let alone change her mind. Was this outburst just the result of an inflexible and obstinate personality, or part of a shrewd and cunning mind beneath the attractive exterior, perhaps planning a hidden agenda? Or was he reading too much into her attitude? Time, in the end, would no doubt provide the answers, he reasoned.

So, by taxi, and in silence, they returned to the car park at Nora. The fifteen-minute walk it took to reach the motorboat was also conducted in silence. Neither felt like breaking the ice that had suddenly formed between them.

North approached the boat first. He had arranged certain things, such as a coiled rope on the deck, in such a way so that he could tell if they had had visitors in their absence. It soon became apparent that someone had indeed been aboard. The padlock to the cabin door was absent. Someone had shown little respect for the mahogany door, which was pitted and splintered where the lock used to be. North told Octavia to stay on the jetty until he said it was safe. Whoever had done this could still be aboard.

Cautiously making his way around the deck, North peered through the portholes. There appeared no sign of life inside. Soon after entering the cabin, this was confirmed. He searched all the way to the anchor locker in the bows. All was intact and untouched, except the door. From the bridge, he waved to Octavia that it was safe for her to come aboard.

So, they had been watched after all, but how could anyone have known that their destination was Nora? Then he knew, and North cursed himself for not picking up on it earlier. Soon after leaving the villa by boat, the word must have gone out that they would probably be heading for Sardinia.

'What about that plane we saw?' said Octavia.

'Yes, my thoughts exactly,' said North.

It had been just a small single-engine machine, too far away to make out any markings, but no doubt its pilot benefited from the use of binoculars in taking a closer look at them.

'That was at first light this morning, and it would have been easy to radio Cagliari and arrange a reception party for us,' said North.

'I don't understand,' said Octavia. 'Where are these Romanians now? Breaking the cabin door makes little sense on its own.'

'The reason is over here.' North's voice had the tired tone of someone who has repeatedly missed the obvious.

He lifted the engine cover, which had inexplicably missed his earlier attention. Someone had ripped out all the wires and hoses he could find, and those that could not be ripped were cut with a very efficient pair of wire cutters. This engine would not be running for quite some time; it would take a mechanic several days of concentrated work to achieve anything like running order again.

North continued his second search of the radio and navigation equipment. The damage here was a little less obvious, but no less crucial. The power supply to the equipment had been severed.

So, they now had no propulsion or means of communication. It would appear that someone wanted them to remain in the area and, what is more, that someone wanted them very much alive. If their 'friend' with the wire cutters had wanted them dead, he would presumably have stayed aboard for that purpose.

From the motorboat, North could see a man bent over amongst the Roman ruins. They had not seen anyone on their outward walk, but Octavia said that she had noticed the man upon their return.

'Why didn't you say something earlier?' said North, angry that Octavia had not communicated this information before.

'You weren't in a listening mood,' said Octavia, throwing her arms up in the air with a gesture of exasperation. 'I thought you were angry with me for wanting to return and pick up my bag.'

'Yes, I was angry with you,' he replied harshly. 'But that's no excuse for not telling me about this man.'

He turned to look at the girl, and thought the dark eyes seemed more attractive and desirable than when he had first seen her face. North also wondered if this theatrical independence represented only an exterior that masked a deeper confusion, and even uncertainty. Or was this nothing more than a usual Sicilian attempt at communication?

'I want to go. I have my bag.'

'An excellent idea,' said North, thinking how impulsive these Sicilians could be with their fluctuations of mood.

Octavia climbed up the wooden steps set into the jetty and North passed her the guns wrapped in a large bag. They had remained hidden, along with their ammunition, amongst blocks of iron used for ballast. Whoever carried out the search had failed in thoroughness. *Somehow,* thought North, *they might come in useful before this whole affair is brought to some kind of conclusion.*

Their waiting taxi drove at a relaxed pace towards Cagliari. The driver did not take an undue interest in the long bag. No doubt he was used to all kinds of luggage.

After ten minutes, North thought he saw a car following, but could not be sure. Maybe the 'archaeologist' Octavia had seen earlier was suddenly taking a closer interest in their movements.

Octavia told the driver, in high pitched Italian, that her aunt was ill in Cagliari and that at the speed he was driving they would be late for her funeral! Her onslaught seemed to have the desired effect, for the man suddenly woke up from his insolent and lazy attitude, and started treating his taxi like a late Grand Prix entry.

The Fiat is an underrated car. Its native country has some of the worst roads in Europe, hence its suspension is among the most enduring. The driver, well-acquainted with his car's capabilities, drove like a possessed maniac. For a while, a long cloud of dust trailed behind them until they reached the well-surfaced main road to Cagliari.

If the Fiat was being followed, whoever was behind them would have an increasingly difficult task to remain discreet. At the speed they were travelling, their pursuers – assuming they really were being followed – would have to view their progress with an increasing amount of importance to continue their interest.

At Octavia's instructions, the driver dropped them off along the Via Roma in front of the harbour. Then, without so much as a goodbye, the taxi departed in a cloud of blue exhaust smoke and with squealing tyres.

'He seemed in nearly as much hurry to leave us as he was in driving us here,' commented North.

Octavia smiled. 'I told him that I had "strong connections" and if my aunt, who is dangerously ill, died before we arrived, my family would hold him responsible.'

North also smiled at this light-hearted interruption to their more serious task of finding Octavia's father. From their view of the harbour, there was no sign of the *Roxana*. Only a large ferry exhibited activity, with hundreds of cars and people disembarking in true Italian chaos.

On the Via Roma, they found a café, its tables shaded from the hot sun by white and blue parasols advertising Cinzano. North ordered a beer, Octavia white wine. The atmosphere was relaxed in spite of the noisy traffic passing so close.

'Cagliari is Sardinia's capital and the port is its centre,' explained Octavia. 'Throughout history the port has played an important part in the town's survival, even during the dark ages. It has always been the leading city of the island since Roman times, mainly due to its natural defences and harbour.'

North was genuinely interested in Octavia's local knowledge, but his eyes constantly watched to see if anyone was taking more than a passing interest in them. So far, from what he could observe, no-one had been. Everyone was either deep in conversation, reading newspapers, or walking purposefully past, but he knew from experience that suspicion was, at times, a healthy frame of mind.

'Did you know, Sebastian...' continued Octavia, with her charming but unfamiliar pronunciation of his name, '...the walls of the citadel that exist today were built by Pisans who seized the city in the 11th century? The Spanish and Sardinian kings made Cagliari their island capital, making it a major centre of commerce to the present day. Unfortunately, during the last war, it sustained extensive damage in parts. These areas have been rebuilt; a few with what I would say are hideous, out of place, modern designs.'

For twenty minutes they walked, before finding a small hotel that commanded a view of the sea. From their room, part of the town and harbour could clearly be seen. Then something caught Octavia's eye, but it was at first too far out to identify clearly. Slowly it grew larger and more distinct. Then finally, she exclaimed in an excited voice, 'It's the *Roxana*!'

'Are you sure?' asked North, his eyes fixed upon the yacht's graceful lines.

'Yes, of course I am sure, I would recognise my father's boat anywhere.'

The *Roxana* had half her sail area up and, as they watched, was reducing more and at the same time slowing her speed as she approached the port. However, she turned at the last moment, as if deciding against navigating into the narrow and crowded harbour. The *Roxana* was expertly brought up into the wind to drop her port anchor with a terrific splash, the spray reaching her decks like a shower. The anchor chain followed with a furious rush, before it slowed. *No doubt controlled by an electrical winch,* thought North, *hidden below deck.*

The *Roxana* drifted, the captain trying to see if the anchor would hold on the seabed, which it did. Several ant-like figures could be seen furling the remaining sails, perched high above the gently heaving deck below.

North recalled what his grandfather – a man who had spent much of his life under sail – always said about using an anchor. To hold a yacht by a secure anchor, three times as much chain must be let out as there is depth under the keel.

So, if the keel depth is four fathoms, then it would need twelve fathoms of chain or seventy-two feet. To those not in the habit of dropping anchors in strange waters, this may seem a lot of chain, but it is a safety margin to prevent the anchor dragging. An anchor will dislodge itself more easily from a vertical pull than from a near-horizontal pull, which is increasingly the case the more chain there is out. It is hoped that the anchor will drag initially, to eventually catch itself on an obstruction along the bottom, or bury its arrow-headed iron prongs into the mud or sand of the seabed.

As they watched from their balcony, Octavia recounted some of *Roxana*'s history.

'A South American from Santiago had her built originally. He was so rich that no expense was spared in fitting her out. Her keel was laid down in Palma at Astilleroc de Mallorca. She was originally named *Ingrid*, reputably after a beautiful Scandinavian mistress he was said to have, but no-one knew for certain.'

North estimated her length at about one hundred and twenty feet, with two masts and three deckhouses, no doubt solid mahogany. Certainly, a beautiful vessel, built for the keen sailing enthusiast, without the compromise of limited resources.

'How long has your father owned her?' asked North, impressed by the Baron's obvious interest in sailing and eye for quality.

'Three or four years, I think,' she replied. 'My father and I sailed a great deal through the Greek Islands after he bought her, but my mother sailed in the *Roxana* only once. She liked firmer ground under her feet than a heaving deck. I think her stomach suffered a great deal, too.'

She paused, thinking. 'Do you think my father is aboard?' she enquired.

'Could be, but one can't be sure,' he replied.

'How are we going to find out?'

North noticed her anxious tone. He had thought up some kind of plan that involved boarding the *Roxana*, but it would be a clandestine visit at night, and he would be going alone.

'I will go tonight, alone, and see what I can discover as to the whereabouts of your father. It's too dangerous for both of us.'

Octavia's large almond-shaped eyes were unsettled. Her face portrayed something more than anxiety, maybe fear.

'I think they want your father's yacht, as well as him, for some purpose which I hope to find out. The whole thing is very odd. There is a reason behind everything that has happened since I met you in France, but I can't quite figure it out yet.

'Those Romanians have a reason for being here and, whatever it is, it's not for our welfare, you can bet your life on it. Especially judging by our recent experiences, not to mention the way the Ceauşescus have run their country over the last few years.'

So, what was Major Vasile's game? If the Baron was aboard, then that is where he would remain, as it would be easier to control an uncooperative kidnapped man on the *Roxana* than ashore.

As North thought, he talked at length with Octavia over all possible motives behind these strange events that had taken place over the last few days. When they had finished, their discussion had not concluded at a logical explanation that fitted all the pieces to this increasingly violent jigsaw puzzle – one that was fast developing around them.

After much protest about wanting to join him, Octavia did finally agree to North's proposed clandestine night investigation of the *Roxana* alone. It might prove to be a useful information-gathering exercise. Once on board, he might find some answers as to what these Romanians were really after.

They left the hotel to walk towards the harbour. After some enquiries conducted by Octavia, they found a small motor cruiser for hire. The owner – a man of about fifty, with a lined, weather-beaten face – was very pleased and helpful, once he caught sight of North's hand that contained a folded bundle of one hundred thousand-lire notes.

Once they had agreed a price and been shown the general layout of the cabin and engine, the owner left, smiling at his new-found wealth.

'This boat will attract less attention than the one we left at Nora,' said North.

Next, North hired a car, which turned out to be a nondescript dark blue Renault. Octavia filled out the numerous forms and North signed each one as required. His identity would, of course, be unknown and meaningless to the over-inquisitive.

After locating a shop specialising in sporting equipment, North and Octavia loaded the Renault with diving gear, in preparation for the evening's activities. North decided to wait until the cover of darkness to transfer the equipment onto the motor cruiser. Upon passing a bakery, the smell of recently cooked bread stimulated Octavia so much that she insisted on buying several freshly baked rolls. She added several cheeses and red wine to her carrier bag before leaving the shop.

They soon found themselves walking down the Viale San Vincenzo towards the ruins of a Roman amphitheatre that Octavia said was close by. The amphitheatre was large, with seating for about fifteen thousand, North estimated.

He walked down one of the aisles to the large stage, then turned around to face the empty seats. It must have been quite a sight when it was full, with thousands of people watching live theatre all those years ago. He saw

Octavia standing at the top of the aisle, and wondered how her tall figure would look in a wide-brimmed hat. Gracefully appealing, he decided, but then he had always held the view that a woman who wears such a hat can only enhance her feminine elegance.

Octavia joined him upon the stage, where they both travelled back in time, each alone with their thoughts as cries from the Roman world filled their ears.

They sat down on one of the stone benches. North opened the bottle of wine and Octavia cut some cheese to have with the bread. They were quite alone as they started eating their lunch under the hot, cloudless sky.

North told Octavia of how she might look in a wide-brimmed hat, and she promised to wear one if he chose the design. At this he laughed and agreed.

It was the first time for days North had seen the Sicilian girl smile and he found it engaging with a hint of charming intrigue. At the hotel, she had changed into a green chiffon blouse, whose thin gauze portrayed ample cleavage below. Around her waist she wore a cream leather skirt that finished mid-thigh, half exposing her athletic-looking legs. Black designer shoes finished the perfect figure.

However, it was her eyes, since he had first seen them in the South of France, that North found most attractive. They were almond-shaped, dark, devastatingly beautiful, and full of mystery that could not be easily defined.

For a while, it was as if their present crisis of circumstance did not exist. They both found each other's company fascinating and enjoyable, and for now, at the amphitheatre, under the hot Sicilian sun, the weight of recent events that hung over them was temporarily lifted. It was the presence of this new-found relationship that they both wished would continue. Octavia wondered if, for her, it represented some kind of security against so much recent distress.

They must have taken a couple of hours over lunch, absorbed in conversation under the very clear blue sky, but neither of them noticed the time.

North picked up the empty wine bottle, and as he did, his hand briefly brushed against the silk of Octavia's blouse. He felt her firm and warm beneath the translucent chiffon. Their eyes met for an instant before the moment passed. Standing up, Octavia suggested they explore a little more of Cagliari.

'It has been a long time since I visited Cagliari,' she said. 'It has much to offer in the way of historical interest and restaurants, several rich in atmosphere.'

Passing through an old part of the city with narrow streets, they found themselves walking down the Via Sardegna, which exhibited many interesting street-fronted cafés. Here the locals passed the time of day and the tourists discussed their latest purchases between taking photographs, all predictably posed, for their album and friends back home.

Then, while browsing in a shop, Octavia found a long black sleeveless dress, cut away low at the back. North bought it for her on the condition that she accepted his offer of dinner later that evening.

This Octavia agreed to, saying that as he liked the dress, too, it would give her pleasure to wear it for him that evening.

Octavia found the wrought-iron gates of *La Valencia*, a Spanish restaurant that overlooked the harbour, which she remembered from visiting the island two years previously.

North opened the gates set into a wall. There was no other sign to say that a restaurant lay beyond, except the name *La Valencia* painted on blue and white tiles off to one side. Due to its out of the way location, Octavia said that the only people who visited were from recommendation.

A path led from the gates to a courtyard enclosed by high walls. Cloisters surrounded the garden, the focal point of which was a pond surrounded by coloured tiles, with waters fed by a bubbling fountain. The air was heavy with the scent of many plants. North reckoned they must be close to the sea, as the smell of salt was faint on the air.

A man appeared from French windows. His dress was traditional Spanish: red shirt, black waistcoat, dark trousers and hat. He greeted them with a wide smile, the droopy moustache only partially hiding his stained teeth. Grasping Octavia's hand, he bowed very low, saying in Spanish, 'Señora, it is a pleasure to welcome you to *La Valencia*.'

North replied in Spanish, the waiter's natural language, that they would like a table for eight-thirty. The waiter bowed again and disappeared, returning a moment later with a large leather book.

'What name should I enter, Señor?' he asked, looking at North; it was the kind of traditional and old-fashioned restaurant that preferred reserving a table in a man's name.

'North,' he replied.

The waiter, with his moustache twitching, entered the name in his ledger and then, with a second deep bow to Octavia and another broad smile with more stained teeth, disappeared through the open doorway from which he had just emerged.

North and Octavia left the way they had come, through the iron gates, to resume their exploration of the town. The Spanish influence along the Via Mannu was evident in its architecture. The Via Mannu in turn led to the Piazza Yennue. Here they found a statue of King Carlo Feline, but the inscription beneath was too faded to read. From the Piazza Yennue, they found themselves in a labyrinth of narrow alleyways which led to the Citadello, an old Pisan fortress. A magnificent marble stairway ascended to the Piazza Consituzione. Here a large plateau, the San Remy Bastion, commanded a spectacular view of Cagliari and its harbour.

The harbour's activity was dominated by the *Roxana*, her presence evoking something splendid and luxurious from another era. The sailing yacht's imposing dignity contrasted with the ugly mechanised container ships and ferries that made up most of the port's activity.

In silence, the two figures leant upon the balustrade, momentarily lost in thought. Their only previous contact had been fleeting, when North's hand had brushed against Octavia's arm at the amphitheatre. A small insignificant thing in itself, but like so much in this world, one wonders afterwards if fate had taken an unseen but purposeful hand in influencing events.

Octavia moved a little closer, remembering their earlier contact. Had this been chance or design? Did this Englishman feel the same way as she did? Then she doubted that it had occurred at all. Was it only an illusion?

He was now quite close. *What can I see in his face?* thought Octavia. The short black hair, strong nose, well-proportioned chin, and those eyes, surrounded by little creases when he smiled or laughed. She had first seen him laugh at the amphitheatre, when he became more Latin and full of life. If only she could make him loosen his emotions a little and bring him out into the open like a true Mediterranean; then he would give everything and hold back nothing.

The Englishman's face seemed to be focused on the *Roxana*. His eyes held a deep faraway look, but she sensed that the mind that controlled them was active, calculating, and measuring, trying to peer into the opaque future.

Suddenly he turned around, perhaps feeling her eyes upon him. Their eyes met, and within that instant she knew without reason that she was not only attracted to him but that she trusted him like no other.

As they stood, a breeze blew up from the south, sending strands of Octavia's hair across her face, like a veil, but her eyes remained un-obscured. With a smile, North saw them change from deep wells of mystery to sparkling streams of exuberance, even the dark rings seeming to recede.

It was down one of the narrow alleyways that they encountered a series of steps. North, taking Octavia's hand, helped her climb them. They continued holding hands after reaching the last step, neither wanting to break the contact.

Such a simple thing, holding hands, but for many it has sadly lost all meaning. However, to the Englishman and Sicilian girl on that late afternoon walking in the old part of Cagliari, this act of unity conveyed countless unspoken words. When they were forced to release their hold for an instant, due to people passing in the opposite direction or some other obstruction, it was renewed with a desire to recapture the pleasure of their first contact.

During their walk through ancient streets and historical buildings, they kept a close watch to see if anyone was following them. Twice North thought he saw a man in a blue shirt not far behind, but he never appeared a third time, if indeed he had existed at all. At the moment, North reckoned, there was a reasonable chance that their exact whereabouts would remain unknown. But Major Vasile would guess that they were not far away due to the discovery of the motor cruiser.

They found another café and ordered coffee and cake. Octavia obtained a copy of the island's newspaper *L'Unione Sarde* and scanned the headlines, then handed it to North.

Apart from local politics, the only other news of interest was that a large freighter of 20,000 tonnes had run aground three miles off Isola di Sant Antiolo, west of Sardinia. It was a Panamanian registered ship called *Belle of the Wind. Unusual name*, thought North. She had run aground on a reef two nights ago in strong winds. It was going to be some time before she could be floated off.

There were a few more lines about dense fog banks that sometimes occurred between the southern coast of Sardinia and Algeria, something to do with the sea temperature and pressure ridges in the area. The article ended by saying that the *Belle of the Wind* had been bound for Istanbul from Caracas. There was no mention as to what her cargo might have been.

Finishing their coffee and sweet cake, they left, making their way to the cathedral in the Piazza Palazzo.

It was built in the 13th century and repaired in the 17th. Once inside its dark interior, it took several minutes to find their bearings, their eyes slowly adapting to the dim light. Their attention was attracted by the beautifully carved wooden pulpits, dating from the 12th century.

Leaving the cathedral, they wandered, often holding hands, through the historical streets of Cagliari just as the mood took them. To their surprise and delight, the dark Sicilian girl and tall Englishman found that many of their thoughts, tastes, and opinions coincided like mirror images, so that they both wondered why life had taken its time in bringing them together.

At last, tired of walking, they returned to *La Valencia* where the same waiter with the ready smile and stained teeth greeted them. *His bow this time was even deeper than before*, thought Octavia.

They passed through a spacious hallway, the walls of which were decorated with crossed swords and old half-faded posters advertising the bullfight. Tall, dark matadors, in various stances of Latin defiance, arrogantly glared down upon them before they entered the low-ceilinged dining room.

The waiter, anticipating their needs, showed them to a secluded corner table, and pulled out a chair for Octavia. Once she was seated, North sat down opposite her. The waiter lit a long red candle, then carefully placed its black wrought-iron holder in the table's centre. Before leaving, he gave them each a menu and North an extensive wine list. The menu was predominantly Spanish, but some local Sardinian dishes were also available. After much discussion, the waiter returned.

After ordering *hors d'oeuvres* and soup, Octavia settled on a prawn and lobster salad. North decided upon poached hake fillets in an almond sauce. He also chose a dry white wine to drink with the main course, a 1985 Grand Cru from Conca de Barbera. He thought that its clean and light flavour from the southeast of Penedes would complement their choice of seafood. It would also be consistent with the convention of white wine with fish and red wine with meat.

Once the waiter had departed, they surveyed with interest the walls of the restaurant, which were partially covered with racks of wine and brightly coloured paintings. Some of these illustrated Spanish castles against dramatic backgrounds of sky and rock. Octavia recognised one from the southeast of Spain called Almansa, near Albacete, that she had visited a few years ago while studying the Moorish influence in the region. Other paintings were of Spanish architecture and colourfully dressed girls dancing the flamenco.

'How very Spanish in atmosphere this restaurant is,' remarked North to Octavia, 'set in Sardinia, of all places.'

'Yes, it is one of my favourites. It reminds me of the real Andalusia. I hoped you would like it.'

Her smile remained intriguing, the dark eyes alluring and beautiful, lit by the backwash from the yellow flame. The lighting was very low, mostly coming from the flickering candles upon the tables, creating dancing shadows across the rough stone walls.

'An excellent choice, Octavia,' replied North.

The waiter arrived with their *hors d'oeuvres* and two glasses of light dry sherry from Jerez de la Frontera. The *hors d'oeuvres* consisted of two small dishes. The first contained mushrooms garnished with garlic and parsley; the second held salmagundi of shellfish and hard-boiled eggs.

For a few minutes, conversation ceased so that justice might be achieved towards their food. Once finished, their table was cleared for the gazpacho – a cold vegetable soup of chopped egg, onions, tomatoes, cucumber, and green and red peppers. 'A very popular and refreshing dish,' commented the waiter, from Andalusia. Once the soup had been consumed, both North and Octavia began to reflect and recount their respective travels and experiences upon that captivating piece of land known as the Iberian Peninsula.

The main course arrived, with the wine chilled to the right temperature. They took a long time over their well-prepared food. Octavia imagined she could feel the spirit of southern Spain from these simple crustaceans of the sea.

Stretching his hand across the table, North held Octavia's hand. He had noticed an interesting gold ring with a large ruby set in its centre. He commented upon its unique design.

'It was given to me by my mother on my twenty-first birthday. It belonged to her mother before, who also received it upon her twenty-first birthday. It's been in the family for many generations. I seem to recall her saying that our family on my mother's side have had it since the 18th century.

"The story is that one of my ancestors brought it back from Persia to Greece, where it was eventually passed down to my mother. It's strange, because family tradition has dictated that it be passed down to the eldest child, even if she is female.

"It has been said that it holds the key to great wealth. Believe it or not, there is some sort of inscription etched onto one of its faces, but I have never seen it. My father told me once that this can be achieved by etching with a diamond. Apparently, this was at one time quite a common practice to record a stone's previous owners.'

'Yes, the hardest and most impervious substance natural or manmade is diamond,' commented North. He continued, 'The only real way to cut or make any impression upon a ruby, which is made of the mineral corundum, is to use a diamond, as its crystallised carbon produces the ideal cutting instrument.

'You have no idea what this inscription means?' enquired North with increasing curiosity at this new information.

'No, none whatever,' replied Octavia.

'It would be an interesting puzzle to solve,' commented North, still holding Octavia's long finger. Then he added with a smile, 'I wonder if the legend has any truth attached to it.'

Octavia laughed. 'Why don't we try to decipher its meaning when we find my father and after all this is over?'

'Let's drink to the legend of your ring,' he replied, raising his glass. There was a satisfying clink when their glasses touched before another sip of the wine.

'Who gave you this ring?' asked North, pointing to a small sapphire Octavia wore on the fourth finger of her left hand.

'My father gave it to me upon my sixteenth birthday. Like the ruby, it has been passed down through the generations on his side. It's been in the Delmonte family a long time, and I value it greatly. The gold leopard with black spots that makes up the ring is often used by the Sicilian aristocracy as a sign of nobility and purity.'

'I noticed at the villa the leopard occurring upon some tiles and woven into one of the large carpets.'

With the cheese selection that followed, North had a glass of vintage port, while Octavia chose a Malmsey Madeira, heavy and rich like a liqueur. Their conversation drifted back to southern Spain covering its people, customs, and music.

'The Spanish guitar is quite the most divine instrument,' remarked Octavia.

'I agree,' replied North. 'In my opinion it does not have a rival in its ability to provoke the emotions.'

'This performance of flamenco I saw performed in Córdoba was quite a sight.'

Octavia laughed again, for she had known the dance from an early age and had performed it countless times. Her teacher had said at the time that, for a Sicilian, she danced like a native of Andalusia. She knew her choice of restaurant was right for the occasion.

They finished their meal with strong coffee and some sort of small chocolate mint cake. Around them, the restaurant had filled up to capacity, but the Englishman and his Sicilian companion had hardly noticed, so deep and interesting had been their conversation.

At their secluded table in the corner, the future was not mentioned. Only the past was discussed, but it was the transient present that the Englishman and the Sicilian girl were trying so courageously to hold on to.

North now wished he had met this girl in different circumstances and that there was no danger for both of them. He knew the present could not last forever. He again stretched his hand across the table, only this time it was not to look at rings but to feel the warmth of the Sicilian's skin. However, it was Octavia who squeezed first, her fingers speaking of sensitivity and understanding. There was also, detected North, a degree of desperation within her grip.

Several tables had been moved at one end of the restaurant and someone started playing the guitar, softly at first, then louder. As its rhythm grew, heads turned, and necks strained for advantage.

Then a flash of red, and a girl who came from nowhere started dancing. She was tall with dark hair tied close behind, exposing a face that was artistically sensitive as well as beautiful. The red dress was traditional flamenco. Her figure was that of one who has always taken dancing seriously, her movements both graceful and energetic.

The atmosphere was charged with expectation. This girl danced the flamenco as few can, in true Andalusian form and style. The flamenco is an art based on several forms of music, developed over time in southern Spain. This dance form has evolved from many places and times: Spanish folk music, gypsy dancing, and the Moorish influence have all left their mark.

She danced the light-hearted *chico*, her lively body moving with vitality and perfect timing to the guitar's rhythm. The audience joined in with clapping, and the girl danced faster and faster as the rhythm quickened.

The girl became a red blur of continuous flowing motion. Then the music stopped, leaving the girl lying exhausted on the floor. She soon rose to stand, smiling, chest heaving, to face the crowded room. Then she bowed very low, thanked the audience, and was gone. The audience was left gasping, clapping, and stomping their feet in appreciation. However, before conversation could be resumed, the dancer reappeared. Another dance? A final encore?

Yes, there was indeed one last performance – a profoundly fiery display of suppressed sensual excitement. The dancer's skill in portraying the emotions was only revealed by her masterful movements and sophisticated vitality. Then all too soon the dance once again came to an end. Exhausted, she bowed twice very low and was gone, and this time, to universal disappointment, for she did not reappear. The audience showed their feelings with more clapping and stomping of feet.

Slowly the crowded restaurant resumed its previous activities of eating, drinking, and talking, but this time their conversation was the same – of universal admiration for the dancer in red.

North settled their bill before escorting Octavia to the courtyard outside. Under the clear sky, the silence was broken only by the fountain, its cheerful noise together with the fragrance of the eucalyptus trees combined to slow their departure, so that the tranquility of the moment might be savoured.

Octavia felt the Englishman's hand upon her waist, and her pulse quickened as he drew her towards him. Clasping both hands around his neck, she felt the strength of his muscles beneath. Her eyes found his, and she recognised the desire mirrored between them, like a flickering flame against a dark wind of uncertainty.

She willed him to kiss her, her body aching with the anticipation. Her breathing quickened, then she felt his lips upon her own. He held her tight against him. Their kissing was eloquent and powerful, its sacred music releasing a deep vibration within the cathedral of their hearts.

North felt the softness of Octavia's body against his own. He ran his fingers through her long, black hair. She leant back, breaking the embrace so he could again run his fingers through its thick mass and delight in the experience. The Englishman could smell the girl's perfume. Faint but intoxicating, it aroused him, like the softness of her skin and the glance of those Sicilian eyes.

They kissed again and again, long and deep, and each time the distressing world around them released a little of its confusion. Octavia gave herself to the moment, not caring for past or future; only the present commanded relevance. She wanted his kisses to last for a thousand years and then another thousand. The first thousand would not be long enough, only the beginning of living free from a cruel and emotionally starved world.

North broke the embrace, content for a moment to look at the Sicilian's face, but he did not speak. He saw her dark eyes once more become deep wells of Latin mystery, wanting to share their secrets of life and joy with him. He kissed her for the last time at *La Valencia*, and once again experienced the intensity of emotion that a Sicilian girl can incite when she surrenders to her emotions.

At last, they drew breath, lingering in each other's arms, not wanting to break the enchantment. But time was now waiting, daring them to face the challenge of their uncertain future.

Holding hands, they passed through the courtyard to the wrought-iron gates. After carefully closing them behind them, they left the enchanted garden, its bubbling fountain, the memory of a dance, and made their way out into the night.

Chapter Four

North's head disappeared under the Mediterranean at 3.05am. It was early September, and a wind from the northwest had increased its strength so that the surface of the sea was no longer smooth, but broken by waves just beginning to form white caps. The water made a monotonous lapping noise against the exposed hulls of moored boats.

Under the surface, North was in a silent world of his own. His first sensation was a jab of cold across his back, the wet suit leaking as it was designed to. He knew it would not last long, as his body heat would in time warm the thin film of trapped water between suit and skin, providing insulation from the cold. Some water had found its way into his mask; this he soon cleared by blowing air through his nostrils, thus forcing out the unwanted water.

He checked his descent by following one of the pier supports to the bottom. In a bag held in his left hand, he carried a full set of diving equipment, including tank. Reaching the harbour bottom, he inspected, with the help of a light, a second bag which was totally waterproof. He did not remove it. Its contents consisted of the handgun, rifle and ammunition. It was as he had left it.

The bottom, composed mainly of limestone, was uneven with little seaweed, but some plant life persisted between the larger rocks. Adjusting the air in his life jacket to give slightly negative buoyancy, North set off on a compass bearing that should take him to the *Roxana*. He swam six feet above the bottom until his depth gauge read nearly 20 feet. This he maintained even though the seabed continued to drop.

Twenty minutes swimming should have brought him directly under the *Roxana*'s hull. Slowly he ascended, until he could see his bubbles break the surface, the cumbersome bag hampering his progress. The dark shadow of what could only be the *Roxana*'s hull was less than 40 feet away. Her large anchor cable disappeared into an outcrop of seaweed growing up between two boulders. The compass bearing had been correct. He was now just slightly short of his objective. The heavy and awkward load had slowed him down more than he had anticipated.

Suddenly his ears picked up a throbbing noise. It slowly increased in pitch until he heard it directly above his head. Then quickly the heavy vibration from churning propellers passed right over his position. Looking up, North saw the outline of a small boat, its present course diverging away from the *Roxana*. Then, as he looked, it suddenly changed direction ninety degrees to a new course towards the open sea. North waited until the throbbing died before continuing his swim towards the *Roxana*'s anchor cable.

The chain was made of half-inch linked steel. To one of these links, about ten feet below the surface, North attached the spare tank. Then, tying his own tank just below this and taking a last breath of air, he rose to the surface. The northwest mistral caught his face, but it was not cold. The waves were steadily increasing in size, with white foam and spray heralding worsening conditions. This suited North, as it would help to make his detection more difficult. He swung round 360 degrees, with just his mask above the waves, looking for any sign of danger.

The boat that had passed directly over him a few minutes before, heading for the open sea, was making for a very large motor cruiser which had recently anchored three hundred yards from the *Roxana*. It must have arrived during his swim. The small motorboat was now alongside, and a figure could be seen climbing steps leading up the cruiser's side.

North wondered if the motorboat had originated from the *Roxana*. Whoever owned that gin palace of a boat wanted to be as far divorced from the elements as possible. It was built for luxurious living in the grand style, not for those wanting to learn the finer points of seamanship.

With great effort, he started to climb the anchor cable. The constantly moving chain with its slippery surface created much more difficulty for his ascent than he had expected. Halfway up, he made a mental note that this, without doubt, would be the last time he would climb an anchor chain in such conditions. The muscles in his arms and legs turned to uncooperative lead as he approached his objective. The last few feet were the most difficult, as the angle of the chain became steeper before it passed through a block onto the deck, then finally disappeared through another block into a concealed locker below.

With a final Herculean effort, North pulled himself over the gunwale to lie exhausted on the deck. It took a full two minutes for him to regain his breath and for his limbs to ease from their intolerable burning to a dull ache. He felt the northwest mistral more strongly now at this increased height. *Today is going to be rough for anyone at sea,* he thought. Looking around him, all was quiet; his unannounced boarding seemed to have escaped notice, at least so far.

Leaning over the side, he jerked the thin rope, the other end of which he had secured around his waist before setting out. The special knot with which he had tied the bag to the anchor cable released, enabling him to haul the bag with its equipment to the deck. Holding the dripping bag, North ran in a crouched position to the other end of the yacht, carefully trying to avoid a maze of obstacles consisting of the usual ropes, bollards, and half-folded sails. At the same time, he watched for any sign that his presence had been discovered. However, all seemed reassuringly quiet.

Arriving safely at the stern, North managed to shelter behind the deckhouse, hidden from possible view. There had been no lookout; at least if there was, he was not doing his job very well, as no hue and cry had yet been sounded. On the way, he had noticed a dinghy moored two-thirds of the way from the bows on the port side. It had a small Yamaha outboard. This, North decided, might prove an easier option than his original plan to swim ashore.

Recalling the map Octavia had drawn earlier, North entered the empty wheelhouse and cautiously descended the steps inside to a large landing area on the main deck. With its generous dimensions, the space would have done credit as the living room of an average-sized house. A passageway led off from the landing, and North knew this ran almost the entire length of the yacht. The doors at this end, he also knew, led to six guest cabins.

Lighting, both in the landing and passageway, came from ornate brass lamps. These gave a period atmosphere with their reflected glow in the highly polished mahogany panelling, which covered the walls and ceiling. The floor was covered with wall-to-wall thick pile carpeting. Clearly this was not an area frequented by the crew.

After putting the bag down, the ache in his shoulder eased. North then turned to face the door that he knew led to the large master cabin in the stern. He pressed his left ear against the door, and within a minute he was sure there was no sound from within. What he did hear was with his right ear. Voices were becoming louder. At least two people, and maybe more, were heading in North's direction from the long corridor.

His field of vision could not take in the entire passageway from the cabin door. However, it was only a matter of seconds before the owners of the voices would see him and make his discovery certain.

There was no time to ascend the stairs he had just come down, so North tried the large brass door handle. To his surprise, the door was not locked. Quickly opening it, he lifted the bag, entered the darkened room, and closed the door behind him. Before his eyes became accustomed to the darkness, his ears strained for any sign of life, but only complete silence greeted his anxiety.

Slowly his eyes picked out various pieces of furniture. It was a comfortable room with dark leather armchairs and a well-stocked bar to one side. Thick pile burgundy carpeting covered the floor and led through adjoining double doors into what must be the bedroom beyond. North heard the same voices of a few moments ago on the other side of the door he had just entered.

Taking four strides, he reached the double doors. Pushing them open, he found himself in the bedroom. If the room he had just left was comfortable, the bedroom was opulent. The accent was oriental, with gold dragons breathing fire, mandarins chasing majestic peacocks, and typical Chinese trees with incredibly twisted trunks and branches supporting various wild creatures. These scenes were depicted in graphic detail on the bedspread, curtains, and the four large lampshades.

North's feet made a squelching noise inside his rubber boots. He left the bag hidden behind a chair off to one side. Then, walking past the bed, he entered the shower and drew the curtain after him. Drawing his knife, he crouched against one of the side walls. He was invisible from the bedroom, because the walls of the shower had a lip of ten inches or so before the curtain started.

The door to the anteroom opened, and now he could hear the voices much more clearly. There was some sort of argument between someone speaking broken Italian with a heavy accent, and another man. A third man spoke to the first in an East European language that North now guessed must be Romanian.

There followed a cry of someone in pain and then a groan that was suddenly cut short. Then the door closed. He heard laughter through it, then more incomprehensible Romanian. A key turned in a lock, then the silence was suddenly broken by a long, deep groaning noise.

North waited a full two minutes before moving. Slowly he straightened, then cautiously drew back the shower curtain, its plastic rings making little sound. Stepping out of the shower basin, he inched across the bedroom towards the other room. The print of a leopard above the bed watched his every move. Reaching the communicating door, North looked into the anteroom, thankful he had not quite closed it. One glance and he relaxed. His precautions were unnecessary, but he kept the knife in his right hand, just in case. Something to do with his rather acute instinct of self-preservation.

Lying face down in the middle of the room was a large man of about fifty, struggling to stand up, his right arm barely supporting him.

The Baron rose hesitatingly to his knees, then slowly to his feet, his back still towards North. The man, in obvious pain, staggered drunkenly towards an armchair. Turning round, he fell heavily into it.

It was then that he caught sight of North's figure. The sight of a black-clad stranger with a knife made him recoil further into the chair. A shadow of fear momentarily passed over his tired features. There was also shock and uncertainty. *Emotions*, thought North, *that until recently this man had not known.* He was, without doubt, the Baron Delmonte.

As Octavia had described, her father was handsome. In recent times, though, he had become the victim of too much high living; the over-sized belly and the beginnings of a double chin bore witness to this.

'You must be the Baron Delmonte,' stated North, hoping to reassure the other man. 'My name is Sebastian North. I have come to help you...'

To put the Baron more at ease, North put the knife away. At the bar, he poured two drinks of 100 per cent malt whisky into two glasses. He had no idea if the Baron drank whisky, but if not, then perhaps this was a good time to start. Handing the Baron a substantial measure of the amber liquid, he sat down in a chair opposite with the second glass.

'Let's drink to liberty and a long life. It might sound a bit premature, considering our present circumstances, but I like to be optimistic.'

The Baron, as if in a trance, obediently raised his glass. When he lowered it, there was fifty per cent less fluid in it. Colour came back to his cheeks as he slowly regained his composure. He spoke for the first time, in perfect English.

'How did you manage to board the *Roxana*? How can you help me? It's impossible to escape from these people you know...' His voice was a little unsteady as he continued, 'The Sicilian mafia, as well as this Balkan Government, are involved in this whole affair.'

Now it was North's turn to be surprised. 'The mafia involved? How?'

'It will take a few minutes to explain, though I am myself only just beginning to understand...'

'Before you continue, I think I had better interrupt. I regret to say I have some very difficult news for you.'

Over the next fifteen minutes, North related recent events as he knew them: the failed kidnapping attempt in the South of France; His wife's tragic death; the boat trip to Sardinia; and his swim to the *Roxana*. The personal involvement between himself and Octavia was the only detail that he chose not to mention.

The Baron was visibly shaken at the news of his wife's death, and North refilled his half empty glass. With a slightly steadier hand holding the glass, he consumed more of the strong spirit. Under his breath, he swore in Italian to avenge his wife's murder. Then after regaining some of his former composure, and with frequent pauses, the Baron told North all he knew.

Under normal circumstances, the Baron would never have confided so much in a stranger, but it seemed this man had risked so much to help Octavia and was now prepared to assist in his own escape, that he felt he had little choice but to trust him.

Over the last six months, the Baron had experienced difficulties with his various business interests, not only in Sicily but in other parts of Europe. His plans and efforts were met with unseen obstacles at every turn. Finally, he contacted a friend with close mafia connections for help. Some days later, through this friend, he had learnt that it was all the work of Roberto Fambino, who was engaged to his daughter Octavia. North recalled her mentioning her former fiancé for the first time soon after they had met on the French Rivieria.

Twelve months ago, Octavia and Roberto had become engaged, and the Baron admitted to being of influence during the matchmaking. Roberto was in his early thirties, Octavia twenty-four. Roberto's family, like his own, was old Sicilian that could trace its ancestry back several generations.

'However, there was a difference; Roberto's family was mafia in every sense of the word. I knew this, of course, and so did Octavia, but she did not appreciate at the time that Roberto and his family did not want her or anyone else changing the strict mafia traditions.'

'Even though they were engaged to be married?' interrupted North.

'That's right. A mafia family is run and controlled by men only. Women have no place in their world or operations. Roberto expected Octavia to participate only in domestic chores and to stay home. Of course, they shared experiences together, expensive foreign trips, exclusive parties and so on, but then they were – how do you say in English – "courting". After the engagement, for Roberto the courtship was over. He then thought he had Octavia forever. He took her for granted and was proved terribly wrong.

'Octavia is beautiful in the physical sense, yes, even if I say so myself about my own daughter. She is also much more. I have seen her develop over the years, and she will give much of herself for a noble cause or someone she loves. Everyone, including myself, greatly underestimated Octavia's reaction to marrying into the Sicilian mafia. Her high principles in this matter did not come from me, I regret to say, for I am a realist. To succeed in business here, you must be. It came from her mother's side, from Greece, at a time when eminence was given to principles.

'Six months later, Octavia wanted to call the engagement off. She claimed Roberto was unfaithful. He should have had more sense than to carry his playboy past into the engagement.

'Finally, after much arguing and distress, she would have nothing more to do with him. She returned the diamond engagement ring he had chosen only a few months before. Roberto had bought it at Cartier's in Geneva. It was a very rare "blue-white" diamond of oval brilliant cut. Ninety-eight per cent of the so-called blue-white diamonds are not true blue-white. The two per cent that truly are, and Octavia's was from the two per cent, are very valuable indeed. Hers was also nearly flawless. To be completely flawless, a diamond must be totally transparent – that is, without any internal imperfections under a lens of 10x magnification. Her engagement ring had a small imperfection called a cleavage crack or tiny bubble within its structure. Perhaps the internal imperfection was somehow symbolic of Roberto's true self. I have sometimes wondered this.

'Roberto destroyed Octavia's love by his arrogant behaviour and inability to recognise the difference between her and those other girls that hung around him. They were mesmerised by his superficial charm and great wealth.

'He threw away the one true flawless diamond that was Octavia so that he could keep the many worthless imitations, under the illusion that he could have both. His true self could never be hidden from Octavia once under the searching light of her love.

'Once she realised her love was not going to be returned, it almost broke her heart. From that point on, the relationship was over and could never fulfil its promise as it should have of love everlasting.

'The mafia connection only compounded the situation. I knew of the deep underworld involvement, but Roberto had apparently always been careful to keep much of it in the background. He assumed Octavia knew or guessed the full extent of the Cosa Nostra involvement and accepted it. Perhaps she was naive in the beginning, but having discovered the reality, she tried to separate her fiancé from his previous life, confident that love could bridge the difficulties and conquer the future.

'They could marry and so begin anew, free from his past. This dream was irretrievably shattered when Roberto would not change. Octavia refused to face a life of not knowing what her husband-to-be was fully engaged in.

'Everyone tried on both sides to come to some solution. Roberto's family put pressure on Octavia to stop asking so many questions and being generally inquisitive about their underworld involvement. They maintained Octavia was lucky to have the chance to marry into their family at all. Many girls would leap at the chance and be grateful, they said, instead of being so awkward. There seemed to be no common ground, no solution.

'One day, Octavia refused to see Roberto. Then he turned on me, blaming the family for poisoning the air between Octavia and him. He vowed vengeance unless she returned. Thus, you see my business difficulties; the mafia has a long reach.

'A kidnapping was attempted on Octavia soon after. It failed by chance, perhaps conducted by incompetent *piccolo* or foot soldiers who took the wrong girl in the hotel room next to Octavia's. I insisted on my daughter staying close to me. She never went anywhere without two bodyguards.

'Then one day, she decided to up and go. She had finally had enough of being chaperoned and she drifted amongst friends in Milan and France. I since learned that she kept in close contact with her best friend, Claudia, who is like a sister to her.'

'It would appear,' continued the Baron, 'that the second attempt at kidnapping Octavia was not Roberto-connected, but Balkan.'

'So, what's their angle?' interrupted North.

'They want the ring. The one she wears on the fourth finger of her right hand.'

'The one with the large ruby?' asked North, his face showing puzzlement at this new piece of information.

'Yes, the one that was passed down to her by her mother, nearly four years ago, on her 21st birthday.'

'She showed it to me last night at the restaurant. I commented upon its unique design. How valuable is it?'

'We had it valued some years ago before giving it to Octavia. It was estimated then at $250,000 – this, we were told, being attributed to its unique design and antique value, rather than the quality of the stone.'

The Romanians could hardly be that interested in it for a mere $250,000, thought North. Certainly not enough to warrant kidnapping and murder. It must have been something to do with the inscription on the stone itself that was attracting their interest.

'What does the inscription say?' asked North.

'It's a strange combination of letters, numbers, and symbols that has never, to my knowledge, been translated. Some of the lettering is in the Cyrillic alphabet. It is very small, and it can only be seen under magnification. The legend of the ring is that it holds the key to great wealth and power. I assumed, like most people who knew of it, that its so-called "great wealth and power" was pure mythology. Perhaps there is a more tangible side to this stone that the Romanians know about.'

'Someone is going to a lot of trouble about something,' agreed North. 'If, as you suggest, they are in possession of some secret knowledge about the ring, it certainly seems to be worth a lot to someone. Whatever this knowledge is, I think these Romanians are going to be more than a little reluctant to share it with anyone else. Who were the men that brought you here?'

'One is called Mario; he seemed to be in charge. He is the big man with the beard. The other is the same height but not as broad. I did not catch his name. The big man kicked me just before they left. They are without doubt from the Balkans somewhere. Someone called Nicu and two others brought me to Sicily from Athens, where they had been holding me.'

'That is why you could not contact your wife?'

'Exactly. I flew to Athens in response to an urgent telephone call from one of my directors. He said my presence was required at once. Trusting him implicitly – he has worked for me for fifteen years – I went, intending to phone my wife after I arrived. I had no chance. It was, how you say, "a set up".

'Two men were holding the director of my Greek operations at gunpoint, so he'd made the phone call to me with a gun at his head. Upon arriving at the hotel, they held me, demanding to know where Octavia was. I told them I did not know, which was the truth.

'I recounted the story of Roberto and Octavia's doomed match. At first, they did not believe me, but I think I managed to convince them. Mario was in communication with someone by phone who seemed to be directing everything. Apparently, this someone wanted Octavia at all costs. I think at this stage he had not told Mario why. Perhaps he did not totally trust him.

'I learnt of their orders later by overhearing a conversation between Mario and one of the other men. I learnt a little Romanian when I had some business interests there. Octavia was to be taken and searched for all her jewellery, which was to be removed. Hearing this, I guessed at once it must be the ruby they were after. She wears little else approaching its value, real or imagined.

'Several days later, we flew by private jet to Palermo, then on to the villa. They captured Octavia a few hours after I had arrived. Apparently, she just walked in. However, I never saw her to communicate with. Now they had all three of us, including my poor wife. This someone was perhaps over-cautious in not giving Mario the real reason for Octavia's capture.

'They split Octavia and her mother into different rooms, thinking they had plenty of time to strip and search Octavia later. Then another problem developed. Neither of them trusted each other to be alone with Octavia. Each one figured he could have his turn with her later, but Mario wanted her for himself, so they delayed their search. Whoever was on the end of that phone won't be pleased with them now as she promptly escaped with her jewellery. I wouldn't want to be in their shoes when whoever it is learns the details of their failure.'

'It must have been at this point that Octavia managed to reach a phone to contact me in France, asking for help,' interrupted North.

'Unfortunately, they must have found out, so they put her and her mother in the cellar as punishment. There they remained until you arrived.'

'Then what happened to you? Where were you all this time?' asked North.

'I was tied up in one of the horse boxes in the stable block, chained to a ring, hand and foot,' replied the Baron.

North could have kicked himself; he should have searched the stable block as well as the villa.

So, it had been this Mario who must have guessed from Octavia's interrupted phone call that her situation was known to someone outside. Whoever this was now posed a possible threat to their future plans.

When North first arrived at the villa, Mario must have been with the Baron in the stables. Then, upon discovering the carnage in the kitchen, he must have set about quickly organising resistance, hence the rifle shots at their intended escape by motorboat. There must have been several of them, as North was certain he had hit two gunmen before the pier blew up. He wondered if it was Mario who had killed Octavia's mother.

'Why did they bring you and the *Roxana* here? I can't see how that helps their side,' said North.

'I can only guess, but I think the reason is that having lost Octavia, this same someone threatened Mario in no uncertain terms with the salt mines, or whatever their equivalent is in Romania, unless he found the girl and her jewellery. At this point, he could have told Mario about the ring, for I overheard them talking about jewellery again during the passage over, but I could not be certain.

'Bringing the *Roxana* and myself to Sardinia was done, I think, for two reasons. Firstly, it would look as if I had my liberty, and thus Octavia would be more likely to contact me. Secondly, Roberto was in Sardinia – Porto Cervo to be exact. And after what I told them of his engagement to Octavia, they perhaps thought that he, with the weight of the Cosa Nostra behind him, would be able to help find Octavia. What the plan was after she was found is far from certain. Perhaps the Romanians did a deal by which they would keep the ring and Roberto would have Octavia.'

'Her opinion not being taken into account?' said North.

'Of course not. She would then be Roberto's prisoner.'

The Baron finished his glass. It was the third one of the conversation.

'However things started, it increasingly looks as if these Balkan people as well as the Cosa Nostra are becoming well-established at having a strong interest in this whole business. Whether they are willing partners or not is far from clear.

'What I will say is that Roberto is now taking a much closer interest. You can't stage this sort of thing, holding me, moving my yacht around the place, to say nothing of leaving a bloody trail, without the mafia taking some interest. The *L'Ora* newspaper is going to have a field day once all this comes out. They have a certain reputation for recording violent deaths, you know.

'That motor cruiser over there,' the Baron said, pointing to a porthole on the port side, 'belongs to Roberto's uncle, Giovanni, also of the Cosa Nostra who control Sicily. They also have much influence on the mainland, as far north as Naples. His boat is here for a reason, and it's not fishing.'

North mentioned to the Baron that before he had surfaced a motorboat had passed over his head in the direction of the large cruiser. It could have come from the *Roxana*.

'That would add fuel to my theory of both sides working together,' said the Baron.

North took a sip of his whisky, then asked, 'If Roberto learns of the wealth, imagined or otherwise, attached to the ring, what will his next move be? To ignore the ring and concentrate on trying to win Octavia over again? Or to separate the ring from her in order to pursue the legend for what it is worth?'

The Baron thought before replying. 'Knowing Roberto as I do, I think he will try by whatever means at his disposal to bend Octavia's mind towards him. He will try to cajole her to begin with. If that fails, he will threaten to force her into submission in order to win her over a second time.

'Roberto's real interest is in Octavia. The ring is of secondary importance, though he might, if he thinks a sufficiently large amount of money is involved, do some sort of deal with the Romanians. However, with Roberto nothing is certain except his treachery.'

There was silence as North thought through the Baron's last few words. This whole bizarre tale unfolding before him was becoming more complicated with each new twist. *Damn it*, thought North, *if I was not so involved with the girl I would walk out now and leave them all to it, legend and all.* But he couldn't, and he knew it. The girl had done something to him. Maybe it was those dark eyes, the way she moved, or the way she had done her hair last night, raked up on top of her head and tied with the red ribbon, that had touched him.

So, he was committed to seeing this whole thing through to its end, whatever that might be. The stakes were getting higher, with death already showing its hand. Would there be room for romance? *Just maybe, just maybe*, he thought.

North looked at his watch. It was 4.15. Time they were away. They had talked far too long already. The door was locked. The Baron said they would be back to check on him in thirty minutes, at 4.45. They always checked up on half-past the hour.

Both men waited the fifteen minutes in silence, while the Baron changed into the wetsuit North had carried with him. Then North briefed him about his intended escape plan.

The Baron went into the bedroom to arrange the bed so that it looked as if he was asleep under the duvet. North thought about removing the light bulbs in the two rooms, but quickly rejected this course of action. Anyone entering and finding the lights not working would immediately become suspicious.

A few minutes after 4.30, the key sounded in the lock. A man entered the room. He turned on the light by the switch at the door, and then closed it softly behind him. He was thickset with dark hair; North wondered if it was Mario. He had a beard, so it was more than likely. He was dressed in wet oilskins. It must be rough outside, thought North.

Before Mario crossed to the bedroom, North caught sight of an automatic held in his right hand. His left hand held a torch which he now switched off with a distinctive click. North saw all this from his partially concealed position, crouched behind the bar.

The man cautiously progressed towards the bedroom. With his torch, he prodded the arranged duvet. Before he could analyse the result, the Baron stepped out from the shower, his right arm poised above his head, the intention obvious. However, his movements were a little slow. Maybe the shock of his wife's death or the strain of the last few days had taken more of a toll than North had been led to believe.

There should have been ample time to make good his intended blow with the glass to the bearded man's head. But the impact was avoided by the Baron's intended target twisting backwards and to the side. It was then that he could have brought his right arm round so that his gun would bear onto the Baron, but the man's orders could not have included murder – at least, not yet. The gun exploded with a deafening noise, the bullet passing harmlessly into the wood panelling. At the same time, the Baron's bottle fell harmlessly onto the bed and he swore for the second time that night. Picking up the bottle, he aimed a second blow.

The bearded man's right hand moved slightly, just enough to ensure that the next bullet covered its intended target and this time would not miss. His unblinking eyes exhibited a complete absence of emotion, his features remaining cold and impassive. Perhaps here, death was no stranger.

Leaving his previously concealed position, North leapt forward. The bearded man must have been possessed with some kind of sixth sense, for in the same instant he turned round, revolver poised.

However, he was surprised to see this new threat from such an unexpected quarter, and for a split second he hesitated. It was this indecision that sealed the bearded man's fate. Within that critical moment, North pulled the trigger of the spear gun with devastating consequences.

The bolt pierced the big man's chest before carrying him with it to the wooden panelled wall behind. A spear gun is designed to be fired through the medium of water; when fired in air, the steel bolt has a much greater velocity. The bolt released by North pinned the bearded man's considerable frame against the polished woodwork.

A dark pool of blood rapidly spread out from where the razor-sharp steel bolt had entered the man's chest. He might as well have been made of soft cheese for all the resistance his flesh and organs offered.

North, closely followed by the Baron, left the cabin with the now motionless man still held against the blood-soaked wood. Locking the door behind them, and holding their diving masks, both men suddenly picked up the sounds of laughter and the distinctive shattering of broken glass. Obviously, some sort of party must be, if not in full swing, then certainly warming up. *At this rate*, thought North, *the* Roxana *would quickly run out of fine crystal.*

Leaving the party below, the two men silently mounted the steps to the deck above. North noticed that the Baron held his right arm in an awkward position, and so questioned the reason. It had been injured earlier by a savage blow with a blunt instrument by one of the Romanians. North became a little more concerned. It was a long swim and the current was running at an angle that would not aid their progress. The Baron would need every bit of strength if they were going to make good their escape.

Upon reaching the port side, North peered over the safety rail to the darkness beyond. His view, though in deep shadow from the deck lights behind him, was given a little illumination from several half-covered portholes below. North found the water line clear, the inflatable he had seen earlier gone. The starboard side soon revealed the same result: someone had moved it!

'So, it looks as if you are going to have a swim tonight,' said North to the Baron with a smile.

'Escape is always a good excuse for a swim,' replied the Baron, studying the dark, turbulent waters below.

The glow from a lighted cigarette was first spotted by the Baron. It came from a position just forward of the first mast on the starboard side. Whoever it was must have had his back to them, for every time the cigarette rose for the man to take a drag, it disappeared.

Whoever it was must have been looking to starboard and slightly forward. This would take in the view of the motor cruiser, now awash with lights like a Christmas tree. In spite of the strong wind, a disco could be heard across the water, and figures could be seen on one of the decks, moving in synchronisation with the music. Roberto's uncle seemed to be having quite a party.

North took one last glance in the direction of the smoker before fitting his mask. If he was a lookout for the bearded man, he was looking in the wrong direction. The smoker had not altered position since he had looked through a pair of binoculars; perhaps the disco was more interesting than watching the *Roxana*'s deck all night.

North and the Baron climbed over the port side support rail and dropped from the moving deck as quietly as they could into the water below. Once in the water, and using their snorkels, the two men swam to the anchor cable and then dived to where North had tied the tanks ten feet below. After considerable difficulty, they secured their equipment and, now breathing successfully from their compressed air, set off upon North's compass bearing for the shore.

The Baron's progress was slow. *Perhaps his injured arm is more serious than he made out,* thought North. They swam at a depth of ten feet, as there was no point going any deeper. Speed was all important to put as much distance between them and the *Roxana*. When Mario's fate was discovered, all hell would break loose.

After twenty minutes, North indicated to the Baron with the thumbs-up sign that he was going to surface.

Once on the surface, he saw that they had drifted, most likely due to the current. Re-establishing his bearing, he dived back to the Baron.

Another ten minutes of hard finning brought them to within twenty yards of the recently hired motorboat, so they used their snorkels for the remaining distance. A quick glance behind showed that all was quiet aboard the *Roxana*. So far, so good. Rounding the end of the pier, they climbed aboard out of sight, after North had first retrieved the bag that contained the rifle and ammunition from the bottom of the pier support.

At last North breathed a sigh of relief at having so far escaped detection. The Baron, breathing heavily from his exertion, climbed into the stairwell. Both men changed into dry clothes. The Baron, feeling a little better, insisted on raising a glass to mark their success. North joined him, but could not help thinking it a bit premature. He also thought that the Baron had a prodigious capacity for alcohol. The time was 5.20. Their next priority was to pick up Octavia.

Both men quickly made their way to a side street not far from the waterfront, where North had parked the blue Renault he had hired previously. They drove with caution for eleven minutes through deserted streets to the hotel. North drove beyond the entrance, then parked out of sight, as he thought it possible that someone might be watching.

The lobby was deserted, and they both climbed the steps to Octavia's room. North knocked the agreed signal. There was no response. He tried again, with the same result. His mind started to race: was she just asleep, or could something have happened? He had told her not to leave the room until his return.

Inserting the key, he found to his surprise that the door was not locked. Was this an oversight on her part? Could she have left for something only to return, and then forget to bolt the door? With his left hand, North slowly opened the door. In his right, he carried the gun that had recently belonged to the harpoon victim, now dead on the *Roxana*. Somehow, deep down he knew something was wrong. Switching on the light, he entered the room with the Baron close behind.

The room was a complete shambles. Octavia was not there. The two beds were smashed into matchwood. The wooden frames made a pile in the middle of the room. Feathers from ripped pillowcases lay everywhere.

'They have taken her,' cried the Baron. He sat down on the edge of an armchair which was lying on its side.

'I wonder who?' said North. 'Roberto or the Romanians?'

'It must be Roberto,' said the Baron.

The Baron's thinking, thought North, *was bound to be somewhat coloured by Roberto's recent personal vendetta against Octavia and the family.* On the other hand, if that was true, then Roberto must now be well aware of the Romanian interest in the ring; after all, why search the room? People don't wreck a hotel room just for the hell of it. But wait a minute, if the ring was on Octavia's finger, why the search?

Whoever they were, they had abducted Octavia with every scrap of her personal possessions, along with North's clothes and personal effects. Nothing of great value, but strange why someone should be so efficient in clearing the room.

Leaving the Baron, his face in his hands, pondering the situation, North went out of the room and descended the stairs to do some further investigating.

He quickly woke up the hotel owner, who protested in no uncertain terms that it was most irregular behaviour to be disturbed at this early hour. At first, he was reluctant to answer North's persistent line of questioning, his ferret-like eyes constantly shifting in their refusal to face North's unblinking gaze.

However, North was in no mood for this lack of cooperation. With a few bank notes upon the table, followed by threats, the hotel owner slowly told his story of events earlier that morning.

Apparently, two men had arrived about two hours after his wife had gone out to see her sick cousin, which would make it about 1am or just after. They wanted to know the room numbers of anyone who had checked in that day, but the hotel owner said that he had to have a reason to release such information. Then the man wearing a blue shirt produced a gun and said, 'This is the reason.'

The hotel owner gave them the information they requested, which included the occupancy of room 5, Octavia's room. He thought they were Cosa Nostra. They looked like *Piccolo*. He told North that he'd had to comply or he would have been swimming that night in Cagliari harbour with very heavy boots indeed! 'Then they told me not to show my face till the sun rose.'

That was exactly what he had been intending to do until North interrupted his sleep. He had no other information except that there was a lot of shouting and a girl screamed twice – the second time much longer than the first.

'How about other guests in the hotel, they must have heard something?' questioned North further.

'Their rooms are on the other side of the building. I doubt if they heard much, but feel free to ask them. Only two rooms are occupied.'

North returned to the Baron and told him all that he had learned from his recent talk with the owner. After he had finished, the Baron said little. He was still deep in thought, still trying to make some kind of sense from this half-finished jigsaw of a problem.

North suddenly felt tired. In the bathroom, he ran the cold tap and splashed his unshaven face with the refreshingly cold liquid.

Looking up, he caught his reflection in the mirror. The eyes that stared back at him exhibited weariness. They were eyes that desperately needed sleep. His mind, in spite of his physical fatigue, tried to focus on the implications of Octavia's dramatic disappearance. His eyes reluctantly wandered around the cramped bathroom, the hideous and peeling wallpaper seeming to mock his efforts.

Then he saw red shapes. No, they were letters, written in the upper right-hand corner of the mirror. North leant forward for a closer inspection. *Must be Russian or Greek*, he thought, recognising a Cyrillic letter.

'Come here quick. I think I have something,' said North.

The Baron came to the doorway of the bathroom and North showed him the lettering written in what both men now recognised as Octavia's very red lipstick. *Beautiful colour*, thought North.

'What does it say?' he asked.

'It says "soap" in Greek.' The Baron did not speak Greek fluently, but having a Greek wife he had acquired a certain amount of knowledge.

What did it mean? What was Octavia trying to tell them? North picked up the bar of soap on the side of the basin. Just an ordinary bar of mass-produced white soap which could be found anywhere. He turned it over. Again, nothing remarkable about it. On one side, the name of the manufacturer was gone.

Strange, thought North. It was a new bar when he had checked into the room the previous day and would have needed quite a lot of use to obliterate the name. Far more than could be explained by normal use. In any case, Octavia had bought some more expensive soap when they were shopping, so it would be unlike her to then use this soap as well.

North squeezed the bar of soap until it resembled spent toothpaste. As he did, he felt something hard, and knew instinctively what it was. Extracting the hard object from the centre of the slippery mass, he held up Octavia's ring – the one with the ruby in its centre, given to her on her 21st birthday.

Chapter Five

The operator took her time to connect North's long-distance telephone call. Continuous background chatter could be heard, another crossed line, which seemed an all too regular occurrence recently. At last the connection was completed, then the familiar tone peculiar to the British telephone system became audible.

North pictured the large house set in spacious grounds. He glanced at his watch, the hands of which told him 7.30am. In England, the time would be 6.30am, as London was one hour behind most of Western Europe. He wondered if the sun was far enough above the horizon to bathe the classical eastern façade, with its six Grecian columns, in gold.

The telephone continued to ring. It must have rung at least ten times, and still the receiver remained fixed upon its cradle.

This particular example of Sir John Vanbrugh's architecture might have been partially lost, but for the careful landscaping of the extensive grounds. These had taken many decades to improve and develop, from numerous grottos surrounding the lake to the planting of early cedar trees, now well over one hundred feet tall. All this had been brought about under the direction and watchful eye of the 18th-century English landscape architect Capability Brown.

The interrelationship between man and nature reaches completion when house and grounds arrive at a flawless correspondence to each other. The result is a paradise of tranquillity, and an inspiration for the spirit.

At sixty-seven, the present owner of Mansfield Court welcomed his surroundings, for much of his life had been of a stressful nature.

Suddenly the ringing stopped. 'Metcalf Residence,' said the female voice.

'Good morning, Mrs Caversham,' replied North, instantly recognising the Highland accent. 'Sorry to disturb you at this unearthly hour...'

He could picture the middle-aged woman in her dressing gown and tartan slippers, standing in the elegant wood panelled hall.

'This is Sebastian North. I am calling long distance. How are you this morning?'

His need to speak to Colonel Metcalf – the owner of Mansfield Court – was urgent, but that did not supersede exchanging pleasantries with such an old friend. Mrs Caversham had been Colonel Metcalf's housekeeper since her late teens. Her reply was predictably sharp, but retained the warmth of her character.

'As you might imagine, tired...' There was a pause before she continued so that the hour would sink in. 'I had an enjoyable holiday visiting my brother in Dornoch last month. The air is so much more invigorating in the Highlands than that found south of the border.'

Her words left no room for doubt, and North knew from experience that it was far better to agree with Mrs Caversham than to argue when it came to the subject of the pure air of Scotland compared to the polluted variety frequently found in England.

'I will awaken the Colonel, as it must be urgent, you ringing at this hour, but I warn you he won't be pleased.' Silence followed, the receiver left upon the hall table while Mrs Caversham climbed the stairs to awaken the master of Mansfield Court.

North reflected upon the immediate past after leaving the hotel, from where Octavia had so completely disappeared.

From a window of the hotel, the Baron had observed the street below to discover that the main entrance was possibly watched. A car neither of them had previously noticed was parked a little further up the deserted street on the opposite side.

Whoever had successfully kidnapped Octavia would logically have the hotel watched just to see who might show up, and so reveal who her companion was.

North did not think that enough time had elapsed for the Baron's absence, let alone Mario's fate, to translate from pandemonium to an organised search of all the hotels in Cagliari.

After waking up the hotel owner for the second time that morning, both North and the Baron left by another exit, through the kitchen. Unless the hotel owner informed whoever was watching the main entrance, they would have a little time before their absence was discovered.

Within minutes of leaving Cagliari, North pointed the blue Renault north towards the Central Campidano Plain. Soon they reached Sanluri, a town some 40 kilometres from the outskirts of Cagliari.

The Baron directed North to a castle situated in the centre of town. Parking discreetly, both men hurried to the imposing gates.

'A friend of mine lives here,' the Baron explained. 'Count Santorini.' It was from his castle that North was contacting England.

Colonel Metcalf had been deep in sleep when the urgent shaking of his right shoulder by Mrs Caversham suddenly destroyed his pleasant dream of achieving a hole in one at St Andrews golf course. Mrs Caversham's sharp voice cut across his subconscious mind as he was about to continue his game.

'Mr Sebastian North is on the telephone, sir. He is calling long distance, did not say where. It must be urgent.'

With great effort, Colonel Metcalf opened his one good eye – the left having been damaged in Malaya by a mine in the 1950s whilst he had been fighting communist guerrillas.

'Thank you, Mrs Caversham. Perhaps some coffee in the library.' Colonel Metcalf was already anticipating the content of the telephone conversation.

'Right away, sir,' she answered, leaving for the kitchen.

Colonel Metcalf propped himself up on one elbow, then lifted the telephone receiver.

'North, is that you?' rasped the clipped military voice.

'Yes, sir,' replied North.

Before he could continue, the Colonel interrupted, 'I hear you're in antiques now, started your own business somewhere near Pangbourne.'

'I was becoming increasingly restless,' North replied. 'A steady diet of paperwork and an ever-increasing straight jacket of short-sighted rules and regulations, dictated by Foreign Office red tape, began to compromise my initiative and independence. So I started my own consultancy business, specialising in international art and antique fraud.'

North was surprised that his explanation had been so candid. Maybe he just needed to say how he felt. Maybe, in part, his honesty had something to do with Colonel Metcalf becoming a close friend in spite of being his superior for many years.

'Where are you?'

'Sardinia.'

'Then you can damn well send some of that Mediterranean sun over here; it's been raining continuously for three weeks! My new secretary from Cape Town has claimed recently that she is suffering from withdrawal symptoms due to a lack of ultra-violet light. I last heard her mentioning something about now spending her spare time on one of those awful sunbeds.'

North smiled at the humour.

'Sorry to wake you up at this hour, but something urgent has come up.'

'Fire away, North.'

'Copy this exactly.' North dictated the inscription he had taken under magnification from Octavia's ring. Then in broad outline he described recent events, with particular emphasis upon the ring's inscription and its possible importance in relation to the girl's whereabouts.

North asked the Colonel if he could find out all he could about Count Roberto Fambino, the Baron Delmonte, and any additional information on the *Belle of the Wind* – the freighter stranded off the Sardinian south coast. It might or might not be relevant.

Once translated, the Colonel would transfer information to the British Embassy in Rome, and then to Sardinia. Before replacing the receiver, North asked for the information to be in a certain code known only to himself and the Colonel. This the Colonel promised to do.

'No need to apologise, son, for the early call. It will help stimulate the little grey cells, and who knows, it might even help the hair grow.' The Colonel had the annoying habit of calling anyone younger than himself 'son'.

North also learnt from him that the shooting incident in the South of France a few days previously had been mentioned in the London newspapers. Not headlines, but three or four pages in, under 'Death on the Côte D'Azur'. The following articles had centred on the incident's almost certain relationship to organised crime. There was no mention of North or the foiled kidnapping attempt.

Colonel Metcalf replaced the receiver. Then, after stepping out of his huge four-poster bed, he put on his silk dressing gown, slippers, and made his way downstairs to the library. The room was large, some seventy by thirty feet, accommodating nearly five thousand volumes on a wide range of subjects, including many valuable first editions.

The Colonel's favourite volumes included such authors as John Buchan, Anthony Hope, and Ryder Haggard. Their heroes, as portrayed in their day, won battles against overwhelming adversity, without moral compromise or weakness in the face of danger. One section of a bookcase was devoted to biographies of famous military leaders throughout history. These leather-bound editions had etched in gold upon their spines such names as Alexander the Great, Julius Caesar, Hannibal, Cromwell, and Napoleon.

At the west end of the room stood a large 18th-century English partners desk. Its worn green-leather surface was bare except for an angle-poise light, a letter opener in the form of a miniature machete, a sixteen-pound cannon ball mounted upon a brass base, and a jade chess set.

The chess set exhibited a game well advanced, with several pieces now off the board. Black seemed to have the upper hand, judging by the more numerous white pieces no longer participating. A collection of papers and envelopes, with postmarks stamped in Prague, added a little untidy confusion to the otherwise orderly scene. All the half-folded pieces of paper had, written in black ink, a letter and a number, which to a non-chess player would have little meaning.

The Colonel was, in fact, playing chess via post with someone in Prague who, it appeared, was a more experienced player than himself. These games could take many months to complete, but to Colonel Metcalf they were a source of mental stimulation and intrigue. And having retired, at least officially, time was now less important than it had once been.

After closing the door behind him, the Colonel sat behind the desk, then turned on the angle-poise light to illuminate the paper with North's curious jumble of letters, numbers, and symbols.

Mrs Caversham knocked before entering the library. Then, taking care not to spill any of the hot coffee, she made her way over to the Colonel seated behind his desk. She set down the tray, with its Georgian silver pot and fine china, slightly to one side so as not to disturb the man's concentration. There was no milk or sugar, for the Colonel never took milk in coffee and sugar only after dinner. His doctor had recently advised that in the interests of future health his sugar consumption needed to be drastically reduced. The Colonel had conceded, but had drawn the line at his after-dinner coffee; some traditions in life were obviously non-negotiable.

For a moment, Mrs Caversham hesitated before leaving, studying the rugged face with the Roman nose that she knew so well. A gold-framed monocle was firmly attached to his right ocular orbit, the eye behind totally absorbed by the paper before it.

Mrs Caversham was mildly curious as to the content of the recent telephone conversation, but she knew better than to ask questions. Closing the double mahogany doors behind her, she left the Colonel in the library, alone studying the paper before him.

During the following hour, Colonel Metcalf wrote many notes and racked his brain in trying to make some kind of sense from the puzzle before him. However, his efforts were in vain. The mystery of letters, numbers, and symbols remained without explanation, their comprehension frustratingly out of reach.

At last, he picked up the telephone receiver and dialled a London number. Immediately it rang through to an apartment in Kew. A woman's voice answered.

'Yes?' Her accent sounded Canadian but her tone was unmistakably irate, possibly due to the early hour.

'Is Tony up yet?' asked the Colonel, knowing full well that this was highly unlikely during his holiday.

'No, he is asleep, and sleeping is what you should be doing.' The Canadian was becoming increasingly annoyed at the early intrusion. 'Who is calling?'

'It's George. Tell Tony it's rather urgent; he will understand.'

Colonel Metcalf's first name was not George. He had been christened Nigel, but George was the name he had previously agreed to use in communication about something of importance. It was the first time he had used the pseudonym since his retirement nearly two years ago.

'Yes, George.' The familiar voice was genuinely surprised.

'Sorry for the early wake-up call, but I have something of interest for you. Can you meet me at the Bohemian Club for breakfast, say at 10.30?'

'Yes, of course, George,' replied Tony, glancing at the digital figures displayed on his alarm clock.

'Apologise to the girl for interrupting her beauty sleep, but may her dreams come true.'

'I will pass it on.'

The Colonel replaced the receiver with a distinctive click. It would take him longer to reach his rendezvous than the man he had just spoken to, as Mansfield Court was in Berkshire.

Once behind the wheel of his 1955 S1 Continental Bentley, the Colonel made good time on the M4 motorway until commuter traffic started to thicken and slow his speed near Windsor.

Tony, however, managed another half hour's sleep before the hand of the Canadian girl, who had answered the telephone earlier, moved across his chest. She liked to run her fingers through the few blond chest hairs that she could find. This was also her usual technique of attracting his attention. Since she had met Tony three months before in Vancouver, this had proved a most efficient means of turning the man's thoughts towards her.

However, on this particular occasion, Cindy's fingers failed to achieve their desired effect. Planting a kiss upon Cindy's soft right cheek, Tony reluctantly left the bed for his urgent meeting. He said something about phoning later, but Cindy could not be sure, her disappointed face buried deep under the duvet folds.

The Bohemian Club did not exist – at least, there was not an institution by that name known to either the Colonel or to the man he was meeting. The Bohemian Club was another pseudonym previously agreed. It was, in fact, the main dining room of the Ritz Hotel in Piccadilly.

The Colonel arrived at the hotel by taxi, having previously parked his car off Cromwell Road, knowing that finding a parking space in Piccadilly was next to impossible.

From the uninterrupted view of the dining room entrance, he discovered that Tony had not yet arrived. At his request, the foreign waiter with the oily smile seated him at a table with a strategic view of new arrivals, overlooking the terrace and Green Park beyond.

Two minutes after the Colonel was seated, Tony Western arrived at the hotel. He indicated to the waiter that he had just spotted someone and that he would not be needing his further assistance in finding a table. Upon seeing him, the Colonel stood up from his chair to greet the younger man, they shook hands.

'Early bird today,' said Tony, sitting down in the chair opposite. 'What type of worm are you after this time?'

"To tell you the truth, I am not really sure.' The Colonel handed over the piece of paper that contained North's mysterious letters, numbers, and symbols. 'I tried earlier this morning to make some kind of sense from this mess. I came up with a large blank, as you now might guess, hence your early phone call. Hope the girl was not too put out?'

The younger man made a gesture with his right hand, as if to say that it was not an inconvenience. His mind was already focused upon the paper before him.

Colonel Metcalf studied the man opposite. His age could be little more than thirty: his light sandy hair, blue eyes, and a liberal sprinkling of freckles across the bridge of his nose and cheeks, gave an overall boyish impression. The bright green and brown checked sports jacket was crumpled, and the sky-blue shirt beneath could not possibly have been close to an iron any time recently. The tie knot, a half-Windsor, had slipped – assuming it had once been correctly positioned – so that it now exposed the shirt's top button.

The Colonel could not help thinking again about his theory that the more intelligent someone was, the more disregard they had for their personal appearance. Perhaps it had something to do with the brain's capacity for a certain number of cells, and if an exceptionally large number of these were taken up with furthering the intelligence quota then there was a shortage elsewhere. The paper now held by Tony was just another challenge to focus his very fertile and imaginative mind upon.

Tony Western was currently head of F Section at GCHQ, Cheltenham – a division involved with the countless radio signals that are picked up and recorded every hour by this top-secret Government listening station. Ninety-nine per cent of these turn out to be harmless clutter, but the remaining fraction contains secret and possibly damaging information with regard to the security of Her Majesty's Government. It was upon this encoded radio traffic that the Government paid a large sum to have Tony Western's mind concentrate.

Tony Western had been promoted after a brilliant breakthrough in deciphering Czechoslovakian cyphers three years previously. Information subsequently gained led to the discovery of a very highly placed mole deep within British intelligence. This someone, who was supposedly working for the British, was in fact working for a foreign power; in other words, a double agent.

It wasn't until the identity of the mole was discovered that the enormous implications for national security were even guessed at. This person's identity could not be revealed under any circumstances, including to the Prime Minister, because the very credibility of the Government was at stake. The long-term ramifications were almost too frightening to contemplate, especially concerning the 'special relationship' with the Americans which still suffers to this day from the echoes of Kim Philby's defection.

Only four people knew the identity of the mole, including Colonel Metcalf and Tony Western. After intense discussion, a plan had been agreed, then executed. A car accident for the traitor was arranged and carried out; it had, of course, proved fatal.

The waiter arrived and the Colonel ordered for both of them. Tony wanted coffee and croissants; *the usual totally inadequate continental snack,* thought the Colonel. He, of course, ordered his usual full English breakfast, consisting of two fried eggs, well-done bacon, mushrooms, sausages, beans, and a double order of brown toast. He could never understand how anyone could possibly start the day with anything less.

At last, Tony Western looked up.

'It's difficult to make much from this without a bit of time and access to a computer. What might help is some line as to its possible contents.'

The Colonel briefly outlined the events, as recently told by North, that had led up to his previous telephone conversation. He stressed the urgency of the matter due to the Sicilian girl's disappearance.

'So, it's a sort of treasure hunt with a damsel in distress?' said Tony with a grin, still not quite sure if he should take the Colonel seriously. 'It does seem a bit far-fetched,' he continued, now concentrating on spreading butter over his croissants. 'Both the Mafia and Romanians showing an interest in this particular ring, a girl disappears, possibly kidnapped, her father incredibly wealthy, with this North chap doing the Don Quixote bit to save her from certain death!'

With his second croissant finished, he added, 'If I did not know you better Colonel Metcalf, I would say this whole story came straight out of a tale from *A Thousand and One Arabian Nights*. You're telling me that this collection of letters, numbers, and symbols really came from the etchings on a precious stone, possibly Greek in origin.' He paused a moment while eating his third butter-laden croissant, then washed the remains from his mouth with more hot black coffee.

'I find the whole tale quite unbelievable. Tell me something, Colonel, is there a grain of truth in what you have just told me?'

'You may be interested to know that Lord North, to give him his title, is a a hereditary peer of England, who comes form a very distinguished family indeed. His great great grandfather was Lord Alexander North who was governor of Madras in British India. His great grandfather Sir Trevelyon North was decorated in the late 19th century for services in the Indian Intelligence Service, which included North West Frontier action against Russian intrigue.

Another ancestor, Captain Edward North, died at the battle of Quebec in 1759, whilst storming the city. This decisive British victory led by General James Wolfe ensured that the French would lose virtually all their possessions in North America and as a consequence Canada would always remain British.

'Sebastian North is an equally capable individual and is not a person to waste my time on something inconsequential, and I, as you know, would not waste yours. North used to work for us some years ago. He was, I may add, very good at his job.'

'Why did he leave?' enquired Tony Western, his interest aroused. What type of man could generate so much respect from Colonel Metcalf? A man who was known to be singularly unimpressed by most people's inadequate dedication to duty, insufficient hard work, and weak loyalties?

'He suddenly resigned after internal department changes resulted in new restrictions placed upon previous *laissez faire* attitudes to operations. North resigned, then disappeared into seclusion and was rumoured to have left the country. We eventually traced him to South America – Peru, in fact – then lost him in the suburbs of Lima. It was another six months before we caught up with him, this time in Patagonia, travelling south to Tierra del Fuego.'

'Rather carrying the getting-away-from-it-all concept to extremes,' commented Tony Western, trying to imagine what life would be like at the bottom of the world.

'There was a helicopter that crashed somewhere down there during the Falklands War, I seem to recall,' he added.

'Yes,' replied the Colonel. 'It crashed in the Strait of Magellan. Three men were arrested, probably a British undercover operation that went wrong. Nothing to do with our department at the time.' The Colonel paused for thought and then continued, 'The captured men ended up in Ushuaia, which incidentally, for your information, is the most southerly town in the world.'

'I don't think I will be visiting the area soon,' said Tony Western. 'Cold climates lost their appeal ever since I enjoyed three months sailing the Greek islands five years ago.'

He drained his coffee cup and then announced that the afternoon was free, thus allowing him to pursue the 'mystery message'.

'I have a meeting with my American opposite number in the NSA. It's classified, of course, but I know how you like to keep in touch.'

'What are our American friends up to this time?' asked Colonel Metcalf, who found retirement difficult, having to adjust to his recent isolation.

'Something to do with the disappearance of a top-secret plane – an advanced prototype called the X-30. It's a hypersonic aircraft, capable of 25,000mph. It vanished into thin air on altitude trials over Uruguay last month, however, the Americans haven't told us exactly where it is supposed to have disappeared yet. The US Air Force are a bit anxious, which is understandable considering the plane's considerable research budget to date. The cost militarily, if this plane fell into the wrong hands, is not worth thinking about.'

'It sounds as if you are going to have an interesting morning and a puzzling afternoon,' said the Colonel, finishing his substantial meal. 'Once again, Tony, many thanks for your time and help. It is very much appreciated.'

'Don't mention it, Colonel Metcalf, I owe you a favour.' The Colonel had personally recommended Tony Western for his present position after his outstanding success with the Czech cyphers.

Tony Western left in high spirits, his mind now occupied with the Colonel's intriguing story and urgent request. *It is certainly going to be more interesting trying to make head or tail of this piece of paper than sifting through more mundane foreign radio traffic*, he thought.

After ordering a fresh pot of coffee, Colonel Metcalf leaned back in his chair, satisfied that in Tony Western he had the right man working upon the task of solving this mysterious inscription. Information on the two names mentioned by North and details of the freighter should prove relatively easy by comparison. Before his evening whisky at six o'clock, he hoped to be in possession of the relevant facts.

His eyes wandered across the busy dining room. For no particular reason, they came to rest upon a couple three tables away. A dark Middle Eastern-looking gentleman with a moustache was engaged in light-hearted conversation with a young blonde girl. She wore a tight-fitting, and expensively tailored, bright blue suit. She looked about thirty-something, Colonel Metcalf reckoned.

When she laughed, her whole body joined with the motion, so that the rather too large blue and gold earrings energetically swung back and forth like an accelerated clock's pendulum. The man opposite had the habit of gesticulating far too much with his arms for a dining room. *This*, thought the Colonel, *confirmed with certainty that his origins weren't local.* He wondered what their topic of conversation could be; perhaps the previous evening's entertainment had been particularly amusing.

The Colonel thought at first that she could be English, but upon reflection decided that American nationality would be more likely, as the blue of her dress was very bright.

Colonel Metcalf wondered why this particular couple had caught his attention. Most of the other tables were occupied by businessmen, their concentration absorbed with important papers and the urgent talk of finance. A large table situated to one side was crowded with Japanese men in dark suits and regulation white shirts.

The tourists that morning were easy to distinguish from those whose reasons for conversation had more to do with accumulating wealth. It was due to these obvious tourists that Colonel Metcalf thought there should be a dress code. A few men, much to the

Colonel's irritation, had refused to wear a tie and jacket. After all, if he had taken the trouble to dress in appropriate fashion, then why couldn't they? He was of a different generation to those around him, but perhaps it had more to do with thirty years in the army that had bound him to formality and tradition.

The same foreign waiter arrived with his pot of coffee, his previous oily smile now absent; obviously, mornings were not a good time for exhibiting a friendly attitude.

Colonel Metcalf's blue-grey eyes finally settled back upon the girl in blue, her blonde hair and bright clothes the only splash of colour contrasting with the dark grey of London's business community.

He reflected once more upon North's recent phone call and its possible implications. The principal players in this unfolding drama included the Baron Delmonte – immensely wealthy with interests on a global scale. The Colonel wondered what future enquiries in his direction might reveal.

Octavia, the Baron's strong-willed daughter, vanishes in the middle of the night. How much was the Cosa Nostra and her former fiancé Count Roberto Fambino involved?

Then there was this eastern connection. What were the Romanians after? Were they connected in some way with the Sicilian Mafia? How did this stranded freighter, *Belle of the Wind*, tie in? Was the Baron's doctor a sympathetic physician, or did he harbour other motives?

Colonel Metcalf possessed a highly-trained and active mind that was naturally suspicious of everyone, until either accurate information or their motives were revealed. His near-infallible sixth sense had proved invaluable over the years.

He paid his bill with a small tip, deciding the waiter's borderline surly attitude did not deserve a more generous consideration. Once outside the hotel, he found to his surprise that the sun was shining. With cautious optimism, he predicted a positive change in the local weather. Maybe North's Mediterranean warmth was beginning to penetrate the monotonous English gloom.

* * * * *

North replaced the receiver with a distinctive click. For a moment he remained motionless, alone in Count Santorini's study, surrounded by partially illuminated paintings from previous centuries.

If the inscription made any sense at all, then Colonel Metcalf, with his various contacts in the Foreign Office and British Intelligence, should be able to come up with something.

North thought of Octavia for the hundredth time that day. *What had happened to her? Where was she now? What was she thinking?*

His mind began to race, driving his imagination unchecked, until it became impulsive and illogical. Then at last, with great effort, he willed his mind to close these persistent questions that had no easy answers.

North left the study to find Count Santorini with a worried expression on his face.

'The Baron,' he explained, 'is unwell and presently sleeps. It seems the stress of the last few days has finally taken its toll. I have also sent for his doctor.

I think he is in need of medical attention, perhaps some sort of tranquilliser to relax him. I have given him something for the time being, but I fear it won't be strong enough.'

North admitted that the Baron had been more than a little tense and agitated, quite understandable considering the circumstances, of course.

'He explained everything to you?' asked North, not sure how much the Count knew of recent events.

'He mentioned the disappearance of his daughter in the early hours of this morning and that you are helping him to find her. He also outlined the circumstances of his wife's tragic death. Such misfortune and disaster striking the illustrious Delmonte family so quickly has been a terrible punishment for the Baron to endure.'

Count Santorini showed North to the Baron's room. They found him lying on his back, asleep. He looked ghastly, pale, and haggard. The room had the antiseptic smell of a hospital.

'What time is his doctor due to arrive?' enquired North, his face transfixed upon the corpse-like figure before him.

'Tomorrow evening. I phoned Dr. Carlos Lacombe, who said he would take the next available flight via Rome. If the Baron's condition deteriorates in the meantime, I will ask a local doctor that I trust to visit at once. He is a relation of mine, so there will be complete confidence.'

North used Count Santorini's telephone once again before retiring to his room. Once the heavy door had closed firmly behind him, he lay supine and exhausted upon the bed. With his eyes closed, he thought for a long time, his mind preoccupied with the recent unfolding drama of mysterious events.

* * * * *

Dr. Carlos Lacombe flew from Nice to Palermo via Rome. From when his plane landed in Rome to his departure for Cagliari, he found just enough time to briefly visit the British Embassy.

Deep within the Embassy building, Dr. Lacombe was handed a brown envelope upon which was written a single name in blue ink. The man who handed him the envelope was very particular in making sure that the doctor was who he claimed to be. Dr. Lacombe left the British Embassy for Sardinia, promising to deliver the important envelope to Sebastian North the moment he saw him.

After his plane had landed in Cagliari, Dr. Lacombe caught a taxi to the castle in Sanluri. Count Santorini's butler showed the tired doctor into the drawing room, where he was met by Count Santorini and Sebastian North. After enquiring after North's shoulder injury, Dr. Lacombe was taken to Baron Delmonte's room.

Before Dr. Lacombe attended to his patient, he handed Sebastian North the brown envelope given to him at the British Embassy in Rome.

So, Colonel Metcalf has been working overtime, thought North. It had been his sudden idea, upon hearing of Dr. Lacombe's intended journey to Sardinia, to use him to carry any information that the Colonel might already have. It would appear that Colonel Metcalf had perhaps achieved some positive results with the inscription sooner than anticipated.

After examining his patient, Dr. Lacombe prescribed a sedative that he administered by injection. His prognosis was optimistic but guarded.

'He must be left alone to sleep and for the drug to take effect. The physical and emotional stress over the last few days have, I fear, taken their inevitable toll,' commented Dr. Lacombe.

He softly closed the door behind him, his face lined with anxiety and concern for the health of his patient.

Over the next hour, North narrated the developments since their previous meeting. Dr. Lacombe listened in silence until the Englishman had finished his curious account.

'It is a bad business, Signor North. I fear there will be much blood spilt before all this is concluded. If the Mafia are involved, as you suggest, my advice to you is to leave Sardinia immediately.

'There is no chance of your survival against Count Roberto Fambino. You are after Octavia, yes?' The doctor did not wait for an answer, as he had already guessed the Englishman's motive. 'You invite an early grave, Signor North.'

North thanked Dr. Lacombe for his advice, but his mind was made up and could not be influenced, no matter how sincere the warning.

Once alone in his room, North opened the brown envelope given to him by Dr. Lacombe. Inside was a single piece of paper containing a neat collection of letters and symbols. They made little sense. As previously agreed, for security Colonel Metcalf had used a cypher known only to himself and North to convey the enclosed information.

With the aid of this secret cypher, North proceeded to transcribe the inscription from Octavia's ring.

Chapter Six

Octavia felt tremendous pressure upon the back of her head. Something hard and unyielding was forcing itself relentlessly down upon her, so that she had the sensation of being trapped in a slowly closing vice. Unseen hands pinned her arms and legs, rendering resistance futile. She wanted to scream, but the cruel fingers under her chin prevented any such sound.

A voice hissed close to her right ear. The warm, moist air from his breath reeked of garlic and alcohol, and Octavia was immediately repulsed.

'Contessa...' The tone was mocking. 'Do not struggle...' The voice spoke Italian, the accent Sicilian. There was a pause to allow the words to sink in. 'You are coming with us. Firstly, I am going to cover your eyes with tape. Just a precaution, you understand?'

Octavia could not see the man because she was lying face down on the bed. The hand around her neck relaxed its grip, thus enabling her to breathe more easily. She felt tape being applied over both eye sockets, then tightly wound around the back of her head. Several strands were applied before the distinctive sound of cutting completed the operation. During the process, her hair was roughly pulled so that her neck muscles became taught and painful.

Octavia's strained imagination now fuelled the fear that spread throughout her nervous system like high voltage through a circuit.

'Sit up. We have selected some clothes for you to wear. They are beside you. Put them on, then we go, and remember, don't make a sound.'

Octavia prayed the nightmare would go away. She willed her panic-stricken mind to bring some sort of detached perspective to the enveloping turmoil around her. This proved impossible; only an ever-increasing circle of apprehension and rising fear could be found.

Once free from the unseen hands, Octavia rolled over onto her back, a single sheet covering her near-naked body. A pair of black silk panties was all that she wore and she cursed herself, for she had chosen them for their sex appeal, they left little to the imagination.

Octavia's eyes, though open, registered only blackness. She sensed the man through the darkness, close and menacing. His unseen presence was acutely uncomfortable in the silence. He was no doubt waiting to see how she would comply with his orders.

The situation, thought Octavia, *does not encourage resistance*. Perhaps with a change in circumstances and an increase in courage, she would try something...

Octavia had never felt so vulnerable in her life. With all her strength she again tried to suppress the rising tide of fear that threatened to paralyse all rational thinking. She was only partially successful, for what little courage she possessed was quickly draining away.

Then she heard voices a little further away. They came from near the window. The conversation was held in whispers. One voice she recognised was that of the man who had recently spoken to her. The second man's accent was difficult to distinguish. Both men were arguing about her ability to dress herself while blindfolded.

What am I to do? thought Octavia. *Question my captors?*

'Supposing I don't want to go with you?' said Octavia. Her voice was slow and controlled, but the pounding in her chest increased.

'You have no choice,' spat the first man.

'Where are you taking me? Why are you doing this?' Octavia's voice was now less steady as it rose in pitch.

'You will find out soon enough,' said the second man.

Octavia thought she would appeal to these strangers with an opportunity for them to demonstrate their sense of honour and respect towards a woman, though she knew these men could possess little esteem in this direction.

'I am not wearing any clothes,' she told them. In the circumstances, she did not count the black silk panties as clothing. 'You surely can't expect me to dress in front of two strange men. I have never met you before. You cannot be afraid of an unprotected and defenceless woman?'

Octavia, with her vision still obscured, managed to sit upright, drawing the single sheet tightly around her body. However, she did not hear one of the men position himself to one side and slightly behind her.

The man hit Octavia on the back of her head, the impact so hard that she flew halfway across the room. She screamed twice before a second, particularly vicious blow connected with the same area of her skull.

From the second blow, Octavia experienced indescribable pain. She tried to scream again, but this proved impossible; her lungs contained no air. Octavia's pain was so acute that she thought she was drowning in a continuous sea of nausea, devoid of oxygen. Unconsciousness must surely follow.

She felt warm blood run down her left cheek; somehow her forehead had been cut. The wound must be deep, as its location throbbed painfully. The second blow had partially dislodged the tape from around Octavia's head, so that it was now no longer tight but loose and hanging.

Her head pounded like a pneumatic drill out of control. She was convinced that it must explode any moment into a thousand fragments. Waves of nausea engulfed her body, threatening exhaustion. Only the sleep of unconsciousness could offer any meaningful relief. But even this was denied her.

Octavia's mind overflowed with fear. What would these men do next? From her parents, Octavia had inherited a unique and powerful blend of qualities. She would need these attributes, which included fortitude, courage, and patience, in the unfolding of her increasingly perilous future.

With her right hand, Octavia wrenched the remaining tape from her face. She tried to focus her eyes, but the room swam in circles, as if she was the axle of a giant centrifuge, spinning much too fast. Her dark eyes, that had only a few hours before expressed such excitement and joy in North's arms, now became clouded with tears of desperation and hopelessness.

Slowly the room ceased to revolve. Octavia wiped her tear-stained face with a corner of white sheet that she still clutched, the material now stained red from her wound. She could taste the distinctive sweet trickle of blood somewhere within her mouth.

From across the room, two figures gradually assumed human form. One wore dark trousers and a leather jacket; his black hair brushed straight back from a receding hairline. Octavia put his age at about forty. The second man, who stood close to the window, wore a bright blue shirt that was drawn tight around him so that it accentuated his powerful chest and forearms. His thick moustache drooped below the corners of his mouth to form two fine points, in the manner of an oriental. He looked about thirty. Maybe it was this man's blue shirt that Sebastian thought he'd seen following them earlier.

Octavia knew instinctively that it was the first man who had struck her. His impassive face remained untouched and oblivious to her suffering. The watchful eyes were sunk deep into their sockets, the nose was too small, the tightly stretched skin that covered his face resembled yellow parchment giving an overall grotesque and gargoyle like appearance. Octavia felt new waves of fear and nausea drop through her delicate mind like corrosive acid.

'That will teach you, to disobey my orders, woman. Now do as I say, put your clothes on, or worse things will happen to you.'

There was no pretence at being civil with this new threat. The man's true ruthless and callous nature, totally devoid of civility, lay open and without shame.

The man with the oriental moustache interrupted.

'Signorina,' his tone softer, more conciliatory than that of his companion, '…if you wish, you may put your clothes on in the bathroom. But remember, we will be just outside, so don't try making any stupid noises.'

Octavia needed no more encouragement, keeping the sheet tightly around her she picked up her clothes and ran for the bathroom, acutely aware of the staring eyes constantly watching her as she moved.

Once behind the door, Octavia carefully locked it. *Those men will not now have the satisfaction of watching me dress,* she thought. For a moment she had a breathing space and time to think, though she knew it was a brief respite from these fiends.

What could they want with her? Where did they intend on taking her? Octavia knew their presence was somehow connected with the higher echelons of the Cosa Nostra. This could not be a straightforward kidnapping-for-ransom scenario. There had to be a more sinister reason which she could only guess at.

The previous kidnapping attempt in the South of France had been a much more sedate affair. The men who had come to her hotel room had been firm in their intentions, but not violent towards her. Perhaps if she had struggled at the time, subsequent events might have become much more uncomfortable.

Octavia looked deep into the mirror. Disbelief gave way to shock. Familiar recognition was absent, and she shuddered and shrank back from the image before her. Her hair was unrestrained and wild, as if blown by an angry wind. The right side of her face and neck was a hideous dark red from blood, which ran from the gash on her forehead. Down her neck and chest, the blood had started to congeal in an ugly mass.

Octavia heard the two men arguing on the other side of the locked door. Their voices became louder. Now and again she recognised the odd word, such as 'gold' and 'jewellery'. After more shouting, Octavia became certain that one of the men was blaming the other for not searching her properly and taking all her jewellery, as ordered.

While forcing her muddled mind to make some kind of sense from this new information, Octavia held resolutely to the sides of the hand basin. With another look in the mirror, she observed the absence of her jewellery. She had removed her earrings and necklace earlier before slipping under the sheet.

Octavia ran cold water into the basin. When it was almost full, she slid both hands into the water, then proceeded to splash the cold water over her face, endeavouring to wash away some of the blood.

Through the water, she noticed the five rings she always wore – three on her left hand, and two on her right. She tried to smile as one of them caught her attention. It was a fine octagonal emerald – the love expressed by a previous flame in Copenhagen a long time ago, or so it seemed.

Suddenly Octavia was jolted back to reality by the sound of the two men tearing the room apart. Then she realised they must be after only one piece of jewellery – the ring that contained the ruby. They must think that she had already removed it and were at this very moment trying to find it.

Octavia's heart beat faster. She tried to extract the ring, but it was firmly placed upon the fourth finger of her left hand and would not move. She was now convinced that this was what the men were after.

In order to gain a few more precious moments, she yelled out, 'I am almost finished, Signor.' Her tone was respectful, perhaps even courteous.

However, these last few moments were not conceded. The lock proved no match for the large man on the other side and the cardboard-thin door flew open with the sound of splintering wood. The large man stood where the door had been two seconds before. His arms moved impatiently, his face flushed with anger. But it was the man's cold and calculating eyes that Octavia feared most.

'I am waiting, Contessa,' again the mocking tone. 'No doubt you are accustomed to more time for presenting yourself. I am not one of your playboys. We go now!'

Octavia became alarmed. The man was watching her every move. Both her hands were in the basin, clear and defined through the water. She splashed more water upon her face, pretending to wash it further. The performance must have looked pretty convincing, as the clotted blood, now breaking up, dissolved in the water, turning it pink and opaque.

Taking the bar of soap from the side, Octavia created the illusion of further washing, this time of her hands. The water turned even more opaque from the added soap, thus completely obscuring her hands. Then with a last desperate effort Octavia tried to free the ring fixed to her finger.

When she had almost given up, the ring came free. Then, carefully under the water, she pushed the ring into the bar of soap. Now Octavia had to let North know where she had hidden the ring, but how? It must be written somewhere so that he would not miss it.

After a final wash to her face and rinsing of her hands, Octavia told the man at the door that she needed to finish her toilet. Then without waiting for a reply, she glared at him before slamming the damaged door in his face.

Quickly, Octavia took out her lipstick and wrote on a corner of the mirror. Flushing the toilet for the sound effects, she quickly put on a revealing green blouse and mid-thigh length, white cotton skirt that revealed her athletic legs to advantage. Attention must now be directed away from the bathroom. The cut on her forehead had stopped bleeding but her head still throbbed painfully. However, Octavia told herself that this was no time to dwell on pain and discomfort.

After opening the door, she announced to the two men beyond, 'Let's go,' in a tone now positively friendly.

Both men paused from their angry discussion, surprised at her sudden change of attitude. Octavia wondered if their suspicions would be aroused.

'I am glad you see things our way, Contessa,' said the man with the moustache.

'A very wise choice,' added the other man.

It was then that they ordered Octavia to remove her remaining jewellery, which consisted of her remaining four rings. Once this had been completed, they placed them carefully in a plastic bag along with the pieces she had removed earlier before sleeping.

Whoever these men were working for, Octavia realised, had not informed them as to the true reason for removing her jewellery. Someone knew of the ruby's true potential value but did not trust his subordinates with this information. So, by collecting all her jewellery, this someone hoped to gain possession of the ruby without drawing specific attention to it. *Someone is going to be very disappointed*, she thought.

Octavia was shocked by the destruction of the room. Whilst she had been in the bathroom, these men must have been searching for any other valuables she might have hidden.

Only after the door was closed behind them did she breathe a cautious sigh of relief. Her short skirt and long brown legs had aroused enough interest to distract their attention away from the bathroom. Strangely, Octavia found renewed confidence in knowing that she had been secretly able to thwart their plans.

The hotel manager was nowhere to be seen. No doubt he had been threatened or paid in advance to take little notice of the commotion, including her screams for help. A car was waiting in the silent street, fifty yards from the hotel entrance. Its engine sprang to life as soon as the three figures emerged from the shadows.

The large car moved quietly, its powerful engine making little noise, and came to a stop beside them. The man who had struck Octavia threatened her with another warning about being difficult, but Octavia needed little encouragement to remain silent. She was pushed roughly into the back seat so that she was sandwiched between the two men. The movement sent additional shock waves of pain across her back and neck. Her head throbbed continuously.

Within the confined space of the car, Octavia smelt stale cigarette smoke mingled with strong body odour. The combined effect was unpleasant and nauseating. In the rear-view mirror, Octavia caught the driver's face. His dark eyes conveyed hostility. His features looked anaemic from the glow of his cigarette, firmly clamped between thin, bloodless lips.

The car pulled away from the curb without a word from the driver, accelerating to just below the speed limit. Never once was it exceeded during the twenty-minute journey to the international airport, north west of Cagliari. The man behind the wheel was well-practised in his ability to drive without drawing attention in the near-deserted streets.

The driver parked the car close to the deserted terminal building and one of the men got out to make a phone call. When he had finished, he ordered Octavia out of the car. The airport showed little in the way of life.

Then somewhere close by, the distinctive high-pitched whine of a jet engine sounded. The man with the moustache held Octavia's arm. Everyone, including the driver, now walked onto the concrete runway towards the increasing noise. A small private jet was preparing for take-off, its port and starboard lights flashing their eerie glow with intermittent sweeps of fluorescent red and green.

As they approached the aircraft, Octavia felt the grip tighten upon her arm. These men were taking little chance with any last-minute escape plans that she might contemplate.

Now the ear-splitting whine of jet engines filled the air. Conversation in the car had been minimal, but possible. Now, any conversation was out of the question.

When Octavia reached the bottom of the steps, a man in a dark suit emerged from the fuselage exit. He was about six foot, well suntanned, and very blond. His youthful features suggested an age of about 35, and Octavia thought he looked strangely familiar.

Her escorts and driver were apparently not invited further than the steps. The blond man shook her hand and, with a ready smile, motioned for her to enter the plane. Once inside, the door immediately closed, reducing the engine whine to conversation level. Through a window, Octavia saw the three men, their backs turned, walking back towards their waiting car.

The Mafia hierarchy believes in keeping the stresses and strains of long-distance travel to a minimum. And Octavia herself was no stranger to the opulent lifestyle of the rich and famous, both from her own family and from being courted. Various wealthy and titled men had sought to demonstrate their many charms across the cities of the world. Many travelled on a regular basis by private plane.

She was the first to admit that she enjoyed the grandiose taste of champagne and the extravagance of an intemperate lifestyle. However, Octavia possessed a set of principles that governed a moral code that was an integral part of her finely balanced conscience. She would not compromise from this code, whatever the circumstances.

She had discussed at length with her childhood friend Claudia, that the means of acquiring wealth would reflect the ethical fibre of the person. Thus, it always surprised her that others saw only importance in the creation of wealth. The means for them was not relevant.

A risk taking spirit, combined with hard work, would ultimately produce financial success, for example by developing a useful product or service. An equal profit could also be achieved by the sale of a narcotic, such as heroin – a drug responsible for the slow death of countless people. The moral difference between these two paths of wealth creation, in Octavia's view, was not less than that between night and day.

'Welcome, Contessa Octavia. You look tired. Please sit down and make yourself comfortable.' The blond man's tone was positively friendly, and the contrast in attitude from her previous escorts could not have been more complete.

Octavia was weary, and welcomed the relief offered by the large armchair behind her.

'What is all this about?' she ventured, feeling a little more comfortable. 'Why have I been brought here? Where are you taking me?'

'One question at a time,' replied the blond man, throwing up his arms in mock protest. 'Firstly, I know it's early but what can I fix you to drink?'

Octavia hesitated before replying. She did need a drink – something strong and alcoholic. However, the situation demanded a clear head and rational thinking, and alcohol had never been renowned for enhancing these qualities.

'Cappuccino would be fine,' replied Octavia.

With another smile, the blond man took her suitcase and disappeared behind a curtain near the rear of the plane. She observed him place the plastic bag containing her jewellery – passed to him earlier by the man with the moustache – into an inside pocket of his expensive suit.

A moment later, a steward appeared from behind the curtain with a large steaming cup of white frothy liquid. At that particular moment Octavia thought the smell of freshly ground coffee had to be one of life's great pleasures. As she sipped the hot foam, she felt new energy seep back into her painful and tired body.

'Scotch after we take off, Rocco. We don't want spilt drinks like last time, such a waste of good whisky,' said the blond man to the impassively faced steward hovering at the rear of the fuselage.

'These small jets,' explained the blond man, 'are notorious for their steep angle of ascent.'

The plane paused for a moment at the start of the runway, like a bird gathering strength. Then the pilot opened up the throttles, causing the engines to roar with increasing power. Slowly at first, but with ever increasing speed and purpose, the plane launched itself into the blood red dawn of a new day.

The blond, blue-eyed man studied the girl sitting opposite with renewed interest. Octavia felt his eyes upon her. Superficial observation gave way to curiosity as his eyebrows knitted together.

Those very blue eyes now questioned her recent wound, which was an ugly blemish upon her otherwise flawless complexion. Her attempts at disguise only been partially successful.

'What happened to your forehead?' he asked.

Octavia's reply was an explosion of burning Sicilian wrath. Her body shook and her eyes flashed with anger.

'If you had noticed earlier, you might have asked the men who brought me here,' said Octavia.

'Al and Joe did this to you?' The man sounded genuine in his surprise.

'Yes. They most certainly did. I was treated like trash by those animals.'

'What did they do exactly?' asked the blond man, before he took another sip of his drink.

Octavia explained in detail what had taken place following the two men entering her hotel room uninvited. The account was complete, apart from where she had hidden the ring.

When Octavia had finished, the blond man was left in little doubt as to her feelings for what had taken place. An inexcusable injustice had occurred that was totally devoid of provocation. This was not a misguided misdemeanour in bad manners, but a reprehensible act of transgression against a defenceless woman.

Octavia had never before felt the hot consuming flame of vengeance burn through her desires, but the fury that now simmered deep within her Sicilian blood, fuelled by pain, would need little to light the torch of revenge.

The blond man's face showed concern, but the very blue eyes reflected no such compassion. It was at this moment that he introduced himself.

'Forgive me, Octavia, my name is Camillio. I am a cousin of Roberto. You have perhaps forgotten we last met three years ago in New York at a party given by Vlademer Klugman.'

Octavia now remembered why he had looked familiar. The South American tin magnet's party in a huge apartment on Park Avenue somewhere. There had been a mixed collection of guests, ranging from American billionaires to English rock stars. Her mother would not have approved, Octavia recalled thinking at the time.

'You wore something red,' said Camillio. 'Off the shoulders and very long. It was attractive. I believe your escort was called Alfonso. He never left your side.'

Octavia recalled the heir apparent to the Spanish throne with what, in different circumstances, would have been termed a smile.

At the time, Alfonso had been a rebel like herself. However, the chemistry between them had proved to be unbalanced, in spite of her mother's initial enthusiasm for the match. It had been fun while it lasted, and as a consequence she had graced the front covers of many European and American fashion magazines.

In the end, Octavia had admitted that she was too frivolous and independent. The heir apparent to the Spanish throne could exercise no authority over her fiery and wild temperament.

Octavia's mind suddenly came crashing back to the present.

'So, Roberto is behind this.' It was a statement of fact that Octavia found difficult to grasp. 'He ordered you to meet me at the airport, then take me to him. Yes?' Octavia did not pause, her anger rising deep within her. 'What does he want? Where is he now? Somewhere on the Costa Smeralda?'

'Roberto phoned me from Porto Cervo to ask if I could divert to Cagliari as he was expecting your arrival at the airport early this morning. His own plane was grounded with an engine fault. Cagliari airport is only a slight change of course from Paris to Palermo.

'We have been in close contact over the last six months with business interests in the States. In the past, we had our differences with operations in Sicily, but we recently patched up our previous problems in order to work on a very big deal with global dimensions.

'Roberto did not mention that there would be any trouble. Only that you might be stranded at Cagliari, with no means at this early hour of reaching Porto Cervo.

'I am sure Roberto will reveal all when you meet him. Perhaps he genuinely wants to amend his previous ways and start the future anew with you. Why don't you give him a chance? Maybe he still loves you?'

Octavia's eyes smouldered with pain and anger.

'And this,' she said, throwing back her hair to once again expose the ugly red line across the right side of her forehead. 'Is this his token of the future?'

'The last chance of love between us was destroyed a long time ago when he threw my heart into the dust, with the consideration of one throwing away an empty wine bottle.'

Octavia did not trust Camillio. She felt he knew more about her present circumstances than he had so far revealed. She also found his smile too quick and false.

At his request, Rocco the steward dressed Octavia's wound, then finished it off with a neat strip of white elastic tape. Then, after exchanging Octavia's empty coffee cup for a full one, and pouring another drink for Camillio, he promptly disappeared behind the curtain.

'I was sorry to hear about your mother. I only heard yesterday. Both *L'Ora* and *La Repubblica* had leading articles.'

'It is not surprising,' replied Octavia. 'Anything to do with the Delmontes is news.'

'The articles concluded that robbery was the most likely motivation. The police apparently discovered that various items were missing from the villa.

'*L'Ora* mentioned something about your father's launch leaving the area soon after a large explosion was heard. This must have accounted for the completely wrecked pier. Gunfire was heard being exchanged between the boat and the shore. Clothing in the water that was picked up later, suggested your mother's fate.

'*L'Ora* must have had a reporter on the scene fairly quickly, judging by their detailed account. At the villa, the police found a dead man and women in the kitchen.

Two more bodies were found outside the villa and path leading down to the sea.

'The only person not dead was a man found inside the villa, bound hand and foot. So far, little information has been gained from this individual who has proved reluctant to talk. All very mysterious, don't you think?'

'My father disappeared in Athens while on business,' Octavia told him. 'I was in the South of France when an attempt was made to kidnap me – the second within a few months. This time, they were not Italian. They were a different bunch, Eastern-European. I escaped with the help of a certain Sebastian North, an Englishman.

'My mother was upset and worried about my father's lack of communication. I returned home, only to be re-captured by the same Eastern-Europeans, then held prisoner with my mother in the cellar of our family villa.

'Sebastian North showed up again after I secretly managed to phone him. We escaped to the launch. During the process, my mother was caught in the crossfire on the jetty, then the explosion...'

'Who is this Englishman?'

'He happened to be on the same beach in the South of France when I made a break for it. They shot him in the arm as we ran for the car. Carlos, my father's doctor, attended to him. He lost some blood, but it wasn't too serious.'

'Where is he now?' asked Camillio.

'I don't know,' replied Octavia truthfully.

She suddenly regretted telling Camillio so much, but she was confused and distraught. She wondered what had become of her father and Sebastian's attempt to board the *Roxana*. *What was Roberto's hand in all this?* They'd had so much once; bittersweet memories came in a well of emotion. Her eyes became moist as the light of the sun grew brighter in the eastern sky.

Conversation abruptly came to an end until the plane touched down on the runway at Olbia in Northern Sardinia.

The early history of Olbia is unclear, its origins uncertain. Probably founded by Carthaginians from North Africa, they were later defeated by the Romans in both Sardinia and Corsica.

A man in a nondescript suit, whom she had never seen before, greeted her at the foot of the steps. He motioned to a waiting silver helicopter, its blades turning. Before escorting her, he received the suitcase and bag containing her jewellery from Camillio.

In the helicopter, they were alone apart from the pilot, but Octavia did not even look at the man next to her. Instead, she looked out of the window, watching the ground disappear. Her thoughts were now of Roberto and their inevitable meeting.

The helicopter climbed until Octavia thought she could see over to the Bonifacio strait, beyond which lay Corsica, the island where Napoleon was born. From the window, she followed the helicopter's passage deep into the sparsely populated region of Gallura.

Suddenly Octavia saw their objective. The ground to the west rose up, forming a steep rise, upon which stood the majestic ruins of a huge crusader castle. From the high battlements, a dominant position was achieved over the valley and plains below.

For over three hundred years, the crusaders built castles along the eastern edge of the Mediterranean to consolidate advances in Palestine and Syria. Their objective was to secure Jerusalem for Christianity.

In 1099, the first crusade under Alexius Comnenus, the Emperor of Byzantium, captured Jerusalem. Eighty-eight years later in 1187, the Muslims recaptured the city under Saladin. The Christians endeavoured to give unrestricted access to Jerusalem, free from Muslim intervention. However, in reality, the pilgrims never enjoyed totally free passage to the Holy City.

For once, Christian Europe was united by a common purpose in its self-appointed quest to claim Jerusalem for the cross. Richard Coeur-de-Lion of England, and others such as Frederick Barbarossa, King of Germany and the Holy Roman Empire, led with courage and gallantry.

In military terms, historians have viewed them almost universally as failures, because supply lines were exposed and much too long for any significant influence in the region.

Economically, these campaigns proved too costly, with no corresponding or meaningful return. Along with their ruins, only the inspiration of a noble cause and its associated romance have endured to the present day.

As they descended towards the castle's towers and crumbled walls, Octavia was momentarily mesmerised by the colossal edifice that slowly increased in size and stature. Parts of the building remained remarkably intact after so many centuries. From the main courtyard rose the central tower or keep, easily two hundred feet above the surrounding ramparts.

At this point, she recalled the legend of the blue diamond and its association with Castle Zehra.

During a storm off the Northern Coast of Cyprus, a ship was wrecked. This particular vessel happened to be carrying a passenger of some importance.

Some of the crew drowned while trying to swim ashore. However, most survived, only to be captured by the island's cruel governor. Amongst these survivors was a daughter of one of the Emirates of Persia, a Princess Zehra.

The governor tortured the ship's crew by putting their eyes out before turning them loose. The Princess was held for ransom. Her fate would follow that of the crew unless the Emirate paid a large ransom.

King Richard Coeur-de-Lion of England, upon hearing of the Princess's fate, ordered his fleet which happened to be in the vicinity to change course for Northern Cyprus. He landed in force, then quickly defeated the governor's soldiers who proved no match for the veteran crusader army. The governor was killed during the conflict.

The Princess was released unharmed, and personally escorted by Richard to Palestine. To show his appreciation, the Emirate gave Richard seven chests containing countless precious and semi precious stones, together with huge amounts of gold and silver.

Amongst this unprecedented wealth was a large uncut diamond, known as the *Darya-i-Nur* or Sea of Light.

King Richard employed most of the sultan's treasure to finance the third crusade. The English king was so taken with Princess Zehra's beauty that he ordered the construction of a castle, in Northern Sardinia, and named it after her.

The fate of the *Darya-i-Nur* became a mystery. Some rumours said that after King Richard left for Europe, the Emirate seized the remainder of the seven chests, which included the great diamond.

Others said that bandits, attracted by rumours of a fabulous stone, somehow found it and from there it passed through several hands to end up lost in the Far East. Its real fate and present location was never discovered.

As a child, Octavia and friends had acted out countless times the extraordinary tale of Princess Zehra's rescue from the evil Governor of Cyprus by courageous King Richard. She had always wanted to play Princess Zehra. To feel the quivering of fear and excitement at being rescued just before her eyes were to be put out. Then the long journey with the heroic King Richard to meet her grateful father.

Was there love between them? Octavia's romantic nature insisted there must have been, but the legend does not say. She liked to think that King Richard kept the diamond to remind him of Princess Zehra on his long military campaign through Palestine.

The helicopter lost more height upon its Eastern approach to the ancient monument. The castle had three protective walls, the innermost protecting the courtyard and central tower, off which ran a long gallery and various other utility buildings, such as stables and barracks. Each wall had a large gate recessed into it. The innermost being by far the most elaborate.

The two outer walls must have been twelve feet thick, the inner one closer to fifteen. Each wall had a walkway behind the battlements for the defenders to shoot arrows and pour oil, or some other equally unpleasant substance, upon those below.

Arrow slits crisscrossed the main tower, on the top of which was a pole that flew an ensign. There was little wind, making its design difficult to distinguish, but it appeared to be a tricolour with the colours arranged vertically. Then Octavia realised that the ensign flew at half mast.

How strange, thought Octavia. *Who would fly an ensign here?*

Upon further inspection from her window, Octavia observed Castle Zehra in more detail. The main walls and central tower were undoubtedly twelfth century, but it was obvious that someone had recently been restoring the structure to its original state. Some of the battlements, the main tower, and various out-buildings, looked much more recent.

Tyre tracks, clear in the loose sand, led from the outer walled entrance down the steep hill to the valley below, to ultimately disappear in the south west. Clearly, Castle Zehra was inhabited.

Then something caught her eye – a slight movement far to the west. After a moment, she made out two horses, their riders urging their animals on at a great pace, so that a small dust cloud was left behind to mark their passage.

The helicopter banked steeply before its final approach to land two hundred yards from the main gate. It was the only flat piece of ground near the castle, and markings on the ground suggested frequent traffic.

Once outside and away from the helicopter's rotating blades, the bright morning sunlight hit Octavia's face with a hope that only a Mediterranean dawn can announce. She paused a moment to breathe in a few lungfuls of clean air, the experience seemed to bring new life to her tired limbs. Even her nausea became less acute. *Perhaps*, she thought, *this nightmare might turn into a pleasant dream after all.* Though she knew there was no rational reason why it should.

'We go this way, Octavia,' shouted her companion above the roar of the engine, his arm pointing to the main gates.

Looking up, she now clearly saw the colours of the tricolour above the tower. Blue, yellow, and red. It was not a design that she recognised.

The man at Octavia's side, once they reached the drawbridge, shouted to whoever was concealed within the gatehouse to 'open up, I have the Contessa'.

The portcullis was down – an arrangement that pointed towards someone being very security conscious – but Octavia thought she saw a slight movement behind one of the arrow slits above the archway. Suddenly, with a noise of rattling chain, the iron portcullis slowly rose until it hung suspended, ten feet above their heads.

The man waited for Octavia to move first. Cautiously, she passed under a row of steel points, her leather shoes scraping across the unfamiliar rough cobblestones as she went.

Within the extensive courtyard, the main tower or keep rose up before them, its entrance reached by stone steps, located some twenty feet above ground.

At the first stone step, Octavia hesitated. Rattling chain announced the lowering of the portcullis, and she tried once again to suppress her increasing fears.

What could Roberto really want? Was it the ring he was after, with its possible key to great wealth? Or did he want to rekindle the dead coals of her once-burning love?

Octavia stumbled up ancient steps, escorted by the steward from the helicopter. Before they reached the door, it opened.

The man who stood there was some sort of servant; his clothes were that of a waiter, his manner polite and accommodating.

'Ah, you have arrived, Contessa Octavia Delmonte. We have been expecting you. Come in, breakfast awaits.'

The servant led the way along a dimly lit, cool passageway, though Octavia noticed wrought iron torches protruding from the walls at intervals. *When lit*, she thought, *they must give an eerie glow.*

The passageway ended with polished wooden doors, opening into a large room or hall with a high wooden ceiling. In the middle of the room stretched a long dining table, with a capacity for at least forty people. The walls were covered with paintings and tapestries. Above an enormous fireplace were two crossed swords, their blades set at right angles.

The table was laid with breakfast crockery and the smell of strong coffee and freshly baked bread was heavy in the air. *The kitchen must be close by*, thought Octavia.

The smiling servant drew out a chair in front of her, and at the same time motioned for her to sit.

'The croissants are hot,' he said. His voice carried little warmth, and Octavia got the impression that he was not a happy man beneath his superficial charm.

Once she was sitting, the man poured steaming hot coffee from a silver pot. After the first taste of hot croissant and melted butter, Octavia had to admit she was hungry. There was no sign of her companion or anyone else while she ate, but at that moment she did not care very much. Breakfast was much more interesting.

When she had finally finished her food, she leant back in her chair, but she had little time for contemplation. The door she had recently passed through suddenly opened. A tall man was momentarily silhouetted before he entered the great hall with purpose in his step.

Octavia's former fiancé, Count Roberto Fambino, wore fine black leather riding boots with light tan breeches. His white silk shirt was worn loose with the top three buttons unfastened, exposing the thick, dark hairs of his powerful chest.

Octavia stood up and turned to face the Count, who had now almost reached her.

'Octavia, it has been so long…'

He stretched out his arms to hold Octavia's slim shoulders at arm's length, then drew her towards him and kissed her lightly on both cheeks. The Count's black eyes studied her closely, missing nothing, and came to rest on the tape across her forehead. His eyebrows drew together with what could be anxiety, his mouth compressed in concentration.

'My dear Octavia, I am so terribly sorry to hear how badly you have been treated.' For a moment, he paused as if in thought, his handsome features showing only concern for Octavia's obvious distress.

'I had no idea…' the Count's words momentarily failed. 'Those idiots will pay heavily for their clumsiness. I asked them to try to persuade you to join me here at Castle Zehra, nothing more.

'Camillio, who tells me that you have met before, has just told me the background to recent events. I am greatly saddened to hear of your mother's death. She was such a wonderful person. I am truly sorry.'

Octavia felt her eyes become moist with the memory of her mother. She also felt a lump in her throat, knowing that her father's safety was still very much in question.

Octavia's wet eyes stared at the face she once knew so well. The Counts' inquisitive eyes searched her face analysing, but was his concern genuine? His mouth was always just ready to break into that attractive smile that accentuated the old duelling scar down his left cheek. His upper lip was outlined by the same pencil-thin black moustache, the ends of which drew down either side of his aristocratic chin. This was a face that Octavia remembered from another life; the same face that had once dominated her emotional existence.

Octavia felt his closeness. She smelt his sweat from the recent ride, together with the animal smell of leather. She felt primitive emotions stir deep within her solar plexus.

Then the Count's frown gave way to a smile. His eyes became less worried and more friendly. *He must enjoy holding me*, thought Octavia. Perhaps as much as she enjoyed being held. She could feel Roberto's potent magnetism relentlessly draw her towards him. She felt half-forgotten memories of their passionate past come flooding back, so that her resistance to his invisible net became dangerously weakened and fatigued.

Chapter Seven

Bucharest is a city without a soul. The citizens of this city were once a dignified people, possessing great spirit and all the confidence that is inherent within an independent and sovereign country. Now only suspicion and fear remained. Everyone was afraid of everyone else. When Nicholas Ceauşescu became dictator Romanian destiny became hopelessly cracked and fragmented under the yoke of communism.

The government that ruled Romania used an extensive state network for gathering information, borne from a paranoid desire to know everything about its citizens. To achieve this, a huge and intricate web of spies and informers was woven throughout the government, civil service, armed forces, industry, and universities.

Ceauşescu's myopic vision of his Utopia translated into a living funeral pyre of hope for a people whose aspirations were constantly mummified in an endless web of tyranny and repression. When the helmsman has no check upon his course, then a country's inability to question its current direction will expose its future to a dangerous dystopia. Nicolae Ceauşescu set himself so far above the suffering of his people that he could no longer see or understand their distress through the dark and consuming clouds of his megalomania.

General Vlademer Kerenskiy, of the Romanian DIE (Foreign Intelligence Service), sped through the dark streets of Bucharest, cushioned from the misery around him by the thick glass and dark curtains of his Zil limousine.

The General's thoughts were oblivious to the suffering around him, however his fertile mind was far from inactive. It was, in fact, at this very moment keenly focused on one subject: the secret mission that Nicolae Ceauşescu had given him less than an hour before.

General Kerenskiy had been suddenly recalled from his luxurious villa on the Black Sea near Constanta, where he had just started a long-overdue holiday. President Nicolae Ceauşescu had demanded his presence in Bucharest.

Once inside the President's private study within the dictator's palace, General Kerenskiy was told a most bizarre story. The dictator's anger was so great that his face had become the colour of a ripe tomato, and the words he spoke were spat, as if he had consumed some life-threatening poison.

Apparently, the President's idiotic nephew, Major Vasile, had been running a delicate operation for the dictator's psychotic wife Elena, who some would say was the real power behind the throne. This operation had suddenly started to blow up in his face, threatening to create an international incident.

General Kerenskiy's mission was damage control for Major Vasile's latest untutored incompetence. From what the General had so far heard of this particular operation, he was not looking forward to picking up the pieces of what he already regarded as little less than an inevitable tragedy of immense proportions.

Leaving the exclusive Primaveri district of Bucharest, the government car travelled for thirty minutes before reaching a military air base. The long black limousine passed through two security checks without slowing down. Advance warning of their impending arrival had been radioed an hour before from President Ceaușescu's palace in northern Bucharest to the base commander.

The Russian-built Ilyushin 11-36 airliner, with Romanian colours clearly marked on its tail, waited at the end of the runway. The civil plane's white fuselage contrasted with the grey, green, and brown of various parked military aircraft.

The limousine came to an abrupt halt under the huge tail and the driver left his seat to open the passenger door. General Kerenskiy climbed out and immediately started walking towards the uniformed figure waiting beside the steps leading to the plane's rear port exit.

The base commander saluted before informing General Kerenskiy that everything was ready, including advanced clearance to land in Palermo. The General returned the salute, thanked the base commander, then mounted the staircase.

Thirty minutes later, the Ilyushin passed over the silver Danube to enter Yugoslavian air space at 25,000 feet, on course for Sicily.

The unscheduled flight from Bucharest landed at Punta Raisi airport with difficulty. The pilot had never landed there before and was unfamiliar with its heavy crosswinds. Two abortive attempts were made before the wheels touched the volcanic island.

The landing was far from smooth, with two blown tyres, a near overshoot of the runway, and one very agitated passenger. General Kerenskiy disliked flying, especially with his mind preoccupied by the present looming crisis.

Kerenskiy walked stiffly down the steps to the concrete runway, into the brilliant Mediterranean sun. Under different circumstances, he might have felt a welcome cheer from the sun's warmth after the overcast skies and damp of Bucharest. However, the nature of his mission and the interruption of his long-overdue holiday had created an atmosphere that was anything but cheerful.

A senior Sicilian immigration officer, proud of the extensive gold braid upon his peaked cap and epaulettes, met General Kerenskiy with an extended hand and broad smile. Kerenskiy shook Signor Viliaro's hand enthusiastically, grateful for his indispensable help in removing the usually impossible red tape of landing a foreign flight on unofficial business.

Engineering undetected visits by aircraft on some sort of dark business had, however, become a speciality of Signor Viliaro. And for this unique skill, a suitably thick brown envelope was the oil that ensured the continuous smooth running of clandestine operations in and out of Punta Raisi Airport.

Signor Viliaro knew far more about the reasons for General Kerenskiy's flight than the Romanian intelligence officer realised, due to a very close relationship with the Fambino crime family.

Both men walked to a waiting midnight-blue Mercedes, exchanging small talk, then General Kerenskiy climbed into the right rear passenger seat. Before Signor Viliaro shut the door, he wished the visitor a successful trip. Then the chauffeur slowly guided the car off the runway to the main road that led east towards Palermo.

Twenty minutes later, the blue Mercedes drew up to the ornate entrance of a once-luxurious, turn-of-the-century hotel. Its past grandeur had long since given way to barely concealed neglect.

General Kerenskiy walked with purpose through the foyer's frayed elegance to the elevators. Once inside the mirror-lined box, he pressed the third-floor button. Ninety seconds later, he found the room number he had been looking for.

General Kerenskiy knocked twice and the door opened almost immediately to reveal a thin, nervous young man of about thirty. He wore a crumpled blue suit, and his black hair was an untidy mop of curls. He obviously had not shaved for several days, suggesting a general departure from normal routine. He was sweating profusely despite the air conditioning, giving his face an unhealthy sheen.

The blue-suited man's nervous state was such that a first attempt at conversation proved useless, his sentences only half-formed before another one started. In the end, General Kerenskiy had to put up his hand to silence the incoherent ramble.

'Dimitro, start at the beginning. We don't have much time, but enough for you to slow down a bit and tell me exactly what has happened. I understand you and your incompetent companions, and that includes Major Vasile...' His tone suggested that there was little room for doubt with regard to his feelings towards the dictator's nephew, '...after kidnapping the Baron Delmonte's daughter, you let her go. And what is more, in the process killed the Baroness, to say nothing of the high casualty rate sustained by your companions.

'All very pointless and too much publicity. The incident has even made *La Repubblica* and, of course, *L'Ora* devotes extensive coverage to it. The Baron and his family are not just any family. The Delmonte name is one of the most famous not only in Sicily, but throughout Europe.'

General Kerenskiy paused to let his words sink in.

'Where is Major Vasile now?'

'He has taken the Baron Delmonte to Sardinia. The Baron goes there aboard his yacht at this time every year. Comrade Vasile's plan was for everything to be as normal as possible after the problems at the Delmonte villa.'

'How do you mean "normal as possible"...?' Now it was General Kerenskiy's turn to have trouble finishing his sentence.

'Start at the beginning, Dimitro.' The General gathered his self-control. If he frightened Dimitro too much, he might clam up altogether, judging by his present state. General Kerenskiy poured himself a generous measure of Russian vodka with a dash of tonic from a well-stocked drinks tray.

After sitting down, Dimitro began his tale.

'Major Vasile gave us orders to kidnap the Baron Delmonte. We held one of his senior directors in Athens, who at our request phoned the Baron here in Sicily at the family villa, saying that something urgent had come up which demanded his immediate personal attention.

'Later the same day, the Baron Delmonte arrived in Athens. At the hotel suggested by us, Gheorghe and Diaconescu, old friends of Major Vasile, met the Baron. As previously arranged, the ransom was for five million American dollars. A note was to be delivered to the Baron's wife in due course.

'Then everything changed, but no-one seemed to know why; Major Vasile kept us in the dark. An urgent phone call came through and Major Vasile answered it. I did not hear the conversation, but apparently something much more important had come up that made this kidnapping game for five million American dollars seem like peanuts. Whatever it was, it was important for us all to pack everything up, including the Baron, and travel that night from Athens to Palermo by private plane.'

'Who was this phone call from?' questioned Kerenskiy.

'Gheorghe thought it was from Elena Ceauşescu herself.'

General Kerenskiy's response was to roll his eyes and take another gulp of his drink.

Slouched in his seat, Dimitro continued his story. His voice was a little steadier, his sentences now more coherent; perhaps the alcoholic drink was proving a relaxing factor.

'Major Vasile had been in touch with Signor Viliaro, via our embassy in Rome, and he was waiting at Punta Raisi Airport. Major Vasile was very careful not to let the Baron be seen. They took him off the plane on a stretcher, heavily sedated, explaining something about a sick friend. His head was well bandaged, obscuring any features. Two cars were arranged to take everyone directly to the Delmonte villa.

'At the villa, we found the Baron's wife and several servants. Oh yes, and there was a girl called Claudia, who was a close friend of the Baron's daughter, Countess Octavia. Major Vasile demanded from the Baroness the whereabouts of the Countess Octavia, but she claimed complete ignorance of her daughter's whereabouts. This sudden interest in the Countess and subsequent change of plans must have resulted from Elena Ceauşescu's phone call.

'She was a strong woman, the Baroness, and gave little away under pressure from Comrade Vasile. Then, miracle of miracles, the Countess Octavia turns up at the villa, out of the blue. She is much more beautiful than any photograph I have seen of her. Apparently, her mother had been talking to her only a few hours before we arrived – not a few months before, as she had led us to believe. She had been trying to persuade her daughter to return home as she was worried at her husband's recent hasty departure for Athens.

'Later, I caught the girl making a phone call, so we tied her up with the Baroness in the cellar.'

'Did you find out who she tried to contact?' interrupted General Kerenskiy.

'No, but she could not have been on the phone more than a moment.'

Long enough, thought General Kerenskiy, *for someone to learn of her distress.*

Avoiding the General's eyes, Dimitro seemed to sink deeper into his chair, his own eyes focused on an indeterminate point upon the worn carpet at his feet.

General Kerenskiy stood up. 'So, you and your friends had everyone in one place: the Baron, his wife, and their daughter. What was Comrade Vasile's next move? What was part two of Elena Ceaușescu's scheme?'

'I have no idea how much of all this was Elena Ceaușescu's plan and how much Major Vasile added to the original scheme, but I do know...' said Dimitro with a wicked grin spreading across his face, '...his next move.

'Comrade Vasile took the girl Claudia, who I mentioned was one of Countess Octavia's friends, to one of the large bedrooms. There was a scream, but the noise did not last long. She had been wearing a bright green dress, but it was in shreds after Major Vasile had finished with her.'

General Kerenskiy was now almost at a loss for words at the sheer stupidity of Comrade Vasile's behaviour.

'You see,' continued Dimitro, 'he liked this Claudia a lot. You know how possessive he is about new things; he sort of latches onto them. Well, that's what happened with his new acquisition. You see, by this time, Major Vasile was quite crazy about this Claudia. He was really touched by her, quite a soft spot you might say, much more than any of the others I have seen him with.'

'For the love of Lenin, one hell of a time to start a relationship!' said General Kerenskiy.

For the hundredth time he wondered just how incompetent Elena Ceauşescu was to choose this relation of her husband's for such an operation. What was more, this was just the beginning. God only knew where this whole scenario would end.

'Please continue,' murmured General Kerenskiy, knowing there was worse to come in this unfolding drama. He helped himself to another drink – his third that morning. At this rate, the previously full vodka bottle was in serious danger of becoming half empty.

'Major Vasile ordered Gheorghe, Diaconescu, Ion, Nicu, and me to stay at the villa. We were to watch over the two women and the Baron, who was tied up in the stables. The Baroness and her daughter were not aware that we held the Baron as well. Major Vasile, Mario, and the girl Claudia left in one of the cars. They did not say where they were going.

'In their absence, someone arrived at the villa – perhaps the result of the Countess Octavia's phone call.'

Most likely, thought General Kerenskiy.

'Whoever this person was, there was a ferocious struggle that resulted in Gheorghe dying, in the company of a dead kitchen maid, with a knife stuck between his shoulder blades.'

'How did the kitchen maid die?' asked General Kerenskiy.

'Her throat was slit. Though the contents of a hot frying pan could not have done her much good either.'

'Could Gheorghe have killed the girl? Or was this the work of someone else?' enquired General Kerenskiy.

'There was so much blood everywhere, it was near impossible to tell exactly what happened in that kitchen,' said Dimitro, recalling the terrible scene. 'I was with Diaconescu and Ion, walking through the grounds of the villa, when this someone must have entered the house.

'When we returned to the villa, we found Nicu tied up and the two women trying to leave, with a man, in the motorboat. We tried to prevent them leaving by sinking the boat. Unfortunately, the pier blew up, which must have killed one of the women, because I don't think anyone could have survived the huge explosion that followed.'

'This was confirmed by the *L'Ora* newspaper articles that followed,' said General Kerenskiy. 'What happened to Diaconescu and Ion?'

'We did not know that this stranger was armed with a high-velocity rifle. He hit both Diaconescu and Ion, at very long range, before escaping with the Countess Octavia, aboard the motorboat.

'Then Major Vasile returned, somewhat the worse for alcohol. When he saw what had happened, he went into a terrible rage. He then left in a car for the Baron's yacht, *Roxana*, moored further along the coast, taking with him Mario, the Baron, and Claudia. He told me to contact Elena Ceauşescu directly and explain what had just happened.'

'And she in turn spoke to her husband President Nicolae Ceauşescu, who in turn summoned me,' finished General Kerenskiy, still hardly able to believe what he had just been told.

'So, what was Major Vasile's plan then?' enquired General Kerenskiy, now almost afraid of what he might hear next.

'To sail the *Roxana* to Sardinia, with the Baron Delmonte very much alive and visible, in order to attract his daughter Octavia to join him. Then Major Vasile would have her, which is what I think the original plan was, as conceived by Elena Ceauşescu.'

'What a mess,' commented General Kerenskiy. He walked over to pick up the phone. Whilst waiting to be put through to an outside line, he poured some more Russian vodka into his empty glass, and this time he did not bother to soften its fierce impact with tonic water.

The object of General Kerenskiy's phone call was to arrange a meeting with the Cosa Nostra. He knew that sooner or later they would become extensively involved with these recent events. In fact the Cosa Nostra probably would already be well aware of this unfolding drama.

After finishing his drink, he told Dimitro to remain in the hotel room until he contacted him. Dimitro was only too glad to have someone else assume responsibility for what looked like an increasingly dangerous future.

* * * * *

From the bridge of the luxurious motor cruiser, *Riflettere Delce Amore*, recently anchored off Cagliari harbour, the sound of an approaching helicopter could be heard. The noise was faint, barely audible above the moaning wind. Slowly at first, then more persistently, its navigation lights could be seen winking relentlessly in the darkness towards the moving platform, now floodlit for landing.

With great difficulty, the helicopter landed on the rolling helipad, mounted astern. A single passenger disembarked from the machine before it launched ghost-like back into the night. He wore a long raincoat with its collar turned up against the increasing wind and driving rain.

A second figure emerged from a doorway to greet the ship's new arrival with a handshake. Then both figures promptly disappeared to shelter within the cruiser's ample interior.

Count Roberto Fambino gave up his soaked raincoat, thankful to be out of the elements, and the officer who greeted him directed him to a large stateroom. In the mirror of the well-equipped and luxurious stateroom, he ran a comb through his thick black hair. Then, with his pencil-thin moustache set at just the right angle and the black bow tie rearranged to achieve a balanced knot, he dismissed the officer and made his way to the cruiser's main stateroom.

Upon entering the stateroom, Count Fambino hesitated to become more accustomed to the bright lighting and to gain his bearings. His hesitation was also designed to give more impact to his already late arrival.

There was a sudden drop in the level of conversation as heads turned to see who had just arrived. The Count made his way through the crowded room, nodding and smiling as he went, as he recognised most of the assembled guests aboard his uncle's yacht that evening as being friends and acquaintances.

Don Giovanni, supreme head of the Sicilian Cosa Nostra, warmly embraced his nephew with all the enthusiasm that is common to a closely knit Sicilian family.

Roberto asked his uncle if everything was in order and going as planned. Don Giovanni replied that there were some problems, not directly connected with the current operation, but distractions that would be taken care of in due course.

The operation referred to by Don Giovanni had been long in the planning stage, and was now on the point of being implemented, with the financial gain potentially very lucrative for all those who participated.

Don Giovanni motioned with his right hand and the drone of conversation quickly died to silence. The assembled men were uniformly dressed in dark suits, except for Don Giovanni who wore a white jacket. Every head turned upon strained necks for an advantageous view, and the audience assumed an atmosphere of expectation.

'Good evening, gentlemen. Our meeting here this evening on the *Riflettere Delce Amore* will in time be regarded as historic. Firstly, not everyone has met before. Let me introduce you…' Don Giovanni paused for a moment, clearly enjoying the audience's total attention.

'Señor Max Santiago, who has concluded with our people here in Sicily a far-reaching agreement on laundering money derived from sales of heroin in

North America. As you know, we control the raw morphine, which is imported from the Bekaa Valley then shipped to Sicily, where it is processed in labs to a finished product. From Sicily, the heroin is transported by container ship to the United States via our usual links in New York and other cities on the East Coast, including Miami.

'That is the easy part. The huge profits, as you all appreciate, have been more difficult to dispose of. Increasing co-operation, spearheaded by Interpol, the Italian DCSA, and the American DEA, along with the other European agencies, has been making life increasingly difficult. So, laundering of money will now be primarily centred in Panama. Once again, my sincere appreciation and thanks to Señor Max Santiago.

'On my left is Señor Sancho Largo of the Medellin Cartel.' A short, overweight man bowed to the assembled guests. His thick moustache, overall dark complexion, and pockmarked face conveyed not a flicker of emotion.

'Their reputation, I am sure, speaks for itself,' continued Don Giovanni. 'The Medellin Cartel controls most of the North American cocaine distribution and ninety per cent of the politicians in Bogota. Little occurs in Colombia without Señor Largo being informed.

'Over the last two years, the North American market has become flooded with cocaine. A kilo of cocaine, which sold for $42,000 four years ago, now sells for $12,000 in New York. So, a deal has been worked out between Señor Largo and our friend here, Signor Vincenzo Lenzane.

'Signor Lenzane is from Naples and is head of the Camorra family, which controls the distribution of cocaine in Europe. Our Columbian friends will export their excess cocaine to Europe by utilising our own well-established networks, for 50 per cent of the profits. A deal, I think you will all agree, that is to everyone's benefit.'

Don Giovanni's gaze across the sea of faces left no room for doubt.

Outside, the officer of the watch observed the flashing lights of another helicopter through the driving rain. Warning of its approach had come several minutes earlier via the green fluorescent radar screen.

The same officer who had greeted Count Roberto Fambino welcomed the single, well-built passenger, who detached himself hesitantly from the helicopter door. This new arrival was also extended the same courtesy of a stateroom to freshen up in, before being escorted to the private day cabin of Don Giovanni. Here, General Kerenskiy waited for his host to appear. He was more than a little curious as to how Don Giovanni would react to the news he carried.

As Don Giovanni's brief but historic speech came to an end, the welcome release of champagne corks was quickly followed by a return to excited conversation. Everyone seemed to be in high spirits.

Ten minutes later the four men, now assembled in Don Giovanni's day cabin, were far from being in a mood to celebrate. They included General Kerenskiy, both members of the Fambino family, and a certain Signor Gianni Martelli. This last man was a short, but powerfully built Italian, with black, greased-back hair, and cold insensitive eyes.

A few moments before Don Giovanni had appeared happiness itself to all those gathered aboard his yacht. However, these same people would hardly have recognised the same man now standing behind a large Louis XV desk in his day cabin.

Don Giovanni's tall frame leant partway across the polished wood, partially supported upon his arms. His dark, tanned complexion contrasted with thick, snow-white hair that extended down his cheeks to form a well trimmed goatee. The bird-of-prey-like black eyes stared unblinking at General Kerenskiy standing opposite.

Next to General Kerenskiy stood Signor Gianni Martelli, and off to the other side sat the Count, smoking a cigarette. He had comfortably sunk into the ample dimensions of a well-padded armchair.

Count Roberto Fambino, through the haze of blue smoke, saw various phantoms come and go, ambiguous and vague, seemingly beyond his control or focus. Then an impression slowly became an image that gradually assumed a recognisable shape and form. He saw first one, then two horses, being ridden at terrific speed below the ramparts of Castle Zehra.

At first, he could not distinguish the identity of the figures, except to say that both were riders of some experience. Then, with a shock, the Count recognised Octavia's long, dark hair, streaming out behind her. The other rider was a man whose face remained frustratingly out of focus and his identity just out of reach. The Count wondered who he was and what their destination could be, as the horses were being driven to their limit.

The Count wanted to possess Octavia. It was impossible for a man, having once seen those mysterious dark eyes and witnessed the sheer femininity of her movements, not to become haunted by their memory. Count Roberto Fambino was no exception, and even his cold and cruel heart had begun to melt. For periods he had found his mind half-delirious under the spell of her eyes. He also recognised that, in addition to Octavia's physical beauty, within this woman there resided a unique set of high principles and a philosophy of life that he could never share or fully understand.

The meaning of the image of Octavia upon the galloping horse suddenly became very clear. The Count knew deep down that he could never really posses Octavia, which only added to his frustration and rising anger.

As quickly as the images came, they disappeared through the blue smoke, leaving the Count unsettled and wondering if they had occurred at all.

General Kerenskiy turned his head from Signor Martelli to Count Roberto Fambino, and then back to Don Giovanni's still leaning frame. General Kerenskiy's ice-cold, blue-grey eyes were steady; they contained resolution. The next few minutes would at the very least decide his career, and more than likely how far into the future he would live.

Apart from the political consequences of this looming international crisis, which would break if this whole bewildering collection of events blew up in the way he increasingly anticipated, for the disintegration would be such that Northern Siberia could suddenly become rather attractive.

General Kerenskiy knew he was risking a lot from this meeting with Don Giovanni, but he thought he might be able to turn this predictably difficult meeting to his advantage.

Those present might already hold him partially responsible for Major Vasile's unwelcome rampage through what was regarded as their exclusive sphere of influence. The sheer audacity of meddling in Mafia territory, at the very heart of local operations, would have attracted quite a lot of attention from the 'Ndrangheta of Calabria.

This was confirmed by the presence of Signor Martelli, who had recently arrived from Taranto in Calabria, after receiving news of the Baron's disappearance and the ensuing mess at the Delmonte villa. Close communication had taken place between the 'Ndrangheta and the Cosa Nostra in coordinating a common approach to the recent and perplexing chain of events.

'Gentlemen...' General Kerenskiy paused to make quite sure he had their attention. 'There has been an unfortunate incident involving a Romanian citizen who I am sure is not a stranger to any of you, at least to those of you who read newspapers.'

It was obvious that everyone knew of Nicolae Ceauşescu's notorious nephew, Major Vasile. His flamboyant lifestyle was well publicised by an ever scandal-hungry Western press. His playboy reputation and drug-taking were followed in glaring detail as an almost continuous saga.

'For some reason best known to himself, Major Vasile set out and subsequently succeeded in kidnapping the Baron Delmonte. From this, several unfortunate consequences have developed, including the probable death of his wife. I say probable because only a few articles of her clothing were found after a large explosion blew up the pier at the Delmonte villa in northern Sicily. Apparently, to date, no body has been found.

'This despicable action, I will categorically state, did not have the backing of the Romanian government. In fact, President Nicolae Ceauşescu has sent me personally to see what I can do in bringing about a conclusion to these unhappy events as quickly as possible.'

General Kerenskiy wanted to distance himself further from the Romanians, so he thought it might work in his favour to mention his own background, though he suspected they already knew of it. Don Giovanni had a reputation for meticulous attention to detail when it came to finding out information about those he did business with, or those unlucky enough to cross his path.

'I have worked for the Romanian government in various different capacities, sometimes as an advisor, sometimes controlling specific clandestine and delicate operations when called upon to do so. As my name suggests, I am not Romanian but Russian. I previously worked for the Russian Intelligence Service. The Romanians wanted to learn some of our methods, but as you can see, they have some way to go before reaching any degree of proficiency.'

At this point, General Kerenskiy did not think it worth going into how Elena Ceaușescu controlled the strings that governed her husband's actions, and that the orders had come from her for this particular mad scheme.

'Major Vasile was acting totally independently of anyone in the Romanian Government,' he added. 'He did not have clearance for an operation on foreign soil.'

General Kerenskiy was pleased that he had everyone's undivided attention. Now perhaps he could convince their sceptical minds with his argument before he finished.

'I flew direct from Bucharest to Palermo this morning when I first heard the awful news. I obtained an up-to-date account of events from one of Major Vasile's men, who escaped the Delmonte villa before the Palermo *Carabinieri* arrived. I learnt that Major Vasile had taken the Baron Delmonte from Athens to Palermo and then on to the family villa. There, he found the Baroness, and later Countess Octavia. Both women were held, then someone arrived who tried to rescue the two women. However, only the Countess Octavia made a successful escape by motorboat. During the resulting struggle, three of Major Vasile's men were killed, and as already mentioned the Baroness probably died in the pier explosion.

'Apparently, for reasons best known to himself, Major Vasile, who had temporarily left the Delmonte villa, decided to leave Sicily for Sardinia with the Baron. He must have had quite a surprise to find so many bodies, together with the escape of the Countess Octavia.'

General Kerenskiy was making little effort to cover up Major Vasile's actions, as he saw the Mafia as a means of helping him locate the man.

'This Romanian has also taken with him a young girl by the name of Claudia. I believe she is a close friend of Countess Octavia.'

The three men continued to listen in silence to the Russian's narration, hardly daring to believe the unfolding story or guess its eventual conclusion. Reading their thoughts, General Kerenskiy finished his account.

'I agree, this young relation of Nicolae Ceauşescu is the *enfant terrible*. He must be found and stopped by whatever means available. And I would, of course, appreciate your help, gentlemen, in bringing this whole unhappy affair to an end.'

For Don Giovanni and the Count, the problem was not only that this Romanian had kidnapped the Baron and caused so much chaos already, but also that he had taken a Sicilian girl against her will for his own pleasure. This was an even more heinous crime, because this outsider had dared to break what all Sicilian men regard as an unwritten law – that only Sicilian men have a right to Sicilian women. Foreigners are never welcome, especially those who have designs upon local women.

'We will assist in finding this Romanian,' said Don Giovanni, in reply to General Kerenskiy's request for help. 'No-one can hide for long when we search for someone such as this Major Vasile.'

'Alive or dead,' interrupted Count Roberto Fambino, through a haze of cigarette smoke, 'he won't last long. I have had my people searching for him since the moment I heard of the mess at the Delmonte villa,' he continued. 'I believe he may be aboard the *Roxana*, with the Baron Delmonte, anchored less than two hundred yards from where we are now. I also have my people searching the immediate coastline and the streets of Cagliari for anything suspicious.'

He paused, obviously pleased at his own efficiency, knowing how impressed his uncle Don Giovanni would be with his prompt action.

Then General Kerenskiy realised why Signor Martelli was present, and remembered the man's face. He was head of the 'Ndrangheta, the Calabria-based crime family which was widely reputed to be the group responsible for several famous kidnappings.

These included the 1973 kidnapping of John Paul Getty III, a sixteen-year-old boy. To increase pressure on his famous grandfather, founder of Getty Oil, they cut off part of the boy's right ear. A ransom of more than one million dollars was reputed to have been paid, but no-one knows exactly how much money changed hands.

The nature of the game is that as soon as one prisoner has been released, another is taken. Sometimes they are passed onto other gangs specialising in kidnapping. They in turn make additional demands, thus increasing the ransom as more people become involved.

General Kerenskiy could not help smiling to himself at the shock the 'Ndrangheta must have had with Major Vasile's successful kidnapping of the Baron Delmonte. No doubt Signor Martelli had little experience of responding to foreign competition in his almost complete monopoly of kidnapping wealthy individuals.

'There is another question that puzzles me,' said Count Roberto, as he stubbed out his cigarette. 'Who was it that helped Countess Octavia to escape from the Delmonte villa, and who also appears responsible for the deaths of at least three of Major Vasile's men, General Kerenskiy?'

The General thought before replying, because he did not know the answer to the question.

'Apparently, there have been two previous attempts to kidnap the Countess Octavia. One of these took place near Monte Carlo within the last week, but both attempts failed. The first, because Major Vasile's men broke into the wrong hotel room and took someone else. Very stupid, I know.

'The second attempt failed because someone shot one of the kidnappers and seriously wounded another on the beach, before helping Countess Octavia escape by car.'

'Whoever this someone is,' said Count Roberto Fambino, 'he appears to be rather efficient at disrupting Major Vasile's operations.'

'I am sure whoever this person is,' commented General Kerenskiy, 'he will prove little match for the Cosa Nostra. With your help in this matter, Count Roberto Fambino, I am sure we can bring this whole affair to a satisfactory conclusion, with the neutralisation of not only Major Vasile, but also this mysterious stranger, whoever he is.'

'Let's hope your predictions prove correct, General Kerenskiy,' said Don Giovanni. He fixed the Russian with an unblinking stare that strongly suggested any failure would not be tolerated.

The meeting in Don Giovanni's day cabin quickly came to an end, and Count Roberto Fambino left for Castle Zehra in northern Sardinia, where urgent business awaited. He would be kept informed of future developments there.

As soon as the weather improved enough to make a safe passage possible, Don Giovanni and General Kerenskiy would take a launch to the *Roxana* anchored two hundred yards away. There they hoped to find Major Vasile and the Baron, and possibly gain new information that might lead to Countess Octavia's present whereabouts.

Once alone in his cabin, General Kerenskiy heard a knock at the door. After opening it, he welcomed Señor Max Santiago into the room and for fifteen minutes listened with undivided attention to what the Panamanian had to say.

Apparently, the freighter known as the *Belle of the Wind*, with its precious cargo, was still aground. Tugs had been sent from Cagliari, but would take time due to deteriorating weather conditions. There was a real chance she might soon break up on a sand bar in heavy seas.

'Has anyone shown any unusual interest in her cargo?' asked General Kerenskiy.

'No, not yet. Her details record a cargo of "heavy industrial machinery" making up the bulk of her cargo. So far, media interest has been focused on the plight of the crew still aboard, and her chances of being refloated before she breaks up.

'The freighter's insurers, Lloyds of London, have been in contact with manufacturers Salamaca Trust, the ship's owners. They are understandably worried, as you can imagine, as when working out this, ah, little enterprise...' Señor Max Santiago's eyes twinkled mischievously at this point, '...at your suggestion we insured the cargo for $25,000,000 – just in case we had problems with the cargo reaching its destination.'

'Yes,' said General Kerenskiy, smiling for the first time since leaving Bucharest.

'Lloyds took a lot of persuading but relented in the end, with an appropriately high premium. Your cut, General Kerenskiy, of the total insurance value is over one-twelfth – a reasonable sum in the West, and a fortune behind the Iron Curtain.

'Either way, we will become wealthy. If the *Belle of the Wind* lifts off, your friends will receive a most valuable cargo, and what is more your future is secured for life. If the freighter can't be refloated, we will destroy its hull with explosives, to avoid its cargo from falling into the wrong hands. However, I think in this weather, the *Belle of the Wind* can't last many more hours of those waves that are continuously pounding her exposed hull.'

Again, the mischievous twinkle in Señor Santiago's eye was much in evidence. His overweight face creased into numerous lines that revealed a truly malicious smile. General Kerenskiy responded with a smile of his own in response to the Panamanian's obvious enjoyment. However, his mind was rather more thoughtful than his face suggested.

The outcome for the stranded freighter's cargo was far from certain. Also, Lloyds had an excellent track record of discovering fraud against them. He recalled, two to three years previously, when an oil tanker sank off the South African coast but Lloyds refused to pay up because her tanks had been drained before her last sailing. She was empty when she went down, as the oil slick on the water did not match 200,000 tonnes of crude.

At last, Señor Max Santiago left General Kerenskiy alone in his cabin to ponder their brief conversation without interruption. However, at 5am the silence was broken by the persistent buzz of a modern phone.

General Kerenskiy leapt out of the armchair he had been slumped in, wondering what additional bad news awaited him at the other end of the line. He was still dressed in his suit, which was now crumpled, his tie loose at the neck. The ashtray beside him overflowed with the remains of numerous American cigarettes. On the same table, a three-quarters empty bottle of Russian vodka testified to his state of mind.

General Kerenskiy had been trying to produce some sort of order and possible solution to recent events, but success had been somewhat elusive. Too many questions remained unanswered, their explanation ambiguous and out of reach. Most of all, General Kerenskiy wondered as to the identity of the man who had so successfully helped the Countess Octavia Delmonte escape. An unease crept through the General's veins, because he knew from the dead men left behind that out there, somewhere, was a man with notable qualities.

After his meeting with Señor Max Santiago, it had been General Kerenskiy's intention to accompany Don Giovanni to the *Roxana* and release the Baron Delmonte if he was indeed aboard.

In the end, their departure for the *Roxana* was delayed until dawn, when the latest forecast predicted less of a swell and a reduction in wind speed. It was too dangerous in those seas to attempt a crossing in a small boat.

General Kerenskiy picked up the receiver.

'Yes, General Kerenskiy speaking.'

'This is the communications officer. Urgent radio-telephone call from the *Roxana*. I am putting you through now.' The communications officer within the ship's radio room pressed the appropriate buttons to divert the incoming phone call to General Kerenskiy's cabin.

'Is that you, General Kerenskiy?' The voice sounded agitated. "This is Stefan. I am with Major Vasile. I have just discovered that the Baron Delmonte has disappeared, and what is more someone has killed Mario with a spear gun. He is, as I speak, attached to the wall – a most terrible death. You must come at once, General Kerenskiy.'

Kerenskiy could hardly believe what he had just heard. How was this latest twist to Major Vasile's exploits possible?

'Where is Major Vasile now?' snapped General Kerenskiy.

'I don't know. He left in an outboard with a woman. His orders were for the rest of us to hold the Baron Delmonte until his return.'

General Kerenskiy felt his pulse quicken with rage at these amateur fools. When all this reached the international press, Romania's carefully cultivated standing with the West, even if it was built upon deceit, was about to be ruined by a few hours of unspeakable negligence and stupidity.

'I will be over immediately, regardless of the weather conditions,' replied General Kerenskiy.

When Don Giovanni and the Count heard about the Baron's disappearance, and Major Vasile's further carry-on with this Sicilian girl, Claudia, the consequences when he was eventually caught did not bear thinking about. Especially given the Cosa Nostra's track record for vengeance.

Chapter Eight

The ring of steel upon steel echoed from the walls of Castle Zehra to the valley below, a sound unheard in those parts for many centuries.

To the east, dawn was still very young, so that the long shadows of the two men moving across the smooth sandstone appeared locked in some sort of insane dance.

Upon closer inspection, it became obvious that the movements of this dance were greatly unbalanced. Each man held a weapon in the form of a sword. The shorter of the two, wearing a red shirt, was wild in his lunges, un-coordinated in his parrying, and his ripostes were much too slow to achieve successful hits.

On the other hand, his opponent, wearing a loose black shirt open from the neck to near his navel, was a master of considerable experience and dexterity in the fine art of swordsmanship. Count Roberto Fambino had learnt his skill at the traditional Italian fencing schools based in Milan, who traced their origins back to the 14th century.

The invention of gunpowder by the Chinese changed the need for body armour and heavy weapons, such as the two-handed crusader sword. The heaviest fencing weapon in use today is the duelling sabre, related to the curved Hungarian Cavalry sabre. Hits are scored with a cutting edge rather than a point.

In previous centuries, the Italians quickly established themselves as the undisputed masters of skilful fencing, using the point contact of foil and *épée*. Other European countries developed their own swordsmanship, such as the rapier fencing that became popular with the nobility of Spain. This particular form of combat comprised of a long rapier held in the right hand, and a short dagger held in the left, for effective parrying.

On this particular morning, the two men were using the modern *épée* – heavier than the foil but lighter than the sabre. The *épée* has developed into the most popular duelling sword of the 20th century.

Elements of the Cosa Nostra had finally caught Major Vasile in a state of *flagrante delicto* with Countess Octavia's friend Claudia.

When they were discovered naked in some rundown hotel on the outskirts of Cagliari by Count Roberto Fambino's men, the girl was by this time an emotional wreck. She would probably need years of psychiatric treatment to overcome her ordeal at the hands of this Romanian maniac.

Major Vasile, under the influence of alcohol, had put up some resistance but proved no match for those who found him. The girl's parents, on holiday in Vienna at the time, were quickly contacted by the Count. They were devastated at the ordeal that their only daughter had been through.

The Count persuaded them that vengeance would be swift, and without interference from the police. Claudia's parents agreed, knowing something of the Count's reputation for dealing with those who crossed his path. The dark side of Count Roberto Fambino's nature was like an overflowing caldron of consuming fire, continuously bubbling and burning, but never full. To the Fambino crime family, vengeance through violence was a way of life.

Major Vasile's fate had been sealed the moment he touched Claudia, Countess Octavia's lifelong friend.

A fencer will try to evaluate his opponent's weaknesses and strengths through his judgement of distance, sensitivity of timing, accuracy of movement, courage of execution, and above all, strategy to win. This constant evaluation of his opponent is known as *sentiment due fer,* or contact of the blade.

The Romanian playboy, who it could be judged had so far squandered his life, knew with certainty that his inevitable death would now come sooner rather than later.

The insane contest was staged solely for the Count to demonstrate his fencing ability and skill before invited friends and guests. He was pleasantly surprised when the Romanian had shown some unexpected flair with his sword., but the outcome of this unbalanced contest was never in doubt.

Major Vasile quickly became bathed in glistening sweat, and his breathing soon resembled that of a spent runner who instinctively knows deep down that the race was never going to be his to win.

The Romanian tried his best with a series of compound attacks comprising of several feints, but the Sicilian always saw through these with successful parrying. Soon a patch of dark blood appeared through Major Vasile's red shirt. He could feel its warm trickle run briefly before the thin cotton soaked up the crimson liquid.

Finally, a well-executed series of feints by the Count, followed by a brilliantly timed point attack to Major

Vasile's head, reduced the space previously occupied by his right eye to a red gelatinous mass. It was, of course, afterwards quite useless as an instrument of sight.

The impact was an explosion of blinding light in a kaleidoscope of indescribable pain. With a sweep of his left hand across his face, Major Vasile found new blood gushing from his right eye socket. Through his remaining good eye, the Romanian saw the satisfied smile of the Count, clearly enjoying the results of his swordplay.

A man fighting for his life will become irrational in his desperation to avoid death. Actions become excited and impulsive, reflexes no longer automatic, but wild and senseless.

Major Vasile knew his life was finally running out. The hourglass of time was releasing the last grains of a wasted life. His days of rich extravagance and bloated self-indulgence were fast drawing to a close. His brutality towards Countess Octavia's friend Claudia had been just the latest violence against a long line of women, who would remain emotionally scarred for many years as a result of his cruel and barbaric behaviour. Rehabilitation for such ill-treatment is commonly measured by degrees of insanity.

The Romanian made a last desperate attempt to gain the initiative with a lunge for the Count's throat, but his attack proved too slow and poorly executed to gain any meaningful chance of success. The Count effortlessly neutralised the Romanian's attack with a semi-circular parry from the high to the low plane, thus deflecting his opponent's sword to leave the Romanian once again dangerously exposed.

With his face twisted into a triumphant smile, the Count launched his counterattack. His right arm straightened, sending the steel point of his sword into Major Vasile's remaining good eye. The Romanian's left eye now suffered a similar fate to that of his right.

The *épée*'s lethal point entered Major Vasile's left eye socket slightly off centre, so that as the steel point travelled forward, it half-turned the eyeball, leaving its lens and pupil fixed facing the unfocused outline of his nose. Once again, the impact resulted in an explosion of blinding light and indescribable pain.

Major Vasile lowered his head like a bull before the charge after the powerful neck muscles have been severed by the picadors before the matador delivers his *coup de grâce*. Only, Major Vasile's reasons were somewhat different. His neck muscles, though a little tense, were working perfectly well. His strange half turned gait was adopted in an attempt to bring his opponent into view through his near-sightless left eye.

To the Romanian, the Count was a constant vanishing apparition, proving time and again to be just out of range for his sword to successfully target. His attacks would frustratingly only connect with elusive phantoms of his smiling opponent.

Then Major Vasile stumbled, not surprisingly, considering he now saw with less than ten per cent of normal vision. He fell, arms outstretched, trying to break his fall, and dropped his sword in the process. His head hit the sandstone with an impact that split open his forehead, so that additional blood now ran with that already trickling from each eye socket.

With his boot, the Count turned the moaning figure over onto his back. Then, with the point of his sword just under Major Vasile's chin, he announced that he had 'something rather special' for him.

The Count motioned with his left hand. Two men detached themselves from the group who had been watching the duel with amusement. Upon reaching Major Vasile's body, they dropped to their knees so that each held a leg, rendering resistance from the Romanian practically impossible.

Then one of the two dark, swarthy men produced a twelve-inch scimitar, its curved blade gleaming wickedly in the early morning sun. He quickly and efficiently cut away the Romanian's trousers and white underwear to expose his genitals. At this point, it must have dawned on Major Vasile what was about to happen. He started struggling in a vain attempt to throw off the two men who so effectively pinned him to the smooth sandstone.

A desperate cry of help came from the doomed man's mouth, but there was no-one to listen, only a faint echo returned upon the northwest wind from the valley below.

'Justice will soon be achieved. Your death will, of course, be much too quick. However, Major Vasile, the punishment will, I think, be in keeping with your crime of interfering with a Sicilian girl. You see, Sicilian women can only be touched by Sicilian men. Foreigners with dishonourable intentions have never been welcome here.'

Then Major Vasile gave the one piece of information that could save his life. He proceeded, in considerable pain and with frequent pauses, to tell an amazing story. The Count leant closer, so as not to miss any detail from this now helpless near blind man.

'I was sent by Elena Ceaușescu to kidnap the Countess Octavia Delmonte for the purpose of finding her ring, the one that contained the ruby. This, the

President's wife said, had an inscription that would lead, once translated, to the famous *Darya-i-Nur* diamond, and the remains of the Sultan's treasure.'

'So Elena Ceauşescu wanted you to find this ring, decipher the inscription, then locate the *Darya-i-Nur* and the rest of the Sultan's treasure, if it was still around, and then transport it all back to Romania. Only you were greedy, and so became fatally side-tracked with Countess Octavia's friend Claudia.'

The Count thought for a moment. *Was Major Vasile really telling the truth or simply buying time with a story of fiction?* He thought it unlikely, considering his present circumstances, that Major Vasile would hold anything back now, with the scimitar's blade poised in such a delicate position. Incredible as the story sounded, it was probably true.

From his extremely uncomfortable position lying on his back, racked with pain, Major Vasile continued his remarkable account.

'It was Elena Ceauşescu who ordered us to kidnap the Baron, because we lost sight of the Countess Octavia in the South of France. By holding the Baron Delmonte, we hoped to learn the whereabouts of his daughter. However, he could not provide us with any useful information as to her recent movements.

'You see, Elena Ceauşescu had learnt of the legend attached to the Countess's ring. You must have heard the history of why King Richard I of England built Castle Zehra?'

'Yes, of course I have, who hasn't?' said the Count, trying to piece the details together. 'So, Countess Octavia's ring, according to Elena Ceauşescu, holds the key to discovering the remains of this treasure?

'You don't, I suppose,' added the Count, leaning even closer to the mutilated face of Major Vasile, 'know of this treasure's location?'

'No, I swear I don't,' gasped the doomed man.

'Such a pity, Major Vasile,' replied the Count smoothly. 'In any case, providing the information would not have changed your fate to any meaningful extent.'

What Major Vasile did not know was that the Count was fully aware of the legend attached to the ring and was already taking steps to retrieve the ring himself.

The Count gave a light nod to the man with the scimitar. In one clean sweep of the razor-sharp blade, Major Vasile's genitals were severed from his body.

The screaming started immediately, and the terrible sound could be heard throughout the castle and a long way down the valley below. A man screaming in pain for his life is a frightening sound few have heard, but once experienced, it is never forgotten.

The Count backed away first, and managed to avoid the fountain of blood that spurted up from Major Vasile's groin. The man who held the scimitar was not so lucky; before he could move, a curtain of blood arched up, catching him full in the face. His companion was luckier; by leaping back, he managed to avoid a similar experience.

Major Vasile was left to die an unpleasant death, writhing in agony upon the blood-soaked sandstone.

Deep within Castle Zehra, Octavia heard the appalling sound that must surely darken the most resolute heart, and send it leaping aghast against the faith of its very foundations. Her heart pounded, not sure what meaning to attach to this chilling intrusion upon her breakfast.

Eight hundred yards away, the entire scene had been witnessed by North, through powerful binoculars. Every detail of the duel had been followed, from the Count's faultless footwork to his consistent parrying and accuracy in riposte.

To North, the identity of the loser of this unbalanced and bloody contest remained a complete mystery. The undisputed winner, he guessed, must be none other than Count Roberto Fambino, Octavia's former fiancé.

With increasing unease, North continued to watch the wounded and helpless man clutch his injured groin in a futile attempt to ease his terrible pain. He wondered what events had led to this bizarre contest below the walls of Castle Zehra.

North could not influence the outcome, even if he had wanted to, as his rifle was in the car, parked a quarter of a mile further down the valley. The Beretta in his pocket was useless at this range. In any case, there were too many of them: at least eight, excluding the Count; and four of the men were armed with machine guns.

North's unease turned to horror as someone poured liquid over the still writhing and screaming man. The red plastic can moved in a wide arc, soaking the prostrate man from head to foot.

A cigarette was then dropped, and a sheet of yellow flame shot up into the air as the man's clothing burnt with a ferocious intensity. The doomed man threw his legs and arms about as he struggled in vain for his life. Eventually, the human torch stopped moving, but the flames continued to shoot skywards, fed by the consuming fires from the red-hot centre of human tissue.

A light wind from the west blew the black smoke, before it finally dissipated into the clear morning air above. The screaming, carried by the same wind, continued briefly before it too was lost to the silence of the Sardinian dawn.

The body of Major Vasile lay motionless, the human remains smouldering, the previous fire now containing little enthusiasm to continue. Now and again, on the wind North caught the unmistakable smell of burnt flesh, and even at eight hundred yards he found it unpleasant and nauseating.

The spectators disappeared, some riding magnificent Arabian horses, others walking, all heading towards the entrance gates of Castle Zehra.

North lowered his binoculars before turning around and sitting up. He had been watching events from a concealed position, hidden from the castle by the crest of a small hill. However, he was exposed from the air, and twice – upon hearing the sound of approaching aircraft, including a helicopter –he'd had to scramble for cover under some nearby boulders.

North reflected upon recent events that had brought him to his present position, within sight of Castle Zehra. The Baron had only partially recovered from his illness. 'Too much stress, together with a weak heart, has proved an unstable combination,' commented Dr. Lacombe. On the doctor's orders, he remained sedated and confined to his bed.

Around the Baron's bed a conference had taken place with Dr. Lacombe, Count Santorini, and North. After much discussion, it had generally been decided to 'go public'. The authorities, as everyone knew, were little guarantee of help in trying to find Octavia and discovering information about those responsible for the death of the Baron's wife, but recent events were fast spiralling out of control, and keeping the lid on future media attention seemed almost impossible.

The Italian media, hungry and impetuous as ever, already sensed a story of sensational proportions that threatened to dominate headlines and push all other news items to mere footnotes of insignificance. Rome's *La Repubblica* had captured the mood with the headline 'Heiress to Delmonte Fortune Disappears in Mysterious Circumstances'. The article continued with detailed descriptions of the worldwide Delmonte empire and two photographs. One was of the imposing Delmonte villa on the Sicilian north coast; the other a glamorous picture of Octavia in a low-cut dress at a party three months previously.

Further discussion was devoted to Octavia's illustrious ancestors on both sides of her family, with particular emphasis on the wealthy Baron Delmonte – the latest in a long line of Sicily's few remaining aristocratic families. The article continued with speculation on the Countess's family paying the ransom in time; in recent years local kidnappers had set very short deadlines for the payment of a ransom. The author gave the Countess's chances of living at one in three, based upon the high mortality rate of recent kidnapping victims in Calabria during the last five years.

A few lines mentioned one or two peculiar and mysterious aspects of this latest case, such as reports from the Palermo Carabinieri that the three bodies found at the Delmonte villa were those of Romanian nationals. This suggested some sort of foreign involvement; certainly a new twist to the usual straightforward Calabrian kidnapping and ransom routine.

The Romanian Embassy had so far not responded to media enquiries of possible Romanian involvement in international kidnapping, or of interfering in the domestic affairs of a foreign country.

The second part of *La Repubblica's* article centred on the previous engagement of Countess Octavia Delmonte to a member of the Fambino family, with glowing descriptions of the very handsome Count Roberto Fambino, reputed to be the most eligible bachelor in Europe.

The Sicilian newspaper, *L'Ora*, devoted much of its front page to the Baron Delmonte's wife, Baroness Sayonnara – a Greek beauty in her time, from Athens. Apparently, along with the three Romanians, she was rumoured to have lost her life in a mysterious explosion that had demolished the wooden pier below the Delmonte villa. However, no body had been found.

The Mayor of Palermo had promised to do all within his power to bring to justice those responsible for this outrageous crime.

An emergency meeting, scheduled in Rome for the following day, was rumoured to include the Prime Minister and various intelligence chiefs to discuss this latest outrage of organised crime and its possible international implications. Full assistance and cooperation with the local authorities in Palermo and Cagliari was also pledged.

A police source, who did not want to be named, suggested that recent events indicated a possible link between the Romanians and the Cosa Nostra. If this information contained an element of truth, then times were indeed changing, for the Cosa Nostra were not renowned for cooperating with anyone.

North lifted his head above the lip of the ridge that commanded his previous view. Through his binoculars, he viewed the area previously occupied by the group watching the duel. There was no-one around and the area was quite empty, apart from the charred and smoking remains of the Count's opponent. The smell of burnt flesh continued upon the air.

Then North noticed something very strange: the flag flying from the white pole above the gatehouse now flew at half-mast. It could only have some sort of bizarre connection with the duel he had just witnessed. He did not recognize its design.

A second flag flew from the main tower, twice the size of the first. Just then, a stronger gust of wind caught the material so that its device was, for a moment, clear and exposed. North saw double black eagle heads facing outwards upon a bright yellow background. This imposing ensign looked vaguely familiar, but for the moment he could not remember the circumstances under which he had seen it before.

North spent most of the day circumventing Castle Zehra, so that by the time he had finished, he was thoroughly familiar with its external dimensions and the surrounding landscape. Cover was offered only to the south, by small trees, bushes, and a few large boulders. It was the same side from which he had viewed the recent duel.

North's reconnoitre took several hours, as the radius of his path from Castle Zehra had to be far enough from the walls to minimise any possible chance of detection from the ramparts and windows.

The sun slowly sank towards the west, its passage turning the horizon briefly deep red before it disappeared altogether. Presently the entire sky was full with the brilliance of countless stars, their needle points of light giving a theatrical backdrop to the imposing silhouette of the castle.

Judging by the yellow glow here and there provided by the illumination of electric light through arrow slits and windows, human activity within Castle Zehra was concentrated in the main tower and three of the six smaller, outer turrets. The rest of the castle was in darkness, except for some lanterns on either side of the gate towers, which were built to a design of substantial proportions in order to guard access to the inside of the castle.

To enter the castle, North had to either first enter through the main gate, which was barred by a portcullis, or scale the formidable walls. He had decided earlier in the day that persuading someone on the inside to open the portcullis was the more difficult of the two options; hence his extensive daylight study of the walls.

North had noted that erosion and vandalism had taken their toll over the centuries, resulting in a certain amount of disrepair in places to the outer and inner walls. Recent restoration work had been undertaken at one point on the outer western wall, marked by mounds of rubble here and there. The distance between one of these mounds of discarded bricks and the top of the wall was about twenty feet. It was to this point, under the cover of darkness, that North carefully made his way.

It took him longer than he had anticipated to climb the wall, using the grappling iron brought for the purpose. A fifth throw had eventually achieved enough purchase, with the hooked iron points snagging the battlements.

Upon reaching the top of the wall, North swore this would be the last time he would attempt to climb using a rope. What he would have given for the use of a ladder; his left shoulder and arm burned with shock waves of pain from the muscle strain imposed upon his previously injured joint. After a moment's rest, his left shoulder eased to an ill-defined ache and cold numbness.

Out of breath, North smiled to himself as he remembered his late father's philosophy that a constant and determined approach to physical training will not only gain a level of physical fitness, but is vital in helping to create a confident belief in one's own capabilities.

Right now, thought North, *it is a race to see which would endure the longest: the physical ability of my injured left shoulder to carry on functioning; or my mental capacity to ignore the joint's increasingly persistent pain.*

North watched several helicopters land on flattened ground to the east. They deposited numerous passengers before disappearing off into the night, their navigation lights winking far over the barren landscape.

He observed that Castle Zehra was well patrolled by guards with automatic rifles. Two were posted just beyond the raised portcullis, checking the identity of all those who sought entry. He also observed that the passengers from the last three helicopters, about thirty in total, were all young, elegantly dressed women.

The second outer wall, and even higher inner wall, North scaled in a similar fashion to the first, using the grappling iron. The forty-foot high inner wall took longer to scale, as he found it increasingly difficult to ignore the reawakened burning pain in his left shoulder and arm.

Standing exhausted on the battlements of the fifteen-foot thick inner wall, North had to agree that whoever had designed Castle Zehra had succeeded in designing a structure that positively discouraged the uninvited from gaining an easy entry.

Unobserved, he carefully slid down his rope into the deep shadow of the courtyard, which was partially lit at intervals by lanterns. The unmistakable smell of horses became stronger, indicating that the stables were close by.

North found the stable block against the inside wall. In the dim courtyard light, the top halves of their split doors were open to reveal the dark flanks of Arabian thoroughbreds. Someone clearly had an eye for the very finest equestrian travel.

The sound of laughter and music could be heard from the direction of the main tower and what must be the principal rooms of the castle, including the great hall. Now and again, a girl's mock scream would be followed by more uncontrollable laughter. *If this is the beginning of the evening celebrations,* thought North, *then the tempo will be wild indeed by the small hours of the morning.*

He had no idea where Octavia might be held within the walls of Castle Zehra. He had memorized the plan given to him by a carpenter who had worked on recent restoration work, and it had provided some ideas. Forty bedrooms had been finished. Several of these were larger and much more elegant than others, with the most elaborate situated in the west and southern towers. They all commanded fine, unobstructed views. A suite of rooms in the large south west corner tower seemed a good place to start.

The Count, reasoned North, would try charm before using other, less noble, methods of winning Octavia back, which implied the best accommodation. Castle Zehra was rumoured to still have accessible dungeons, but North decided to try these last.

He walked across the cobblestone courtyard, which must have been recently swept, as sand was piled in little mounds off to one side here and there. He cautiously made out his way from the glow of the numerous lanterns that lit the courtyard walls, all the time keeping to the shadows as closely as his direction made possible. The lanterns gave a fairy-tale appearance to the castle walls.

The door at the base of the southwest tower was new and made of thick wood, with large wrought-iron hinges. North turned the large ring recessed into the wood. And the door yielded to his pressure with ease, the hinges – evidently well-oiled – making no sound.

North entered the blackness beyond, and the door clicked shut behind him. He hesitated a moment, trying to orientate himself to this new environment. He found himself in the middle of a rough-hewn stone passageway that seemed to run the circumference of the tower base. A spiral staircase was located opposite the door he had just used, according to the carpenter's plan. This staircase linked all six floors, including the tower's battlements.

The sixth floor contained one of the most luxurious suites of rooms, rivalled only by the Count's own set of rooms situated in the central tower.

The passageway was harshly lit by single electric light bulbs hanging from the ceiling, spaced at uniform intervals throughout its course. North took a right turn for his intended objective of the staircase.

After covering only twenty yards, he stopped dead in his tracks. All the lights had been extinguished, plunging the passageway into complete darkness.

North thought he then heard the door he had just used close with a click. The noise was so slight that he could well have imagined it. However, he grimly acknowledged the fact that he was still without light and only his hands could now guide future progress towards the staircase.

Without warning, a hand grabbed his neck in a vice-like grip from behind. Upon his back, he felt the touch of a sharp object to the point of pain. Any second it must pierce the skin. Then an artery or vein would spill his lifeblood, and he would lose consciousness. Death would quickly follow.

Whoever was behind him must have seen or heard him earlier, and followed his movements into the tower. This same individual had no doubt cut the electric power supply.

North's only chance of survival was to lull his attacker into a false sense of security. Trying to breathe slowly, North went completely limp, his heart rate the pulse of a world record sprinter waiting for the starter's gun. His adrenal glands secreted powerful hormones, at what could only have been an alarming rate, into his bloodstream.

The pressure from the knife point became less, but North could still feel its threatening presence. He somehow knew that his situation was going to be less than favourable from a survival point of view, unless something positive was done very soon to change his predicament.

The gun in North's right hand would not be easy to use upon the man now pressed right up behind him. He had to try something that would gain him enough space, and a split second, to manoeuvre his position for advantage.

Suddenly North raised his right foot, then brought his heel down hard where he thought his attacker's right foot should be. His heel caught the edge of something hard, which fortunately must have been part of his attacker's foot, another half inch and North would have missed it altogether.

The man cried out in pain, and at the same time loosened his grip on North's neck, but not enough to release the unyielding point of the knife at his back.

North jerked his body forward, turning as he did to the left. Then his attacker lashed out with a leg. His toe caught him just below his left kneecap. North's knee immediately exploded in searing pain, the impact knocking him to the ground.

As North fell, he twisted round drawing his gun, and aimed for where he thought his attacker would be. From the ground, North fired at spaced intervals into the blackness. The first bullet missed as its ricochet whined against the stone walls, the report deafening within the narrow corridor. The second bullet must have found its mark, for he heard the man fall heavily, with the sound of what must have been the knife clattering upon the stonework. North fired a third bullet just for good measure. This one must have also found its target for there was no answering whine of a ricochet.

With light from the dead man's lighter, North took five minutes to drag the body back along the passageway to a side door he had noticed earlier. The door led into some sort of storage room, with various wooden crates stacked up neatly at one end.

By the lighter's harsh flame, North saw that his first bullet had travelled through the dead man's heart. The second had entered low and to the left, no doubt piercing his stomach or related organs.

Before leaving, North paused. The room had a peculiar odour – strong and sweet. He recognised it as the distinctive smell of heroin.

North knew that he did not have long to find Octavia before his recent attacker was reported missing and a search was mounted. Once the body was found with bullet holes, everyone within Castle Zehra would be looking for him, and the Count would double the guard over Octavia to prevent her escape.

The spiral staircase ended its tortuous assent at the top of the southwest tower on the sixth floor. North found himself in a short corridor lit by wrought-iron mounted torches spaced at regular intervals. They were positioned halfway between arrow slits situated in the outside wall in order to maximise their feeble light. Electricity did not apparently reach to the top of this tower.

North saw a source of light from the room at the end of the passageway. The thick, wooden door was open a slight crack, obscuring most of the room's interior. Now and again, the light from within the room would be interrupted, as if someone was pacing to and fro.

The light source must have been an unguarded flame, for its flickering created a narrow strip, through the partially open door, of dancing shadows upon the passageway walls beyond.

As North cautiously made his way towards what appeared to be a surprisingly large room for one situated at the top of a turret, he saw beyond the door that someone dressed in red was indeed pacing the floor.

Upon reaching the end of the passageway, he peered through the crack between partially open door and wooden frame. Whoever was inside the room must have paused in their movements, for now the room's light was uninterrupted in its illuminated reach beyond the door's aperture. There was no sound from within the room. North wondered if someone had heard his footsteps.

With his left hand, he pushed the door wide open, then in one fluid motion stepped forward into the room, closing the door behind him. The gun in his right hand covered the single figure standing in the middle of the room.

Immediately, North recognised Octavia. Only half of her face was visible, illuminated by the steady yellow flame of a candle, while the other half remained in deep shadow.

Octavia gasped, astounded at North's sudden and unexpected entry. Her dark eyes were the same deep wells of mysterious attraction that had been forever imprinted upon North's memory from the moment they had first met.

'Sebastian...' Octavia left her sentence unfinished, her eyes now questioning the gun pointed in her direction.

Realising her apprehension, he lowered his forearm and replaced the gun in an inside pocket.

'Octavia, are you alright? What happened at the hotel?'

Octavia was dressed for the grandest of balls. Her long hair was appealingly piled high on top of her head, which together with large circular gold earrings gave her a statuesque profile. The effect reminded North of how she had looked when he had been recovering in the South of France, only this time the design of the earrings was much more elaborate.

Dividing neck and shoulders was a diamond encrusted necklace that sparkled in spite of the dim light. Each forearm and wrist was endowed with several ebony and gold bangles, some boasting various animal heads.

Octavia's ball gown was cut well off her shoulders, its numerous folds creating shadows that would rise and disappear as she moved. Her generous breasts were barely concealed, so that North found his imagination tormented as to how they would look without the benefit of the gown's partial concealment.

Most of the room was in shadow, with the entire source of light coming from three candles. Two were situated on either side of a mirror upon a dressing table, and the third upon a side table in front of a window overlooking the courtyard. North could make out a large wardrobe against one wall, and a four-poster bed with an extensive canopy of blue material elaborately tied above.

Octavia rushed to North and clasped both her hands very tightly around his neck, her face buried submissively in the left side of his neck. He found Octavia's face pleasantly warm, her perfume intriguing, and her mouth sensuously moist. He suddenly wished he had shaved, but normal routine had somehow paled into insignificance with so much more important things to worry about.

Reluctantly, Octavia relaxed her stranglehold and drew back to lean against North's arms, firmly locked behind her waist. Under his fingers, North felt the smooth satin of the ball gown and the warmth of the girl's restless body beneath.

He looked once more into her bewitchingly beautiful eyes, and where a moment ago he had seen intriguing mystery, he now found within her heart deep torment and something more – an unexplained turmoil. Those dark eyes – half Greek, half Sicilian – that North thought he knew so well from *La Valencia*, now told him all was far from well.

They now spoke a different language, and Octavia's heart beat a strange rhythm whose tune he did not understand. North quickly released his arms from Octavia's waist and they drew apart, as if the air between them had been suddenly poisoned.

'I love only Roberto.'

Octavia's words were barely more than a whisper, but they cut through the silence like a knife. The impact of these four words was severe upon North, cutting deep to his solar plexus, leaving him nauseous and drained of emotion.

What had happened to *La Valencia*? North's mind raced back to the restaurant and then over all that had taken place. The holding hands when exploring Cagliari, the warm and intimate conversation over their meal, and the fiery rhythm of the flamenco. North remembered the dance with perfect clarity: slow to begin with, then faster and faster, the dancer moving in time to the guitar, ultimately reaching a feverish pitch, just before the climax in a sea of exhausted red silk and heaving breasts.

The tranquil sound of running water from the fountain, the smell of eucalyptus in the still evening air, and Octavia's soft body against his own, so yielding and responsive to his lead, her mouth inviting with desire. How could a kiss once mean so much, and yet now masquerade as a deceitful phantom to haunt and distort his memory?

Where was the deception? The kiss itself, or his memory now made false by Octavia's revealed love for Roberto?

How could Octavia betray him so convincingly, and for what gain or purpose? North could not find any logical motive behind her actions, except perhaps some deep vein of treachery that had remained undiscovered until now. It must have lain dormant within her like a tripwire, for someone like him to activate at his peril. His love was founded upon an apparition; hers was a mask of deceit, and had therefore never existed.

North had learnt to hide his true feelings from the time of his youth. A great uncle of his, who had spent most of his life at sea in the service of the Royal Navy, was a poker player of some repute. Whenever he had visited Great Uncle Nigel in Scotland, the evenings had usually ended up with much whisky being consumed over cards until the early hours of the following morning. It was during these times that his great uncle had taught him always, no matter what the value of his cards, to conceal the true worth of his hand from showing on his face.

It was partly from these experiences that North drew on to try to overcome the unbearable situation, but he was not entirely successful. Concealing one's hand at cards was a very different game to that of masking affairs of the heart.

'Does *La Valencia* mean anything to you, Octavia, or was it designed all along as an exercise in emotional deception? For if this was indeed the case, congratulations; you succeeded beyond your wildest dreams! With all this talent, you should be playing "The Sorceress Seduces the Unweary Man" in the next Hollywood production. I can personally guarantee that its spellbinding plot of seductive treachery would be a runaway success!'

Tearing his eyes away from Octavia's still beautiful face, North took three steps over to an elegantly carved side table that contained an assortment of bottles and glasses.

Without looking up, he said, 'I hope you don't mind if I help myself, it's been a long day.' His voice was heavy with sarcasm.

North found a bottle of Glenfiddich whisky and, unscrewing the top, poured a generous portion into a large cut crystal glass. After taking a mouthful, he felt the strong liquid pleasantly burn the back of his throat.

Two high-backed Queen Anne grandfather chairs stood either side of a small table made from dark wood. The table was situated in front of a window that overlooked the courtyard below. The considerable width of the walls could be seen from the 18-inch depth of the inclined windowsill.

North carried the bottle and glass over to the table, setting them both down upon its rough and uneven surface. A single red candle in a simple brass holder gave an eerie flickering light from a slight draught, sending hideous and grotesque shadows across North's features. He thought the dripping red wax of the candle matched the rouge of Octavia's lips and the colour of her dress.

North sat down heavily in one of the chairs, and this immediately brought some relief to his aching muscles. The whisky would soon work upon his mind and dull his thinking. Maybe Octavia's words would then become easier to understand. However, North somehow knew that this would be another illusion.

Octavia walked over to the table, the extensive folds of red satin making a swishing sound as she moved. She now stood very close to his chair. North was hunched over the table, his elbows resting upon its surface, his hands cradling his head. His eyes stared at the amber liquid in the glass, but they would not focus.

'Sebastian, Sebastian...' Where Octavia's voice had once caressed, it now worked like corrosive acid upon North's still reeling mind and poisoned heart.

'...did you find the ring at the hotel?' she asked.

'Yes, I found it hidden in the soap,' replied North.

'Do you have it with you?' she asked.

'At a time like this, what difference does it make whether I have the ring or not?' he questioned, amazed that after what Octavia had just said, she was so concerned about something so seemingly unimportant.

North hesitated for a moment before replying, trying to understand the Sicilian's motives. 'As a matter of fact, I do have the ring,' he said, taking another mouthful of whisky.

'Sebastian...' Octavia's voice faltered, its tone unsteady. 'Please give my ring back.'

North reached into an inside pocket, his fingers finding the warm metal of the ring. Slowly he withdrew his hand, holding the ring between the thumb and index finger of his right hand, close to the candle's yellow flame. As the ruby reflected the light from its many surfaces, North found himself wondering what sort of a talisman this precious stone really was.

'From whom were you trying to hide this ring, Octavia? And why is it so important now?' he asked.

Octavia sat down in the chair opposite. North noticed that her perfume was a little too heavy; he did not believe it could have been her choice.

'Two men broke into the hotel room after you left. They must have been after this ring, only they did not know it at the time. Whoever gave them their instructions hoped that this particular ring would be included in the haul after seizing all my personal jewellery.'

'If this is true,' said North, 'whoever this someone was, he or she did not trust these men very far, and also did not want to draw undue attention to the ring itself.'

North looked up from his curious observation of the ancient ring and mysterious stone to see Octavia's face, now illuminated more evenly in the glare of the candlelight. His stomach tensed when he saw part of the cut across her forehead. Her clever use of makeup had, until now, reduced the previously hideous scar to a small, thin line.

'They weren't very friendly, I see,' he said. His voice carried little feeling, but Octavia thought she detected a trace of genuine concern beyond his sarcastic words.

'It was Roberto who gave the orders for my jewellery to be taken, and my subsequent removal by plane to Castle Zehra. He had shown an interest in the legend of the ring and the possibility of it leading to great wealth, since I first knew him.'

It seems, thought North, that Roberto was one step ahead of the Romanians in pursuing the ring and it's legend.

Octavia paused in her search for the right words, evidently finding the story difficult to recount.

'When Roberto saw how these repulsive, callous men who carried this out had treated me, he said they would be taken care of. I am sure it was not Roberto's fault this happened.'

Octavia must be crazy, thought North. Her mind should have registered doubt and uncertainty, but apparently she saw only Roberto. That could only be explained by a rekindling of their previous passion.

'The Count gave orders for you to be brought to Castle Zehra, and in the process his lackeys do this! You fail to question the Count's motives, and what is more you seem to accept his explanation at face value. It doesn't make any sense, Octavia. In fact, it's all quite crazy.

'Of course, your love for the Count would explain everything, for love is the one emotion that resides well outside the normal bounds of reason!'

North wondered if one of the previously mentioned men had been the unfortunate duellist whose death he had so recently witnessed.

Octavia stretched out her right hand and her slim fingers took the ring. She placed it with care upon the fourth finger of her right hand while North poured himself another two fingers' worth of malt whisky. He welcomed the strong liquid as it continued to work upon his tired nervous system.

He changed the subject. 'So, the Count also thinks that this ring holds the key to untold wealth? Strange, as I would not have taken the Count as someone who gave much weight to mere legends.'

'You have heard the legend of the Sultan's treasure: a gift to King Richard Coeur-De-Lion for rescuing his daughter Princess Zehra in Cyprus during the third crusade?' asked Octavia.

'Yes, your father mentioned the story to me when we discovered your whereabouts at Castle Zehra.'

Octavia's face went completely white at the mention of her father. Her discussion with North had completely sidetracked her concern for his safety and health.

'How is Papa?' she asked, her voice a bare whisper of emotion.

'Your father is in poor health after his recent ordeal,' he told her. 'I found him held prisoner aboard the *Roxana* soon after I left you in the hotel. The same night we made a successful escape from the Romanians, for it was they who held him.'

'Thank you, Sebastian. My family owes you a great debt,' said Octavia. Because of their recent conversation, her words fell rather flat.

North diverted their talk back to the previous discussion, still puzzled as to how Octavia could forget to ask about the fate of her father so easily.

'Why does Roberto want the ring? It has to be something to do with the legend, does it not?'

'Yes, Roberto says the Sultan's treasure, or at least part of it, does in fact exist, and that the transcribed inscription from the ring will reveal its location.'

'Do you believe in the legend?' asked North.

'I don't know what to believe,' she replied truthfully.

North took another mouthful of whisky before asking his next question. 'Tell me, Octavia, did the Count ask you to find out if I had the ring's inscription transcribed?'

She seemed shocked by the question. 'How could he ask this? How could he have known that you would arrive at Castle Zehra?' she replied.

North became certain that he had walked into a trap. The Count, realising that the ring was missing from Octavia's finger and the jewellery found in the hotel room, had calculated that North would make an attempt to rescue her. After all, he had succeeded in rescuing her both in the South of France and Sicily, so why not a third attempt?

North abruptly stood up, suddenly realising how blinded he had become by his own stupidity.

Of course, it wasn't the Count who had calculated that he would try a third time to rescue her, but Octavia herself.

'The Count could not have known for sure that I would try to aid your escape from Castle Zehra, but you knew for certain that I would make the attempt, because of *La Valencia*. Deep down, you alone knew I had fallen for you. The kiss in the garden at *La Valencia* was the basis for accurately predicting my future journey to Castle Zehra.'

Octavia's dark eyes filled with tears as she protested that none of it was true, and that she was totally innocent of the treachery that North now accused her of.

'You may now have the ring, Octavia, but only I possess the key to the Sultan's treasure, if indeed it really does exist. I recently had the inscription transcribed through a friend of mine in England who knows one of Europe's leading code-breakers.'

Octavia turned her head, her eyes meeting North's. It was then that he saw deep into her soul. His confused heart dared to hope, but his rational mind would not listen, and yet he saw without disorientation or compromise that his memory of *La Valencia* was indeed true and accurate. Octavia's heart had been reached at

La Valencia, just as his had at that unequivocal moment of their decisive first kiss. And this now only added to North's emotional uncertainty and present turmoil.

Before Octavia could reply, a knock sounded on the closed but unlocked door. Both she and North were brought back to the present by the sudden intrusion.

'Octavia, are you ready?' North had never heard Count Roberto Fambino's voice before, but he knew beyond question that it was him on the other side of the door.

Chapter Nine

Within the high turret room occupied by Octavia and North, silence reigned unbroken for what seemed an age, but in reality could only have been but a few brief moments.

Octavia relived the last few hours in horrific detail, though she tried with all her might and weakened fortitude to erase the recorded tape of her emotional memory. She felt hope run through her hands like water so that a terrible despair engulfed her mind.

The Count's treachery, through revenge fuelled by jealousy and now hate, was swift and ruthless in its undisguised brutality. Revenge for his rejected proposal of marriage to Octavia had created within his cold and cruel heart a minotaur of truly daunting proportions.

As predicted by the Baron to North earlier aboard the *Roxana*, the Count had tried first to persuade his former fiancée to forget their past differences with a flattery full of charm and persuasion. From the moment Octavia arrived at Castle Zehra, she had felt the Count's presence close enough to rekindle past and half-forgotten memories of desire, even excitement.

However, with a supreme effort Octavia rallied her strength of mind, just in time to check Roberto's amorous intentions before they progressed beyond the point of no return. From her past relationship with Roberto she had begun to learn the terrible pain of betrayal just before it was too late. Like so many women throughout history, a man of mysterious and evil repute, wielding great power, could and often did prove irresistible to women.

Octavia had learnt her lesson by painful experience, and she now prayed with all her heart that she would never repeat the terrible mistake of falling for Roberto again.

Her illustrious ancestors, many richly endowed with noble qualities, reaching back to ancient Greece and Rome, had ensured that her blood would flow with resolution and fortitude in time of need. She also knew that courage on her part must not be found wanting.

She began to realise that she had previously abandoned her young heart to impulsive and naive winds of passion that contained little of substance and were, in the end, of no value. The consequence for the refined and tender flame of her heart was acute disappointment when fool's gold was discovered, once again masquerading as something of value.

Count Roberto Fambino was a man whose whole life was dedicated to the sole aim of increasing his power and influence within the Sicilian Mafia, whose tentacles were worldwide and governed without the constraint of morality.

The Count's rewards, reaped from these evil-fashioned activities conducted on such a massive scale, left a grim wake of misery for the living and an early death for countless thousands.

His activities spanned from the distribution of heroin to child prostitution. Everywhere, he had encountered only success, until his rejection by Octavia – the first and only woman who finally saw him as he really was.

His attempts to possess the one jewel he would never own had ended in complete failure.

Soon after Octavia's arrival, having quickly exhausted his considerable but impatient charm, the Count became consumed by the fires of vengeance. He knew deep down that Octavia's heart now belonged to someone else and would never have a place for him.

The Count had repeatedly struck Octavia in a frenzy of madness that was incomprehensible to her. She had fought back with every ounce of strength her body possessed, but was not strong enough to repel his maniacal onslaught. Cunningly, the blows he rained against Octavia's body were positioned so that the heavy bruising that would inevitably follow was upon areas not easily visible to the casual observer.

Fear and anger all but paralysed Octavia's mind. The ferocity of the Count's attack was such that she felt sure a broken arm or rib must surely follow. Perhaps a wheelchair was her fate, rendering her dream of life a taunting illusion.

Once, Octavia was pushed so hard against a chair that she dared not move from the floor, sure that her back was broken. However, at that moment the gods must have been on her side, because eventually painful and hesitating movement returned to her legs, after an hour or so of frightening numbness.

The Count was oblivious to her distress. No words of apology were forthcoming, only a continuous stream of obscenities and additional threats of more violence or even death! Octavia now believed that he was even capable of this, such was her fear.

She begged on her knees, pleading with him to cease this madness and promised to do anything he asked, if only he would stop. Octavia was fast approaching the point where sanity and insanity become blurred and ill-defined. Soon she would mentally break and join the Count on the dark side of sanity, and so become his willing slave.

For a moment Octavia had contemplated offering him her body in a vain attempt at stopping his physical abuse, but the very thought now proved too repulsive and hideous. She seriously doubted her ability to carry the act through. There had to be another way out of this wide-awake screaming nightmare.

Octavia's whole body shook with the shuddering convulsions of the truly desperate. Tears of hopelessness welled up in her beautiful dark eyes to cascade in floods down her cheeks, like so much life running away from a future too black to understand.

The Count wasn't fooled for a moment by Octavia's attempts at submission. He had guessed her true feelings towards the Englishman, and had fashioned his plans accordingly in order to destroy what her heart held close. He had cunningly played his hand, so that the knife of his burning vengeance would produce the greatest of pain and suffering for his former fiancée.

The Count instinctively knew, as the devil shrinks from the light, that deep inside Octavia there was a substance he could never completely destroy. Her heart was like the rare flawless diamond that men only dream of. It would remain beyond his influence and forever indestructible to someone like himself.

Thalia was one of Octavia's two middle names, given by her mother after one of the three graces from Greek mythology. She was by reputation very beautiful, and full of grace, charm, and favour. These qualities were incomprehensible to Count Roberto Fambino.

The Count had insisted upon hearing the words 'I love only Roberto' from Octavia's lips, said straight to the impostor's face. He knew that he had lost the battle for Octavia's heart, but somehow these false words would give his own black heart a twisted and dishonourable sense of satisfaction.

Suddenly the draught of air from the window fluctuated in strength, so that the candle's flame now burnt with hesitation. Watching it, Octavia reflected how like her previous search for true love it was, continuously caught in a dark wind of misfortune, false hope, and infatuations.

The door was violently flung open. There was no second knock or waiting for Octavia to reply to the earlier question as to her state of readiness. Framed in the doorway was the erect and confident figure of Count Roberto Fambino.

He wore evening dress cut from the very finest of cloth and tailored by the best that Milan could offer. The snow white of the Count's starched shirt contrasted well with his dark, chiselled features. The black tie was tied with perfect symmetry, the black hair combed straight back without a parting, the pencil thin moustache drooped either side of a narrow mouth. His piercing charcoal eyes swept the room, taking in every detail, missing nothing of consequence, before settling upon the tall figure of Sebastian North.

The gun, held steady in the Count's right hand, discouraged any sudden motion on North's part. Octavia froze, her face turned to white marble.

Her heart pounded with anticipation of the future, now heavily pregnant with foreboding.

The Count, seeing that the moment was entirely his to play as he wished, allowed a slow smile of triumph to play over his lips. Octavia observed the face that she knew so well. A handsome mask that concealed to perfection his true thoughts of treachery and deceit. She found ill-defined ominous clouds, full of future menace, deep within his eyes.

'Octavia, I don't recall you mentioning that we were to expect an extra guest tonight.' The Count's English was nearly perfect, with only the faintest trace of an accent to suggest that he was not a native of the language.

She felt sick. 'You deliberately set up this whole hideous thing, and now you pretend that you had no hand in its conception.' Her eyes flashed anger.

'I wasn't invited by the Countess,' said North. 'I forced an entry upon my own account.'

This was not exactly true, as he and Octavia both knew, for the door had been open and she had not demanded or suggested his immediate withdrawal. It was then that North felt the first trace of doubt that all was not quite as it seemed.

Was his appearance at Castle Zehra such a surprise, after all?

The Count ignored North's explanation.

'So, Englishman, we meet at last. Your reputation grows by the hour. Since arriving first in Sicily and now in Sardinia, you have succeeded in interfering in other people's business to a remarkable extent.'

The Count continued with obvious enjoyment, 'As you admitted, Englishman, your entry was forced without invitation. Therefore, I am compelled to conclude that your intentions are less than honourable.

'Before we continue, Englishman, perhaps you will be so kind as to introduce yourself and state the nature of your business?'

'My name is Sebastian North, and the reason for my visit to these islands is purely medical; my doctor suggested a change of climate would be good for my health.'

North's expression was one of amusement. He seemed to be outwardly quite unconcerned at looking into the barrel of the Count's gun.

The Count's smile of triumph evaporated into lines of fury.

North knew that explaining to the Count about his intentions of rescuing the Countess Octavia – now obviously in love with her former fiancé, either for the second time or having never really stopped loving him since their engagement – was ridiculous in the extreme. So, he thought it high time to change the direction of their increasingly strained conversation before his circumstances developed from the merely difficult to the impossible.

'May I return the compliments, Count Roberto Fambino?' said North. 'Your reputation is well known to most of the European police forces and Interpol, as a member of the most successful Sicilian crime family of all time.'

The Count's previous anger at North's insolence subsided and he quickly returned to his all-too-easy and treacherous smile. He was proud of his own distinction within the Cosa Nostra and their ever-increasing notoriety.

'I understand, Count Fambino, that you are interested in a certain ring belonging to the Countess – the one that contains a mounted ruby, given to her by her mother on the occasion of her twenty-first birthday?'

The Count was suddenly intrigued by the stranger before him. The man was about his own height and build, tall, with an athlete's physique, but there was something more. Something he had never encountered in a man before. It was sensed rather than felt, an uneasy experience that was both undeniable and irrefutable in its passing intensity, like someone adept at reading the depths of other people's desires. An uncomfortable sensation, acknowledged the Count, of being momentarily caught naked and graphically exposed under a revealing flash of light.

The Count found in the Englishman's eyes qualities that seemed to mirror or emphasise his own weaknesses.

'Yes, you are quite correct. I am very interested in the ring that you mentioned. I believe you stole the ring from the Countess, is that not correct?' The Count's tone carried contempt, as one confronting a common thief.

Before North could reply, Octavia walked over to the Count and held out her right palm containing the ring. Its oval, brilliant cut caught the light, so that it briefly sparkled before the Count's eager left hand took possession of the ring and his eyes became transfixed upon its unique design.

North's muscles tightened in anticipation of sudden and violent movement, as he gauged his chances, but the Count would easily be able to fire his gun before he could draw his own.

North became fascinated by the almost hypnotic effect this little piece of corundum had upon the Count.

The invisible influence of this precious stone seemed to totally captivate him to such an extent that he had to, with obvious effort, tear his eyes away.

The Count continued speaking, his voice still heavy with contempt.

'Of course, I know that the ring is useless without the correct transcription of its inscription. However, I have a most reliable source in the Italian Security Services who has recently informed me that you are now in possession of just such a transcription. Is this not true?'

The Count's smile broadened to a grin of amusement and self-congratulation at North's obvious surprise at his competent intelligence work.

Quickly recovering from his surprise, North replied, 'You seem to know quite a lot, my dear Count. Let us suppose for a moment that your information is accurate, and that I do indeed possess such a correctly transcribed copy of the inscription. What makes you think I would give it to you?'

The Count burst out laughing until he almost shook with the exercise, but his gun never wavered for an instant from covering North's position.

'Mr North, your situation is, shall we say, a delicate one, and your position with regard to negotiation, I suggest, is definitely on the weak side.

'Believe me, Englishman, it would not be in your best interests to withhold this information. However, in view of the circumstances, I am prepared to resolve this little problem to our mutual satisfaction. I enjoy games of chance, but I enjoy contests that involve an element of skill even more, so I propose that we stage a contest as a way of concluding this difference of opinion.'

The Count paused, enjoying the uncomfortable curiosity of both Octavia and North.

'I propose we settle this little problem of you being here uninvited, and as a consequence the Contessa's reputation being most certainly compromised, along with this stubborn reluctance to part with a copy of the transcription, with a duel. Winner takes all.

'We all know that this transcription is the only key to the exact location of the remaining portion of the Sultan's treasure, which includes the largest uncut diamond ever found, needless to say beyond price.'

North's mind started to race as the full implications of the Count's challenge sank in. The very recent memory of the man's fate he had witnessed earlier hung vivid and fresh upon his mind.

Without looking at Octavia, the Count continued his conversation with the Englishman.

'I believe you have met Countess Octavia before in, how shall I say, more relaxed circumstances. I throw her in as a bonus, so it really will be winner takes all!'

The Count's attitude towards his former fiancée, thought North, *is more than obvious. He treats her as a chattel, a piece of his property to do with as he wishes.*

Octavia's eyes found North's but her vocal cords would not function, silenced by a paralysing fear that produced only soundless bewilderment and hesitation.

North, however, had assumed the appearance of someone quite unconcerned, almost detached, after the Count's monumental throw of a gauntlet in the form of a duel.

'Just suppose I don't survive this duel,' said North. 'You will be no nearer to finding the Sultan's treasure and the *Darya-i-Nur* – assuming that it really does exist.'

'My dear Mr North, you give me far too much credit,' replied the Count, his voice smooth and full of confidence.

The Count had found the desire to defeat the Englishman in a duel much too tempting to resist, for here was another chance to show his partners in crime how good his swordsmanship really was. It bothered him little that, as with Major Vasile previously, the contest would be hopelessly loaded in his own favour. The master against the novice.

The double prize of possessing the *Darya-i-Nur* and breaking Octavia's heart by killing the Englishman worked deep within his mind like a powerful narcotic. She would then at last be his, a conquered chattel, irretrievably broken, and too weak to fight back.

'If wounded, as often occurs in a duel, there is a certain space of time before death is certain. It is during this time that you will tell me the whereabouts of this transcribed inscription, yes?'

North knew then with certainty that one of them would never see the coming dawn. 'As you are so sure as to the outcome of this duel, I hope you have no objection if I help myself to some more of your excellent whisky?'

Without waiting for a reply, North poured a generous portion of the straw-coloured liquid into his glass. 'The condemned man is always allowed a last request?' he questioned, after taking a satisfactory mouthful of the Highland malt.

'That depends, Mr North, upon your request,' said the Count, now curious as to what this could be. He remained alert to North's every move, his gun never wavering for an instant.

'One of your cigars? I see a fine box by the window and, judging by its size, an extensive selection must be contained within.'

'Ah, yes, the traditional last smoke; English observance of formality to the end. But if you think playing for time will greatly change your position, I fear you will be very much mistaken.'

North, having selected a long cigar, took his time in first cutting the end, then lighting it from the candle. When the end was a burning glow to his satisfaction, he blew from between his lips blue smoke that eddied briefly upwards before disappearing into the vaulted ceiling. Octavia watched North incredulously. Here he was facing certain death and his only thought was of whisky and a last smoke!

The distinctive smell of expensive cigar smoke drifted across the room. For a moment, the aroma reminded Octavia of her father, who enjoyed a smoke, mostly at weekends when he found time to reminisce with exciting stories from his youth. Strange how a smell can stimulate such strong images from the past.

Octavia once more found North's eyes. She held them for a moment, before he turned back to the Count. What did she find there? It was impossible to read his thoughts; she wanted to see so much but had to confess uncertainty.

Then the Count asked a surprise question, directed at North.

'What do you know, Mr North, about the Manila Galleons?'

Octavia watched North's initial reaction to the strange question with puzzlement. His face gave nothing away, even the slow smile that developed across his handsome features assumed the impenetrable veneer of a mask. Octavia wondered how this question related to the present circumstances.

Before replying, North blew more cigar smoke, that again hung momentarily in the air before drifting in layers above their heads.

'Dangerous, but very profitable, is how I would describe the passage of Spanish galleons and their cargos of rich oriental treasures from the ports of India, Siam, and China, in exchange for New World silver and European manufactured goods. From the early 1500s to the early 1800s, the Manila galleons carried the riches of the East to Europe, and provided a vital trade link between two continents. Previous searches for wrecked galleons have traditionally been directed in the Caribbean Sea – a vast area with notorious hurricanes and treacherous reefs, where conditions claimed many a galleon.

'However, recent salvage operations have been conducted on the Pacific leg of the long nine-thousand-mile journey from the Philippines to Europe via the New World ports of Acapulco and Vera Cruz. The difficult and often slow crossing of the Pan American isthmus was performed overland by mule train to the Gulf of Mexico.

'I seem to recall a recent successful salvage operation upon the *Nuestra Señora De Le Conception*, off the southern coast of Saipan, one of the northern Marianna Islands. She went down in a typhoon on 20th September, 1638. Her cargo at the time was one of the largest of any ship to sail for the New World, valued at four million pesos, which would be many millions of dollars in today's currency. It included silks, porcelain, ivory, silver, gold, and many precious and semi-precious jewels.

'A second successful salvage operation was conducted on her sister ship, the *Nuestra Señora De La Isabella*, which sank a year later in almost the same position as the *Conception*. The *Isabella*'s cargo was even larger than her sister ship.

'According to archives found in Seville, Mexico City, and Madrid, her cargo was many times more valuable. These archives confirmed that, in addition to Oriental silks, porcelain, ivory, silver, and precious jewels, huge quantities of gold bullion and hundreds of yards of gold chain were on board. In addition, she held 1,900 pieces of gold jewellery of exceptional quality and unique design, as well as jewel-encrusted boxes set with fine emeralds and sapphires.

'I heard,' continued North, to the increasing astonishment of Octavia and the Count, 'that figures such as nearly half a billion dollars could be a close estimate of the true value of her cargo.

'However, I also recall that a large portion of what was brought to the surface mysteriously disappeared without trace before it reached California, the salvage company's intended destination for their bounty.'

Count Fambino's previous self-confidence was somewhat shaken by this unexpected and profound appreciation for the subject of his enquiry so adequately displayed by the Englishman. The result was to produce a great degree of uncertainty and suspicion as to what possible motive lay behind this detailed knowledge. The Count wondered again what the real reason was for North's presence first in Sicily and now in Sardinia.

Octavia became captivated and curious with North's detailed account of the majestic galleons and their cargos all those years ago. Graveyards for so long, veiled by the sea, now giving up their secrets as man probed the deep in his quest for riches.

Where is the missing cargo from the Nuestra Señora De La Isabella *now?* she wondered. *Is it really worth hundreds of millions of dollars? Who could have stolen it, without trace? And why does North know so much about the Manila galleons?*

'Well, Mr North, having shown us your knowledge of the Manila galleons, perhaps you can tell us something of the famous *Darya-i-Nur*?' asked the Count.

With more thick, blue cigar smoke and another sip of his whisky, North proceeded to answer the Count's next question with as much enthusiasm and attention to detail as the previous one.

'According to certain archives held in Mecca, Riyadh, and confirmed by others in Baghdad and Damascus, the Sultan's gift to King Richard of England originally consisted of seven chests containing a treasure of unimaginable proportions at that time. Perhaps not on the scale of the *Isabella*'s cargo, but still considerable at present value.

'I assume that you are familiar with the legend of why these seven chests were paid to King Richard of England, and therefore, will concentrate on other aspects of this so-called legend.

'Of course, Richard had to finance his crusade, as well as the building of Castle Zehra. The first drew notoriously on national resources, and the second could not have been inexpensive, so how much was left of the original seven chests is very uncertain. However, one chest half-filled with gold, silver, precious and semi-precious stones, as described in the archives, would be worth a King's ransom today.

'The famous *Darya-i-Nur*, meaning Sea of Light or blue mogul as it later became known, is reputed to be a diamond of truly staggering proportions, according to recorded descriptions of the few individuals privileged to have actually seen it. It is a huge blue-white uncut diamond of a colossal 3,400 carats which, if true, would make it the largest ever found.

'The previous largest known diamond was the *Cullinan* of about 3,100 carats, well over a pound in weight. The *Darya-i-Nur*, if these archives are to be believed, would be even heavier. The *Cullinan* stone was cut up in Amsterdam in 1908. The two largest pieces from the cutting resulted in nine major stones, which ended up in the British crown jewels.'

At this point, the Count found himself struggling to regain the initiative, which should have been his by virtue of his gun but was now fast approaching question.

'So, Mr North, you are some sort of professional treasure hunter?'

North laughed at the question, perhaps enjoying the surprise he had caused. Or was this seemingly relaxed attitude only a cover, at facing certain death after the Count's challenge to a duel?

'I have, shall we say, a natural curiosity with regard to antiques, and in particular those that disappear in rather mysterious circumstances.'

'What of the Sultan's treasure chests? Does this possible discovery stimulate your natural curiosity, too? Is it the legendary blue fire of the *Darya-i-Nur* that drives you far from home to this island? Or perhaps there are other reasons for your Mediterranean travels...'

The Count left his sentence unfinished and hanging, but there was no doubt that his interest had been aroused as to what North's presence really meant.

After another sip of his whisky, North thought that it was his turn to ask some questions.

'I hope, Count Fambino, that I have answered your questions adequately. Perhaps you might answer one of mine in fair exchange?' Without waiting for the Count to object, North asked his first question.

'From a distance, I saw two flags flying – one from the battlements of the main tower, a double black-headed eagle upon a yellow background; the other from above the gatehouse, a blue, yellow and red vertical tricolour. I now recognise it as the colours of Romania.

'What puzzles me most is that the tricolour flies at half-mast. Was there someone you knew who is now no longer with us?' North believed it must have something to do with the duel he had so recently witnessed.

The Count sensed the chance to restore the initiative in what was quickly becoming a sort of uncomfortable contest in answering questions between himself and the Englishman.

'My dear Englishman, it is all very simple. The double black eagle heads facing outwards against a yellow background is my own coat of arms. It dates, for your information, from the 14th century when my ancestors controlled Sicily and most of what is now Calabria.'

'I am sure you and your family, through the sale of narcotics, control a much larger area now,' interrupted North.

The Count tried to ignore North's tone and continued his explanation.

'The Romanian flag flies at half-mast out of respect for someone who recently found an early grave, through tragic circumstances. He was indeed Romanian. However, his death was, I may add, somewhat self-inflicted.'

'Out of respect for the dead, or as a warning to those who were not among the privileged few to witness his grizzly end? I guess it was he whom I saw go up in smoke this morning?'

'Once again, Englishman, you seem to be remarkably well-informed about my affairs. This unfortunate Romanian was a certain Major Vasile – a young nephew of President Ceauşescu, dictator of Romania. His reputation with the ladies was notorious, with numerous scandals constantly reaching the international newspapers. He was caught by our people in a compromising situation with a Sicilian girl called Claudia, against her will. I believe she is a friend of yours,' he said, glancing at Octavia.

The Count paused to let his words sink in. 'So, justice was carried out on Major Vasile. You see, in the Cosa Nostra we have always operated independently of the police or the courts. They are mere amateurs in the administration of justice.'

Octavia gasped at the horrific news; Claudia was her closest friend since childhood. 'Wh-where is Claudia now?' she stammered. 'How long have you known this news without telling me?'

Octavia could not conceive of a reason why the Count had withheld such devastating news from her. The true nature and full extent of her former fiancé's insensitivity and callousness was beginning to sink in.

'It doesn't matter. The incident occurred and the culprit was quickly punished,' said the Count without feeling.

Large tears of despair cascaded down Octavia's cheeks. She covered her face with trembling hands, but the tears ran through her fingers in uncontrollable floods. Her whole body shook with the sudden shock of Claudia's ordeal, on top of her own continuing nightmare. Everything seemed to be occurring so fast, a continuous screaming rollercoaster of events and heart-breaking emotions.

How much more could she take before breaking point was reached? Instinct told her that this moment would not be long in coming.

Octavia dared not show her true feelings for Sebastian. There was no knowing what the Count might do, including murder. Somehow, she must think of a plan to stop this duel from taking place, as it was nothing less than a death sentence for North. Life after North's death could only be a living hell of an existence for her, so she had to come up with something before North's time ran out altogether.

With a slow understanding that gathered increasing clarity, North perceived that everything was not as he had originally been led to believe.

Was it possible that Octavia's words were indeed counterfeit? Was her declared love, so convincingly spoken for the Count, false? If so, then what kind of hold did the Count exercise over her?

The Count interrupted his train of thought.

'Major Vasile was sent by that evil woman, Elena Ceauşescu, who some would say is the real power behind the presidency of her husband.'

'For what purpose? The Sultan's treasure is, after all, only a legend. She must be completely crazy,' said North.

'Her aim, according to a certain General Kerenskiy with whom I have recently had conversation, was for her nephew to obtain the Sultan's treasure for the future "King and Queen of Romania".'

'You mean to tell me that they are attempting to re-establish the monarchy with Nicolae Ceauşescu on the throne?' said North incredulously.

'Yes, exactly. You see, every monarch, and his consort, needs a set of crown jewels. Hence Elena Ceauşescu's fanatical interest in the legend.'

North could not help but wonder how much importance the Count now attached to the legend of the Sultan's treasure.

'Mr North, it is time. My guests are waiting. Our duel will provide some unexpected entertainment that is most in keeping with our celebrations.'

'A last question, my dear Count, for my cigar is not yet finished. What is the significance of these celebrations?'

The Count smiled, proud to inform North of his latest plans and ambitions.

'Of course, I should have told you earlier. Forgive me for keeping you in the dark for so long. Sicily has always been the centre of the heroin trade. Poppy fields in the Bekaa Valley in Lebanon and elsewhere are harvested. The juice of the unripe seed capsule contains several alkaloids, one of which is morphine.

'The raw morphine – a bitter, white crystalline structure – is transported to Palermo by container ship, to be in turn secretly distributed to laboratories. Within these laboratories it is refined into an extremely powerful white, powdered narcotic, commonly known as heroin. It is one of the most habit-forming substances that man has ever encountered.

'I am sure you are not entirely ignorant of these facts.' But the Count did not wait for a reply; his tone suggested a statement rather than a question.

'From Palermo, the heroin is shipped to the east coast of America to such ports as New York, Boston, and more recently Miami. Lately things have been difficult, with the greatly increased activities of the Palermo *Carabinieri* resulting in many arrests. So, we have switched to Cagliari and the Costa Smeralda, Sardinia, where so far things have been much quieter.

'Profits from sky-high sales within the United States have proved to be an ever-increasing problem during these last few years, due to difficulties in laundering money. This is where Señor Max Santiago from Panama comes in. You will meet him presently. He has been most helpful with various financial investments on our behalf, for a reasonable percentage of the substantial profits.

'Señor Sancho Largo is from the Medellin Cartel, which I am sure you have heard of.' The Count's smile was perfect, but his unfeeling ice-cold eyes perfectly betrayed his true nature. 'He will supply us with cocaine. For while North America has been saturated, Europe is, by comparison, untouched. We were offered fifty per cent of the profits to distribute their cocaine through our already well-established networks.

'Due to the colossal scale of this deal, we have enlisted the help of Signor Vincenzo Lezane of the Camorra, another one of my distinguished guests tonight.

'Come, it is time we joined our guests. Contessa, you will lead the way to the great hall, Mr North will follow you. I will be directly behind, but not close enough for Mr North to try anything suicidal. I need not remind you again that I will not hesitate to use my gun.'

As the steady barrel of the Count's gun continued to cover North's every movement, he needed little additional encouragement to comply with his host's wishes. Under the present arrangement there was no chance of using his own gun.

In the order suggested by the Count, the two men and one woman filed their way out of the turret room and into the badly lit passageway. Beyond, their descent of the spiral staircase produced slow progress on account of Octavia's ball gown, its numerous folds hindering her movement. North's mind was constantly searching for a plan of escape, but so far he had to admit that he was rather short of ideas.

Octavia was breathing fast, partly from fear and partly from frustration, as the ball gown's substantial material several times threatened to pitch her forwards down the stone steps.

Once North reached the last stone step, he knew that he had made the right decision not to try anything violent, as a second man with a gun stood waiting to welcome him.

The man had snow white hair and a goatee of the same colour. His pitiless coal-black eyes were set within a forehead and cheeks of dark olive skin. His nose was hooked like a bird of prey, his mouth devoid of compassion. When Octavia, followed by the Count, arrived at the bottom of the narrow stairs, the man with the eagle nose opened a conversation with the Count. Now North was covered by two guns.

'Roberto, I had wondered what kept you and the Contessa for so long. I see you have found an extra guest,' he said, sounding surprised.

'Excuse my memory, but I don't recall having met you before,' he said to North.

'I just happened to be passing through when the Count here very kindly invited me to your party which, judging by the noise, must already be approaching full swing.'

The sound of music came from a room not too far away, its rhythm broken now and again by a woman crying out. Whether her cries were the result of pain or ecstasy was impossible to tell.

'Tell me,' continued North, 'do you always welcome strangers with the barrel of a gun? I am starting to become quite used to it, for your colleague here,' he gestured to the Count positioned behind him, 'gave me a similar welcome only a moment ago. Sort of guilty until proven innocent routine?'

'We waste more time,' said the Count. 'This impostor, Uncle, who invited himself tonight so cavalierly to Castle Zehra, has in his possession the transcribed inscription that solves the mystery of the Sultan's treasure.'

Don Giovanni Fambino smiled. 'And where is this transcribed inscription now?'

'I have challenged this stranger, who is an Englishman by the name of Sebastian North, to a duel – the outcome of which, I believe, will produce the information we desire.'

'You have, of course, searched him?' asked Don Giovanni Fambino.

'There is no need. Only a fool would bring it with him, and this Englishman may turn out to be many things, but I doubt a fool is one of them.'

'And what reasons do you have for adopting this opinion, Roberto?'

'It seems that Mr North was directly responsible for the Romanians failing so spectacularly to kidnap the Contessa. He is also the reason why General Kerenskiy is here. You see, Uncle, a steady trail of bodies has followed this Englishman from the South of France to the Delmonte villa not to mention the recent discovery of a Romanian pinned to a wall by a spear gun bolt aboard the *Roxana*. So far the body count is at least five if not more. I intend to end this annoying habit of his.'

'If all this is true, what makes you think Mr North will oblige you and part with the transcribed inscription?'

'He is, dear Uncle, more than a little reluctant to release the information at the moment. So, I thought a means of resolving this problem in a satisfactory fashion would be to introduce Mr North to some cold steel. Then there is every possibility that he will see the issue my way. It will also provide our guests with some added entertainment.

'The result of this duel will perhaps speed up our inevitable success in locating the remains of the Sultan's treasure,' finished the Count, with a laugh that echoed down the narrow stone corridor.

Twelve-foot-high, double wooden doors opened to allow in first North, then the Count – holding Octavia by the hand – followed by Don Giovanni, his gun hand still very steady.

The party could only be described as being at its height in terms of exuberance, perhaps even in danger of running out of control.

Three thirty-foot-long tables were covered with the remains of a meal which, judging from the number of empty bottles and glasses, must have been extensive in terms of consumed alcohol. The scene would have done credit to any grand celebration hosted by a 19th century Russian prince in his castle.

A hundred or more men and women sat at the three tables. Several of the men had discarded their dinner jackets and lost their ties. The women, all young and pretty, added much colour, with their elegant dresses exhibiting various shades of red, blue, turquoise, green, and yellow, many with eye-catching patterns and designs.

The great hall was lit by torches spaced every ten feet around the walls, their moving flames of strong yellow giving a festive and almost medieval atmosphere to the gathering below.

A tall, dark haired girl was belly dancing upon the centre table. She wore only pants and bra, both in bright blue silk. Extensive gold jewellery glinted around her neck and arms.

Her legs straddled a particularly fat man, who lay unconscious, but remained seated. His head lay firmly on his plate, its previous contents impossible to identify, except for some brown liquid that oozed around the man's face and spilled over onto the table. It could have been anything from gravy to chocolate ice cream.

Music from a group of musicians in one corner dictated the speed of the gyrating pelvis. Faster and faster her hips moved, all eyes fixed with hypnotic concentration upon the impossible feats being performed by the girl's navel. The final crescendo, during which the girl's pelvis became a blur of continuous sensual motion, brought loud applause. The music stopped at last, bringing relief to the girl's exhausted muscles, her skin now glistening with sweat from the exertion.

The audience went wild with excitement. Applause was immediate, with everyone clapping their hands, except for the man with his face on his plate, quite oblivious to his surroundings.

A girl screamed as the man she was sitting on squeezed a particularly sensitive part of her anatomy, and more applause followed from men around her. Clearly the party had much life left, even at this late hour.

Suddenly everyone noticed the four figures who had just entered the great hall. A new focal point of interest had been found, and even the numerous and smartly dressed waiters with over-laden trays paused from their busy activities.

Leaving his uncle to cover North, the Count let go of Octavia's arm and leapt onto the partially cleared centre table. Then, with the sole of his right shoe under the chin of the seated fat man, he violently pushed the bloated face and head. This resulted in the man leaning first to his right, then backwards over the chair, to fall with a crash to the ground with the remains of his unfinished food and plate still firmly stuck to his right ear. This incident proved immensely amusing to everyone, with added encouragement shown by more clapping and shouts of excitement.

The unfortunate heap now lying on the floor did not rise to the occasion. It seemed that even this trauma failed to bring him to the land of the conscious.

Standing next to the still sweating belly dancer, the Count put his left arm around her and held her close. All eyes were now upon him and the scantily clad dancer, her breasts rising and falling as she struggled to regain her breath.

'Ladies and gentlemen, welcome to Castle Zehra. The celebrations are not yet over, for I now offer you something sensational – a final piece of spectacular entertainment that you will never forget!'

The gathered audience became quiet at this interruption of their celebrations, and an expectant silence followed, full of anticipation at the Count's enthusiastic words.

'This man,' said the Count, pointing to North, 'has invited himself to our party. He has also tried to take that which does not belong to him…'

The Count turned his head to look in Octavia's direction. Her face looked very white, her eyes flashing the anger and fear of a frightened animal.

'So, I have challenged him to a duel…'

There was loud applause from the inebriated audience, with men yelling incoherent encouragement. Several more women screamed as their escort's hands and mouths found even more sensitive flesh, firstly to explore and then to excite.

'…to the death,' finished the Count.

The applause died immediately. The great hall for a moment or two was transformed to the semblance of a morgue, silent and full of foreboding.

However, this was only a temporary state, for their intoxicated minds were soon lusting after blood, like spectators at the Colosseum in Rome years ago, cheering two gladiators before the fight.

A cry went out, 'Let the duel begin!' Soon tables and chairs were moved by darting waiters, who quickly cleared a space in the centre of the hall.

Leaving the belly dancer, the Count jumped off the table and strode over to the cavernous fireplace above which, attached to the wall, were two crossed swords. Reaching up, he released each one from its brackets, and then turned to face his guests.

Five yards from the double doors, inside the great hall, stood North, Octavia and, just behind them, Don Giovanni Fambino. His gun continued to cover North, who slowly walked to the now-cleared centre of the room. Two waiters stood guard in front of the doors, blocking any hope of escape.

For a moment, North found himself alone in the middle of the room, aware that every curious eye was upon him. Then the Count threw one of the sabres to North from about ten feet away. The move was quite unexpected, but drew murmurs of approval when North caught the handle with his right hand.

However, the Count remained unimpressed. 'Are you as proficient with the sabre as you are at pushing your nose into other people's business, Englishman?'

The Count's words were spat with complete contempt. His handsome face twisted into a hideous grin, his cruel eyes boring through North's face, trying to reach the Englishman's very soul with a feverish intensity of hate and rage. For the first time in his life, the Count had recognised a man he could never control or influence, and he found the experience unsettling in the extreme.

They were all there: the Sicilians, Italians, and South Americans, including several Panamanians led by Señor

Max Santiago – all very intoxicated, each with an equally drunk woman on their lap, several in various stages of undress.

The blonde-haired beauty sitting on Signor Martelli's lap had long since discarded her bra, leaving only large turquoise earrings and a matching necklace to decorate her upper half. Her waist was covered by the remains of a green dress that still made some pretence of covering the girl's well-proportioned pelvis. However, the green silk was torn in several places; perhaps it was her that had been screaming earlier.

Señor Max Santiago had a dark-haired girl straddling him so that her breasts were inches from his narrow and stoat-like face, her long legs firmly locked somewhere behind the chair.

The South Americans were equally busy. Certainly, Señor Sancho Largo from Colombia was enjoying the undivided attention of another dark-haired girl, whose enormous breasts seemed to be straining within the narrow confines of her black strapless dress. Another member of the Medellin Cartel had not one but two women, perched on either knee – one blonde, one dark. The combined weight apparently did little to dampen his enthusiasm for such close company.

For a handful of Count Fambino's guests, the celebrations were taking a heavy toll. Several of the South Americans and one of the Count's own cousins were now too drunk to partake in any further entertainment. Their heads were either extended back upon their chairs or resting comfortably upon the hard, wooden table in a semiconscious state of numbness.

General Kerenskiy was one of the few who remained in complete control of his faculties. His sleepless eyes were always alert, constantly feeding his over-active mind, whose whole function and purpose in life was to calculate and analyse other people's intentions.

North grasped the sabre and raised the point to the 'on guard' position. It felt cold in his right hand. In a moment, the steel would be the only contact between them. Their eyes locked only for a second, the Count's portraying jealousy and hate. North's were impossible to read; they gave nothing away.

A man before the gallows knows that death is certain, but he still hopes and prays that a last-minute reprieve will change his circumstances so that life may last a little longer.

Faith is irrational and defies logic, because it cannot be measured in terms of understanding. Faith alone ignites the torch of supreme endurance. Combined with the indomitable will to survive, it will challenge without hesitation all uncertainties and danger. For faith is built upon rock that cannot break or fragment. Holding onto this philosophy, North proceeded to focus his mind upon the duel ahead. It would not only dictate his fate but also that of Octavia's.

It was at that moment that Octavia cracked emotionally. She could not take this living nightmare any more. In trying to run, her ball gown caught, so that a stumbling gait was all she could manage.

Finally, she tripped and fell, landing at Roberto's feet. She barely noticed the physical blow; the far greater pain was in her heart. Sobbing, her whole body was engulfed by violent convulsions of fear and despair.

Roberto looked down with surprise at her prostrate form. Octavia looked up with a tear-stained face that pleaded with him to listen.

'Roberto, you must stop this insanity. Let him go, he has done you no harm. Don't kill him, please; you must let him go free. If you let him go, I will never leave you. You can do as you like with me, even marriage. I beseech you; I will love you always if only you will spare his life.'

The Count's eyes burned with cruelty, while his lips parted to form the grin of a possessed demon. 'Move out of my way and watch this lover of yours die before your eyes.' He laughed without pity at her pain and desperation.

Without waiting for a response, the Count sidestepped her prostrate form, still violently shaking, as one might a piece of dirt on the street.

Taking several paces, North reached one of the waiters. Changing the sword from one hand to the other, he took off his jacket and handed it to the waiter in preparation for the coming duel.

It was then that Octavia felt North very close. She had not heard him approach because her still-violent shaking and sobs of despair had dulled her senses. Yet she knew instinctively it was him.

The first tangible proof of her intuition was an arm across her shaking shoulders. Then, with firm gentle strokes, his left hand wiped her tears away, his fingers warm and reassuring. Through eyes filled with more tears, Octavia looked up into Sebastian's face, still the face of a stranger and yet somehow so familiar. His eyes illuminated a hope that she desperately wanted to believe in, to be consumed by his electricity now dancing before her.

Octavia's previous life had been a phantom of an existence, misshapen and crippled by illusions of past love that always cracked and fragmented under the inevitable hammer of truth.

'Octavia…' His voice was barely a whisper. No-one else could have heard, but its strength carried deep within her. 'Have faith. You must hold the dream, no matter how desperate and impossible the struggle.'

Octavia's eyes, those big sensitive pools of desire and emotion, welled up with still more tears that cascaded endlessly down her cheeks. This time, North found he could not stem the flow. They were like a river after a huge flood, running with complete abandon towards the sea of no tomorrow.

'Sebastian, I love you. I love you so much I ache with the pain…'

It was pure relief to say the words, and an enormous, invisible weight was lifted from deep within her soul. Suddenly Octavia could breathe again, like someone who has held their breath until their lungs would burst with the pain. She felt a strange completeness that was quite illogical under the circumstances.

'Don't you understand?' she continued in a hoarse whisper. 'The Count will kill you, and if you die, I can't continue this life any more.' Her eyes pleaded with him to understand.

'Give Roberto the transcribed inscription; at least you will be alive,' she urged. 'I wasted everything before meeting you. If you die, my heart will break and shatter forever. There will be no meaning or purpose, only a chasm devoid of life. I can't take it any more, please, please understand.'

Octavia waited for his reply, for him to say something, anything… Anything that would send her relief.

'Giving Roberto the transcribed inscription will be no use now,' said Sebastian. 'He is set on vengeance too deep to retreat from. If he did not know of our love before, he is in no doubt now. The duel cannot be changed, or the challenge withdrawn; the scene must be fought to its end, whatever the outcome.'

Octavia felt the strength of his arms as Sebastian lifted her slowly to her feet. His muscles bulging with the strain as she was limp like a puppet whose strings no longer work.

'Octavia...' She was moved by the way he said her name, so deep snd soft. Her near hysteria responded to the calm of his voice. '... You must let your uncertainties go, for faith alone shall ensure your future, you have to believe this'

The Englishman leant forward to kiss her on the mouth. His words echoed through her mind, giving her strength. His kiss was the electricity of life itself. The flame of her soul leapt as if by magic, its fires now burning with defiance against the unknown void that was her only path.

North kissed Octavia on the mouth a second time, and her eyes met his for an instant. At this point, fixed in time, the world ceased to exist. Octavia felt deeper and more complete than anything she had yet experienced.

This man's magnetic attraction pulsated through her nervous system, and the surge of high voltage was hope regained. Her mind ceased for a moment to build phantoms of fear. Again, Octavia let his electricity wash through her, bathing her every fibre so that she felt part of him.

Octavia watched the two men face each other, the Count with the reckless arrogant grin of one who is certain of his triumph. The Englishman at first glance showed little emotion, but upon a second look Octavia thought she perceived a slight smile upon the corners of his mouth. Or was it her imagination?

Then he looked straight at her. She knew then it wasn't an illusion but very real, the secret smile that is only exchanged between lovers...

Chapter Ten

The sound of two sabres striking pierced the silence; and also fractured like cracked glass Octavia's hope of seeing Sebastian alive for much longer.

Embraced in a dance with death were two men. One represented previous excitement and passion. The other something inexplicably different: sexual desire, yes; but there was more, far more – a kind of raw power that kindled emotions of a deeper fire. If the Count died and North lived, there was hope, but this Octavia knew was impossible. North would die, leaving the Count triumphant. She shook with the anticipated consequences.

The conclusion was certain; the die was heavily loaded against the Englishman. When it finally ceased to roll, she knew its reading would announce only her loss.

Concentration was complete, with necks straining and eyes riveted upon the unfolding engagement. First this way, then that, the two men would move, each trying to gain an advantage. The spectators began to spread out towards the walls of the great hall, for the duel was beginning to take up an increasing amount of space.

It began to emerge at an early stage of the duel that the outcome was not going to be as certain as everyone had first imagined. True, the Count seemed to have the upper hand with skilful footwork and proficient reflexes. With every minute, each attack became more sophisticated and cunning than the previous. However, something strange was happening. Octavia felt sure that North was improving, like someone out of practice but quickly regaining a former skill.

The Englishman began to emerge, not as the Count's cornered animal to be played with as he chose, with death the prize, but as the Count's worthy adversary. *How was this possible? Where had the Englishman learnt his skill? The tactical insight, the excellent sense of timing, such confidence that seemed to grow by the moment?*

Octavia was not the only one surprised; indeed, the entire audience was becoming breathless with anticipation as to the Count's now increasingly uncertain future. With every second the duel continued, it became more and more difficult to predict a clear winner. The evenness of the two combatants was starting to resemble a set of finely balanced scales. The attacks were pressed home with greater enthusiasm, the parrying became fiercer, the ripostes near-blurs of motion.

Steel flashed in the dim light.

A woman screamed, then another. It must have been the Count's sword, for the Englishman's shirt had a long cut from the left shoulder down the arm to just below the elbow. The white cotton absorbed the increasing spread of crimson like blotting paper.

Then it was the Count's turn to experience the sabre's razor edge. The Englishman had noticed that his opponent had left his right forearm exposed on several occasions. Scoring the first hit in front of those he most wanted to impress filled his disdainful mind with self-importance and a little too much confidence. The Count was a man who had the necessary skill and experience to win this duel of death. However, he had exercised and practised little of this ancient art in recent months.

Arrogance told him that his natural inherited ability as a swordsman, now driven by vengeance to kill this foreigner, gave him more than enough reason to win. Justification for death was absolute. This Englishman had tried to take his former fiancée after she had started to show a desired interest to return. True, he had brought Octavia to Castle Zehra against her will, but he, the most eligible bachelor in Europe could never accept defeat easily.

With a flick of the wrist, North cut across the Count's exposed right forearm. It must have been deep, cutting nerve and disabling tendons, for the Count's game from that point on became flawed and transparent.

The audience let out a gasp of amazement. Their concentration was greater than the customers in an Italian café equipped with a television during the World Cup soccer final, with Italy the favourites to win. How could this be? How could the famous Count Roberto Fambino take such insult from this stranger?

The most surprised person of all was the Count himself. He had been certain of an easy victory. Defeat was a conclusion that did not need thinking about. He also became curious as to how the Englishman had acquired such skill without becoming noticed by the international fencing community.

Then slow realisation dawned like a terrible pain. The answer he suspected before now became a certainty; this jigsaw of a mystery was becoming clearer.

Five years ago, the world fencing championships had been held at Würzburg Castle, where Luther many years before had worked on the German Bible. At the last minute, the world number three had pulled out. The official reason was 'personal grounds'. To the international fencing community, it had been a great disappointment, for this particular duellist had been fencing so well that he was favourite to win against Francisco Rodrigo, the Spanish World Champion at the time.

The duel that did take place was between Francisco Rodrigo and the then world number two, a Sicilian aristocrat by the name of Count Roberto Fambino. The resultant contest was ranked as being amongst the most exciting world champion duels ever recorded between two fencing masters. In the end, Count Roberto Fambino had won with a hit delivered by a well-executed fleche attack. The Spaniard should have won, for he was the more experienced swordsman of the two, but on the day he had to bow to the Count's superior game.

The strange thing was that no-one knew who the world's number three really was, for the mysterious man never took his mask off in public. His real face was never seen, thus concealing his identity.

He was known as the 'Indigo Fencer', because a long scarf of indigo silk would be wound round his neck. After he won a duel, which was most of the time, the stranger would untie and then throw the silk scarf to whichever girl in the audience had caught his eye. This ritual had developed into quite a tradition, so that the girl who caught the scarf would be hounded by the media as to who she thought the identity of the 'Indigo Fencer' really was.

Rumours abounded as to the reasons for this inexplicable show of creating such mystery. They ranged from the cynics who said he must have had a disfiguring accident, to the romantics who thought only of a handsome, wealthy aristocrat.

He was only recognised by his game, fencing with a style that was both distinctive and unique. The flowing movements with well-coordinated attacks combined with just enough flair to ensure a dull contest impossible.

The Germans all thought this 'Indigo Fencer' must have been a member of their elitist student fraternity, the *Burschenschaften*, and therefore German. Out of the top one hundred world-class fencers, seventy were German, thus demonstrating the popularity of the Burschenschaften – a fraternity founded as student resistance to Napoleonic rule in the early 1800s. However, proof remained elusive in spite of exhaustive enquiries to expose the identity of the 'Indigo Fencer'. In the end, all leads produced little of consequence.

Count Fambino's composure slipped for only a moment with the pain of understanding. He was finally able to find answers to previous incomprehensible and troublesome problems. This foreign mischief-maker had suddenly transformed himself from an unwelcome guest to a very lethal threat. This was the stranger who had caused so much havoc and mayhem in France, Sicily, and now Sardinia. He was without doubt the mysterious indigo fencer.

'So, Englishman, you have decided to show your face at last. Your skill and style as a swordsman are distinctive; you give yourself away. Mask and mystery no longer hide the face the world craves to see.' The Count paused in his revelations, like someone purposely and maliciously exposing a conjurer at a children's party. 'I see no disfigurement, so who are you, Englishman? A misguided noble or a skilful peasant?'

'Under the present circumstance I believe it is of little consequence to you, my dear Count. What is more to the point is that your skill with a sword seems to be rather rusty. I fail to see as to how this affects the situation.'

'It doesn't but you could have explained yourself a little more fully. Such information as to who you work for and for what purpose would have been helpful. Instead, you resort to insults. Perhaps you have overstayed your welcome in Sardinia, Englishman.'

'In that case, Count, you will have to go unsatisfied a while longer.'

The duel continued at ferocious speed and momentum. Up and down the great hall both men fought for advantage in position. Through constant probing they sought to discover any sign of weakness that could be exploited into a successful hit.

A stage was reached when North, in spite of his opponents forearm cut, became increasingly hard-pressed after a series of shrewdly planned attacks by the Count. At this point, North had to think of something, whatever the risk, to turn the tables in his favour.

Once again North found himself retreating, then twisting like a corkscrew. He partially turned to leap four feet into the air, his left hand outstretched to grasp the wrought iron of the large chandelier above.

The move was not anticipated by the Count and his attack fell short and wide, with his sword cutting nothing thicker than air. In a smooth, powerful movement, North straightened his legs, previously crouched from the leap, so that his feet caught the Count in the face. The impact sent the Count sprawling backwards, his sword clattering across the floor.

North seized his chance. Dropping from the swinging chandelier, he leaped upon the Count who, in spite of his bleeding face, was struggling to stand up. North's sword point connected with skin just under the Count's chin. Now it was the Count who was experiencing the same uncomfortable position he had engineered earlier for Comrade Vasile.

The atmosphere was electric. No-one had expected this turn of events, and the stage was now set for the finale. Through broken teeth and bruised lips, the Count talked with threats, Sicilian pride defiant to the end.

'If you run me through, Englishman, you will never leave this room alive. My death will only serve to hasten your own. Kill me and you sign your own death warrant.'

North laughed. 'What sort of crazy logic is this? You will be telling me next that if I spare your life, I will be free to leave when I want, even take the girl with me! Somehow, my dear Count, I believe you stretch what is reasonable to beyond the realms of fantasy.'

'Where is the diamond, Englishman? Where is the blue fire known as the *Darya-i-Nur*? What secrets did you learn? Where is this mother of all diamonds hidden? Give me the plans of its concealed retreat and you may yet live.'

The Count spoke with difficulty, his face starting to swell, making speech painful and distorted. 'You cheated by using the chandelier, Englishman. A great pity, for now we will never know who was the finer swordsman.'

'My dear Count, some questions in life will always remain unanswered and I believe this will be one of them. Your game, Count, was good, very good. In fact, too good for me to try to live on the difference.'

Suddenly a dagger appeared in the Count's left hand. He must have had it concealed, anticipating just such a moment.

Octavia screamed with a breath of wind that exploded with fear.

The dagger flashed in the flickering light and the Count seemed to emerge from the floor, twisting like a half-dead snake miraculously experiencing a new lease of life.

The Count's left arm shot up to reach North's chest, a near lethal thrust for the Englishman, until fate played its unexpected hand. The still-swinging chandelier was dripping hot wax from its dozens of candles; one such piece, with the consistency of oil, fell on the Count's face, spoiling his aim at the crucial moment.

Before realising the Count had missed his target, North thrust his sword tip through the Count's throat. Blood spurted and gurgled, then ever-increasing pools formed rapidly behind his head. Still conscious, and breathing rapidly with fits of coughing that sent blood splattering deep red over North's legs, the Count then fixed North with what would become a staring death mask of arrogance and defiance to the end.

North turned to shout to Octavia. 'The door!'

Octavia galvanised her previously sleeping limbs and they both ran towards the double doors, still guarded by two waiters. Their approach and intended escape was blocked by one producing a long knife, the other a flaming torch which he detached from the wall.

Holding it before him, the impassive face behind the yellow flame spoke only of savagery, with murder mirrored in lifeless black eyes.

North moved with speed and uncompromising ruthlessness once he was within range of initiating his attack. He slashed across the man's unguarded hand and the torch fell in a smouldering mass of flame and ash; several sparks thrown up in the process burnt through North's shirt. The second cut flayed open the man's face in a five-inch line from the left eye to the chin. The man's hands flew up to hold his haemorrhaging cheek; blood ran in rivers through clenched fingers.

The second waiter launched his attack with the machete, using much bravery and courage, but his action was coarse and he relied on brute force alone. The cut to North's head lacked refinement and practical skill. The heavy machete proved much too heavy to be used as a duelling weapon.

North successfully protected his head with his sword lying horizontally. However, he forgot to take into account that his opponent was using something far heavier than a duelling sabre, and North's blade broke clean in two. Leaning back at the last moment, he just avoided his head following the fate of his sword.

Surprised and pleased with his new-found skill and success at cutting North's sword, the waiter left himself unguarded.

North's sabre was now two-thirds its normal length and, without wasting time, he lunged far forward to strike the man's torso, between his fifth and sixth ribs. The waiter fell forward, dropping the machete in the process, so that the sabre shaft was driven deeper through the left lung. The waiter slumped forward completely, forcing his entire weight upon the weapon, so that its broken shaft emerged from his back. North gave up any hope of recovering his weapon.

For the second time that evening, this band of cut-throats and master criminals were shocked and startled at another new and unexpected turn of events. Women screamed hysterically, the men either stood immobilised and numb or yelled for pursuit and revenge.

North thought his life was now worth less than at any time he could remember.

The double doors yielded to his urgent pressure and Octavia followed him to the other side. Once the doors closed behind them, North ran two heavy steel bolts home, effectively blocking pursuit, at least by that route. However, he knew this was not the only exit from the Great Hall.

North's victory sent ecstatic relief cascading through Octavia's previously uncontrolled and penetrating fear. She knew then just how much in love with the Englishman she was, and that he was none other than the mysterious 'Indigo Fencer'.

Strangely, she felt little for her former fiancé, now dying only a few feet away. The grandiose and lavish life she had once desired and craved in Roberto was finally exposed as empty and devoid of substance.

Beyond the door, the Englishman's blood was being demanded. Giovanni Fambino's voice could be heard above the others, furious but controlled and unquestionably in charge.

'The radio, where is it?' shouted North.

Octavia's eyes still spoke of uncertainty and fear, but she managed to gather herself enough to answer the question.

'In the basement of the tower,' replied Octavia.

'Find it now before they find us.'

With her knowledge of the castle, Octavia led the way through a labyrinth of rooms and passageways, many with little or no light.

Deep down in the bowels of the castle, under the foundations of the tower, was the radio room, secure from outside assault. From here, when visiting Castle Zehra, the mafia hierarchy could maintain their many worldwide contacts without interruption.

The remoteness from the rest of the castle suggested this was where in times past prisoners were kept – the original dungeons. And this was confirmed when Octavia pointed out ancient iron rings placed at intervals along the walls in some of the alcoves they passed.

The room that contained the radio served as a communication centre of some magnitude; it also acted as some sort of storeroom with boxes and packing cases piled high all over the place. The radio itself was a very modern piece of high-tech equipment located against one wall, with a chair for the operator. The room showed little sign of human life except for a crowded ashtray.

North put on headphones, then, with the microphone in his left hand, pushed buttons and turned knobs with his right. He spoke a series of short sentences in what must be some sort of code, as Octavia understood none of it.

For the next ninety seconds, North listened intently, then finished by throwing the headphones onto the table. His face remained expressionless throughout. He stood up, walked over to a pile of packing cases then broke one open. Inside he found small plastic bags, containing sugar-like white crystals. North did not have to open them to know it wasn't sugar.

After a three-minute search, North found several bottles of whisky. Opening one, he poured nearly all of its contents over some of the equipment and wooden cases. The last drop he saved for himself, its familiar flavour a welcome relief for his dry mouth. Striking a match, he flicked it at the wooden cases and immediately blue and yellow flames leapt up to produce dense black smoke.

North grabbed Octavia's hand and together they ran back down the passageway to a junction, where they took a different turn from their previous route. Octavia led the way through a series of corridors that would be a complete maze to those unfamiliar with its extensive layout.

She could not help but think of her second middle name 'Ariadne' – The Way of the Labyrinth. According to legend, she showed the hero Theseus, by way of a silver thread, an escape route through the labyrinth to freedom after he had slain the Minotaur. Was Octavia now like a page torn from the ancient world, involved in some sort of strange re-enactment of mythology?

Octavia reflected on their progress. They were not out of the labyrinth yet and this particular maze was anything but straightforward.

Suddenly one of the passageways abruptly opened up into a large room. From the opposite side of the room, through a second entrance, a lot of noise could be heard. Men were talking in a strange language with intermittent groans, and every now and then a scraping noise could be heard as if a very heavy object was being moved.

A few seconds later, the source of the noise could be identified.

Two men emerged from the second entrance into the room. General Kerenskiy and another man carried something very heavy; indeed, their backs hunched with the strain.

With Octavia holding the torch they had brought with them to illuminate their passage, North was upon General Kerenskiy before the others had time to react. In the confusion, Kerenskiy dropped whatever he was carrying, which landed on one of his feet. A loud yell told those present that its weight was indeed considerable.

The struggle was brief, aided in no small part by General Kerenskiy's injured foot. North managed to relieve Kerenskiy of his gun, located in an inside pocket of his jacket. Stepping back with the weapon, he covered both men.

General Kerenskiy's accomplice was unable to offer any resistance, his stance suggested his back was at the point of being inadequate to support his frame any more.

By dropping the load, the other man's back must have jolted so violently that it had totally seized up, to produce a stance of almost comical appearance. Then a sudden sharp spasm of pain evidently proved too much and, with a cry, he collapsed in a heap of writhing agony. Perhaps he was now experiencing the initial stages of a collapsed disc. With little doubt, Kerenskiy's friend would be experiencing a painful future.

'Well, well, if it isn't General Kerenskiy, the Russian who is Head of the Romanian Foreign Intelligence Service. We meet at last. It couldn't be anyone else talking Romanian. Not a common language in Sardinia, I am sure you would agree?

'What could your purpose be at this time of night, here in the foundations of Castle Zehra? I bet it's not of a noble design.' The box lying at General Kerenskiy's feet was made of wood, with heavy ornate metal clasps.

'What's in the box, General Kerenskiy?'

'Ah, you must be Mr North. We don't encounter many Englishmen in Sardinia either.' General Kerenskiy had recovered from the interruption and was approaching his normal smooth and controlled self.

'Well, I didn't know that you Balkans had a sense of humour,' said North.

'Where is the Count? How did you escape from the hall? How did you evade your death?'

'Ah yes, well it's like this,' replied North. 'The Count is no longer with us.' He paused, studying General Kerenskiy's reaction to the news.

'Dead?' Said General Kerenskiy, incredulously.

'Well, if not in hell yet, certainly on his way. And hell is no doubt where you will eventually end up too General Kerenskiy, given the death rate under the communist regime of Romania, that you have had such a dark hand in.

'So how did the Count die? He was perfectly healthy the last time I saw him. In fact, you were about to suffer the consequences of the Count's sword.'

'It seems, General Kerenskiy, you left a little early. Your greed persuaded you that the duel's end was a foregone conclusion – a rash decision, as it turns out.'

'You out-fenced the Count?' General Kerenskiy was still finding it difficult to fully comprehend this incredible piece of information.

'He was a fine swordsman, one of the best,' North acknowledged.

'You saw this, Contessa?' asked General Kerenskiy, acknowledging Octavia's presence for the first time.

'Yes, it's true, the Count is dead,' reassured Octavia, '...but not the finest swordsman, as it turns out.' There were a few more moments of silence as General Kerenskiy digested this now obvious fact.

'Now, General Kerenskiy, to more pressing issues. The contents of this box? It can't possibly belong to you.'

'The Sultan's treasure, or at least what's left out of the original seven chests. There is only one now.'

'How did you find it? Where was it?'

'For that, I must thank you, Englishman. Countess Octavia held your jacket carelessly over her arm. From an inside pocket, a piece of paper protruded. Her attention was naturally, like everyone else's, focused on the duel. She did not see my hand extract the paper. You also left your gun within an inside pocket – very careless, I may add, but then you really had little chance to use it.

'With Alexandrov's help,' he gestured to the prostrate figure on the ground beside him, 'and your clear instructions, we had little problem in finding this box.

'We had to remove several stone blocks with a pickaxe from under a flagstone not too far from here. Only a ten-minute job, which was surprising after eight hundred odd years. The exact directions outlined in your paper made it easy.'

He continued, 'Your information source is very good. Am I right in assuming the directions came from the Countess's ring?'

'Absolutely correct,' replied North. 'What did the Ceauşescus want with the treasure?'

'Elena Ceauşescu had some crazy idea of becoming Queen, and her husband King, of Romania, hence the need for crown jewels.

'Hearing of the legend, she sent her husband's nephew, Comrade Vasile, to investigate. First, to establish the authenticity; and if confirmed, then to locate its whereabouts. You are no doubt aware he became a little sidetracked.'

'Yes, I was also witness to Comrade Vasile's end by the hand of the Count.'

'It's rather irrelevant now, but I wonder how much you were intending to inform the Count of your successful treasure hunt?' General Kerenskiy was less than enthusiastic with this line of questioning. So, he tried a new subject.

'Englishman, do you know of the *Belle of the Wind* and its cargo? For I am sure we could do a little business that would be to our mutual benefit.'

General Kerenskiy talked about his offer with a fever borne of desperation; he sensed his possession of the chest fast becoming doubtful. For the first time in his life, he was unsure of his immediate future. For a man wed to certainties, this was unsettling.

North refused Kerenskiy's offer, so Kerenskiy made a last desperate attempt to live. He lunged at North, hands outstretched, reaching for his neck, strangulation the obvious intention. The Russian was a big man, powerful and heavy set, and it was easy to imagine previous victims succumbing to his strength.

However, North moved faster, side-stepping to the right, and fired twice, each bullet hitting chest height. With a scream, General Kerenskiy staggered back, both hands desperately clutching his chest. He hit the ground, his head contacting the rock wall on the way down. Bending over him, North observed complete absence of movement. His pulse quickly diminished to nothing.

North and Octavia should have then resumed running down the passage and made good their escape, but caution was thrown to the wind by the possible fortune at their feet. Their curiosity worked like a narcotic by igniting their interest to discover the contents of this ancient chest.

The lock had already been forced; General Kerenskiy had also been eager to learn of its contents. The chest was two feet wide, three long, and one and a half deep, made of wood with finely worked metal reinforced throughout. The hinges looked stout and substantial for supporting such a heavy lid.

Octavia held the torch closer for a clearer view of what lay inside.

Time stood still. North heard the girl breathing heavily with excitement that matched his own.

He lifted the lid with difficulty, for it was both stiff and heavy. Octavia brought the flickering torch even closer, focusing its light upon the now open box.

A thousand or more precious and semi-precious stones refracted the light spectrum in an explosion of splendid colours, brilliant in its intensity and peerless in quality.

The faces of the two that held this unprecedented spectacle adopted a fluorescent glow in the backwash of light. Pushing his hands deep within the chest, North discovered hidden treasures beyond the reality of his imagination.

Octavia secured the torch to help him. Her long fingers lifted to the surface objects hidden in pieces of ancient cloth, linen and fine cotton decorated with extensive embroidery.

Jewel encrusted necklaces, solid gold bracelet pendants, some used for earrings, others perhaps amulets made from amethyst and lapis. Full body girdles worked with precious stones and alloys such as electrum in the shape of animals were found, others in deified human form. This suggested an origin of some pieces older than the 8th century, for the Prophet Mohammed discouraged images of the human form to avoid deification.

Turquoise, ebony, and gold abounded in intricate patterns – some bold, others delicate in structure. All beautiful and glorious as only a sophisticated and advanced civilisation could produce.

Suddenly Octavia held up two earrings to examine their design more clearly.

Heavy gold, fashioned in the shape of a cobra's head, the eyes ebony, the loop of the snake's body alternated with gold and turquoise. The loop was not quite round, so that the cobra's head would always face forward, to protect the wearer from evil.

Like a wind that was both from deep within her and far away at the same instant, Octavia was possessed with a desire to wear these earrings. An ancient and tangible bridge with the past.

Octavia threw off her modern imitations. She held the ancient gold with dexterous fingers, working the delicate golden pins with ease. Their mechanism functioned as perfectly as the day they were made.

Once in place, she asked North how she looked. Her face in the light radiated liquid gold.

'Divine, positively divine. No lady throughout history wore them with as much distinction as you.'

There was a pause as they savoured the moment. 'You had better replace them; you don't want to lose them.'

She laughed, then reluctantly removed the two precious pieces of history.

Upon a last sweep of the chest, North found a hard object much larger than any previously encountered. The hard object was contained in some sort of blue velvet. It was tied by a single golden thread. Untying it, he turned the sack upside down so its contents fell out into his palm.

Chapter Eleven

Octavia gasped in awe as the diamond before them – a huge, uncut blue stone – glowed with an intense wild fire. North handed it to her and she held it closer; its very heart seemed to burn with a penetrating translucent blue flame.

A rare piece of carbon crystal, forged by the limitless hand of nature millions of years before mortal man discovered the wheel, thought North, unable to take his eyes from the rock crystal. It was the hardest and most durable substance known to man. Capable of resisting the strongest steel, yet composed of the common element carbon. Its very name derived from the Greek Adamas, meaning unconquerable or invincible.

Throughout history, the diamond has been sought after for wealth and power. It has for thousands of years been exchanged between lovers as a symbol of devotion. Its possession drives the king and gypsy alike; there is no other substance known to man that means so much. The *Darya-i-Nur* was, without doubt, one of the largest diamonds ever discovered by man.

Without saying a word, Octavia's eyes met North's, and she knew he also felt the hypnotic effect of the stone's spell.

He also knew they had already spent far too long there. With great effort, Octavia reluctantly handed him back the huge stone. Slowly, he put it back into its velvet sack, and then concealed it deep within an inside pocket.

To carry the chest was out of the question. It was too heavy, and their progress, even if he and Octavia could lift it, would be suicidally slow. Octavia's dress contained no pockets of any description, so they each stuffed as many diamonds and other precious stones into North's jacket pockets, including the earrings Octavia had tried on. They left rich beyond dreams, but with their future more uncertain than ever before.

Octavia gave directions as they ran, while North held General Kerenskiy's gun. It took them many minutes and they got lost twice before they found a passageway that Octavia recognised. It sloped gently up, to end with a closed door.

The door was unlocked, North opened it cautiously to find an unlit part of the courtyard. He hesitated, making sure they were unobserved.

'The stables, where are they?' he asked. They would have more chance with horses to cover the ground across the large courtyard, pass through the gatehouse, and to the open ground beyond.

Staying close to the courtyard wall for forty yards, they turned a corner to find the stables. They were unattended. Selecting two horses, they saddled them, taking several more valuable minutes as they were hampered by not daring to turn on a light in the darkness.

That was the easy part. Now they had to cross the courtyard to the gatehouse and portcullis, which thankfully was still raised.

Riding in her ball gown was out of the question, quickly Octavia took off the cumbersome material. She found a pair of riding boots several sizes too big and, hanging up, a bolero.

As they each mounted their magnificent animals, North could not help admiring the Count's equestrian eye.

These Arabian pure-breds, he recalled learning from an Arab friend of his who raced horses in Syria and Northern Arabia, were referred to as the 'asl' or 'known race'. They were the aristocrats of horses, combining a rare balance of intelligence, good form, and of course, legendary speed.

They made their way across the courtyard, the horses' shoes making a little noise upon the cobblestones.

'You can ride?' North asked, knowing that if they made it out of the castle, they faced a hard ride beyond.

Octavia's eyes flashed with Sicilian fire, her voice full of pride, perhaps a hint of aristocratic defiance, even arrogance. For a moment she lost all concern and previous anxiety for danger.

'Since the day I was born. I ride like the Levante wind: strong, hot, and with gathering strength.'

Her smile broke the tension. But it was short-lived, as someone started shooting. A bullet ricocheted upon the cobblestones of the courtyard, its echo loud against so much surrounding stonework. Before its sound had died, a second and third followed. This time, the range was wide. Perhaps the first shot had been lucky; it was impossible to tell.

Disaster struck. The portcullis dropped with a clanking of chains, cutting off their escape route. The mechanism must be operated from one of the two towers that made up the gatehouse.

North jumped off his horse, handed the reins to Octavia, then sprinted eighty yards to the gatehouse. He made for the left tower, where a light showing from a half-open door suggested that the controls for lifting the portcullis might be located.

Beyond the door, North was confronted by steep stairs that led up to a wooden trap door in the floor of the room above. This room was small, its function to house huge cog wheels linked by lengths of chain, with a system of gears – the controlling mechanism for the portcullis.

A man, his back to North's slowly emerging shape, was crouched over several levers. He seemed preoccupied with the controlling mechanism and North's presence behind him must have been the last thing on his mind.

However, a sixth sense must have suddenly made the man turn round to find North just eight feet away. In other circumstances, the man's face would have been comical, such was his expression of surprise.

With a wrench in one hand, the man made a leap for North. So quick was his action that he succeeded in knocking the gun out of North's hand. North cursed himself: first, for not anticipating the move, and secondly for being too slow.

He grabbed the man's right arm, which held the wrench. Failure to immediately restrain this arm communicated lurid images of his skull turning into a mixture of blood and bone meal.

The two men struggled for a time in the confined space above the portcullis. The struggle continued after North managed to disarm his opponent of the wrench with various headlocks, attempts at strangulation, and blows using fists, when space and time allowed.

For a time, it looked as if North was going to succumb to the other man's superior strength. However, through the unexpected use of a feint, North managed to deliver a blow of sufficient strength to topple his adversary. The man fell so that his right foot became entangled in part of the lifting machinery.

It took several minutes for North to work out how the controls functioned. An electric motor provided the power for lifting the heavy portcullis, but the motor would not work. No matter what switches he touched or what sequence he pressed them, it refused to function.

There was no time to find out what the problem was, so North started to lift the portcullis by hand. This involved pulling a lever back and forth, both time consuming and hard work.

But there was another benefit of this action. His recent opponent's right ankle rose as a result of the moving pulleys and chains, so that he became suspended by his leg. His position was such that freeing himself would not come easily. Through a window, North could see his progress as the portcullis slowly moved up to disappear into an aperture above.

With a kick from her heels, Octavia's horse shot forward even before the gate had been fully raised; its steel points passed inches from her lowered head.

More shots rang out, again impossible to tell their source, but so far relatively inaccurate as Octavia and her horse passed untouched. There was no other exit from the tower to the outside, North had to return the way he had entered.

His escape involved exiting the gatehouse, mounting his horse, traversing part of the tower's huge circumference – say twenty yards – then passing the fifteen yards through the gatehouse and under the raised portcullis. Exposed ground lay between the two outer-walled defences. There, no portcullis or gate threatened their passage.

North descended the stairs to ground level. Opening the door, he stepped out into the courtyard, hesitating, his senses strained, judging the hostile atmosphere.

The gunmen were strangely silent. The hue and cry had momentarily fallen silent. Perhaps the Sultan's chest had been discovered, creating a diversion of interest. North could picture them all fighting over its contents.

With a leap, he mounted the patiently waiting horse. A tug at the reins and slight pressure with his heels brought an instant response. Only twenty yards to the gatehouse, but it was unexpectedly going to be made much more difficult. A clanking of chain sounded, heralding the lowering of the portcullis – again!

What had gone wrong? Either he had not secured the locking mechanism properly, or the man left inside had managed to free himself, enabling him to release the lock.

Whatever the cause, the result was going to be the same problem in the end: a prisoner in Castle Zehra with a very short future. North raced for the decreasing aperture of space between the unyielding steel points and hard cobblestone. The great horse was gathering speed all the time, its powerful body beneath him eager to obey his command. It too must have seen the lowering portcullis but was unswayed in direction or speed.

The first explosion was deep within the castle – a low rumble, felt as much as heard. Within seconds, a second and third explosion followed, much louder. Bits of masonry started falling all over the courtyard, smoke appeared in thick, dense pockets, the smell of burning was strong, almost nauseating.

The explosions – no doubt a result of him setting fire to the radio room – would act as a welcome diversion for his escape from Castle Zehra.

Single rifle shots rang out with increasing frequency, and an automatic joined in, but whoever controlled the shooting was not firing at North. With all these explosions, it must look as if the entire castle was under attack.

North knew he was not going to make it. At his present rate of progress, it was simply a question of speed.

There were only three variables in the equation of reaching the other side of the descending portcullis. The speed of the gate's descent, the acceleration of his horse, and his height.

He could do little about the gate's rate of descent and the horse's acceleration, for the animal was doing its utmost. That left his height.

Taking his left foot out of the stirrup, he leant far over to the right, holding on as he did to the saddle with both hands. With his reduced height, it was still going to be close, but possible. The gate loomed closer, the noise of the chain now very loud as it echoed from the surrounding stonework.

The steel points were now only feet away. North was leaning so far over to his right that he was in real danger of losing his grip. The cobblestones were now a blur, barely three feet from his face.

If the portcullis hit the horse, it was dead, pinned under its lethal points. He might then have a chance, scraping beneath the gap produced by the dead animal.

The gate continued its relentless descent, the horse's head cleared first, its speed still increasing, but there was not enough time for the back and hind quarters. With a sudden pull on the right rein, the responsive animal jerked its right flank, the steel points grazing the horse just behind the saddle. The wounded animal let out a cry but incredibly continued its former speed and direction.

The two outer walls had gatehouses, which were much less substantial and, as it turned out, unguarded. North passed under their arches unchallenged.

Once he was through the last arch of the outer defence wall, he turned sharp left, following a rough path to a small plateau upon which several helicopters were neatly parked.

After dismounting, he ran to a large shed off to one side. The door was not locked and no-one seemed to be around. Inside were various sophisticated-looking pieces of equipment, probably for the purpose of repairing helicopters.

Selecting an axe, North used it to puncture a hole in the first helicopter's fuel tank. This he repeated with all the other helicopters, except the fourth. No matter how hard he tried, it proved impossible to penetrate. Perhaps it had some kind of reinforced protection common in military aircraft. So, he opted to smash the fuses surrounding the cockpit. With a bit of luck, it would go up with the others in sympathy.

North ignited one of the aviation fuel pools that had formed and spread over an increasing area. The effect was instantaneous and spectacular, the heat intense.

The fuel tanks went up in deafening explosions that lit up the surrounding area for many miles around. North ran back to his patient horse, remarkably untroubled by the noise and heat. *Very well trained,* thought North, because all animals are naturally afraid of fire.

With the horse at full gallop, North concentrated on putting as much distance as possible between him and the firework display.

He found Octavia waiting as planned, three miles from Castle Zehra, behind an outcrop of rocks in a small valley. The Sicilian girl's hair was wild and full of spirit, blown by the speed of the ride. She cut a striking figure upon the Arabian horse.

Almost-knee-length riding boots contrasted with the skin of her legs. Black panties and a tan bolero partially covered the contour of her breasts; her profile was complete. She smiled upon seeing him, full of relief and remembered hope.

Their horses drew together from opposite directions, and North lent over to kiss her full on the lips without restriction or condition. To Octavia, the kiss was refreshing, even promising.

Dawn was fast approaching in the east and the sky had already begun to pale. The stars were fading; another day was being born. Below, the two riders rode with speed, their lives depending upon their horses.

They rode for nearly an hour, during which time the sun rose to a full orange orb, at last free of the horizon. Now there was no cover of darkness, except from the shadows left by the various rock formations they passed.

For the last half hour, the terrain had become increasingly rough, with no natural path. Octavia could not help wondering how North knew his way. Their speed had slowed to a walk several times in order to negotiate particularly steep and difficult tracks.

She wondered what their course was, what destination was North aiming for? His face seemed set and preoccupied, as if deep in thought.

She felt discouraged from questioning him, which was unlike her! Where was her famous Sicilian fiery and troublesome temperament? What invisible power did this stranger exercise over her? What did it mean? These questions again and again echoed through her mind.

Behind an outcrop of rock, North brought his horse to a stop, then dismounted. He motioned to Octavia to follow.

Leaving the horses, they walked on foot through a narrow gorge. Here, the sun could not reach, and Octavia felt the coolness after a hard ride. Suddenly the gorge opened up to reveal a flat piece of ground about a quarter of a mile in front of them. Beyond that was the grey concrete control tower of an air base.

The United States Air Force had built a base in Northern Sardinia soon after World War II. The base was small by the standards of other U.S.A.F. bases around the world, but size in this case had little to do with importance.

Sardinia's strategic influence was primarily due to its location, straddling the shipping and communication lines of the Western Mediterranean. Its other attractions included a remote and rocky interior, and a population that was to the point of being sparse, with miles of uninhabited coastline.

These qualities were precisely what attracted the U.S.A.F. An ideal location for conducting secret and clandestine activities in the Western Mediterranean. It was known as WM-3.

The Italian government, like the American, would only admit to the base's existence: 'a small NATO Communication Centre' was the only official piece of information that could be obtained.

Octavia could not believe her eyes. What was an air base doing here?

As if reading her mind, North said, 'There is no time to explain. Either you stay here and wait, or you come with me?'

Curiosity was burning, questions abounded, but finally she gave vent to her curiosity. Her Sicilian fire could not be muzzled any longer and the pair became involved in a very heated discussion. While it ran its course, Octavia admitted that her hot Sicilian blood knew little about control or compromise.

In the end, North had to give Octavia an ultimatum: she either settled down, or she would stay where she was until his return, which he could not guarantee.

Octavia was not used to being restrained by a man, any man, but she swallowed her pride and vanity to the point of adopting a stubborn silence, at least for now.

Trying to keep a low profile, they scrambled down a collection of loose rocks to level ground. Once reached, they sprinted to the perimeter fence.

A new sound could now be heard, far off but getting closer. North chose to ignore it, at least for the moment. In any case, there was little he could do about it.

With some difficulty and effort, Octavia managed to scramble under the fine meshed wire which she then held for North. Once inside, he told her to stay close to him.

North ran towards a line of military aircraft 150 yards away, Octavia kept close on his heels. There were sixteen planes in all, parked neatly in a long line. North slowed his pace after passing the first plane, but only after reaching the third did he resume a speed to something approaching a walk.

Finding a ladder, he lent it against the plane, positioned for access to the cockpit. Climbing with care, he came within reach of the clasps that secured the transparent canopy, and unfastened them.

North looked down to Octavia's waiting face below. 'Climb up, Octavia, we're going flying.'

'Where are we going? To my father? To the police? I notice from the plane's markings that this is an American base, why not tell everything to them?'

'You don't understand. They can't help. What I have to do involves taking this plane, with or without the American Air Force's cooperation. The State Department has been penetrated by a very high-level mole that has paralysed American foreign policy and compromised sensitive intelligence going in and out of the White House. The latest analysis involves the possibility of a second mole existing deep within the Pentagon, either independently or in tandem with the first.

'You have to realise that there are people out there that will stop at nothing to prevent me from taking this plane and doing what I have to do.

'Your father was well the last time I saw him, and the police are next to useless, as you mentioned before. Mafia informers are everywhere.'

Octavia's last grains of self-control vanished in an explosion of Sicilian anger and vexation. She screamed at the Englishman, her language deteriorating to new depths.

North stepped down from the ladder, then from behind grabbed hold of her hair as close to the roots as he could to ensure control. He brought her face within inches of his own, her arms fell limp to her sides. They had been in continuous motion lashing out, attempting to hurt him. In a vain attempt to understand, her accumulated frustration driven, by recent events including the death of her mother and kidnapping of her father led to Octavia's patience disintegrating.

'For once you have encountered a situation you can't influence as you would like. You must let go, there is no other path.'

'If you want to stay, please yourself, but I have more pressing things to attend to.'

Octavia fell silent, resenting North's words. She did manage to whisper, 'I want to come with you.'

'Fine, but at the moment, leave the decisions to me.'

The plane, a U.S.A.F. A-50, had space for two people sitting in tandem, the pilot and his navigator/observer, with dual controls. It was an updated version of the A-10 tank buster plane, deployed in West Germany to help blunt a possible Soviet-led armoured attack.

Octavia climbed into the navigator's position, directly behind the pilot. A helmet had been conveniently left on the seat. *Was this such a surprise flight, after all?* North told her to put it on and, after seeing that she was secure, put his own helmet on and settled into the pilot's position. Then he slid the transparent cover forward.

North started the engines and their high-pitched whine rose to an almost deafening pitch, breaking the silence of the morning air.

The instrumentation came to life with a fluorescent glow. Opening the throttles further, the aircraft slowly moved forward. Once clear of the other planes in the line, North kicked the rudder and the plane turned out of its neat row, then taxied to the runway.

Octavia could make out several figures at the base of the control tower, pointing and gesticulating with their arms. This was not going to be a scheduled flight, judging by their excited behaviour.

North's eyes scanned the instruments, and he gave a pre-flight check of no more than five seconds – oil pressure, rpms, ammeter, etc. All was as it should be. The radio was off; he did not feel like talking to the control tower, the response would be all too predictable.

North saw the jeep first, at the perimeter fence. Someone was standing up, firing a machine gun. This was the noise they had heard earlier, the far-off noise of an engine in low gear, negotiating difficult terrain.

At last, the plane reached the runway and North turned the aircraft so that its nose pointed directly down the centre of the concrete. He pushed the throttle forward for maximum power, the jets screamed louder as the plane slowly gathered speed.

Now the man in the jeep had found their range, machine gun fire raked the fuselage. North prayed nothing vital would be hit.

Then the jeep appeared right in front of them. They must have cut a hole in the perimeter fence; the jeep now lay directly in their path on the runway, driving towards them. The machine gun was now firing almost continuously. Bullets splattered against the windshield but failed to break the bulletproof Perspex.

Even with the throttles fully open, the distance was too short for the plane's wheels to clear the top of the jeep.

With delicate adjustments of the rudder, North held the jeep directly in front of him. He now attempted something never performed with an A-50 before. He fired its cannon while the plane's wheels were still in contact with the runway.

During the two-second burst, the whole plane shook and shuddered with the enormous vibration, as if caught in a strong wind. The 30mm cannon discharged 140 armour-piercing shells, the size of pint milk bottles, at a rate of 70 rounds per second.

One moment the jeep was speeding towards them; the next it disappeared in a brilliant explosion of yellow and red fire. Little remained except dense black smoke.

The explosion was close enough to rock the whole plane. North kicked the rudder to yank the plane around the burning wreck. The wheels smoked and squealed with the huge pressure and friction of trying to avoid the obstruction.

Once the plane had resumed its original course, North soon reached take-off speed, at which point he pulled the joystick back, the wheels released their grip, and they were airborne.

Once clear of the air base, North waited until he was out of sight before changing his northerly course for one almost due south. He set his course parallel and ten miles off the west coast of Sardinia. His height was very low, two hundred feet above sea level. At this height, he should be almost invisible to any radar screens in the area.

Over the intercom, he told Octavia their destination.

'You may have read in the papers or heard about a freighter *Belle of the Wind* that ran aground off the southern coast of Sardinia?'

'Yes, I remember you pointed it out to me while we had coffee at a café in Cagliari. Curious name, you said.'

'Well, that ship is our destination.'

'What? How can we land near a ship? And what is so interesting about this ship? Who is on it?'

'It's the cargo that the ship contains that makes it so interesting. We are going to sink it, if we can find it. Still glad you came?'

'What!' cried Octavia, shocked. 'Sink the ship! What for? What is her cargo?'

'Her cargo contains parts of an American top-secret experimental spy plane that crashed a few weeks ago in Mexico. Someone located the plane, then found out its importance before the Americans found the crash site and decided to sell it to the Russians. General Kerenskiy had a lot to do with it, so did some of the South Americans at the party we just left.'

So, was the pursuit of this freighter and its cargo what Sebastian North had planned all along? Was his apparent interest in her some sort of smokescreen? No, it couldn't be, she told herself. He loved her; he had demonstrated it often enough by risking his life. She suddenly longed to know more about this Englishman. What was his background, and what would she find in his past?

There was silence until North found, then began to circle, the position where the freighter had run aground. He checked, then rechecked, his coordinates, only to find his position correct the first time.

There was only one problem – the *Belle of the Wind* was nowhere to be seen. They must have floated her off the reef the night before last.

According to his source of information, the freighter had not moved during the previous three days. North had learned this with other information during his brief time from Castle Zehra's radio.

'Damn, damn, where the hell is she?' he muttered. If they had floated her during the previous night, their course must either be through the Strait of Messina or between North Africa and the coast of southern Sicily.

Assuming the *Belle of the Wind's* destination was the Black Sea, which was the only logical course, she would have to navigate the Aegean Sea, Bosphorus and Dardanelles Strait, to one of the Romanian Black Sea ports. Perhaps Constantia or Silina. Unless a deal with the Russians had already been made, in which case the destination would more than likely be Odessa.

North again became acutely aware that he was now the only person who could stop the *Belle of the Wind* reaching its destination.

When all this was over, the Americans had to find and neutralise this high-level mole or their foreign policy and military intentions would continue to be thwarted and compromised for many years to come.

He smiled at Colonel Metcalf's ability, even in retirement, to bypass both the Pentagon and the White House in providing this U.S.A.F. plane. The Colonel's personal relationship with the Deputy Director of the C.I.A. had proved to be a most valuable friendship in time of need.

There had been no time for the air base to gather any real resistance to their take off. The trouble with the jeep must have been mafia-inspired; its source had to have been Castle Zehra.

North decided to search the Messina route, this being, he reasoned, the most likely course of the freighter. It was shorter than sailing around the Sicilian coast, and time was vital for them to reach friendly waters.

Two hundred and eighty miles later, North located the *Belle of the Wind* in bright sunlight. He had memorised her profile from the newspaper article that illustrated her silhouette. Someone had been doing some painting, though, as her superstructure was now blue; it had been white. However, in spite of the disguise, North knew it was the same ship.

He circled twice, very low, for another look. On the second pass, Octavia could make out the name on the stern as *Paradise Found,* with country of origin painted neatly in black 'Liberia'. They must have changed the name as well as the colour. *Clever mind, whoever was behind this operation,* thought North.

She could see small figures on the deck and bridge, motionless as they scrutinised the intruder circling above. Two figures were now running along the port side towards the bow. They reached it and stopped running to bend over what looked like a small wooden box.

Over the intercom, North spoke briefly. 'We're going in, Octavia. This could be quite a ride, so hold tight.'

He guided the plane down so that he was no more than 150ft above sea level. With the throttle wide open, the jet reached 380 knots.

As the freighter slowly became larger, North concentrated on holding his course and height steady. The *Belle of the Wind* had started to turn with maximum port rudder. She was approaching 45° of her intended 90° turn.

Slowly, the distance between the plane and its target closed from 6,000 yards to 5,000; at 4,000 yards, North knew the A-50's 30mm cannon could punch holes right through the ship's tissue-paper-thin hull. If the 30mm cannon could penetrate the armour of a tank at

3,500 yards, what would it do to a ship with no armour plating?

At 3,000 yards, the ship had almost completed 60° of its turn. At 2,000 yards, North, on a straight and level course, held the blue bridge of the freighter under the crosshairs of the gun sights. Then he squeezed the button and, as before, the whole plane shook with the strong vibration.

The cannon discharged alternating rounds of incendiary and armour-piercing shells at the rate of 70 rounds a second. North's thumb held the firing button for exactly four seconds. Enough time for 280 rounds to be fired.

The paper-thin metal of the unprotected bridge presented little resistance to such a devastating onslaught. The armour-piercing shells with their core of depleted uranium – one of the densest materials there is – travelled uninterrupted right through the entire bridge structure.

The high explosive rounds detonated, blowing the whole bridge to matchwood. As soon as he took his thumb off the firing button, North violently banked the plane to starboard.

The gaping hole where the bridge had once been was now a mass of red fire that licked upward into bright yellow flame. Black smoke spread up and out like dense fog. Soon it would obscure the ship completely.

North climbed to 2,000ft for a better view of the stricken vessel. He turned to observe dense black smoke spreading over an increasingly large area from the burning freighter.

She was badly damaged, but not sinking. If the fires were extinguished, she could be towed to some port.

North knew he had to sink her now to avoid, however slim, the chance of the precious cargo falling into Russian hands.

The second attack was easier than the first, as the freighter's course was set hard to port, producing a tight but predictable circle. Her speed had slowed to about ten knots.

With the bridge now a smoking hole, previous communication between engine room and officer of the watch was no longer possible.

At 3,200 yards, North resumed the attack, focusing the crosshairs on the waterline amidships. With his thumb on the firing button, once more the cannon violently erupted into life. He fish-tailed the rudder left and right, yawing the aircraft so that the shells would cover the entire length of the ship's exposed hull.

The shells reached their target, exploding with lethal consequences. Huge holes were punched through the thin metal at the water line immediately letting in thousands of gallons of water, which soon produced a listing to port. Fires now raged out of control on much of the upper decks.

Pulling back on the control column, North cleared the stricken ship by 50ft. It was hard to separate the next few seconds into coherent understanding; a sudden thunderclap of noise blasted the aircraft, unexpected and brutal in its huge impact. The plane shook under the hurricane-like force.

The plane's controls now responded sluggishly. No longer was North in control of a modern military jet, but of an unresponsive and crippled piece of near-useless metal. He knew, as only a pilot can, that they would not be airborne much longer.

The mystery of the men observed surrounding the box in the bows was now obvious. It must have contained a shoulder-launched ground-to-air missile of some sort, such as the American 'Stinger' or Russian 'Sam'.

The doomed ship was wracked by several internal explosions. She must have been badly holed below the water line, for her list became more acute. Water washed over her bows and the forward deck was now completely under water. Her stern rose high to reveal the twin screws still turning, bright silver in the sunlight.

The *Belle of the Wind* was almost lost under an ever-increasing cloud of black smoke. The stricken ship suddenly tilted further down at the bows, then quickly sank under the blue sea. A little debris remained, with an oil slick that spread with the current. There was no sign of survivors, though it was difficult to tell now amongst the wreckage and smoke. In any case, there was little the stricken plane could do under the circumstances, as she continued to lose height at an alarming rate.

North spoke through the intercom. 'Octavia, are you alright? ... Can you hear me?' He repeated the questions, but there was no reply. Something was wrong – obviously the explosion – but there was no time to ponder.

North now concentrated his whole mind on putting the plane down in one piece, if possible. If the jet broke up on impact, she would sink like a stone. Their only chance was to remain afloat long enough to get out and, if Octavia was injured, that could take time.

He set a course straight for Panarea – the closest of the Lipari Islands. Black smoke trailed from the starboard engine behind them, it was only a matter of time before it blew up or caught fire. The oil pressure on the port engine so far was holding steady.

The speed of the aircraft dropped to 210 knots, its fuselage barely 50ft above the waves. During the next twenty-two minutes, North wrestled with the controls that frustratingly continued to thwart his efforts to keep the plane from losing more height.

The island of Panarea rose majestically from the sea, its mostly black volcanic rock contrasting with the blue Mediterranean. Much of its coast exhibited sheer rock to the surrounding water; its main port was located on the east coast.

The volcano Stromboli came into view, located on a neighbouring island, as the plane sank still lower.

The aircraft must hit the water any second. North continued his struggle with the controls, but it was a battle he could not win. The impact was only seconds away, the sea's surface was smooth with only a little swell. North found himself wondering how death would come from drowning.

The plane crashed in shallow water and the impact was surprisingly light, resulting in the air frame remaining intact.

Forward movement was enough to carry the plane so that it ran part-way up a smooth beach composed of very fine sand. North had spotted it as being the only break in an inhospitable coastline of irregular and dangerous rocks.

When it finally came to rest with the last jolt, North slid open the canopy, enabling him to lift himself out of the cockpit. The strong smell of aviation fuel and burning greeted his nose, he felt nauseous and slightly disorientated.

North saw Octavia frantically trying to open the canopy above her, which must have jammed on impact. In what seemed like an age, he managed to free the mechanism with the aid of some tools he found in the cockpit.

'Are you alright?' he asked. 'I tried to talk to you via the intercom but there was no reply.'

'It can't be working, damaged in the explosion. My neck aches like crazy and I feel sick. Must be the impact.'

'Let's get you out of here before the whole thing goes up. It's still burning back there.'

With difficulty, North helped Octavia out of the cramped space and into the water. It was a swim of only a few strokes before they felt sand under foot.

For a moment they lay exhausted on the white sand. Then, turning round, they saw fire creep along the fuselage. The sea was alight from leaking aviation fuel. Suddenly the plane exploded in a thunderous display of spellbinding fireworks. The wind carried the black smoke out to sea, but it would not last long, for the fires would soon die as the fuel ran out.

North held Octavia in his arms and looked down at her frightened and troubled face.

'It's all over, Octavia. Today is the start of a new beginning, free from the obstacles of the past.' His voice was steady and full of reassurance.

'Roberto made me do it. He made me say to you that I loved only him,' she told him. 'You must understand, Sebastian, that it is not true. I may have loved him once, but that was long ago. Ever since you helped me in the South of France, I love only you!'

'No need to explain…' said North, stroking her thick hair. 'When you threw yourself at Roberto's feet to prevent the duel from taking place, and I helped you to your feet, I knew from your eyes that your heart was mine.'

'I know so little about you, but that doesn't matter. You have risked your life so many times for me, which only demonstrates your complete and unconditional love for a woman who, I pray, deserves all that you have risked.'

'You have given me something very precious,' North replied. 'Through you, I have found renewed faith in the very breath of life itself.'

Octavia looked at Sebastian's face with tears pooling in both her eyes from the full realisation and emotional impact of her love for this complete stranger. She ached inside from a spiritual pain that she never knew it was possible to experience, and she prayed with all the fire in her soul that it would last forever.

In reply, North bent and kissed the waiting lips. Octavia's mouth yielded to his pressure. Strange how they both found the faint taste of salt only adding to the pleasure.

Chapter Twelve

Panarea is one of an archipelago of seven main islands located some 30 miles off the northern coast of Sicily. They are known as the Lipari Islands, home to the wind god, Aeolus, and made famous by their warm romantic breezes.

Six weeks after the plane crash, Octavia and North escaped the constant glare of publicity to return to Panarea. If fate had brought them to this island paradise, why not return to enjoy its natural beauty of exotic plants, rugged coastline, and complete isolation, all within sight of the active volcano Stromboli?

The villa they rented was on the west coast, its vistas always commanding magnificent sunsets. The wisdom of the architect was adequately demonstrated by the creation of a Moorish courtyard garden. A square central pool was surrounded by intricately carved stone columns, linked by proportioned arches above the white marble floor that covered the surrounding cloisters. The shallow pool of blue patterned tiles spoke of life and magic with its gurgling fountain.

Connected to the garden was the main villa, comprising some twenty rooms on two levels. A green marble patio ran its entire length, broken here and there by plants in brightly tiled boxes that gave off a rich fragrance.

North stood for a moment framed in the open French windows that paralleled the marble patio. In one hand he held two glasses, in the other a bottle of champagne. His attention was captivated by the figure wearing a black dress.

Octavia must have felt his eyes, for she suddenly turned to face him. Her hair was piled high upon the top of her head. She wore gold earrings fashioned in the shape of cobra heads – the same ones she had tried on in Castle Zehra – now with a necklace of turquoise beads strung between large double gold leopard heads. The grandeur of the jewellery only served to emphasise her long aristocratic neck.

North had asked for, then Octavia had demanded, a share of the treasure. This had resulted in a tense argument with both the Italian and Egyptian governments, as well as with various representatives of leading museums and private collectors from around the world, who all laid claim to part or all of the Sultan's treasure. North insisted on keeping nine pieces from the incredible collection. Three of these, which included the earrings and necklace, were now being worn with such distinction by Octavia.

The Cairo Museum lay a strong and eventually unrivalled claim to the earrings and necklace, for they were authenticated as originating from Egypt, during the time of the Sixth Dynasty Old Kingdom (2345-2181BC). As a special concession for helping to discover them, along with various other important pieces of Egyptian jewellery, the Cairo Museum would allow her to wear them whenever she wished during her lifetime. However, as they belonged to Egypt, they otherwise had to remain in the Cairo Museum on display for the world to see. They were second to none, and superior to anything yet discovered from the Sixth Dynasty.

One other condition had been imposed by the museum's directors: that she could only wear them within the borders of Egypt. This she agreed to, on the condition that before officially handing them over, she could take them to the island of Panarea for a period of one month.

When North had presented them to her barely two hours before, Octavia had lost her voice with emotion, but this time with joy and happiness. She had cried with tenderness and sentimentality, for few women throughout history had seen such beauty fashioned by the hand of man, let alone worn such priceless antiques. She wondered for which princess or queen they had been designed.

North set the two glasses upon the white marble table, and the cork flew off with a loud bang. He poured slowly, first one glass then the other, to avoid overflowing the bubbling liquid. When both glasses were full to his satisfaction, he set the bottle in the ice bucket and then handed Octavia her glass.

The two glasses touched. 'Here's to us at last,' he said, and they both drank deeply, their eyes exploring… waiting…

Octavia felt madness envelope her senses. It was almost too much to anticipate. She wondered how it would be to make love with such a man. A man who had three times risked his life for her. A man who had proved his worth indeed beyond question.

When Sebastian North had been lying asleep in her father's villa in Monte Carlo, recovering from his shoulder injury, she had quietly and secretly entered his room. Standing over him, watching his slow breathing, she had pretended to herself to reposition the sheet that lay over him. Deep down, though, she admitted it had been an excuse to touch him, to see what it felt like to feel his skin against her own.

Octavia savoured his confident movements when opening the champagne bottle, pouring the bubbling liquid, and the extended arm offering her the glass. A simple gesture, but it meant so much more, as he was doing it all for her.

What was it about his movements that influenced her so much? What was it that set this man apart?

To be close to him was like fingertips caressing her spine, so that a delicious blindness enveloped her mind, rendering thinking irrelevant; archaic even.

Within fifteen minutes, the champagne was finished. They said little, for conversation became unnecessary, even a waste of time. Instead, they rested their arms upon the marble trellis that divided the patio from the sheer drop to volcanic rocks below, partially submerged under a restful sea.

At last they held each other. Slowly, ever so slowly, Octavia felt North's hands tighten behind her. His left hand was warm against the bare flesh of her exposed back, where the black chiffon was cut low to the waist. His right hand held her left buttock, gently squeezing, and Octavia felt herself tighten with increased desire.

The smell of aftershave became stronger, its effect stimulating. She wondered what brand it was. His mouth was wet upon her neck, its impact sending wonderful shock waves throughout her starving nervous system.

Octavia's pulse quickened as the memory of *La Valencia* rushed to her heightened senses. Only, this time the danger that had threatened their previously doubtful future had given way to a feverish hope that grew by the moment.

She felt his cheek very smooth, for the shave was close. Their lips touched, sealing the circuit between them, creating a single chamber of dynamic sensitive expression.

Octavia waited, willing him to enter her mouth, to answer her hunger. She hesitated, waiting for his lead.

North eased his tongue into the waiting aperture of her mouth and experienced once more the moist eloquent movements of her tongue. In this way they danced together in circles full of flowing and confident pleasure.

The Englishman and Sicilian played this endless game of drawing circles, first in her mouth, then his, and back to hers, and then it would begin all over again. North could extend his tongue so far that she felt him explore her many sensitive surfaces at will.

They kissed with an unquenchable thirst from a glass full and rich with future promise.

Real love is a solution that is mixed with a fine balance between dynamic physical attraction and emotional sensitivity. It is a unique drink whose potent measure can focus its amorous energy, so that all present and future obstacles become solvable and everything else obsolete.

Octavia and North had each lived previous lives of desolate and emotional lonely wandering in an endless and meaningless wasteland of nothing.

North relaxed, then disengaged his hold altogether. Octavia opened her eyes, the long embrace at last broken. *A kiss*, she reflected. *A kiss... What could one find in a kiss?* So simple and natural, and yet so deep and profound. Strange how she had previously never considered it at all, except for the moment. *This kiss, she decided, was a symphony of deep passion straight from her wildest fantasy.*

Octavia felt North's left arm outstretched, reaching for her hand. He found it warm and waiting. They turned to face the open sea, the sun's rays upon it delivering a deep blue of moving light. Octavia felt the sparkling waves were dancing just for them. The warm wind across her face seemed to sing only for their love.

North squeezed her hand, a secret symbol between them, a communication that spoke with more power than mere words. He then led the tall Sicilian girl wearing black chiffon through the open windows to the room beyond.

The room was spacious, set parallel to the patio and separated by seven-foot floor-to-ceiling glass doors. When these were open, the room became part of the patio, allowing natural light and fragrance into the room's cool interior.

At the end stood a large bed with an ornate gold-framed mirror for a headboard. On either side were two statues, carved from green marble. They supported matching green lamp shades of oriental patterns. One was of Cupid, the Roman god of love; the other of Eos, the Greek goddess of the dawn, reputed to drive her horse-drawn chariot every day across the morning sky.

In the middle of the room stood a circular glass table upon a large circular oriental carpet with a lot of blue and gold. Upon the centre of the table stood a white marble statue of Julius Caesar, with the date 52BC carved into the base – the date he defeated the

Gallic tribes at the battle of Alesia and thus increased Rome's influence from a Mediterranean centric to a West European power.

The rest of the room was sparingly furnished with a few chairs and coffee tables, surfaced with brightly coloured tiles in the Spanish style.

Hung on the walls were views of monuments, depicting classical architecture from various Italian cities. North had admired them earlier; both he and Octavia had discovered more common ground in appreciation of Greek and Roman designs. They found close agreement in their respective views of disappointment towards many 20th century buildings. How could modern construction turn its back on thousands of years of symmetry and balance, to be replaced by asymmetric shapes and a total disregard of anything that pleases the eye and uplifts the spirit.

North pulled the girl across the room to the foot of the bed. Octavia had deliberately drawn back so that North had to almost drag her the last few feet.

She could not explain why she acted in this way, except in some sort of deep primitive desire for the man to exercise his superior strength over her. A last struggle for him to win her over before she submitted to both their desires.

Octavia actively wanted to feel helpless in this man's arms, to feel the strength of a man she could trust. To throw the key to her heart at his feet became an overpowering urge, an acute craving that she did not entirely understand.

North turned round. Octavia hesitated, still holding back, but there was no point fighting what she wanted. She wanted him more than ever.

He kissed her again, then drew apart so that she fell backwards upon the bed. North guided his body over hers, the softness of it yielding to his grasp. He slid his fingers down and around her back, their lips moving with greater intensity.

Octavia ran her fingers through North's short hair, then down his spine to the middle of his back. Here the muscles were well-defined and taut as he held her. She untucked his shirt to feel his strength – firm and so wonderfully sensuous. She longed to feel more of him. Anticipation was building higher and faster.

Suddenly North released his hold to rise up above her onto his knees, so that he could take off his white cotton shirt and throw it to the floor.

Octavia took this opportunity to explore further. She traced the line of his trousers round to the front. There, after some difficulty, she managed to unfasten the clasp, single button, and finally zipper that held them. Now she could pass the fingertips of her right hand between the top of his shorts and the skin of his stomach.

Octavia found him strong, and the end of his penis incredibly soft. *Like silk,* she thought. Her fingers ran slowly down the warm shaft and North's whole body tensed with the effect.

She withdrew her hands and North relaxed. He slipped her dress off, carefully up and over her head, as Octavia still wore the priceless jewellery. The black chiffon came free to reveal Octavia naked except for very brief black panties. They were arched high over the thigh, accentuating her long legs. The kind that, if viewed from behind, were impossible to see as the thin black silk tapered so much that it completely disappeared between her buttocks.

North was struck by how well proportioned she was: her breasts were large but balanced to her above-average height, the nipples dark and prominent.

He moved his left leg so that he was no longer straddling her, then stepped off the bed to undress.

Octavia also left the bed, but for a different reason. She wanted to see how she looked in the large mirror, standing up, wearing only the jewellery and panties. She walked the full length of the room. Below a print called 'Isolotto', showing a water garden created by Alfonso Parigi at the Boboli Gardens, Florence, she turned round with a flourish of movement.

'How do I look?' Her expression was of natural self-confidence, borne from her unquestionable physical attractiveness.

'Bravo! Bravo!' North froze in motion, then sat down on a chair, still wearing his trousers, his left shoe on, the right off. *What was all this about? A parade of vanity? Sicilian aristocratic defiance to the end? A last show of fiery spirit before love?*

In a way it was an expression that was all Octavia: spontaneous, sensitive, full of movement and fire, but there was something more. She could, by a glance, kindle a rare sense of mystery, almost intrigue, to those around her.

'Sebastian, I want to dance the tango with you.'

North was surprised but accepted the invitation at once; hesitation had no place for a dance in paradise. Octavia retraced her steps across the floor and, slipping her dress on, turned to face him.

Octavia had dreamed of dancing the tango with the man she would love forever. From the moment she had seen it performed in Buenos Aires a few years before, she had fallen in love with its deep sensuous movements. With her profound sense of timing and rhythm, she had learnt in weeks what normally took years of dedicated practice.

The tango involves unique movements, the legs being most prominent, interlaced and interlocked in various positions. Without warning, the flow is interrupted by the *corte*, the abrupt halt and change of direction. This is followed by a flash of white flesh, as the woman's calf hooks behind the man's thigh. A twist called the *quebrara* is followed with a glide across the room ending in the woman's back arched very low over the floor in submission.

The tall Englishman and aristocratic Sicilian danced with yearning movements of synchronised passion. When the tango first reached Europe from Buenos Aires in the 1920s, people danced under its hypnosis until exhaustion.

Finally, they stopped, bathed in sweat, to reach the patio. There, the cool breeze was welcome.

Octavia had not known how North would react to her request to dance the tango, but she thought he enjoyed it because he danced well. Never once did she feel his hold slip or his feet step wrongly. Then she explained.

'I have always thought of the tango and flamenco as being the two greatest dances in the world. For me, they represent the basic needs of life.

'The tango represents physical attraction, the explosive passion between man and woman. It is only performed by two people, never alone, hence the saying: "it takes two to tango".

'The flamenco represents the spirit. Its haunting music has a way of reaching the divine within us all, like no other music or dance. It is often performed alone, and much of it is sad, but that is only when the spirit is alone, as it craves a kindred spirit to share the inner mysteries of divine love. For love has no cure except fulfilment.'

North and Octavia took their time to recover from the exertion of the tango, for they had all the time in the world. They consumed a bottle of dry white wine from the North Sicilian town of Cefalù. Crisp and light, it glided down, a welcome refreshment after such exertion.

Returning to the bedroom, they were this time more successful in undressing, and their clothes soon lay discarded around them. Octavia's jewellery was carefully placed on the side table under the statue of Eos.

North kissed Octavia once more, but this time without the inhibition of clothes. Octavia felt her whole body tingle with heightened sensitivity, anticipation increasing. It was like a warm wind that was slowly gathering power and strength, carrying all before it.

Closing her eyes, Octavia felt him kiss her neck, his warm and wet tongue setting her skin yearning and making her impatient and restless.

North's tongue found the superior contour of her left breast. He slowly worked his way to its waiting apex. His mouth, after an age, found the dark brown erect nipple. The effect radiated across her left chest in small shock waves of yearning.

The yearning of Octavia's breast suddenly became less, for North's mouth had moved elsewhere. He drew with his tongue a wet line of circles down towards her navel where he found her depression. She thought he must be enjoying the smell, for she had earlier moistened her skin with fine fragrance.

Quivers of desire reached so high that Octavia's breathing became deeper and a little faster. North's beautifully wet mouth, then his tongue, found the outer ring of her dark pubic hair. She felt his head angle so that his mouth sealed with her outer lips.

High voltage now charged her entire body in a series of rippling shock waves, each one bigger and more potent than the one before. Octavia's pelvis moved with the sensual motion of a dream; past and future faded to meaningless memories, as a never-ending present of sacred music became her only reality.

She could wait no longer; the point of no return had been reached. Or had it passed? Then he was on top of her. Quickly, her enthusiastic fingers found him so warm and smooth, then she slowly guided him deep within her, so perfectly, as nature had intended.

Octavia moved her long legs high up and behind so that her ankles locked together, ensuring their motion became one.

With each breath they generated life into their emotionally starved souls. Together they would reach the perfect moment of mystery when all the senses are brought to one point in space and time. At last, on this highest of planes, they would reach complete harmony in mind, body, and spirit, with a climax of liquid fire.

The art of the flamenco is both ancient and diverse in its origins, its mysterious attraction lying deep within its potent influence over the conscious senses. It consists of three basic components: song, dance, and guitar.

The flamenco is performed in three forms: the *chico*, or light flamenco, which consists of a mixture of many emotions but is full of light vitality; the *intermedia*, more elaborate and intense; and the *jondo* or *grand*, which is the most pure and deep emotionally. A good flamenco artist performing the *jondo* will be able to transmit and inspire the spirit within. Out of all flamenco dances, this is the most difficult to achieve; once seen and heard, it is never forgotten, so powerful is its influence upon those lucky enough to experience it.

Slowly at first, then faster and faster, their bodies moved like the *chico* in temperament, sensuous and tender with an easily understood rhythm. This rhythm produced a cohesion that perfectly balanced Octavia's fiery passion with North's strength and stability. She, the sprinter, he, the long-distance runner, combined to produce an enduring contract that could never be broken.

The effect of North's rhythm was both immediate and continuous. Its increasing strength and tempo ignited Octavia's spiritual fuse with fire. This man answered a deep longing that compelled her escape from reality into fantasy. This fuse, once lit, burnt faster and without compromise to its explosive climax.

North's weight compressed her deeper into the bed, his fingers locked with hers, their arms high above her head. She felt his chest hairs against the smooth skin of her breasts, stimulating countless nerve endings, producing exquisite delight. In contrast to her arms held back and high above her head, Octavia squeezed North's pelvis and buttocks with her strong thigh muscles.

At last, a cataclysmic wave of white-hot fire engulfed Octavia's body. Like thousands of volts, it charged her nervous system to reach her first beautiful orgasm. Its sheer strength and delight left her gasping for breath, its supreme energy carrying her on up the scales of divine music.

North's rhythm continued, creating within Octavia an ever-higher note of inflamed heat... *Could this last forever? How long would this dance in paradise last?*

Octavia lost count. She felt as never before, a strange sense of invincibility and eloquence at the same time.

An explosion, followed by several convulsions, announced North's climax deep within Octavia's pelvis. Simultaneously, the Sicilian's orgasm broke with equal burning pleasure.

Three times they resumed this unique dance in paradise. The third time was like a *grande* or *jondo*, the most pure and original flamenco expression that can be performed. The grand finale engulfed them both so completely that time itself became obsolete and meaningless.

When the drive of desire had been temporarily halted, a time of reprieve followed, and conversation was once again possible. Then the Englishman and the Sicilian girl talked in whispers as if a huge secret had been discovered, afraid that the outside world might discover and somehow dilute their new-found love.

Octavia thought for a moment, then decided. Making love is like performing a moving dance that is both dynamic and intensely secret, an art form that is moulded from the very clay of life and fired by the eternal flame of love.

Chapter Thirteen

Octavia stood on the patio wearing only the lower part of a blue and white striped bikini, the kind that economised on material to such an extent that it barely covered her pubic hair. Like the panties she had worn earlier, the attempt at covering up any skin was next to hopeless. She felt good wearing it, knowing her body was being shown at its best.

She took in the view of the coast with all her senses, from its dark volcanic rock to the infinity of the horizon. Here she found only a strange unease, instead of the tranquillity she sought. The surface of the water was more troubled than before, the Levante wind from the east seeming to combine with the sea to produce a swell that gave a feeling of restlessness.

Did she glimpse a forecast of future troubles not yet reached? What could she be afraid of? Surely nothing now. After all, Roberto was dead, and she was now free of his influence. *After so much, why did her mind speculate upon such vague uncertainties?*

A moment later, as if in answer, searing hot pain immediately replaced apprehension. It shot through Octavia's neck and deep into her skull.

Octavia knew she had finally entered the gates of hell, as the pain was of such intensity that her head seemed to swim in an endless lake of burning oil. Pain penetrated every screaming cell so that her mind's

319

delicate fabric, indeed its very language of thought and reason, rapidly ceased to function. She longed for the oblivious sleep of unconsciousness. Octavia managed to scream, just once, with the desperation of the living who are about to die.

Powerful hormones were now being secreted at a rate that could not long be sustained. Octavia's heart pounded at near lethal levels.

Fear once again became the unwelcome architect of Octavia's emotions. It built huge phantoms that assumed the reality of a nightmare.

The force around her neck directed Octavia downwards towards the marble under her feet. Her eyes no longer produced a clear image, but one blurred and out of focus. She felt claustrophobic and unable to communicate, as if she were drowning. She could not resist, and her legs buckled under her. The pain in her neck boiled unbearably. *How much more could she endure? Would she pass out or go insane?*

'Please, God, let me live. I don't want to die. I want to live for Sebastian. If I die, I give my life to him. I will wait for him to join me, for I will be faithful even beyond the grave.'

Then the excruciating pain at the back of her neck eased just enough to bring welcome relief in the form of an intense, throbbing headache. Perhaps she might live after all.

The glass was cold against her lips. The bottle's hard aperture grated on her clenched teeth. The force was sufficient to draw blood. It drained inside her mouth, its taste unmistakable: the bottle contained something with alcohol that was somewhat sweet. Her nose recoiled immediately from the powerful stench. *What could it be? What kind of hellish brew had been prepared? For what purpose? And by whom?*

Slowly, through the still numbing pain, her eyes focused upon the man holding the bottle. She recognised the same deep-set impassive eyes, oblivious now, as they had been before, to her pain and suffering. They were those of the man who with another had kidnapped her in Cagliari at the hotel, when North had left to find her father.

Behind those terrible eyes was only one clear purpose, frightening in its intensity and single-minded madness. This man's sole aim was to make certain that she, Octavia, consumed the contents of this hideous bottle.

Elixir or poison? Deep down, Octavia knew the fearful answer. The skull-like features twisted with a grin that tormented her very soul, like a hideous image from some far off classical play. It was a mask of impending doom that heralded her own tortuous end.

Octavia found herself held hard against the white marble patio. The man with the bottle straddled her so that he sat on her stomach, his overweight grotesque folds smothering any meaningful movements or escape from below. She felt his breath, a toxic wind of contamination that only increased her despair.

Clenching her teeth, Octavia tried to avoid the inevitable fate of consuming the bottle's contents. This brought a swift blow to the side of her head. A second man held her, so further resistance was not possible.

For fifteen seconds, the pain sent explosive fires of excruciating numbness radiating throughout her left cheek and neck. She could not sustain this punishment a second time. Shaking with fear and failure, she admitted that her courage to resist and the will to live itself no longer existed.

Octavia's parents had passed through to her genes of nobility and honour from many illustrious ancestors. The history of Greece held many in high acclaim and distinction from its turbulent and glorious past.

What courage was there left with which to face this last battle? How could she surrender and die like this? Would her love for Sebastian be strong enough to let her live?

Octavia parted her lips to find that the first taste of the liquid was surprisingly pleasant: very strong, like whisky, from what she could remember. It was also sweet at the same time, and was perhaps not going to be so awful, after all. However, this was but a taste, and there was still a whole bottle to finish.

Slowly the bottle's powerful contents took its inevitable effect. Octavia's stomach turned in pain. She felt dizzy and disorientated. The reek of alcohol became unbearable and she felt sick. Unconsciousness could not be far away now. Hysteria became her master.

The man with the pitiless eyes sensed her increased discomfort. He stopped the deadly flow just long enough for the hysteria and nausea to ease. Then it resumed, the fiery liquid burning her throat, its fumes now overpowering. Suddenly, she could take no more. She vomited with such force that the bottle flew out of the man's hands; foul-smelling vomit sprayed everywhere.

The bottle smashed upon the marble, its remaining fluid running away across the smooth surface. Judging by the liquid left, Octavia must have consumed over two-thirds of the original contents.

With a supreme effort Octavia fought back, her arms swinging wildly in front of her. She wanted to live more than anything. She became fuelled by a raw power, an animal potency, a certain irresistible primeval instinct that said, 'I want to live!'

The uncontrollable intensity of facing immediate and violent death wreaks havoc with the average mind, numbing its very machinery so that thoughts of self-preservation and survival become overwhelmed and then retreat to the asylum of uncertainty.

One of the two men spoke, his unpleasant voice talking of a fate perhaps worse than death.

'Contessa!' The tone was smooth, but an element of contempt was present. 'You have drunk enough methyl alcohol. If it does not kill you, it will render your eyes useless, for it has a great appetite for the optic nerve. Either way, you will never see your foreign lover again. Just think, my face is the last face on this earth you will ever see! You rejected the Count, now the Count has avenged you… from the grave.'

His sadistic laugh so distorted his overweight features that they assumed the hellish contours of some Greek mythological creature consumed by barbarous savagery.

Blind. The word rampaged out of control, discharging its cataclysmic meaning with ferocious speed in monstrous proportions. So, this was the powerful poison she had been forced to consume; it would veil her eyes for certain, and maybe take her life.

Octavia now welcomed death with outstretched arms. Was it not now preferable to a condemned darkness? What would life be except a cloaked existence in a world devoid of sunlight forever? The spectre of irreversible blindness produced an image that vandalised and mauled her mind, threatening a nervous breakdown.

Octavia felt cold iron around her ankles. She could make little sense from the images formed by her painful eyes. The focus was blurred, distorted, and out of all proportion, like that from a fairground she remembered as a child. She had stood in front of several mirrors, each one producing a different hideous reflection, distorting her features to impossible proportions of ugliness. Her reaction had been to run away to the safety of her mother.

* * * * *

The helicopter landed on the pad two hundred yards from the villa. Before the blades had finished turning, North jumped out. He had seen something that sent his mind racing.

From the air he had spotted a man on the path from the beach leading to the villa. It was impossible to tell the original direction of the man, for he was motionless. *Was he making towards the villa, or away, down the path to the water?*

Somehow, North knew Octavia was his purpose, and it could not fare well for her.

He ran through an olive grove to find a gravel path lined by conifers and cypresses. The path continued to lead him to a series of stone steps linking three separate terraces, each one bordered on the seaward side by a balustrade of classical design. The terraces contained numerous yuccas and cacti, with terracotta pots filled with plants exhibiting a mosaic of bright colours here and there.

Earlier, he and Octavia had intimately explored this articulation of natural beauty that was wild and graceful in the same moment, a living poetry written in a language that only nature could provide. This natural beauty now made no impression on North's panic-driven mind.

Out of breath, North reached the arched entrance to the cloistered water garden, its harmony momentarily checking his stride. He recalled the previous evening. He had whispered to Octavia, as only lovers can, that they would rise together, free at last from the chains of uncertainty, to live a dream beyond the minds of mere mortals.

Through the villa's numerous rooms he ran, not daring to slow his pace a second time. The door to the bedroom was open, the scene of their lovemaking... Pleasant images and smells flashed through his mind, but now they only served to mock and torment.

The patio was deserted. There was no sign of Octavia, whom he had left sunbathing a few hours earlier. The two chairs and table had not moved since their breakfast together. North's eyes looked to the sea. The terracotta pots and phoenix canariensis palms stood out against the cobalt-blue water.

Then something caught the sunlight, and the ground sparkled in a small area at the far end of the patio. There, steps of blue and yellow painted tiles descended to a long portico supported by white marble pillars.

North took several steps to investigate. Bending over, he found broken glass. The glass had contained a liquid, the remains of which had run and pooled. The ground reeked. North touched his finger to a pool that had not completely dried. He tested it on his tongue, the sensation confirming what his nose had just told him.

The pieces of remaining glass suggested the size and shape of an ordinary wine bottle. Its recent contents must have consisted of a very high proportion of alcohol. That was what his nose and tongue had established.

North observed another curious thing: judging by the spilt liquid, the bottle's contents at the time of being smashed must have been between a quarter and a third of its full capacity, assuming it had been full originally. *Where was the remaining liquid?* If the bottle had a label, it was not now in evidence; a mysterious puzzle indeed. *But where was Octavia?*

Upon further investigation, North found traces of vomit. Clearly the bottle's contents had not agreed with someone.

Then North noticed a rope tied around one of the small pillars that guarded the patio's edge from the sheer drop the other side. It was about a quarter of an inch in diameter. *What could it be doing here?* He could not remember noticing it before.

Straightening up, North ran to the patio's edge and, peering over the balustrade, he found the purpose of the rope's existence.

North's mind seized with what he saw. The appalling truth shrieked up from below. His previously disciplined thinking, militarily trained to react with detached purpose devoid of emotion, now almost refused to respond. The assault on his brain unleashed a poisonous lance that pierced his heart with murderous insanity, for North already feared that Octavia was dead.

She hung suspended by her legs, metal cuffs holding her ankles, tied to which was the rope North had observed earlier. Her head was not visible for it lay under the water; only her hair could be seen, floating like so much dark seaweed.

North galvanised his body into action. Taking hold of the thin rope, he slowly began to haul Octavia up from the depths below. The weight was unbelievably heavy and his left shoulder soon ached with the strain.

He was within a few feet of pulling her over the railings when someone quietly and confidently pressed a sharp knife against his throat. North stopped pulling. *What new threat was this?* Of course, the man he had seen from the helicopter. In his haste to help Octavia, his mind had pushed everything else to irrelevance.

North knew that if Octavia was not dead, she must be close to death, unless he prevented her from drowning. Of course, he might have arrived too late, in which case it would all be a waste of time. The blade pressed closer and a voice sounded in his ear.

'Please continue, Englishman. You have nearly succeeded in saving the Contessa from drowning. Your lover awaits you.'

North hesitated no longer. Hand over hand, he pulled with a will that blocked pain from his burning left shoulder more completely than any man-made analgesic.

Just pull, hand over hand, slow, steady, sure. The way his father had always taught him: that nothing of importance or endurance was ever achieved in a hurry.

At last, North held Octavia's ankles, wet and cold. His left shoulder burnt with the vicious savagery of a deep wound. With a supreme effort, North pulled Octavia's limp form over the parapet and he lay her wet, salt-covered body on the marble. A single strand of black seaweed pressed like a serpent tight across her neck. North pulled, releasing its momentary hold.

Quickly, he untied the bonds that bound her wrists, but her ankles were cuffed with steel too tight for her feet to slide through. Her carotid pulse felt weak but regular, her breathing fast and shallow. Octavia was alive, but only just.

The man previously positioned behind North moved away and to the side, the threat of sharp steel now no longer present. He began to laugh, a deep ominous sound full of foreboding. The key to Octavia's manacles was thrown at her feet. North did not hesitate to unlock her constraints.

North straightened his back after freeing Octavia's ankles, then repositioned her in the recovery position. He now looked for the first time upon the man who stood before him.

The man stood tall, perhaps slightly more than North's above-average height, his hair very blond without sign of balding. His eyes were blue. *Most unusual in these parts*, thought North.

The face was unquestionably handsome, the Roman nose and eyes well proportioned, with almost too-smooth, oily, Mediterranean skin. There was, however, something of the Count's disdainfulness and treachery in the movements of his shifting eyes.

'The girl will perhaps live, but what a life she will lead! She will wish you had left her hanging, waiting to drown here on Panarea. Such a beautiful island; too bad she has looked her last upon this paradise of volcanic rock.'

North was puzzled.

'The stupid Contessa has paid the price for double dealing with my late cousin, the Count.'

'So, you are Camillio. It was you who tried to drown her?'

'Well, it was my idea, but others carried it out. They also gave the Countess a farewell drink, the side effects of which she won't forget – a state of permanent vengeance from the Count.'

The broken glass, the smell of alcohol, the remains of foul-smelling vomit… *What did the bottle contain? What poison had they forced Octavia to consume?*

'What did the bottle contain?' asked North, his shocked mind straining to comprehend the unfolding picture.

'You will never understand Sicily, Englishman, for you are an impostor, a foreigner. What could you know of our customs and ancient traditions?'

But North understood just as much, if not more, Sicilian history than Camillio did. 'Your struggle and survival against Norman invasion to the rule of Bourbon kings might be argued to be once one of noble cause.

'However, the Sicilian Mafia has always lived by the code of Omerta enforced by vengeance. Your treacherous mind is a prism that distorts the light of justice. Through its present diseased dimensions, you create an image devoid of honour and full of corruption.

'You give new meaning to man's inhumanity to man.' North's voice carried only a deep loathing towards the other man and all that he represented.

Camillio exploded with anger. He was not used to being lectured to, and especially not by a foreigner.

'Your beloved Octavia will be totally blind. The Count has wreaked vengeance from the grave!' His face cracked into a grin of evil-hearted triumph, the like of which North had never before witnessed.

'When I learned of my cousin's death in a duel, at the hand of an Englishman, I knew you and I would meet, but only once.'

'If you wish to avenge your cousin's death, let us not delay a moment longer,' stated North, his voice steady and full of challenge.

Camillio observed that his face looked composed and remarkably calm.

'There are two sabres in the hall. If these weapons are to your taste, perhaps we could settle the matter now... To the death...' challenged North.

He knew that Camillio would find it difficult to resist the challenge of a duel, especially for stakes so high and being as experienced as he was. North had knowledge of Camillio's fencing expertise. As well as being the Count's cousin, he had been the man's personal fencing coach for many years.

Hollywood has glamorised the duel between two men in combat, from the mounted knights of King Arthur's court to the fencing duels portrayed by such flamboyant actors as Errol Flynn. Trial by combat arouses something deep within the human character that has not been diminished by time or the discovery of gunpowder. The appeal lies within the age-old struggle between two men, whose strength and skill are pitted one against the other. Sometimes the cause of one is perceived more noble than the other, and then the spectator will naturally take sides.

The fencing duel portrayed on the screen is usually far from realistic. A small error that draws blood from the point or sabre's edge need not be fatal, but the nature of the contest discourages leisurely reflexes and inaccuracy. Duels that ended for at least one of the contestants in blood, damaged eyes, cut cheeks, and punctured lungs, were almost commonplace. It was a practical way of settling disputes with a certain formality outlined by strict rules.

In practice, the time taken to show a clear winner – often through injury – by duelling is very short indeed, measured in minutes rather than a long drawn-out contest.

Camillio and North adopted the on-guard position with their blades close to the perpendicular, ready for either offensive or defensive actions. Their left arms were held behind for balance and to avoid becoming an additional target.

If one plays by the rules, as laid down by the *Federation Internationale d'Escrime*, the target area with sabre duelling is the entire body above the waist. However, right now this was rather irrelevant information, for North and the blond Sicilian were playing by the open rules of survival.

Survival demands only one outcome. To win, whatever the method.

Camillio was angry; in fact, he was furious at the way North had manipulated him by challenging him first to a duel. The initiative had been seized when the advantage should have been his by virtue of his knife. However, he would now show this foreigner how to die.

At that moment, Octavia regained consciousness. Her head throbbed with renewed pulsations pounding relentlessly, creating deep nausea. Through blurred eyes she saw two men, both of whom she recognised. She screamed with naked fear, but neither man turned round. The duel had already begun.

Camillio attacked with a near vertical cut to North's head. His blade was high, but not so high as to expose his forearm, the final movement consisting of a flicking action from the wrist.

Before Camillio could strike home, North countered with the parry of Quinte – the standard blocking action with his blade horizontal and at eye level.

Following his successful parry, North counter-attacked with a cut to Camillio's right flank. However, Camillio lowered his blade just in time to block North's from striking. The Sicilian lost little time in pressing home his next attack, only to be successfully blocked, or sidestepped, by North.

In this fashion the contest continued for several minutes, each man trying to find, then exploit, a weakness in the other.

North forced his mind to concentrate on the single aim of winning. Distracting thoughts of anger towards those responsible for Octavia being so close to death would only serve to dilute his focus and deny him the victory that he so desperately needed. Their fencing skills were so evenly matched that the outcome of the duel was going to be very close indeed.

The duel is not unlike a game of chess, with each player endeavouring to think several moves ahead.

Plans of attack must be countered, false attacks unmasked, and counterattacks exposed, if survival in the field is to be maintained.

The opening of a duel is traditionally played with caution in order to measure one's opponent's strengths and possible weaknesses. It is through the opponent's blade that initial contact and knowledge is accumulated, otherwise known as '*sentiment du fer*'.

At last North began to sense and recognise Camillio's shrewd and skilful game. Each fencer leaves an impression of movement with his distinctive style and rhythm. This can be likened to the way a conductor influences the orchestra by leaving his own unique stamp upon the music.

The duel increased dramatically in tempo, with the movement of the two men and their weapons blurring as Octavia's eyes fought to catch up with reality. Hers were the only eyes to witness this fast unfolding and preposterous event.

With the clever use of double and triple feints, it became apparent to North that Camillio had developed great skill and finesse in the execution of attacks to the head.

Did this suggest a weakness elsewhere? If so, where in his play was it located? So far, in spite of the Sicilian's obvious anger, his game had suffered little. In fact, if anything, it had improved. Try as he might, North could not yet detect a weakness in his opponent's game. In fact, it seemed to North that as the duel progressed Camillio's game improved in its illustration of competence. This blond Sicilian showed a brilliance that would have put him on equal terms with some of the best fencers in the world.

North knew in the pit of his stomach then that he was likely to lose. His win against the Count had been solely due to his use of the overhead chandelier, not because he was the finer swordsman. His dry mouth, sweaty palms, and increased pulse, he recognised as symptoms of failure. He knew now, when it was far too late, that he should have kept up his fencing lessons instead of letting them lapse.

He had to somehow expose a window of vulnerability in Camillio's game. A chance of survival...

Then Camillio executed a successful cut to North's face. A flexing of his wrist brought the last three to four inches of the razor-sharp sabre across North's left cheek. North was a fraction too slow to effectively counter this attack, and suffered the inevitable consequences.

His left cheek and neck turned crimson with blood running from the deep cut. If Camillio had been aiming for his jugular vein, he might not miss a second time. North's blood quickly turned his white cotton shirt a dark ugly red.

The duel was fast reaching its conclusion and Camillio could now taste victory. He had drawn first blood and his face cracked into a grin of satisfaction. It would give him much pleasure to administer the *coup de grâce*. At last the Count's death would not have been in vain.

At that moment, if an outside observer had chanced upon the scene taking place on that white marble, he might be forgiven for thinking that he was watching the final stages of some bizarre Greek tragedy. The villa, with its magical gardens and magnificent vistas, formed the perfect amphitheatre, with the two men duelling for life and death over the near-naked girl.

'How had she influenced the story?' an observer would ask, had there been any that bright sunny morning. Was this the last act in a classical story of immortal love? The kind of love experienced between two people so potent that the threat of death's dark barrier becomes nothing more than a transient sleep.

However, the setting was an Italian island in the 20th century, not classical Greece, and the duel's outcome had not yet been decided.

THE GREEK RING

Pain radiated from North's right cheek. It began to distort his sight by blurring the vision on the same side. He experienced a dull burning sensation from the open wound, while at the same time the warm blood felt strangely soothing as it trickled down his neck and chest. He knew he could not survive a repeat of this sort of treatment. His life and Octavia's would be decided over the next few moments, assuming she did not die first from either the poison in her blood or the water that must still be in her lungs.

North had learnt the Hungarian quadruple feint from a fencing master quite by chance whilst passing through Budapest several years ago. It was this difficult compound attack with a high risk of failure that he decided upon to try and finish his opponent once and for all. Camillio had been, until this point, steadily gaining the upper hand. Again, North cursed himself for not practising his fencing skills frequently enough, as his present situation deteriorated still further.

Camillio, as was to be expected from such an experienced fencer, did well but he only saw through three of North's carefully laid feints. His miscalculation was in thinking that the third feint to his right arm was North's final attack. This miscalculation sealed his fate, for when it was just too late to counter, North's real intention revealed itself. His sabre blade sliced forward at an angle and the point entered Camillio's upper torso with a third of its length piercing the right lung.

With a sudden pull, North withdrew his sword from Camillio's chest. The man fell backwards to the ground, his hands trying in vain to stem the leaking blood from his wound. A coughing fit became a desperate noise of pain, spattering his face in dark blood. His voice became an incoherent mumble, no louder than a whisper. The blue eyes, once so full of disdain, now showed total incomprehension and fear as he, like the Count before him, contemplated death for the first time.

Just before he lost consciousness, Camillio heard North's voice say something about watching out for the Hungarian Quadruple Cross Over, just in case the devil played a devious game, too.

Camillio no longer posed a threat, so North left him in a spasm of convulsions before his inevitable death. Octavia's life was now all that mattered.

She was conscious, but in an alarming state. Her stomach burnt with the ferocity of ignited kerosene. Racked by pain, she lay pathetically with her knees drawn up high, close to her chest.

She saw North move towards her and, looking up, found that his face was very close. It was covered in blood. Through her pain Octavia's eyes became troubled and concerned.

'You are hurt.' It was a statement rather than a question.

'Yes, but don't worry about that now, it can wait. Tell me what you feel, Octavia. You must tell me so that I can help you.'

She told him in slow painful words what they had done to her, from the forcing of the bottle's contents down her throat to being suspended by her ankles half-submerged in the sea.

North's face was full of anxiety and apprehension throughout the telling of her tale.

When Octavia had finished, she paused before continuing, 'Am I dying, Sebastian?' Her physical pain momentarily ceased as the far greater pain of leaving a loved one was felt. 'It is not death that I am afraid of, it is leaving you that I can't face,' she whispered.

'Listen, Octavia, no-one will take your life away. The Count can't in death succeed at what he failed to achieve in life. Not even he can reach you from beyond the grave. His attempt to separate us died a moment ago with Camillio's death,' said North, with so much confidence that Octavia wanted to believe every word he said.

'Sebastian, always remember that your face is my destiny. I will carry your image to the grave...' She paused to let a wave of nausea pass. '...I am so frightened Sebastian. Please tell me that Camillio was lying, that I won't go blind and that I will see your face tomorrow.'

'We have no time to lose, sweetheart. Don't move, for I must go and find the antidote to the poison you have consumed.'

Before leaving her side, North kissed Octavia lightly on the lips.

Deep down North knew he might already be too late to save Octavia's eyesight, let alone her life. So, he moved with the urgency borne of the insane. He recalled a newspaper article two or three years previously; he knew that what he had learnt from its contents had to save Octavia's life.

In 1989, the western state of Gujarat, India, achieved fame when three hundred people died and hundreds more were rendered blind from consuming a local brew called 'Lattha'. This particular batch had been made too strong by the addition of methanol from such sources as melted boot polish and paint thinner.

Methyl alcohol, or methanol as it is more commonly called, is added to a base syrup of fermented sugar. This achieves a final brew that is much more potent than, say, ordinary over-the-counter whisky. What is more, it is much cheaper, and therefore readily available to anyone prepared to risk the horrendous consequences of blindness and possible death for a few hours of alcohol-induced pleasure.

A doctor at a nearby hospital recognised the symptoms associated with methanol poisoning and administered the antidote. None of those treated suffered blindness or died, except one man who lost the sight of a single eye.

North returned from inside the house with a bottle containing a pale golden liquid. Propping up Octavia's head with his left hand, he held the bottle with his right poised above her.

'You must drink this if you want to see again.'

'What is it?' said Octavia, puzzled that an antidote could be found so easily.

'Just drink it, for it will take too long to explain.'

Obediently Octavia opened her mouth. Immediately the taste was strangely familiar, but she could not put a name to this liquid that also burnt.

Suddenly a new fear gripped her mind in a vice of uncertainty. *Was this new liquid really an antidote to the poison or was it a second poison?*

New doubts began to permeate her mind and cloud her reason. *Was Sebastian North in some inexplicable way working against her all along? If so, to what end and purpose? Could she trust his eyes and have faith in those handsome features? Was there real treachery here, or was it only another phantom of her inadequate faith, come to haunt and undermine her self-confidence?*

Chapter Fourteen

The fire burnt deep from below, from its epicentre radiating lines of pain that punished the nervous system, threatening to engulf and destroy.

All pain beyond a certain threshold must be consciously met. High levels of pain demand attention without compromise, for it is relentless and it cannot be ignored. Only in the unconscious state can peace be found. However, there is a second state that affords relief from terrible pain: it is called death.

Octavia was now experiencing such pain from deep within her solar plexus. An unseen hand had filled it with a consuming fire that burnt with a wicked vengeance.

Time passed; how much was difficult to tell. Perhaps only a few moments, maybe days or more. It was impossible to be accurate. At last the pain eased and Octavia's mind became less numb; rational thinking once again became possible.

She opened her eyes. Panic immediately set in, for the retinas of both eyes registered only darkness. She might just as well have not opened them at all, for they produced no measurable impression.

Slowly she became more aware of her surroundings. She was lying on her back, wearing some sort of nightshirt. It felt several sizes too big. She was covered by a single sheet. The room was warm, with an ever-so-faint breeze, the origin of which had to be an open window somewhere off to the left. From the distinctive smell, she was sure the surroundings were those of a room within a hospital. As far as she could tell, she was alone.

Several times she opened and closed her eyelids to make quite sure first impressions were not false. The result always remained constant, complete darkness.

Blind! Blind! Again and again the crushing word ricocheted through Octavia's mind, threatening to muffle and weaken her willpower, as insanity's dark hand beckoned towards the ever-present path of hopelessness.

How could this be?

Camillio's words returned to haunt her. 'You will never see your lover again. My face is the last face on earth you will ever see!'

Octavia's mind recoiled as it grappled in vain against her crippled future.

The antidote! *What happened to the antidote? Did it not work? So, Sebastian had betrayed her after all! How was this possible? Why, why, why did he destroy her so completely? What was it, that pale yellow liquid that he had given her?*

Octavia tried to find answers to this impossible riddle, but she had none. Within her, deep down, she found nothing that was remotely capable of helping her. Acute depression set in. All courage to face the future had fallen.

Octavia felt nauseous and light-headed. The inside of her mouth was dry and her tongue fought to find moisture, but without success. There must be water nearby; on the bedside table there might be some, a bathroom could not be too far away... Her mind drifted somewhere between incoherent thinking and a longing for deep uninterrupted sleep. She tried to ignore her thirst, but it was persistent and would not go away.

More time passed, then she heard her mother's voice, or perhaps it was just her imagination? Its familiar tone was smooth and strong.

'Octavia, you must listen, do not fear. You have to face the unknown with boldness and fortitude. Think of your Greek ancestors, for their lines stretch to antiquity and beyond. They will help you. Your blood is rich in courage and inspiration; you cannot afford to cower from the unknown, no matter how uncertain the future appears.'

Her mother's voice spoke with authority and direction to influence that which was latent within her. Abruptly the voice fell silent, but Octavia had already started to feel the potent genes of her ancestors stir and awaken; a mighty trumpet had sounded in her hour of need.

Octavia slept for a long time. When she awoke, she cried out. Her thirst had become more pronounced. Feeling too weak to leave the bed, she hoped that someone would hear her. Someone did. A door opened, footsteps, then the glass touched her dry lips. Slowly she drank the cool water, and a little dripped down her chin and neck. Her thirst eased, she felt clearer as the previous nausea left. Whoever gave her the water spoke a few words of consolation and advice.

'Try to sleep, you will feel refreshed then.'

Octavia was too weak to contemplate argument, but she wondered who had spoken.

She must have dreamt a great deal. A flood of images and feelings raced through her mind. They lacked any kind of sequence or recognisable form that made sense. Sebastian's face kept appearing and she started to doubt her feelings for him. *What had gone wrong? How could she travel from the paradise on Panarea with the man she loved to her present nightmare of an existence so quickly? What had gone so awfully wrong?*

More time passed, again impossible to measure how much. Someone helped her drink more water, as her burning thirst returned more than once.

A little later Octavia felt the sweet air from the open window brush her cheek again. She opened her eyes, and immediately the previous blackness was not as complete as before.

She could make out a vase upon a table nearby, containing flowers with long stems. The room was very dim, and what light there was must have an external source. A smell waxed and waned according to the strength of moving air. Of course, the scented air was from the flowers, the position of which was in front of the window.

What an elegant vase, she thought. It was black and gold, rather narrow, with high curved twin handles. The rich design of its delicate and unhurried work reminded her of Ancient Greece. She continued to lie on her side looking at this vase, enjoying its appealing contours and graceful shape.

Slowly Octavia became aware that first its outline, then its intricate curved motifs were becoming clearer and more defined. Stronger light was now penetrating the room and striking the vase. The decorations etched in gold glowed back at her with the increasing strength of the sun.

Octavia sat up. She could see! She was not blind, after all! She repeated the words over and over again. 'I can see! I can see!' Her pulse raced with heightened excitement, while she opened and closed her eyelids dozens of times just to make sure; but the vase remained clearly visible and undiminished in all its artistic splendour. She thought its shape strangely enchanting.

Octavia leaped out of bed to look out of the window, beyond the vase and fresh flowers to the scarlet horizon of a new day. The room was situated within a large building, the limited light of the dawn suggesting country rather than an urban site.

The night's darkness combined with her previous delirious state had led her to think that her sight had been lost forever. An incoherent mind left in a darkened room is prone to conjure the worst scenario. Suddenly life seemed worth living again. Octavia breathed deeply, absorbing with each breath new life into her tortured mind and exhausted body.

She quickly became tired. Her legs felt weak, so she resumed her previous position upon the bed, lying on her left side so the vase, now bathed in sunlight, could still be viewed. Soon her eyelids drooped and a welcome sleep followed.

More time passed, again impossible to tell how much. Her father's wonderful face slowly, then with increasing clarity, took shape. Its familiarity conveyed refuge and understanding. His soothing voice was how she imagined gods to speak. Kind and protective, with great intuition for her feelings and the troubled waters of her soul. Then Octavia realised she no longer slept but was fully conscious and awake.

'Welcome back, Octavia, you have endured much...'
He paused, smiling, then continued, 'The doctor says
your eyesight will be 100 per cent normal. You are
very fortunate, for the antidote given by Mr North
worked brilliantly. It not only saved your sight but
probably your life.'

Octavia sat up, her father helping to position several
pillows behind her to support her still delicate head.
This was incredible news! She longed to see the man she
loved, her previous thoughts of his betrayal completely
false. A shadow of guilt passed over her as to how she
could have thought of Sebastian with anything other
than favour and honour.

As lovers do, she lacked patience and tolerance
because she was not within his arms. She wanted
to touch him, to feel the strength of his muscles, to
run her fingers through his short hair, and to once
again make love to him as if tomorrow did not exist.
Octavia longed to balance her body with his and
complete once again, as intended by nature, a perfect
fusion.

Her father had shut the door behind him and was
now sitting at the side of her bed. He carried several
newspapers in one hand. Octavia looked into his eyes:
what a kind, gentle face he had. He continued to
recount events.

'When Mr North found the smashed bottle on the
patio, he correctly suspected someone had tried to
poison you with almost pure alcohol. A methyl alcohol,
in fact, like methylated spirits. When consumed in any
quantity, and you had a lethal dose, it is absorbed via
the stomach into the bloodstream, then circulated
throughout the arterial system.

'Myelin, which acts as an insulator, surrounds each nerve cell throughout the body. It has a great affinity for absorbing methyl alcohol, and when this occurs it inhibits the nerve's ability to transmit electrical impulses. The optic nerve is a delicate and very sensitive structure; any inhibition in its myelin sheath reduces its insulation and thus quickly renders the nerve's ability to transmit a visual image useless. In other words, blindness quickly results.

'The only real antidote is ordinary whisky, which is what Mr North gave you. It was lucky there happened to be a bottle to hand.'

So, thought Octavia, *that was the pale yellow liquid he made me drink. Just whisky!* Her father continued the story.

'Whisky is largely ethyl alcohol, to give it its chemical name. Myelin sheaths, including those surrounding the nerves that supply the eyes, like ethyl alcohol much more than methyl alcohol. So, by consuming ordinary whisky, the ethyl alcohol displaces the methyl alcohol from the myelin sheaths. The process of absorption is the same that occurs when you become drunk in the ordinary way. After a time, the ethyl alcohol is released, so that the myelin sheaths can resume their function of insulation once again.'

So, that's how Sebastian saved her sight and more than likely her life. She wondered how he had hauled her up from the water first. *How clever and how amazing*, she thought.

Her father went on to tell her of the duel with Camillio that had resulted in Camillio's death, and that it had taken place before North could administer the whisky. *My God*, she thought, *his left shoulder must be in an awful state after such physical retribution.*

Like a far-off dream, half remembered, she saw herself lying desperately sick on the patio, watching blurred images of two men fighting with swords that continuously flashed in the bright sunlight. What was more, her first impressions after meeting Camillio aboard the plane, and viewing his intentions with suspicion, were well founded. Members of the Cosa Nostra, so called 'men of honour', were rich in treacherous blood. And vengeance, as always, came easily.

Then Octavia noticed her father's expression, which had suddenly changed from delight at her recovery to one of quivering agitation and distress.

'What is it, Father? What is it that brings out this concern? Is it for me? There is no need to worry, for now that I am alive and can see perfectly, life will begin all over. With Sebastian everything is now possible. Who knows, he might even ask me to marry him! A woman's intuition can see much, you know!'

'I have some news that I find distressing to give you.'

'How long have you had it?'

'A few days; until now only your health, your life, mattered.'

'What is it, Father? Pray tell me.'

'When I tell you, you must face the future with bravery, for I fear you are being tested to the very limit of your endurance, perhaps beyond...' His voice trailed off to a whisper.

'What is it, Father?' persisted Octavia. 'Does it concern Sebastian?'

'Yes,' came the reluctant reply, her father's voice now so quiet she had to strain to listen further.

'Where is he? Where is he now?'

'Listen, Octavia, he can't see you...' Again, she had to strain to pick up his words.

'What do you mean? Is he in England?'

'Yes, in England.' His voice was now that of someone in a trance, husky and far away. It did not seem to belong to him any more. *Cold and detached, even mechanical*, thought Octavia.

'Then I will travel to England to meet him—' Before Octavia could finish, she heard the fatal words.

'Mr North was killed in a car crash seven days ago, three days after saving your life.' He passed over the pile of newspapers he had under his arm. Then he turned his head away to hide his face. It was only for a second, because he knew his daughter would need his strength to lean on, and he desperately wanted to help her in this hour of need.

The headlines screamed up from the newspaper's front page.

'MYSTERIOUS CAR CRASH – MAFIA VENGEANCE?'

The letters, in heavy type, carried pulverising weight, their full significance numbing Octavia's mind and fracturing her heart beyond hope. Tears welled up in her dark eyes, then ran in ever increasing streams down her cheeks.

How deceitful can destiny be! It plays pitiless games with a false-hearted cunning. What use were her eyes now as her doomed fate finally revealed its losing hand by destroying that which she wished so much to have?

The extensive article gave little information with regard to exact cause of death. Only a brief sketch of circumstances relating to the accident was outlined.

Sebastian North's car left the road out of control in wet conditions, moments before it hit a tree at an estimated 100mph. The result left little to the imagination.

Most of the article recounted in some detail the recent discovery of the Sultan's treasure. A smiling photograph of herself, entitled 'The Unlucky Countess Octavia', appeared halfway through the print. Some details of the fight had leaked out, and a graphic account was recorded of the fierce and highly-skilled duel between Count Fambino, a member of the powerful Fambino family, and the Englishman.

The Times recounted with obvious satisfaction how 'a lone Englishman has dared to challenge the legendary Cosa Nostra with, of all things, a duel, and win! Then he escaped with the former fiancée of Count Roberto Fambino, whom he had just killed. Then finally he made a discovery of perhaps the greatest and most valuable archaeological find... since Tutankhamun!'

A local paper continued, '...However, it seems that even this extraordinary individual was not immune from the long reach of the Sicilian Mafia. For this shadowy organisation was cited as having the most likely influence in connection with his death, though there is no proof in this direction as yet. However, due to this possibility, Britain's elite police unit, Scotland Yard, has been brought in to investigate the matter further.

'The private funeral is scheduled for next Thursday in a small village in the Royal County of Berkshire. Only close family are invited to attend. There is a lot of speculation as to whether the reputed lover of the Englishman, the famous Sicilian socialite, Countess Octavia Delmonte, will attend. Since the age of twenty-one, she has worn the antique ring which contained the secret inscription that, once transcribed, gave the position of the Sultan's treasure.'

Octavia paused to look at the ruby upon the fourth finger of her left hand, which had been returned to her by the local Sardinian police after investigating the Count's death, then read further.

The article continued with a few lines about the Countess suffering from a recent illness. 'Rumour has it that a bizarre poisoning attempt, possibly by the Cosa Nostra, had been carried out. The unique international background, so full of intrigue and numerous unnatural deaths including, that of, Sebastian North, gave the doomed lovers a kind of Greek tragedy finish.'

The scale of international interest and media exposure was expressed from California to the Far East and from Oslo to Cape Town.

The Los Angeles Times, the day after the car accident, mentioned that Hollywood was already showing some interest in the film rights to this strange story of romance, hidden treasure, duels, death, and finally vengeance. A spokesman for Columbia Pictures would not 'confirm or deny' their interest. However, 20th Century Fox stated that they would be keeping their 'options open'.

Amongst the collection of newspapers were two later editions printed after the funeral. The service in the local church had been sparsely attended, with reporters kept firmly outside. Apparently, the Countess Octavia Delmonte did not attend. Her father, the Baron Delmonte, stated she was too ill to travel. He would not be drawn into giving an opinion on the poison theory, or speculation on the possible foreign influence of the car 'accident'.

The story did now seem to have some sort of conclusion, with the Count's death, the Englishman's death, and the Countess too ill from the possible effects of poison, to carry the story further.

Octavia threw the newspapers to the floor. A whole week had passed since the fatal car crash. She had missed the funeral, his funeral, now two days ago. She must have been very sick, for she remembered little during the previous week, save a general malaise of disjointed images and emotions that suddenly meant very little.

What direction was her life taking? For the first time in her life Octavia wanted to die. To live now seemed far worse than any imagined fate in hell.

For days at a time Octavia would not listen to anyone, including her father, whose health was also starting to fail him. She refused to leave the villa where she had been recovering. The added strain of seeing his only daughter breaking apart before his eyes, after the recent death of his wife, began to tell throughout the Baron's weakened constitution.

One day, a large bunch of flowers arrived, their colours and shades bringing a cheerfulness to Octavia's room that somehow lifted her distraught spirits a little above irretrievability.

The thoughtful gift was from a convent that had heard of her suffering. Two of the Sisters from the Holy Order of St Crispin's had personally picked and chosen them from the convent's garden. Their stay was only a few moments, just long enough for their kind gift and presence to be appreciated and much remembered.

After many sleepless nights, Octavia recalled the calm serenity of the two sisters, but they of course could not understand the pain and suffering from losing someone you love. How incredibly lucky they were to conduct their lives free from the constraints of a heart yearning for another.

Octavia, in a fit of what some would say was confusion and bewilderment, decided to incarcerate herself within the protective walls of St Crispin's, away from the insensitive chaos of the outside world.

She would seek spiritual answers from the emotional questions that life had insisted on asking, but first she had to go to a place of emotional starvation and isolation, far away from men. There she would try to repair her shattered heart by offering her soul for religious instruction in the pursuit of enlightenment and understanding.

Her father tried to persuade her that the convent could not provide answers for a broken heart; but maybe its routine would offer some sort of short-term stability. In any case, once Octavia had made up her mind there was no turning back.

* * * * *

The narrow window was situated high above Octavia's head. She lay supine upon the simple bed, her eyes focusing on the sunlight that shafted through the restricted aperture. Her eyes followed the constricted beam as it edged across the opposite wall. At last it reached the solitary wooden crucifix that was the only interruption in the wall's bleak white surface.

The mid-morning call sounded from the bell tower. Octavia pictured one of the sisters pulling for all she was worth, her enclosed mind no doubt anticipating a future closeness with the Almighty from this dedicated exertion.

Octavia rose from her bed, hesitating before dressing. This was the third time that day she had performed the ritual. The previous occasions were for the same purpose as this rising, only they had taken place much earlier – at 4.30am and 6.30am – before the inadequate breakfast at 7.30am. She found it hard to imagine life without this routine, though in reality her participation in this structure had been little more than nine months.

The now-familiar black, grey, and white clothes lay on a solitary chair. How she loathed these shapeless garments that hid her body in an indistinguishable formless mass of folds.

She made some last-minute adjustments to her hair with the aid of a small mirror, smuggled in some months earlier. Officially such an instrument of vanity was banned, along with most of the outside world. No-one would be able to see her hair, as it would be totally covered; it was just that she felt better in taking this small amount of effort with her appearance.

The ringing ceased, indicating her lateness for the mid-morning prayers. Octavia left her austere room to descend the worn steps that led from her cell. Then, like a ghost, she passed through the shadow-casting cloisters, her grey cape making a scraping noise as she went. After several cool stone corridors and additional steps, she reached the 14th century chapel.

How many countless thousands of miserable and wretched souls had trod this path before her? The Holy Order of St Crispin's had been founded well before Christopher Columbus discovered the Americas in 1492.

St Crispin, a Roman Christian martyr of the 3rd Century AD, was the patron saint of the After Life or Heaven. Exactly how this martyr came to such an exalted position Octavia was never able to discover.

To ensure future success in this most difficult area, a lifetime of earthly prayer and servitude was called upon. Unquestioned loyalty to St Crispin and, of course, continuous allegiance to Rome was the price of future salvation for all those within the holy order.

The Mother Superior would, God willing, be able to rout out the 'unbelievers and those with doubt in their hearts'. For this purpose, ordained by the Pope and via the Holy Order of St Crispin, she exercised enormous power over those who lived within the confines of the cloisters.

Octavia entered the richly decorated and sombre atmosphere of the chapel. From the half-light of candles, she made out the dark silhouettes of kneeling figures. Her footsteps scraped upon worn marble, the rasping sound carried an echo, ensuring that her lateness would be noted.

Octavia took her allotted place at the end of the first pew, much to the irritation of the Mother Superior. On the end of her long, hooked nose, small gold-rimmed glasses perched at such an angle that the pious black eyes beyond imitated a bird of prey. Somehow the detached coldness reminded Octavia of Roberto's uncle. The difference was that Giovanni Fambino was in no doubt which side he was on, and it wasn't for the good of humanity. The Mother Superior believed that she was saving the souls of those under her for religious instruction, thus 'guaranteeing' her own place at God's exalted right hand.

The Mother Superior would have words about this irresponsibility later. Being late would be viewed as indicative of Octavia's attitude. Her first six months had been those of a model neophyte, but something had changed. Maybe her mind had started to rediscover and explore the dangerous path of independent thought, without reference to those in authority.

Octavia felt those eyes upon her, calculating and penetrating in their endeavour to read the secrets of her heart.

Sister Octavia will need more instruction to purify her soul, thought the Mother Superior. *She is much constrained by aristocratic birth, power and privilege. Her soul is, of course, tainted by having succumbed to the weakness of the flesh. She will need regular and more individual tuition to cleanse this pleasure-seeking mind from earthly temptations.*

Maybe, after a long time, when her beauty fades and does not pose so much of a threat to temptation, then redemption may at last be possible.

The inevitable appointment with the Mother Superior was set for 6pm that evening, between afternoon prayers and the evening meal at 7pm. So, Octavia had until then to contemplate the possible outcome of this meeting. This would be the third such disciplinary meeting in as many months – an unprecedented record at St Crispin's.

That same afternoon, Octavia cried with the uncontrolled convulsions of one who suffers the great pain of heartbreak.

For the past week, she had left her room only to pray in the chapel. *Maybe*, she thought, *God might listen more intently if she knelt on holy ground*. It was all in vain, for Sebastian could not come back to the land of the living. No matter how hard she tried, his only presence was through past memories where the present had no place and the future held no hope.

Each night Octavia had buried her head in her pillow. Face down, she would cry herself to sleep with shallow and uncertain breaths. The pillow's coarse material would always be damp from the silent tears of one who can't find a meaning for their existence.

Her dreams were of the man she loved. How she ached with the vivid memory of their brief but powerful time together. *La Valencia*, the dancing, the first kiss, the island of Panarea, their first lovemaking... What divine music it was!

What intrigue life once held for two such distinct souls in their creation of harmony by the delicate and potent fusion of their bodies.

Octavia recalled every detail. The hair upon Sebastian's chest and how it felt against her own smooth skin. The animal smell of his skin that somehow told of this man's unquestioned masculinity and inherent attraction. Most of all, she would remember his fascinating eyes that conveyed in the same moment such meaning and trust, with perhaps a far-off understanding of life's deeper mysteries. His eyes suggested experience well beyond his years, possibly his soul had learned much from the testing fires of life's sometimes uncompromising course.

More than once Octavia heard his voice, saying something about life being a constantly evolving process, not a destination. That was when he was alive. *Now that the gods had left her, what hope was there for this solo existence?*

Faith in life was a ridiculous idea. She wished with all her broken heart she would die soon. She longed to finish this living crucifixion and reach the soft sands of oblivion, where at last her soul could gain respite from its harrowing burden.

However, Octavia was afraid to take her own life. Fear of this ultimate and unknown path kept her in the land of the living, one step from the concealed precipice of no return. Sometimes the void that is death beckoned her to challenge its prohibited truth; was it so bad, after all? For then she would find her lover, and life would begin anew.

At the appointed hour, Octavia arrived outside the Mother Superior's door. Her secretary – a thin, unhealthy-looking woman with a pronounced hunch and pock-marked cheeks – had the distinction of managing to make the folds of cloth look huge, like a half-folded parachute covering her bent, wiry frame.

Without saying a word, she motioned for Octavia to sit upon an ancient and austere wooden bench. This was no doubt to give her time to contemplate the coming meeting, which was going to be anything but relaxing.

While she sat staring at the cracks in the brick wall opposite, Octavia reflected. *How important was a person's lineage? Could she find strength from the past as told by her mother? Her illustrious ancestors had passed on a certain amount of fortitude, or was she confusing this with her own stubbornness?*

The secretary announced to the space beyond the door that the novice was waiting. There was an expectant pause, but no sound came from within. However, unseen by Octavia, some gesture must have taken place as the stooped secretary motioned for Octavia to enter the forbidding void.

Alone beside a large desk stood the Mother Superior. A little light came from a high window, but it was not enough to penetrate the oppressive gloom. It took Octavia a moment to gain the room's dimensions. It was large and sparse in its lack of furniture and fixtures, save for a few chairs and a wooden cabinet that looked old and somehow valuable.

Dressed in white, the figure before Octavia confronted her. The light from an electric lamp off to one side struck the large linked gold chain and crucifix in such a way that it momentarily dazzled. The reflection forced her to step sideways. Whether this effect was by accident or design, Octavia was uncertain. She felt uncomfortable, her position vulnerable.

'It is time you and I had a little talk…' The Mother Superior paused, pursing her bloodless lips, the black eyes seeming to sink deeper into their hollow sockets, giving her face a deathly appearance. She continued, 'Ever since you arrived at St Crispin's, your presence amongst us has not been a happy experience or one that I could describe as in any way harmonious.

'In particular, your recent attitude has created a distrustful and rebellious atmosphere with all those who have had contact with you. At St Crispin's you will learn that there is little that I don't know about.'

The Mother Superior began to pace up and down, sadistically enjoying the young girl's discomfort and complete subservience in her presence.

'Several of the novices showed promise in their dedication to the scriptures and acceptance of our spiritual authority. Several of these same novices, and even a few of those who have already taken their final vows, now question that which was not even thought of.'

To most of the Sisters at St Crispin's, Octavia was someone to be avoided, though many harboured envy within their hearts. Her previous life beyond the convent walls had filtered through soon after her passing the entrance gates.

Those Sisters that considered themselves the most observant and devoted Christians were found among the middle-aged and elderly. Here the magical flame of youth's curiosity and hope had long been extinguished by years of fanatical obedience to near-useless dogma.

To question authority, as laid down by Rome, was to risk accusations of possessing a compromised mind. The purpose of question and power of reason were condemned as tools belonging to heretics and, worse, those of Lucifer's servants. In blind pursuit of spiritual purity, they rejected the flesh of their own bodies, thus developing an imbalance between the spirit and the organic. Their short-sightedness formed the limitations of their spiritual prison, for its walls remained impervious to the pursuit of liberty in thought.

The occasional newspaper and magazine had been smuggled into the convent. Some of these pages reported Octavia's romantic adventures and the finding of the Sultan's treasure.

Very few within had felt the touch of a man upon them, or had even been kissed by one, let alone known the meaning of love.

'Sit down, Contessa.' It was the first time Octavia had heard the Mother Superior use her title. *Her voice was deep and husky like a man's,* she thought. It grated like a delicate musical instrument being forced to play notes much lower than its original designer intended.

'I prefer to stand,' said Octavia with new-found strength. The advantage of height, for she was several inches taller than the Mother Superior, was worth preserving if possible.

Octavia did not want to risk being intimidated any more than she could help. The Mother Superior had not made it clear as to what position she would adopt: sit behind her large desk, or continue standing off to the side? For the moment, Octavia's height gave her an advantage, perhaps a small comfort. But anything that might help her in what she knew would be a difficult time seemed worth considering.

'As you wish,' came the irritated reply. The woman in white now chose the comfort of her hard, high-backed wooden chair. It commanded a reassuring view from behind the desk's imposing size.

A gold inlay in the shape of Christ being crucified on the Cross was the only ornamentation in the green leather surface. *A constant reminder of earthly pain and suffering,* thought Octavia.

The withered figure perched on the chair's edge leant forward, now supported upon her elbows. The coif was bound so tight Octavia wondered if the woman's skull had not in some way been moulded by its uncompromising tension. Again, the bloodless lips were pursed in preparation. The cold black eyes fixed an unblinking stare.

'Let me give you some of our history, Contessa. This might enable you to understand what we are trying to achieve here at the Order of St Crispin's.

'This may also illuminate your present situation, which you will see has turned out to be quite unique, at least so far as the 20th Century is concerned.

'In previous centuries, the numbers within this convent were made from girls of very varied backgrounds and circumstances.

'Of course, there was always a steady number who had made it an earthly ambition to join us. The reasons vary. A physical defect, or ugly features, might accelerate their desire to leave the outside world and its constant pressures for our more orderly existence.

'For instance, a noble family who could not find a suitable marriage for a daughter might think to avoid shame by passing her over to us, along with a suitable dowry. She, of course, could not leave even as a novice, without her parent's consent.

'The daughters of families that could not produce suitable dowries were known as Sisters of the Orange Scarf. The tradition continues; you will have noticed several amongst us wearing a scarf. Those that came with dowries were known as the Sisters of the Purple Scarf. You will have noticed that this tradition also continues, except that now those who wish to leave can of their own free will.

'The work of those that did not arrive with a dowry would always be manual in nature.

'Unplanned and subsequently unwanted pregnancies of noble families to avoid scandal could be granted a place, and again the same rules apply with regard to a suitable dowry.

'A few will always try to escape; the grass is always greener on the other side for a few misinformed and stupid girls. To my knowledge, only four girls have managed successful escapes in over four hundred years.

'I am not including those that tried and failed. Those that were caught found life here extremely unpleasant for many years afterwards. And as far as I know, no-one succeeded upon a second try.'

'How could you possibly know?' enquired Octavia. 'Those in authority would hardly acknowledge that someone amongst them would try and leave this "garden of Eden".' Her voice now contained heavy sarcasm as sudden anger brought new courage and a strange confidence.

'I wonder what excuse was adopted to account for such occurrences. Were those poor girls guilty of only an intemperate decision corrected with further indoctrination, or was "delirium" their new-found illness?'

'This book…' the Mother Superior pointed with a gnarled finger to a leather-bound volume, '…is a record of most, if not all, of those who have graced the cloisters of St Crispin's since its 14th Century foundation.

'It is also a diary of events that proved of interest during the administration of each Mother Superior.

'The volume's pages were painstakingly compiled by one of us, during the latter nineteenth century, who had access to various letters, manuscripts, and official documents. Many such papers were lost or destroyed. One that survived was a Papal decree. This established St Crispin's close contact with Rome and certified the Pope's sanctioned authority and supremacy over all aspects of the human life.

'Judging from its contents, it was never intended for the eyes of anyone during the lifetime of its author.

It was during restoration work twenty years ago in this very room that its discovery was made, including some human remains.

'One of the skeletons was a woman; the other was, according to medical opinion, without doubt that of a young man.

'If the man had entered the convent illegally, there was only one reason. And if caught with one of the Sisters, which seems the logical explanation, then their fate would have been sealed. In this case, literally bricked up behind this wall.' She pointed behind her.

'The presence of this book was coincidence, it having been concealed a few yards from them many years later.'

Octavia was distressed at this pitiful tale, but worse was to come.

'You may be interested to know that the relative position of the remains and some writing on the walls suggested they were bricked up alive.'

Alive! Octavia's mind froze. Her imagination seized the image that it created, then it ran wild as she pictured the two lovers and their horrendous fate.

My God, what evil had these walls been witness to? What degradation and decay had ruled here? Only those in an advanced state of mental confusion and spiritual disintegration could be remotely capable of carrying out such an act!

The Mother Superior smiled a wicked grin. 'But all this is in the past. The problem we have today, Contessa Octavia Delmonte, is that your father has not kept his part of the contract he agreed with us.'

'What contract?' asked Octavia, bewildered.

'You see, the second instalment of a sum agreed – a donation, you understand, for helping in your particular situation – has failed to arrive.

'We accepted you here because our institution could be of help in healing this licentious mind that you so stubbornly possess.

'From the beginning, I had reservations. Your, ah, reputation somewhat preceded you in penetrating even these walls.' She gestured with her arms to the stone walls around her. 'Finances have been difficult lately, funds increasingly hard to administer, but your father was most generous, or so we were led to believe. As it turns out, my secretary was right, one can never trust a Sicilian!'

She paused, the black eyes, falcon-like, sunk impossibly deep into their cavernous sockets, the whole face now white like a pastry before baking. *Completely drained of blood and life*, thought Octavia.

'You cannot leave until we have word that the entire sum agreed upon by both parties has been delivered to our satisfaction.'

Octavia's blood boiled with an intense fury that fuelled the gathering storm that had long waited to vent its frustration. This witch of a woman who dared to proclaim spiritual enlightenment now became the object of her unmuzzled wrath.

'By what authority do you seek to constrain me? This is the twentieth century, not the Dark Ages!'

The Mother Superior's reply confirmed that her brainwashing was complete and absolute.

'Power is held by the Church to grant or withhold absolution through St Peter to the Pope, and thence to the Roman Catholic Priesthood. It's all in Matthew, if you care to read your Bible, which I am sure you have not.'

She continued, with Octavia finding it almost impossible to believe what was being said, 'By the authority of the Vatican and God, through Jesus Christ, do I hold your person. For by doing so I am helping the Church and its work to obtain much needed funds to carry on God's wishes.'

Octavia stood erect, her heart pounding hot Sicilian blood through her arteries.

'You propose to hold me with authority from God?' said Octavia incredulously. 'You have no more right to consult God and interpret his divine messages, let alone use his authority, than those that play the Ouija board have to communicate with the devil and his servants!'

With a deep breath, Octavia continued, 'From the Vatican's insulated ivory towers through a celibate priesthood to an institution such as this, there runs a wind strong in superstition and averse to independent thought!

'You are but a small wheel in a vast machine of influence that has created this prison, the walls of which are too thick for real learning to penetrate. The windows are fitted with bars too close for the outside world to reach within. To condemn the world beyond is to deny truth and ultimately freedom of choice that can only be found through the illumination of lessons that life teaches us!

'I wonder how many other poor souls St Crispin's keeps restrained within these walls?' Octavia continued to attack, her eyes now smouldering with unrestrained anger.

She had come to St Crispin's seeking solitude, isolation, and even peace from a broken heart. In these aims she had only partially succeeded, but had discovered something infinitely more valuable. Slowly, a much deeper understanding of who she really was, in terms of present awareness and future direction, had grown and assumed shape. The future began to release its thick shroud of apprehension, so that lessons from the past could be applied with something approaching hope, because direction came from within, not the teachings of St Crispin's.

The Mother Superior had never known anyone raise a voice in her presence before, and from someone so young, who dared to question her very existence and belief with such venom. She was shaken to the core by this onslaught – an unwelcome situation that did not come easily to her.

Octavia continued with renewed enthusiasm, 'If you hide away from the outside world and its endless game of chance, you risk nothing and so learn little of life.

'If you do not know the demon defeat, how can you possibly understand the exaltation of success?

'If you have never tasted a man's breath upon you, nor felt his superior strength tighten with love, then much of your enclosed learning ceases to be a measure of meaningful progress. For I believe there must be a balance between that which is spiritual and everyday material existence—'

The Mother Superior could take little more. She stood up, but stayed behind the desk's imposing barrier and, with hate permeating every word, launched into a counterattack.

'Your cursed and despicable indoctrination has warped and twisted your once tender mind into its present evil-fashioned existence. Born to wealth and privilege, you squandered money without a thought for the peasant and starving. You have led a licentious life whose exploits through the world's media spread far and wide for all good Christians to wince and cower from.'

The old woman, strange as it may seem, now started to develop some signs of colour in her previously so pale cheeks, but the words were spat with ill-concealed rage and hatred.

'How dare you speak to me in this way! Only the fires of eternal damnation await your wicked soul. St Peter's gates will be closed, for he will be deaf to your cries of help.'

Then her attitude changed, like a storm passing. The tone became patient, the voice adopting a hint of conciliation, even benevolence. The previous eyes, dark and deep in their sockets, now approached those associated with a serpent – bulging, hypnotic and devoid of all emotion.

'Perhaps I can help by keeping you here, a prisoner until your father's money arrives. I can guarantee that this will be looked upon with favour, for you will be helping the Church and thus helping to atone for your misspent past. I need not remind you that we alone have the power to grant absolution.'

Octavia replied, her voice now low and controlled, 'You can't hold my future to ransom because of my past!'

To the Mother Superior, deception was a habit of mind in the manipulation and control of others if it so suited her purpose.

With the threat of being held, Octavia's mind became oddly detached. *Strange, this state of mind, when monumental events are happening around you and yet one's thoughts are briefly free to wonder in clear reflection.*

Octavia remembered at the age of eighteen having posed topless for a Milan-based magazine. It wasn't the money that had charged her mind with electricity. It was the incredible power generated by her body that could send men half-crazy for her attention.

Men would melt by looking into her eyes; they would promise every material possession money could buy, from diamonds to houses.

She could have married any one of them, except those who participated in drug-taking, which was common. She drew her own line at something that destroyed and corrupted so easily. This principle was to be tested later by Roberto Fambino, whose attention and love for Octavia was thus in the end doomed to failure, for his life was led by the principle of self-interest.

Roberto was more than just money. It was the mysterious mafia background, this secret power, that she first found attractive, whose dark side she later hoped to ignore.

Then at last it became impossible to disregard, for she could not compromise her principles and succumb like so many others impressed by noble looks and money alone.

Yes, she did believe in something, and it was not going to be sacrificed by marrying Roberto under any circumstances. He wrecked any real chance by not being faithful to her after their publicised engagement. At first, Roberto promised to be faithful, but he failed. He also said he would renounce the mafia and his connections with the Cosa Nostra. Such empty words of deceit; he had no intention in this direction. Roberto's values amounted to the fanatical pursuit of money and power by any method available.

Octavia soon realised that she counted in importance as little more than a chattel. So, she left to follow a quest for life that could not be defined or explained. She had to leave Sicily, her destination uncertain.

Her past continued to flicker like a disjointed series of photographs, her mind probing past memories of turmoil and excitement. Searching these various scenes for meaning and understanding, she wondered what truth was or how she would recognise it.

The timely intervention of Sebastian in her life, by risking his own life without a thought for personal safety, was the dawn of something new and which would change her life forever. When this stranger lay wounded at the villa in Monte Carlo and she observed his face asleep, she found her senses amplified as they started to open a new and previously unknown dimension.

Time and again this man helped her in her hour of need. Octavia wanted to cry, the lump in her throat stuck as she recalled how she had denounced him at Roberto's request, to gain possession of the ring.

Octavia could not understand it, but her first meeting with Roberto after so long, at Castle Zehra, had re-kindled old emotions so that she had started to fall for the Count all over again. *How could she come under Roberto's influence once more, when she was so sure he could not reach her on the emotional plane for a second time?*

When Roberto resorted to violence, this confusion had left like an unwelcome visitor in the night. From that point, there was of course no doubt where her emotions lay, perhaps had always been, the moment she had fallen at Sebastian's feet asking for help, now so long ago.

Octavia found herself frightened that there had been uncertainty at all, no matter how brief.

Her past confusion and regret mocked her. The present was now much too late to re-write the past, and the car crash in England had with harsh efficiency rendered the future emotionally irrelevant.

Her father would never turn against her, so why had the second instalment not arrived? With both Roberto and Camillio dead, who could still plot against her? The Mother Superior could not be trusted, but was she telling the truth now? Had there really been an agreement with her father? So many questions remained unanswered.

Who was the owner of the unseen hand that carved these new rules that sought to bind her life to that of a prisoner?

Or was it only a procedural hold-up, a technical hitch, a genuine misunderstanding? In a few days all could be well, when the second instalment arrived. Then she could leave.

Octavia's mind spun in circles with little focus and control. Her imagination shuddered then settled reluctantly once again upon the two lovers bricked up all that time ago, alive!

The interview came to an abrupt end. Octavia remembered little as she left the figure in white and her repulsive secretary.

Octavia knew then that there was only one solution, for insanity was beckoning with a lethal intensity. She had to escape, and very soon.

Chapter Fifteen

The convent was set apart on raised ground overlooking a valley. Its location commanded fine views of the river fast flowing below and a busy town, some two or three miles down river.

When Octavia first saw the convent that housed the Holy Order of St Crispin, she had thought how like Castle Zehra it looked. However, its structure was not as massive, as it had not been designed to withstand a protracted siege. It was the lack of windows in both structures that she noticed first. Not until later did she discover the very different reasons for this common design.

Castle Zehra was designed to keep undesirable people out, while the convent was built to discourage those within its walls from leaving. St Crispin's was originally founded, and maintained until recent times, as a closed order.

Escape now dominated Octavia's entire existence. She pushed aside all other thoughts to this single purpose. *But to escape alone? Was this within the realms of possibility? Who could she trust?*

There was only one person that escape could be mentioned to without risk of exposure: Sister Nicol. She had completed her novice training some five years earlier to take the final vows, thus pledging her earthly existence to the Church and God.

Octavia and Nicol had become close friends soon after Octavia's arrival at St Crispin's. Octavia's mournful expression and constant crying brought out Nicol's sympathy and concern for the Sicilian girl's predicament.

Nicol could not be described as beautiful in the classical sense. The skin on her face was coarse, her features rather too full, suggesting that she was overweight. Octavia had wondered how anyone could be anything other than thin and underweight living off the meagre rations at St Crispin's. Nicol had also since birth been blind in the right eye, so that she looked at people with her head turned slightly to compensate.

When Octavia arrived, Nicol had been at first intimidated by her famous wealth and legendary lifestyle. However, her intense curiosity to find out what it was like to be attractive and desired by men overcame her initial hesitation. Most of all, she wanted to know how it was to be with and love a man.

Over time, Nicol and Octavia developed a friendship that was based on mutual trust and understanding. Whenever they could find an opportunity alone together, Nicol would ask Octavia to recount some incident or experience of a famous person. One that she had met at a party in Rome, Los Angeles, or some such haunt of the rich and famous.

Sometimes Nicol would visit Octavia in the middle of the night and, in shaded light, listen to her stories of shopping trips to Milan and New York. Nicol's eyes became large with the thought of choosing a dress from a wardrobe containing over two hundred – the number kept in the house Octavia's parents had given her outside Madrid. This did not include the rest of the collection in apartments and villas scattered around the world.

Nicol would make Octavia tell her about the men she had met, what attracted them, and why she dated them. What were these experiences like? Did her heart ache the way some books describe at the touch of a man? How did she adjust to breaking up? Was this so very painful, as portrayed in romantic books? How did she, Octavia, cope with this pain?

For hours Nicol listened to Octavia's past experiences of high society, narrated by someone who once thought she had everything, only to discover that in fact she had so very little. Octavia had enjoyed her past, but it was the encounter with Sebastian that had given her life a strange and intangible new meaning. Perspective was now being applied to the material, which Octavia soon learned had no more value than changing scenery on the unpredictable stage of life.

Nicol found it astonishing and fascinating that such enormous differences could be found during the game of courtship. For the Italian man was quite different in his approach to the Scandinavian, recounted Octavia one evening.

'Italian men within Italy itself vary a great deal from north to south. Compared with those closer to Calabria in the south, men from the north are much more European in outlook than those from south of Naples, whose views tend to be insular to the region and suspicious of everything outside it.

'A man's kiss in the south still implies possible engagement, although a following marriage is no longer as certain as it once was. To the north, a kiss has been liberated to come and go as it pleases, but the courtship still remains drawn out, with long candlelight meals on open terraces.

'It is here that the Italian man will demonstrate his great ingenuity and skill at convincing the girl that she literally dropped from heaven. He will tell her the moon worships the very ground she stands on, and that the brightness of the stars pales beside the depths of her eyes. The sun's radiance cannot improve upon her perfect complexion.

'Here he uses flattery on an outrageous scale that no Englishman or Scandinavian would dream of following. A girl who is not used to this approach quickly melts and becomes all too easily caught.

'The Italian male is also cunning, his emotions at times inconsistent and impossible to predict. He is also very possessive of women, and jealousy can arise from something quite trivial. An incident that would attract only a passing comment, if any, in Northern Europe, frequently produces a hurricane of uncontrolled Latin emotion.

'The cold climate of northern Europe is by and large reflected by its people in their cooler approach to courtship, which is much less volatile and more tranquil, at least on the surface. However, it is by no means more predictable than that played out in the south, along the warm shores of the Mediterranean. It is just that the game is played with customs often misunderstood when a north and south match is involved. In both regions, the relationship's course develops and so progresses to any one of a changing and infinite number of situations and conclusions.'

Octavia paused as she gave more consideration to her thoughts.

'Maybe that was part of what Sebastian gave me, a sense of structure and framework to help balance any volatile nature. I know myself well enough to realise that I need a man sufficiently different in temperament from my own to counter my hot Sicilian blood.'

Octavia paused again as she became lost in reflection.

'In this Englishman I found a personality that combined with something within me that was all-powerful and ever so attractive. Until then, I thought Englishmen were always so cold, even remote; for me, they did not come across well. Perhaps their cold wet island, devoid of a hot sun, develops a different outlook. Someone told me that they are notoriously slow to arouse in an argument.'

Nicol's imagination was barely contained, and her attention was absolute, hanging on Octavia's every word.

'My father always said that once you have penetrated that reserve, which could take a long time, the Englishman would be one of the most reliable friends you could wish for. Their method of expression and communication is just so different from our own that misunderstandings arise almost immediately,' Octavia went on.

'The educated Englishman, in the worldly sense of being well-travelled and with a philosophy borne from the wisdom of experience, can be a perfect gentleman, my mother once told me. She knew someone who married such a man and has lived happily ever since in an 18th century house in the county of Hampshire.'

'What about the French?' asked Nicol. 'Is not Paris the city that all lovers go to at least once during their courting? There they hold hands as they walk down the *Avenue du Champs Elysées*, kiss in open air cafés, and stare forever into each other's eyes.'

Octavia laughed. 'How well informed you are for someone who has not been out of this area, let alone travelled abroad.

'The French are a law unto themselves, in most things. The men I found independent and pragmatic, with bouts of high passion and romance. Yes, attractive and a little like our own country in temperament, but not so spontaneous. What is more, they lack Italian style, but exhibit less emotional dishonesty than we do.'

Over the months, Nicol was treated to wonderful stories full of graphic detail and told first-hand so that she came to fantasise some of them almost as if they were her own.

Nicol had tried to help and comfort Octavia during those endless first few weeks of grief, and offered understanding by being open and available to the girl's shattered heart.

Nicol burst into tears when Octavia told her of her plan to escape, because she would be losing a friend, and true friendship was hard to come by at St Crispin's. The Mother Superior had spies everywhere. It was claimed that her intelligence within the convent was so good that she knew what everyone was thinking even before the thought had fully crystallised.

Solitary confinement became Octavia's life after her latest confrontation with the Mother Superior. She had little human contact except her twice daily tray of food brought by the cook's assistant, whose face changed every week.

An almost impossible situation was presented by living in solitary confinement. Nicol provided her with the only chance of escape. Confiding in anyone else would surely be an invitation for disaster. Octavia knew that if her intentions were discovered, they would watch her with the concentration of a hawk seeking its prey.

Sister Nicol had gained a degree of trust and enjoyed a certain amount of freedom within the confines of the cloisters. She was a model student under the strict supervision of St Crispin's ideological straight jacket.

Since having solitary confinement imposed upon her, Octavia and Nicol had developed a system of communication which involved exchanging messages written on pieces of paper hidden in some way. For instance, a message was often smuggled into and out of Octavia's room via her food tray. This was Octavia's vital link beyond the door of her room and the only means of planning for escape, with the risk of detection kept to a minimum.

Isolated in her room and alone for long periods, Octavia gained the liberty to think freely without the interruptions of others.

During the day, when she was allowed out for an hour in the middle of the afternoon, Octavia thought those she saw even at a distance could read her mind and recognise her thoughts of escape. These walks in the cloisters and garden were conducted with almost as much isolation as that found in her room, and two middle-aged Sisters were assigned exclusively to ensure that she remained without communication through word or concealed signal.

This time of intense planning and waiting somehow became easier, as Octavia's mind was now focused upon one aim – the objective of escape. Many plans were at first considered then rejected as impractical and dangerous, because they incorporated too high a risk of detection.

In the end, they decided the escape had to be conducted at night, as it would allow Octavia the greatest amount of time before her absence was discovered.

The traffic in and out of the convent was minimal, and from dawn to dusk the gate was watched with enough thoroughness to deter flight by that route. Again, Octavia found it hard to believe that she was living in the twentieth century and not the Middle Ages.

The night Octavia planned to escape from St Crispin's drew closer. The passing days and nights worked upon her mind like a suppressed spring with ever-increasing pressure, just waiting for release.

Octavia would lie awake at night, going over every detail of the plan in her mind. Then concentration would drift, and again she would silently ask the four walls why the second instalment of money pledged by her father had not arrived.

How was it possible to be held a prisoner in this convent? Was this not the twentieth century? Had she started to enter some terrible time warp, and would wake one morning to find herself in the 1500s? For countless nights, sleep only came through tears as she thought of her beloved Sebastian.

Once asleep, Octavia often dreamed. Only then did she become sure of love's authenticity and realise its enduring truth, as it tried to conquer her uncertainties. If she awoke during the night, tears of disappointment would come, for the experience was almost real.

Then one morning, a letter appeared under Octavia's door. She picked it up with great curiosity, as the colourful stamp and postmark named Córdoba as the place of posting! It was dated six weeks previously. The envelope was written by a cavalier but disciplined hand in blue ink with an italic nib, that suggested by its right slant and elaborate capital letters a certain unconventional attitude and style.

Contained within the white envelope was not a letter, but an invitation printed in black flowing script upon white card that was edged by a single gold line.

'Ten travelling gypsies from Arcus de la Frontera invite you to a Fiesta'

The date was on the 15th of the following month at 7.30pm and dress was formal, for it specifically stated 'Black Tie'. What was most unusual was that no mention was made of a venue or address for reply! Octavia wondered who these gypsies were and how this invitation had been smuggled into the convent.

There was something more: seven stars of gold were arranged in a circle at the top of the card, their significance unclear.

* * * * *

Nicol listened with the door to her room slightly ajar. The passage beyond gave no sound. She opened the door just enough to pass into the dark passage, closing the door behind. It clicked shut. Now the nervous girl hesitated, listening. Octavia's escape had started.

The keys she sought, which included those for Octavia's room, hung in a small anteroom off the kitchens. The Sister on duty occupied it during the night, her job 'general watch keeper' for the entire convent.

The night in question had been chosen because this particular Sister was renowned for indolence and inertia towards any tasks remotely requiring diligence or activity. She was the only one that month whose carelessness could be relied upon. Every week the rota changed, and the other Sisters were much too vigilant in carrying out their duties.

Nicol arrived at the anteroom. From the kitchen, the smell of freshly baked bread mingling with burnt fat greeted her nose. There was no-one around; she could hardly believe her luck. The Sister must be on her rounds or asleep somewhere. She had been known to lose interest in whatever task was at hand and just fall asleep from sheer boredom.

Locating a set of keys from a clearly labelled row of hooks, Nicol quickly retraced her steps past her own room, then up a flight of stairs to the first floor and Octavia's room. Halfway up the stairs, she heard a single scream, its source somewhere behind her. It suddenly ceased and a door clanged shut, then silence. Hardly daring to breathe, Nicol hurried on. Her mind raced with growing apprehension. *Who had screamed and why?*

Three gentle knocks upon the thick wooden door brought an immediate response with three similar knocks from within. Octavia was waiting, fully clothed, on the other side.

Nicol's heart rate soared. She felt the palms of her hands moist with sweat, because apart from the obvious stress of implementing the night's plans, she could not find the right key. She tried each of the dozen keys four times, but in vain. None would turn the mechanism. The key that fitted the lock was just not there!

She must have taken the wrong set of keys and yet her memory would not acknowledge a mistake, for she had taken the correct set, assuming the labels matched against the hooks. Unless someone had incorrectly placed the keys to Octavia's room and corridor on a different hook.

Whatever the explanation, it could not be solved here. She had to go back to the anteroom. Nicol explained the predicament to Octavia, who could do little except listen for and await her return.

Within a few yards of her objective, Nicol heard voices, their source close at hand. Then from beyond a bend in the passageway, four white-robed figures came into view, carrying some sort of load. As they drew closer, Nicol could make out the shape of their burden – a stretcher with perhaps someone lying motionless under a white sheet. *Had this something to do with the scream she had heard earlier?*

For a moment, Nicol panicked, thinking they had somehow discovered Octavia's escape plans and were now carrying her off. Then reason returned, for she had just returned from Octavia's room; there had not been time to have arranged a stretcher, having first persuaded an unwilling participant to lie down. In any case, these four figures with their mysterious patient had come from the opposite direction to Octavia's room. *So, who was it?*

Seizing the initiative, Nicol revealed her presence, saying that she had heard the noise of their passage and had come to investigate further. The figures in white passed, one of them answering her question. Apparently, a novice had been taken ill with suspected food poisoning, and so they were taking her to the emergency room for observation. The Sister on duty had left to call a doctor, who should arrive shortly.

So, thought Nicol, *that explains the recent absence of the Sister from the anteroom.*

After the party had passed on its way, Nicol ran the remaining few yards to the anteroom. Thankfully, it remained deserted. Desperate now, she replaced the previous useless keys and took all the other rings containing numerous keys. One of them must open Octavia's door, she reasoned.

At last Nicol reached Octavia's door and, for the second time, she proceeded to try every key in her possession. There were a great number, only half of which were labelled with such names as 'Library' and 'Storeroom', followed by a number. The rest lacked any form of identification. *A few were worn and rusty with age, which was quite incredible in such an organised place as this*, thought Nicol.

If the right key could not be found, the escape would have to be aborted. Maybe the Mother Superior had deliberately taken custody of this key in the hope of thwarting any escape plan.

Nicol heard Octavia calling from the other side of the door. 'What's wrong, Nicol? Is the key not there?'

Nicol felt her hands moisten again as she carefully tried each key in turn, the laborious process taking an incredible amount of time. She dropped several, the metal striking against the worn flagstones, the sound echoing down the low-ceilinged corridor, causing more concern at possible discovery.

Nicol replied, 'I have a few more left to try.'

Then Octavia heard the key turn. The mechanism worked smoothly and the bolt slid back with a click.

With the door open, Nicol and Octavia hugged each other briefly and then parted company. Nicol retraced her steps to replace the many bunches of keys before their loss was noticed. Even now, their absence could have been found. Octavia left in another direction to complete her escape to the outside world.

The two girls parted for the last time with kisses to both cheeks. Nicol had wanted to accompany Octavia as far as the outside wall, but Octavia had persuaded her not to in case they were both caught. There was no knowing what fate awaited Nicol if she was caught helping her to escape. Octavia did not want to endanger her faithful friend any more than was absolutely necessary. If she was caught with Nicol still unsuspected, there might be another chance at a later date.

They had also agreed weeks before that Nicol was to write every month; if she missed a month, then this would be the signal that all was not well. Octavia would then set about finding out the circumstances of the problem. The letters would be sent to a close relative of Nicol's and in code, to ensure her line of communication stayed open.

Octavia's feet hurried through several passageways, but she was careful not to trip over the many folds in her habit. She thought about the four figures, mentioned by Nicol, carrying the stretcher upon which lay someone unknown, and the single muffled scream. *How could that be accounted for? What did it mean? A genuine case of food poisoning or something more sinister?*

Once in the courtyard, Octavia made sure she kept to the shadows cast by the silvery half-moon. She expected to hear sounds indicating her escape had been discovered, or more likely that Nicol had had difficulty in returning the keys undetected. Again, she wondered who the sick novice was on the stretcher, and the nature of her illness.

After leaving the courtyard behind, Octavia quickly covered the distance to the outside wall. Following instructions from Nicol, she located a ladder hidden behind a garden tool shed. It proved too heavy to carry, so she dragged it with difficulty to the imposing wall that loomed massively above her.

Octavia returned to the tool shed and found a coil of rope, exactly as instructed by Nicol earlier. Carefully, she tied one end to the last rung. Once leant against the stone wall, she found the ladder's top fell just short a few inches.

Climbing was difficult because her cumbersome clothes forced caution against haste. With each step upward, Octavia closed the gap between herself and the waiting parapet.

From a crouched position, perched precariously upon the second last rung of the ladder, Octavia slowly stretched her body. Both eyes followed the uneven stones until they abruptly stopped to reveal an uninhibited view. The valley below was partially lit by the half-moon. From her vantage point, Octavia saw that freedom waited, now so very close. The danger surrounding her vulnerable position set her heart pounding with anxiety, for success and capture were both possible.

On top of the wall, Octavia coiled a loop of rope around her. Then she launched herself into the thin air below, playing out the rope as she went. Her feet scraped across the wall's surface as she tried to steady her descent. Five feet from the ground, the rope slipped too fast through her hands, its passage burning with ferocity.

Upon landing Octavia twisted her left ankle, then fell heavily on her left shoulder. There was little pain to start with; it would, she knew, intensify later. The ankle was not broken, as far as she could tell, as movement with hesitation was possible. A bad sprain was her diagnosis.

It was going to make walking most inconvenient, to say nothing of the pain. Looking around, she found a stick for the purpose of support. Concentrating on where she was placing her feet, Octavia made slow progress over an uneven and rocky surface towards the town below.

There was no sign of pursuit, no cry of alarm had been raised. New pain levels were being reached with every step; soon her injured ankle felt as if someone had packed it in red-hot volcanic ash. The pain travelled its cruel course up her leg to the knee, until Octavia felt a wave of nausea pass through her. She begged her limbs to stop and ease this torture. To collapse would bring relief, but she knew even that would be temporary, for the injury was severe.

Somehow, Octavia managed to reach the road, her progress becoming slower and more painful with every step she took. At last she sat down next to a large rock. Her ankle welcomed the rest, as a constant gnawing ache now replaced the previous burning pain.

Only now did she turn her head and look back towards the path just taken and beyond to the forbidding silhouette that was the convent.

Octavia wondered what fate had befallen Nicol. Perhaps she had succeeded in returning all those keys, after all. What a friend she was in her time of great need, to risk so much! *Dear Nicol*, she thought, *may I send you much happiness in future years.*

Octavia removed her shoe. The once-white skin was black and blue from bruising, and the swelling had increased so much that her ankle was becoming indistinguishable from her calf.

With difficulty and much willpower, Octavia restarted her journey towards the sleeping village. Apart from the occasional dog, all was silent. The light had disappeared, with the moon now obscured behind clouds. Octavia was now not as afraid to walk in the road as before; with every faltering step, her chance of escape increased and that of capture receded. At last, real hope loomed closer.

With tears of pain running down her cheeks, Octavia entered the village. Finding a house with telephone lines, she limped up to the whitewashed door and knocked.

Several minutes passed before an old man answered her knock. The door was partially opened, the hour demanding caution. His surprise was reflected in his expression at having a nun call in the middle of the night.

Octavia spun a story about a sick novice at the convent, which could have been true as she remembered the stretcher case described by Nicol. She continued by saying the phone lines were out of order, and her sprained ankle was a result of too much haste in reaching the village. Once the sympathy of her host was gained, access to a phone was granted without further hesitation.

Hardly daring to breathe, the pain of her ankle temporarily forgotten, Octavia pushed the numbers, praying as she did so that her memory had recalled the sequence correctly.

She heard the phone ring but soon lost count of how many times. Of course, there was no need to be alarmed yet, it was still the middle of the night. Then she thought, *supposing there is no-one to answer it?*

'Hello?' The familiar voice sounded strong and clear as if the person was beside her. Relief washed over her, easing her fear like a powerful tranquilliser.

'Papa, it's me, Octavia…'

'Octavia! My God, how are you? Are you alright?'

'Papa, I am at a house in the village below the convent—'

'Your voice is distressed. In your last letter you said everything was wonderful and that St Crispin's was just the experience you needed.'

Octavia's voice was barely a whisper. 'Papa, you must believe me. I have not written to you for many months, they would not let me. I have been held a prisoner at St Crispin's, I have just managed to escape tonight. Please come and take me away. They will be after me even here, I am sure of it. I don't think I am safe yet!'

Her father reacted at once. 'I am sending my doctor, Carlos, over immediately. You remember him, of course. He is with me now. I can't move my legs. They haven't worked so well these last few months. Carlos will leave now and should be with you in a little over an hour.'

Octavia gave details of the house's location before replacing the telephone receiver. Her last words were, 'Papa, I love you.' She had tears in her eyes as she realised no-one outside St Crispin's knew that she had been held a prisoner for so long.

Her father's final words were, 'I love you, too. Don't worry. Carlos will be there shortly. There will be some enquiries, I tell you. Someone has a lot to answer for! I will see you soon, I miss you.'

Octavia waited in the kitchen with a hot drink provided by the owner's wife, who had come down to see what all the noise was about. How much either of them had heard of her telephone conversation she did not know or care. If they had listened, then what they made of her previous story about the sick novice, telephone lines out of order, and trying to reach a local doctor, was anyone's guess.

Her ankle had turned from a patchy blue and black to an extensive swollen mass that confirmed its serious nature. It ached with a deep-felt throbbing pain, but Octavia's thoughts were a long way off, close to the man she loved but could never reach.

Chapter Sixteen

Octavia's near-naked body felt the sun's divine power as its warmth played over her moist skin like thousands of caressing fingers. After the physical starvation and mental torment of the convent, she found the sun's strength invigorating and somehow strangely comforting.

As the sea water dried upon her body, now the colour of mahogany, it left a thin film of salt. She found the sensation both provocative and refreshing.

While sunbathing on a beach in northern Sardinia, Octavia found herself reflecting upon the previous month's events, since her dramatic escape from St Crispin's. Once her father had listened to her whole story, he became angry, for his side of the bargain with St Crispin's had been kept. Unknown to Octavia, a deal had been struck; her father viewed it as a small price in helping his daughter.

Later, as a result of extensive enquiries, he found that a 'conspiracy of revenge' was still in existence against the Delmonte family, and against Octavia in particular. This was as a direct result of Count Fambino's violent death. This conspiracy extended deep inside the Church hierarchy. Octavia reflected that the Sicilian Mafia has a powerful reach and a long arm of influence.

When the Cosa Nostra learnt, through their extensive network, that Octavia resided within the walls of St Crispin's, they sought revenge by keeping her a prisoner.

It was easy with inside help to pass fictitious correspondence, supposedly from her, to the outside.

The 'late funds' were only a pretext in the plan, and the overall aim was to confine Octavia within St Crispin's indefinitely. The Mother Superior was a willing participant from the plan's inception. With hindsight, Octavia was convinced that the Mother Superior's vindictive attitude was not only due to Cosa Nostra pressure, but also from a consuming jealousy. Octavia's previous high profile and extravagant life, with recent fame over the Sultan's treasure and much romantic speculation with this Englishman, had resulted in a great source of personal friction.

Octavia's physical beauty and constant appetite to question accepted convention had only served to compound an ever-increasing irritation between herself and the convent's hierarchy. The Mother Superior had allowed jealousy to feast upon her plate of resentment so that personal vengeance came easily and without remorse.

The sun had now moved a little higher, its strength increasing accordingly. The Sicilian girl with the long legs wondered if it was time to rub more oil into her already bronzed skin. *Or was it time for another swim in the endless turquoise sea?*

Then she remembered. Tonight was the night of the mysterious party, the one that did not have a venue, only a time. It had stated 'Black Tie', suggesting a formal occasion. For the hundredth time, she thought how strange it was. *Whoever received an invitation without a venue being mentioned? Had the venue been left out by accident or design?* She thought further, *How was it possible to leave out a venue on such an invitation?*

On a beach, time moves forward without urgency or motivation. You cook slowly at first, soon the sun's heat turns into welcome torture, then an increased sensuality permeates. Finally, you can't put off the swim any longer. So, with reluctant determination you rise, exhausted, and within a few steps find the cool joyous waters in which to immerse your over-heated body.

It was in this fashion that Octavia passed much of the day, the heat producing a sort of welcome mental paralysis through physical fatigue.

Sometime in the late afternoon, Octavia had begun to think of leaving. Her thoughts drifted to focus upon that of Sebastian beside her, his body exposed like her own to the sun's heat. Images of past emotions were relived, then reluctantly released back to whence they came.

If he was here now, they would stay a while longer before leaving, then slowly make their way back up the beach. She would hold back a little, so that Sebastian would stretch his arm out, offering to hold her hand up the incline of small sand dunes. She would enjoy wondering, once back at the hotel, when they would make love. Before taking a shower and so taste the salt on each other's skin, or wait till much later, after an evening meal perhaps by candlelight, on the beach under the stars? When reality returned, she cried, as it was only a dream within her imagination that had so captured reality.

Then she heard voices around her. With an effort, Octavia propped herself up on both elbows.

Several people along the beach had stopped what they were doing to stare at the blue horizon. Following their gaze, Octavia found the object of their interest.

A large sailing yacht was passing. At first, Octavia thought it was the *Roxana*, recently sold by her father for a much-needed cash injection. In any case, he was not up to the strains of sailing with the state of his health, at least according to him. As it drew past, it became apparent that it dwarfed even the *Roxana* in size by a considerable margin.

Octavia's interest was soon aroused. Standing up, she walked over to an elderly couple several yards away, whom she had noticed earlier using a set of binoculars.

With the happy smile of someone clearly recently retired and enjoying a holiday in the sun, the grey-haired gentleman handed Octavia the binoculars. While she adjusted the focus, he stared up from the sand at the girl's brown and well-proportioned legs. His wife tactfully chose to ignore her husband's new-found interest by closing both eyes. In this way, her undistracted mind could fully focus and delight upon the many pleasures of Italian cooking.

Once viewed through the powerful binoculars, the yacht's dimensions dramatically increased. Light brown sails were filled from three tall masts that descended into the dark wooden hull. Several flags flew from the masts, but their design was unclear in the prevailing wind.

Someone was not only wealthy but possessed a passion for nature's elements. This was no 'gin palace' so favoured by the *nouveau riche*, but the connoisseur of long-distance cruising. Again, Octavia found herself admiring the graceful lines and uncompromising quality. There was also something more. A stimulation that stirred deeply for foreign travel and unfamiliar ports.

She scanned the bows for the name, her pulse quickening with curiosity. Turning each lens independently, Octavia confirmed what she had first read. The name in bold script, *The Seven Stars*. Then she remembered. The invitation was arranged against the background of seven gold stars placed in a circle!

Later that evening, Octavia and her companion sat at a table overlooking the waterfront, commanding an excellent view of the crowded harbour. Boats of every size and description were moored like sardines, their aluminium masts a forest of grey and white. Intervention came with the occasional dark brown of a traditional wooden mast, a rare sight in these days of modern alloys and composites.

Her companion was a handsome man whose name she hardly remembered. His tall, well-built frame and features would have satisfied many women. He was also wealthy, owning a family telecommunications company with extensive interests in the north of Italy. She had known him a short time. Perhaps he was a perfect gentleman; maybe she would marry him. Who knew? Who cared!

The truth was that Octavia's mind, nearly eighteen months after Sebastian's death, could not let go of his memory. The man she loved still, lived through her blood, but reality mocked her for she could believe only in the past.

Since leaving the convent, Octavia had endeavoured to live a normal life, but no matter how sincere her efforts, it had proved impossible. Daily existence quickly became a crudely fashioned costume only worn to impersonate the joys of life from some far-off stage.

The evening was very pleasant and the view could only be described as picturesque, overlooking this harbour on the Costa Smeralda. Octavia felt the breeze, pleasant against her skin. A smell of salt water and the occasional whiff of diesel oil caught her nostrils.

However, these thoughts and sensations were only distractions, as it is strange how, when confronted by a monumental crisis or crucial decision, one becomes acutely aware of the unimportant and mundane.

This man had asked her three times in as many weeks to marry him. The first time her answer had been definitely 'No'. Sebastian's memory was too strong. In any case, they had only just met and hardly knew each other. The second time, Octavia hesitated before replying. She needed more time to think about his passionate offer. Again, the reply was 'No', but her voice came with hesitation and this time it betrayed her doubt. It was then that she knew her resistance had begun to crumble.

She would always love Sebastian, but did it make sense to love a phantom that was no longer flesh and blood? Reason told her to leave the past and Sebastian's memory, and confront the future with a new man, maybe even this one.

Deep within her heart rang a bell whose vibration she could not ignore, for the Englishman's spirit lived deep in her soul. She knew there would never be another like him, only substitutes to mimic his immortal truth.

At the third proposal of marriage, Octavia's resistance continued to disintegrate. She acknowledged an increasing pressure within her for an unconditional 'Yes' to his question.

Octavia was now discovering just how strong a woman's desire is in finding masculine security and protection. Through marriage she would take the honour and mantle of his name. Strange how these ancient values had suddenly become so important and real to such an independent spirit as she had always considered herself to be!

She looked across the table at the man opposite – young and handsome, with such classic Roman features that Michelangelo might have had a hand in carving them himself. What was more, this man was sensitive and understanding to her needs. This last quality was the more valuable, for vanity and arrogance so often dominate character in the physically attractive.

Octavia turned away from the man's face, while his eyes remained fixed on her appearance. His imagination was fascinated with the curvaceousness of her form, half-veiled by the translucent black chiffon. Street lamps, recently illuminated across the road, produced a reflective gleam from the gold of her earrings and an inner brilliance from the semi-precious stones of her necklace.

Octavia's gaze rested upon *The Seven Stars*. She would make love to this man. Yes, maybe soon, perhaps tomorrow, but definitely not tonight.

She had appointed herself a last twenty-four hours, but that was yesterday. Only a few hours now remained before her last hour of freedom. The hour that ended with midnight drew closer with every moment.

Octavia had known her freedom had started to run out the moment this Italian had come into her life, barely a few weeks before. He offered future hope and a solution to her recent desolation and broken heart.

The luxury of choice was irretrievably limited by the stroke of midnight. Octavia would try to enjoy the present, but her emotions were fatally trapped by the coming of twelve o'clock. Then she would accept this man's offer of marriage and become his devoted wife.

Octavia tore her mind away from this inevitable fate to focus on the rest of the evening. The mysterious party aboard *The Seven Stars* was about to begin. Already she could hear music. Someone was playing the guitar; softly its chords carried across the still evening water.

She thought its tune spoke of past romance, sad and full of remorse. Through her mind she heard the legendary words of Edith Piaf, *Je ne regrette rien*. Those fingers played with sensitivity and passion for someone whose love meant much, long ago...

Some torches had been lit, their bright yellow flames reflected in the still harbour waters. How attractive the yacht appeared. The hull and masts were also lit by numerous white bulbs outlining its shape and emphasising its size. Octavia was reminded of such artists as Turner and the Dutch master Willem van de Velde.

After he had settled the bill, Octavia and her companion lingered a moment, his fingers drawing circles upon her forearm, trying to regain her previous attention and visible enjoyment. This time, the amorous Italian could not reach her. Octavia's head was turned towards the open sea, and her eyes had a strange faraway look he could not understand.

In silence they left the restaurant, Octavia's new suitor not comprehending her detached attitude and unresponsive mood. She was now only barely aware of her companion's presence. She knew the guitar player's rhythm had stirred passions powerful and deep within her.

The silence continued unbroken as they walked around the harbour, eventually arriving at stone steps that descended to the dark water. A launch waited, its engine running. *Its highly polished wood must match the yacht's quality*, thought Octavia. In gold, across its stern, the boldly cut letters *The Seven Stars* were carved.

A collection of people had already gathered in the launch. A brightly coloured dress of turquoise stood out, worn by a blonde girl whose expensive perfume dominated the party.

When everyone was safely aboard, the engines were opened up, the helmsman's course, once clear of the crowded harbour, straightened for *The Seven Stars*.

Conversation amongst the guests was entirely of speculation as to who their host was and the possible owner of this magnificent yacht.

'How very unusual to keep everyone in the dark for so long!' said one voice.

'Maybe our host will not disclose his identity until the very end, like some Agatha Christie suspense novel,' said another.

'Perhaps he is disguised as a guest,' said the blonde woman, obviously enjoying the intrigue, 'who will only reveal himself at some self-appointed moment!'

A mysterious American billionaire who had disappeared ten years previously became the favourite contender for 'host'. This individual had a reputation for turning up in unusual circumstances.

"This,' said an elderly gentleman who spoke with authority, 'was due to being pursued by various government agencies for undisclosed crimes across half the world.'

By now they were practically beside *The Seven Stars*. The launch slowed to a fraction of its previous speed; the yacht's dimensions now overshadowed them.

Octavia heard someone say, 'Not an inch under two hundred and fifty feet.'

'Judging by the size of this yacht, I would say whoever he is has to be doing a pretty good job of living his dream!' said another.

There was unanimous agreement with this last remark.

From somewhere quite close, the guitar player could be heard. Everyone's attention was concentrating upon the yacht and who their wealthy host might be. Only Octavia was listening to the skill of the guitarrista.

A place had been cleared on the main deck, upon which tables and chairs had been arranged for the guests. White tablecloths covered each table; in the centre, a single oil lamp protected by glass was placed. The flaming torches seen earlier from the shore were four in number and marked the corners of the cleared space. At one end, upon a raised platform, was a solitary figure dressed in the traditional black of the Spanish flamenco costume. His face was obscured by a wide brimmed black hat. He was sitting and bending forward, the hat angled, for it was he who played the guitar.

The guests included beautiful women, expensively dressed, each one trying to out-do each other in design, colour, and amount of exposed skin. Those too advanced in years to expose much flesh used expensive jewellery instead to try and capture attention.

Their escorts wore the regulation black dinner jackets and crisp white shirts; the male uniformity was only broken now and again by the glitter of a cufflink or watch. Many were handsome young men; some were older with an ever-decreasing amount of grey hair. Everyone was in high spirits.

Forty minutes elapsed before the guests sat down at the tables, a time usually spent on irrelevant small talk that so characterises a party, especially in its early stages. Topics of lasting interest and ideas of substance don't usually come to light until a certain measure of alcohol and food have had their philosophical effect. At this point, dogma and inflexibility slowly give way to humour and perhaps a more receptive disposition.

Octavia knew the routine well. Before recent events took place that accumulated in her meeting Sebastian, she had been content to be part of this enjoyable and comfortable lifestyle.

She now became much more aware with the clarity of hindsight that many previous acquaintances and so-called 'friends' lacked any meaningful depth of sincerity. *There was another rare quality, too*, she thought. Apart from her parents, Sebastian was the most interesting person she had met. The Englishman's general knowledge was a vast spectrum that encompassed the history, geography, and politics of ancient civilisations to modern-day living and travel. Nor did it end there, for his concepts and philosophy of life were conceived in a profound understanding of the human struggle and enthusiasm for life itself.

Their encounter had been both intense and tragically brief. However, with time, she would hold the privilege of his memory as a superior influence upon the future random turn of her life.

It was to do with something unseen and intangible, a fundamental faith and belief in the principle of controlling one's own destiny. This great truth demanded an expansion of mind that she, Octavia, wanted so much to be part of.

A rare individual, she thought, *was the man whose counsel was unaffected by the expediency and convenience of the moment.*

Octavia forced a smile at her companion, whose eyes had hardly left her all evening. She hoped her true thoughts could not be read or interpreted.

She allowed her eyes to wander over the surrounding tables; the guests must have numbered close to one hundred and fifty. They did not seem to be from any particular common denominator, except that collectively some of Europe's wealthiest and best-known families were represented.

Wealth was apparently not the only criteria for these anonymous invitations. Here and there she recognised an artist, writer, painter, and musician – they were all present.

Her companion mentioned that a well-known architect was also present who he thought 'not progressive enough and lacked imagination.' Octavia remembered it differently. Many ridiculed the man's work for its traditional and classical symmetry in an age of 'modern' thought that seemed only capable of expressing itself as formless confusion and chaos!

Conversation was still dominated by the unknown author of this gathering. For Octavia, it was not only the magical setting aboard *The Seven Stars* but the music; its vibration permeated her mind with the spirit of Andalusia.

The *guitarrista* left, to be replaced by a succession of dancers while they consumed their seven-course meal. Octavia remembered little of the food or conversation, for the time was fast approaching midnight, the hour of her acceptance to marry – the third and last answer to his proposal must be 'Yes'!

When coffee arrived and liqueurs were chosen, Octavia became increasingly detached from her companion and more absorbed with the music's rhythm.

They had introduced themselves as travelling gypsies from Arcus de la Frontera in Andalusia. A few weeks previously, they had been contracted to perform in Northern Sardinia at a fiesta – a most unusual request for them to travel beyond Andalusia, let alone entertain outside Spain!

Their leader, a *guitarrista* of extraordinary talent called Marcellino, announced their great honour and privilege to provide everyone with the flavour of Southern Spain through the unique art of flamenco.

When the delicious and enjoyable meal drew to an end, glasses became filled with champagne by ever-attentive and watchful waiters. Now the atmosphere became expectant and charged with suspense.

Throughout the many courses, music had been provided by Marcellino and his group, consisting of solo guitar pieces, some accompanied by singing. Their tone was heavy with depression and full of *soleares*, confirming love's powerful attraction and agonising pain once lost.

The group consisted of twelve members, six men and six women. To begin with, as a way of introduction, everyone performed a solo piece, with two or three of the men taking it in turn to set the rhythm from their guitars.

These introductions were made by each performer leaving his or her unique impression upon the audience.

Not everyone sang but members, without exception, expressed feelings with great passion and exuberance. These moods ranged from slow sensuous hip and arm movements to intensely fast artistic stances of the human form.

Most of the audience was unfamiliar with the art of flamenco, with the exception of Octavia and one or two others. These few who had previously come into contact with this profound and smouldering description of emotional energy found half-forgotten memories stirred and rekindled.

Even those who witnessed the flamenco for the first time now rediscovered lost thoughts of amorous encounters, for the flamenco is the opera of Andalusia and the raw spirit of romance. It has been said that, if performed well, its ability to touch the heart and arouse emotional hysteria is second to none.

With the enveloping cloak of night, only the harbour lights could be seen from *The Seven Stars* and the occasional cruiser returning from a day of exploring further up the coast. The decks of these boats were usually ablaze with excessive lighting and crowded alcohol-saturated bodies now exhausted, with senses too dulled to notice their disco music or the anchored schooner called *The Seven Stars*.

Aboard this yacht, distractions did not exist, for these artists had struck a chord deep within every heart. They lived for the moment, mesmerising their audience to leave their uncertainties behind, to be replaced by interwoven themes of love, anger, jealousy, and occasional comedy.

Octavia looked for the original *guitarrista* who had played with such sensitivity and passion. She had first heard him from the restaurant. She realised his mastery of the rhythm had struck deep within her, stirring a powerful primeval restlessness. The man dressed in black from his traditional boots, long-sleeved bolero, and wide-brimmed hat angled so low, was not to be seen or heard. Maybe he would play again, perhaps near the end, then once again she could briefly lose her mind and find her soul in the potency and near-uncontrolled fire of his rhythm.

She wondered who he had loved so much to play with such emotion, and why this love had been lost. Through his guitar, a picture of sound was recreated. It told of an amorous encounter that flared with love's consuming flame of attraction before tragedy strikes, conquering all but the romance of a relived memory. With these thoughts, Octavia felt the lump in her throat and her eyes became moist, and from her memory she once again felt Sebastian's lips upon her own...

The entire audience was now responding by either clapping their hands or stamping their feet in time to the rhythm. With smooth synchronised movements of arms, shoulders, and hips, a dancer's dress swirled in a colourful display of yellow and black.

Her face was now a picture of jubilation and happiness for her lover's safety. Motivated by jealousy, he had been successful in killing another suitor, his natural foe by competition for the girl's love and affection. In true gypsy style, a wickedly-curved knife was plunged deep into his heart, much to the satisfaction of the audience, pleased that the lovers were now free to enjoy each other in well-deserved passion.

Marcellino played the unconquerable hero of this well-rehearsed theme of love, jealousy, and anger, to finish with a violent struggle between two suitors that then results in the death of one, and finally ends with the true lover triumphing over his rival. Once again demonstrating true love's immortal ability to be victorious over all adversaries.

Again, the audience showed their approval with cries of *'Olé'*, enthusiastic clapping, and stamping of their feet. Octavia was reminded of when she and Sebastian had spent an evening at *La Valencia*, where the flamenco had also been the entertainment, now so long ago, and yet it could have been yesterday.

Conversation resumed, now almost entirely of commendation for Marcellino, Maria, the beautiful girl who danced so well in the yellow dress with black polka dots, and the rest of their group. Again, cries of *'Olé'* were heard.

Once the applause had died down, Marcellino stepped forward to thank the invited guests for the appreciation of their efforts.

Then he asked if there was anyone amongst them who would care to try their skill and perform the flamenco.

'Is there a *Bailaores* amongst you, willing to try flamenco?' It was difficult to know if the question was in jest or entirely serious.

Without thinking, Octavia stood up. Every head turned towards her, some further away straining their necks for a better view.

'I accept your invitation to dance the flamenco.' Her voice was low, almost a whisper, but it carried in the silence and still night air, for the previous breeze had died.

'Bravo!' said Marcellino. 'There is hope – one amongst you has some spirit! From where do you come, Señora?'

'I am not married, and I come from the South, from Sicily,' answered Octavia. The audience held its breath to hear, as she still spoke just above a whisper, her throat suddenly dry.

Marcellino quickly recovered from his mistake. 'My greatest apologies, Señorita. I had naturally assumed that someone so beautiful had to be married!' The audience responded with laughter.

Then her escort for the evening leapt up, his intentions soon clear. Holding her arms, he informed her that the hour of midnight had been struck. He also reminded Octavia of her promise to answer his proposal.

The flamenco's intoxicating strength had ignited Octavia's soul with fire, so that her blood ran half-crazy with the excitement of love's memory. She knew from years ago in Córdoba, where she practised its eloquent movements and learnt to let the music's rhythm take her to the heights of eternity, that it could possess one like a narcotic.

Pushing her escort aside, she made her way between the tables. Halfway to the stage, she paused and turned to face the Italian, still standing, waiting for her reply. Her voice no longer a whisper, but clear and full of purpose, 'My answer to your proposal will have to wait...'

Then, with her head held high, she proceeded with great determination to reach the stage and the waiting Marcellino. The rest of his group looked on with professional interest; a few had already dismissed her acceptance to dance as some sort of insolent exercise in vanity.

Marcellino took her hand upon the stage. Bending low, he kissed the fingers as only a Spaniard can who wants to flatter and laud a lady's beauty. Octavia felt the brush of his moustache upon her skin; the memory of Roberto flashed past, but it was now meaningless.

Within a few moments, Octavia was led backstage by one of the *Bailaores* who lent her a dress, predominantly red with black polka dots. A brief discussion followed between several of the *guitarristas*, then all was set.

The lights went out, leaving the audience to anticipate Octavia's imminent performance in a darkness full of excited curiosity.

Chapter Seventeen

With the stage in complete darkness, a lone *guitarrista* started the *compás*. Slow and heavy with grief, it began, as a second and third *guitarrista* joined in.

Then a spotlight high up, fixed to one of the masts, cut a shaft of light to centre stage, illuminating the prostrate figure of Octavia. Slowly she rose to her full height, arms poised above her head, the elbows slightly pronounced. Then the focus became the girl's long fingers.

To succeed in flamenco, the artist must be able to communicate any mood he or she wishes so that the audience, if receptive, absorbs this experience and so becomes part of it.

With the movement of her fingers, Octavia extracted the very substance of flamenco, her femininity finding strength of expression in capturing the *duende*, the soul of the flamenco. The dance progressed into something sad and full of desire, her dark eyes swelling with tears that spoke only of torment and unbearable pain.

Octavia illustrated such emotion by her facial expressions and curvaceous body. The audience quickly became aroused, and even the acknowledged masters from Andalusia found themselves curious and reluctantly impressed by someone who danced the difficult *ballet grande* so well.

The next dance continued with the same theme: a broken heart in the depths of wretchedness remembering a past flame that had long been extinguished. The audience now shared Octavia's grief and sorrow to such an extent that several girls felt their eyes become moist with scarcely held back emotion. Many of the men forgot reality and craved this Sicilian dancer for themselves.

The Italian who had recently proposed now felt acute and unbearable jealousy, for he knew the passion that drove Octavia was not for him, but for another.

When she shook her head, Octavia tossed thick masses of wild hair in rhythm to the guitarrista, and with each glance of her dark eyes every man wanted to know her, and every woman imagined they too could dance the flamenco. Octavia's powers of communication with the audience had no limit, they were absolute.

A few of the invited guests now recognised Octavia from previous newspaper and magazine photographs. Her identity quickly spread from table to table with the speed of a strong wind and the comprehension of amazement.

At last, with the audience clapping their hands and stamping their feet, Octavia finished her astounding performance in a prostrate mass of red, as she had begun; only now she buried her face behind black hair and unsteady hands, in a near-useless attempt to hide her inner grief.

The audience rose to their feet with deafening applause and much shouting of 'Olé' from the Spanish, for such a performance from someone other than a native of Andalusia was unheard of.

The lone *guitarrista* stood up, his exertion from playing evident from his stiff and slow manner. *Or was there another reason for his steps towards Octavia's exhausted heap being taken with the hint of a limp?*

Now, for the first time, the *guitarrista's* hat did not conceal his entire face. Under its shadow-casting brim, the audience found his face dark from long exposure to the sun and, unlike the other *guitarristas*, he was clean-shaven, without the usual moustache.

Upon reaching Octavia, a collapsed heap of laboured breathing upon the floor, the *guitarrista* bent over to take her hands within his own. Gently, this tall man drew the girl up towards him. Octavia felt the strength of his arms and wanted to believe in their confidence.

Once standing, Octavia felt the *man's* arm slip around her waist, drawing her very tight against him. *He must feel the dampness of my dress*, she thought. She sensed his eyes upon her bowed head. Her face remained partly hidden by moist hair that clung to flushed cheeks.

Again, Octavia felt the strength of a man run through her emotions. At last, she slowly raised her head to find, in complete amazement, Sebastian's face!

It was the same face that she remembered in her dreams, that was part of her soul; the same face that she would gladly die for was now before her!

'Sebastian!' His name came as a barely heard whisper. Before she could say anything more, he kissed her on the lips. Octavia clasped both hands behind his neck, desperately afraid she might wake up from this fantasy.

For a moment, Octavia lived in a space that had no past or future; only the present contained meaning. She wanted more than anything in the world to believe in his enduring memory and masculinity, to believe in the complete impossibility of his return!

To the audience, Octavia and the *guitarrista's* embrace was a fitting finish to an outstanding performance. Everyone rose to their feet, stamping and clapping in an exuberant and unprecedented show of appreciation.

The *guitarrista* in black and the beautiful girl wearing red at last disengaged themselves, to bow to the near madness of the audience. It was obvious that they demanded a last dance, a last encore with which to lose their minds and witness once again such a wild and crazy desire of the senses.

Only when North resumed his position upon a stool, bent over his instrument, and Octavia stood poised and waiting centre stage, did the audience sit down in a hushed and expectant silence.

North resumed his playing, and whereas before the rhythm spoke only of sorrow and restlessness from a great loss, now the rhythm gave structure and definition to Octavia's *grande* composition.

The last dance was not long in terms of time, but its hypnotic grandeur and sensual energy carried the audience to the point of hysteria.

Octavia became a swirling blur of red and long black hair, her fingers snapping like pistol shots. Her arms, ever eloquent in movement, became the very essence of femininity. Her feet tapped in time to North's rhythm, responding with sensitivity and a mirrored faithfulness to his every mood.

Octavia did not understand how Sebastian's return was possible. Her powers of understanding were at a loss to comprehend his presence, let alone his near-native skill with the guitar. She did, however, recall him mentioning at *La Valencia*, so long ago, that he thought it capable of the most divine music.

Tears of joy ran down Octavia's cheeks and her Sicilian blood ran with fiery passion. She had agreed previously to dance the flamenco for Sebastian's memory, overcome with grief; now that he was alive, she moved the earth with amorous abandon. She danced, fired with the limitless power of her soul, for this man and this man alone she adored without condition.

Did this confirm her insane belief that, through faith in his memory, her dream could conquer the past and dare the impossibility of responding once more to his future kiss, and the truth of his strength?

Octavia performed with the rare skill of an artist who can at will capture that elusive inner soul of flamenco, the *duende*.

When the music finally died to silence, the audience stood up for the last time, hysterical and mad with the emotion they now shared with Octavia and the tall *guitarrista*.

Then a man rushed to the front, holding a gun at arm's length in the classic pose of one taking aim just before firing. In one leap, he was on the low stage, his progress unchecked. Then Octavia saw him. She screamed, 'Sebastian!' It was in his direction that the gun was aimed.

Octavia became faint with fear, Sebastian could not die now, not again. Her heart would only break once; there was no second chance if he was taken from her a second time.

Sebastian responded to the warning by turning to face the closing gun barrel.

The audience watched, unsure how to respond. Could this latest twist to the evening's entertainment be a planned part, or an unscheduled vendetta by a jealous lover bent on eliminating his rival with death?

Octavia's former escort was transfixed, not believing what his eyes were telling him. Secretly, he welcomed this intrusion upon this *guitarrista*. His wounded pride delighted in possible retaliation for losing Octavia with such humiliation. The Italian man does not let a girl go easily.

Sebastian flew into motion, throwing his guitar at the gun while simultaneously diving for the man's legs. The gun went off, its report very loud. Sebastian swept the other man's feet from under him so that both men locked together, struggling and rolling over and over. First this way, then that, they grappled for the uninhibited possession of the gun. Sebastian's hand held the other man's right wrist which controlled the trigger finger, but his hand was becoming more tired and weak with every second. The first bullet had missed him, the second probably would not.

Octavia now felt her mind rapidly approaching the very thin dividing line that separates extreme emotional anxiety from insanity. She again screamed 'Sebastian!' with a desperation that could only accept his survival in his moment of imminent danger.

A second gunshot was followed by a third, both very close together. It was impossible to tell what mark they found as the struggle continued.

Then a third man broke from the audience, his age middle fifties judging from the grey hair, but still fit as testified by his speed and agility in leaping upon the stage. Like the man before him, he also held a gun.

Looking back at the two struggling men, Octavia noticed the dense crimson that could only be blood from a major haemorrhage. She prayed its origin was not Sebastian, and her prayers were answered when, as she looked, he struggled to sit up. The other man remained motionless in an ever-widening dark pool.

She bent over Sebastian. His breathing was laboured from the exertion of the conflict. Her eyes were wide and full of concern.

'Are you hurt, Sebastian? I was so worried.'

'No, just a little tired. I will be alright in a moment,' he replied.

Octavia helped to support him onto his feet. She saw blood upon his arm, but it must have come from his assailant, for he was not in pain from the area. Sebastian turned round to identify the purpose of the second man, but it was this man who recognised Octavia.

'Countess Octavia Delmonte and Mr Sebastian North, I apologise for the intrusion, but we have a certain department in the Paris Police who has been interested in this particular individual for some time.' He gestured with the gun he still held in the direction of the dead man.

'Quick, we must get him off the stage,' said North immediately.

Inspector Ladoux and Sebastian lifted the dead man from either end. Then they took the limp body off the stage, out of sight and away from the audience. Once the corpse was secured below deck, Sebastian took Octavia aside.

'We must try to make this last scene look like a final twist to this evening's entertainment. I will explain everything afterwards.'

'Whatever you think is best, Sebastian. I only want you safe. Nothing else matters.'

He kissed her lightly on the lips then, holding hands as they had first experienced an age before while exploring Cagliari, the Englishman and the Sicilian girl reappeared from the shadows onto the centre stage.

When Marcellino and his group had joined Sebastian and Octavia upon the stage, he could not resist taking hold of Octavia's hand, then bending low, kissing it once more. Her outstanding performance had impressed him. He straightened to find her dark eyes and joyous laughter ever more attractive. He said that she always had a home in Arcos de la Frontera, and a place to dance the flamenco with his group any time she pleased.

Octavia laughed with pleasure at the attention. She thanked the Señor for his offer, adding that she was spoken for by the man whose hand she now held, and that her future interests lay with him.

Then Marcellino announced an end to the evening. The applause reluctantly died, and the guests all left by several launches in the direction of the shore. The only conversation that could be heard was that of how unexpected the final scene had been acted out after the magnificent solo dances by the girl dressed in red, rumoured to be none other than Countess Octavia Delmonte.

Octavia's former escort had in the end found the whole performance too much to take, and had proceeded to drown his wounded vanity in champagne. By the time everyone was boarding boats for the short passage ashore, this particular individual had to be helped, for he was virtually unconscious. He mumbled continuously about his intention of marrying the Countess no matter what. Eventually, he was laid unceremoniously in the bottom of a boat for the trip ashore.

After the last boat became lost amongst the coastline maze of moored boats and jetties, a conference was held. Attending were Inspector Ladoux, North and Octavia.

Briefly, Inspector Ladoux told of his Paris Police Department's interest in Sicilian Mafia activities in France, and particularly those concerned with narcotics.

'Investigations that included close liaison with the local Palermo *Carabinieri* revealed that one of the most powerful and influential criminal minds behind this traffic was a certain Don Giovanni Fambino.

'For some time, we have had him and others within this particular "crime family" watched, made all the more difficult by the fall-out resulting from Mr North's interruption of the party at Castle Zehra. The chaos meant that the Cosa Nostra would never sleep. Giovanni Fambino's right-hand man was here tonight, and the reason was simple. Vengeance. He now sleeps the eternal sleep, as we all witnessed.' All three pairs of eyes glanced at the body lying on the table, covered with a white sheet.

North looked up after removing the sheet.

'I see from a brief examination of the body that two bullet holes suggest our late friend was hit twice, once through the right lung and once through the neck.'

'As I recall, there were three shots in all,' said Inspector Ladoux, 'but as you indicate, only two holes.'

'Quite simple,' replied the Englishman. 'The first shot was our late friend aiming at me. By throwing the guitar in his face, it went wide of its intended target.' He smiled at the narrow escape.

'The second and third shots had only a split second between them. However, I think with some degree of accuracy we can say which bullets landed where. During the struggle, this man's gun went off with the barrel compressed against his chest. Unless the bullet travelled clear through him, his right lung must be the resting place of the second bullet.

'The third shot was fired by yourself, Inspector Ladoux. It sliced clean through this individual's neck, severing the carotid artery, hence the large amount of haemorrhaging blood.

'It is possible that even after the second shot penetrating the right upper lobe of the lung, this *mafioso* was capable of another shot, thus I am grateful for your timely intervention, Inspector Ladoux.'

'Glad to be of help, Mr North.' Now it was the Inspector's turn to concede a smile. 'This party aboard *The Seven Stars* has proved an inexplicable mystery! The Cosa Nostra was involved in keeping Octavia a prisoner in the convent as revenge for Mr North's killing of Count Fambino. Soon after her escape, they had her followed. We know, because we were following them.

'We learned of the party fairly easily, as it has been the major topic of conversation in certain circles over the last several weeks, with the press having a great time speculating as to its purpose and origin. It seems that no-one really guessed that it was aboard a yacht until *The Seven Stars* anchored this evening. No-one of course knew you were hosting the party, as you were already dead!

'I always thought you English liked a bit of intrigue with a certain degree of, how shall I say, drawn out suspense. Now it's completely confirmed! It was by watching this man, a known assassin for the Cosa Nostra, that we hoped to discover the identity of his target.

'The assassin's intention must have been to murder the Countess when the party finished. Maybe when she returned to her hotel, if not before.

'The discovery that Mr North was alive and well must have shocked him so much that he decided to shoot you as well as Octavia. Certainly, if he had succeeded, Giovanni Fambino, the uncle of the late Count Roberto Fambino, would have rewarded him very well indeed.

'Since Dr. Carlos Lancombe's phone call from Monte Carlo last year when Mr North first took a hand in this strange tale by rescuing the Countess, he has kept me informed of recent events. Thus, I am also aware of your father's ill-health.' Facing Octavia, he continued, 'May I wish him all possible haste in his recovery.'

Showing surprising compassion, Inspector Ladoux mentioned the recent strain upon the Baron; from the kidnapping and loss of his wife the previous year, to Sebastian's 'accidental death' and Octavia's imprisonment, to say nothing of his business interests collapsing from the undermining influence of the Cosa Nostra now bent upon revenge against all the Delmontes.

Octavia held Sebastian's hand very tightly, half afraid she might wake up to find he was not there. Looking at it, she noticed scar tissue. She remembered none before.

Sensing her question, Sebastian answered, 'The car crash in England occurred as reported by the media, and as some suspected it was no accident but mafia-inspired vengeance, no doubt for Count Roberto Fambino's death.

'The fuel tank exploded, and my hands and left arm were badly burned trying to escape the wreckage. The emergency services at the scene decided I was dead, and clinically I was. No measurable pulse, and breathing virtually non-existent, with 25% to 30% of my body surface area burned.

'However, I did survive, but only just. I had a long stay in intensive care of nearly eight weeks, with skin grafting initiated almost straight away to reduce the risk of infection.

'The backs of my hands were so badly burned that several tendons were destroyed and had to be replaced with new ones transplanted from other areas.

'My recovery was long and painful. They said that I needed to perform exercise with my fingers to help restore normal function. So, I learned to play the guitar. But it was playing the flamenco that I enjoyed most.

'I spent the early months of my recovery at a military hospital, thus my survival after the near-fatal crash was kept secret from all but a very few.'

Looking at Octavia, Sebastian continued with his story. 'The Government department I used to work for thought that, for my own safety, if I remained 'dead' my chances of survival might improve. Until this evening, they were right.

'My enthusiasm for the guitar grew to such an extent that when I was fit and able enough, I travelled to Southern Spain with the object of perfecting my guitar playing. I visited Seville, Malaga, Córdoba, and Granada where I played practically every day, trying to perfect and capture the spirit of this penetrating and divine music. My fingers gained strength and increased endurance, for the love of a woman ran raw and breathtaking within my soul.'

Octavia looked at his hands and found the scars. Spontaneously, she leant forward to kiss his right hand, as if to say that her love could heal even this. She remembered his limp upon the stage earlier. *It must have been a terrible crash*, she thought.

Sebastian looked into Octavia's dark almond-shaped eyes. It was then that she found what could not be fully explained.

His steady eyes were somehow part of her. She knew they always had been, and that the attraction between them was as enduring and timeless as the dawn.

North continued his fascinating story.

'In Arcos de la Frontera, I met Marcellino and the rest of the group. They were suspicious of me at first, a foreigner, but as my skill improved, they eventually accepted my dedication and sincerity to their music.'

'Through discreet enquiries, I found out about your stay in St Crispin's. You went on a voluntary basis, I heard, because you thought I did not survive the crash.' Sebastian paused, and then continued. 'If I ever needed confirmation of your love, I had it from the moment you entered the gates of St Crispin's. No woman would enter such a place if her love for someone meant less than life itself. When there was no response from my letters, I knew something was wrong, but could not work out what.

'So, one evening while practising a particularly sad tune – in fact, it was the same piece you may have heard across the water before arriving aboard this evening – I remembered the view overlooking a courtyard. In the centre was a fountain, and within its cool moving waters I saw your face, full of despair and devoid of hope.

'It was then that the idea of a party first took hold. I sent out the invitations without a venue, to prevent possible Cosa Nostra involvement, though it appears with hindsight that their shadow was not far behind. An invitation was smuggled into St Crispin's to make sure it reached you. At that stage, even I did not have a venue worked out, but was willing to trust to inspiration alone.'

'Of course!' exclaimed Octavia with excitement, 'how stupid I have been. *The Seven Stars* was the clue! Ariadne is one of my middle names. According to Greek mythology, at their wedding her lover Bacchus gave her a crown of seven stars, because he was so captivated by her beauty.

Sebastian smiled and kissed her on the mouth. 'That is exactly why I named her *The Seven Stars*.

'*The Seven Stars* had just passed the straits of Gibraltar after crossing the Atlantic from South America, then under another name, when I heard that she was for sale. I first set eyes on her in Malaga; there was an attraction I could not ignore.

'After some phone calls to London and Geneva, I bought her, including her present crew. I had recovered sufficiently to do without the close medical supervision that had been so necessary in the early stages of my recovery.

'So, strange as it may seem, I thought the invitation would arouse your curiosity to leave St Crispin's, never guessing that you were in fact held captive. After your escape a few weeks ago, I learnt of the Cosa Nostra scheme to keep you a prisoner, and that previous correspondence could not have reached you.

"Then you completely disappeared without trace, so the invitation was some wild and crazy idea to find you!'

Octavia's face changed from deep concern at Sebastian's injuries to spirited exuberance at the happy outcome resulting in their unscheduled encounter from her accepting the strange invitation aboard *The Seven Stars*.

Inspector Ladoux interjected, 'A fascinating tale, Englishman, but we have a pressing problem before us.' His head nodded to the body lying upon the table.

'You see, bringing him ashore is going to generate a lot of questions with first the local Sardinian police, then with the *Carabinieri* and its Sicilian branch. Of course, politicians in Rome will be screaming; many of them are on mafia payrolls.'

'Being French, the Italians will view my presence here as encroaching upon their territory and interfering, though obviously mafia activity is a worldwide problem, affecting many countries.

'If Mafia political and judicial penetration in Italy is extensive, in Sicily it is complete. Thus, for us in Paris, we prefer to work alone without Italian and Sicilian help, if possible. We have found through experience that success in first catching then convicting organised criminals is significantly higher by doing things our way. Lastly, once in jail, they seldom escape from French prisons. In comparison, the Sicilian jails are like hotels, with the convicted enjoying almost as much freedom!'

Looking suddenly tired, Inspector Ladoux outlined his plan for their unwelcome guest. 'I must leave as quickly as possible for France, as we have an undercover operation that awaits my return.'

'Perhaps you would be so kind, Mr North, as to attach something heavy to our late friend, before sending him for a last swim once you are in deeper waters.'

'It will be my pleasure, Inspector,' replied North. 'It's the least I can do after your well-timed intervention, for which I thank you again.'

'You are a strange man, Mr North.'

Both men shook hands before Inspector Ladoux departed, but not before he had kissed Octavia lightly on both cheeks. 'Your performance tonight was truly splendid,' he told her. 'I will always remember it, far into the future, for through your movements you have given the rest of us hope against the world's uncertainties.'

'My dancing the flamenco tonight was only possible because I love someone without condition or compromise, for love is immortal, it has no limit of endurance,' replied Octavia.

'Ah, my dear Countess, then you are fortunate indeed, for you have discovered something us mere mortals only dream of!' Then he was gone into the night, to continue his struggle against crime and all those who endeavour to perpetuate its cause.

Last to leave was Marcellino and the rest of his group, bound for their home of Arcos de la Frontera. He gave North a look as if to say he knew murder had taken place upon the stage, but he said nothing. North knew the gypsy well enough that the evening's events were safe. He repeated his offer again to Octavia, who declined for the second time saying that her life had another course and destination.

When they too, laughing and singing, disappeared into the night for the distant shore lights, North gave orders for the sails to be unfurled and the anchor to be raised.

A light wind from the north, as if anticipating their intentions, filled their sails, and once the shore lights could be seen no more, North carried out the Inspector's wishes. A faint splash was the only mark that finally sent the weighted gunman for his last swim.

Sleep was out of the question for the two lovers alone upon the foredeck of the yacht known as *The Seven Stars*.

Yes, thought Octavia, *there were practical considerations, such as she did not have any clothes, save the dress she wore.* The dancer she borrowed it from had given it to her before leaving, saying that it was hers until she could equip her wardrobe with the finest flamenco dresses money could buy! However, these thoughts were unimportant practical matters that she soon dismissed, as they had little place in Sebastian's arms.

For hours they kissed and held each other under the brilliant night sky lit by thousands of stars, with the only sound the creak of the rigging.

They talked endlessly about all that had taken place from their first encounter near Monte Carlo. Octavia was intrigued to learn that the *Belle of the Wind* had another cargo to give up. As well as the spy plane, she contained most of the missing treasure from the *Nuestra Señora De La Isabella*, courtesy of a certain Señor Max Santiago and the late General Kerenskiy.

'A chance for future treasure hunting presents itself,' Sebastian said with a smile, 'though the competition from the Cosa Nostra and others will no doubt be strong. However, the few pieces from the Sultan's treasure that I managed to squeeze into my pockets have so far yielded a reasonable sum – as paid by various museums and private collectors – of between forty and fifty million US dollars. Thus, I fear the incentive for diving over the *Belle of the Wind* has been somewhat reduced.'

Octavia smiled at this news, which she translated into extensive future travelling to faraway places with Sebastian.

She listened to him for a long time, because here was a man who believed in what he said.

To first attract and then capture a man was easy, but to hold and appreciate him was much more difficult, especially if he was worth something in terms of moral fibre and honesty. For a woman to be capable and expressive with her own character, but without posing a threat to a man's all-important sense of direction and purpose. *Ah, there was the balance of a successful relationship!* thought Octavia.

Sebastian at last paused, then continued.

'During the journey of life we will all encounter difficulties and sometimes great reversals, but these uncertainties are not the end but only temporary set backs in the longer struggle that defines life's real purpose.

'Victory will always belong to the individual who draws upon resilience in the face of certain defeat.

'We have both been through quite a lot Octavia, including facing death on a number of occasions. But we both survived, and in the process discovered through the intense struggle to live, that our love did indeed triumph against impossible odds after all.

'I am sorry Octavia, I have talked for too long,' said Sebastian.

'No, please continue if you wish...' replied Octavia. 'If you believe in something, you can express yourself to me for as long as you want,' she said smiling.

The wind strengthened, Octavia felt the warm air upon her cheek, and once again she thought upon the two men who had recently, and so dramatically, changed her life. Roberto had represented something dark and malevolent. She had to fight against him with all her strength for her very survival depended upon it. Sebastian represented something quite different, here was a man who was guided by a very different code.

From the beginning he was never a threat to her. He unconditionally offered endurance and fortitude in her hour of need. Sebastian risked everything and in the end the race was won.

Octavia ran her hand inside Sebastian's shirt and across his chest, the hairs felt good between her fingers. *Strange*, she thought, *with Sebastian she would always find comfort and security within his embrace.* To help him achieve his dreams and ambitions would be a noble cause indeed, for now she would be part of that future to share together.

Octavia silently thanked her faithful ancestors. She was convinced that her lineage had somehow assisted her through recent times, when her need was greatest.

Alone at last with the man she wanted to spend the rest of her life with, she sensed an exhilarating release of freedom within the refuge of his presence.

How could the past vanish so completely, when she looked into his eyes? With his smile, the future became all that she wished. Only the present could be measured with meaning, for with every kiss the mysterious equation of life became balanced in a fusion of limitless energy and eternal hope.

They had been together upon the gently heaving deck for a long time when Sebastian said, 'Look, Octavia, there…' and he pointed with his right hand '…the night pales to announce the dawn.'